# The Island

## of the

## Mapmaker's

## Wife

## &

### OTHER TALES

# The Island

# of the

# Mapmaker's

# Wife

# &

## OTHER TALES

## Marilyn Sides

HARMONY BOOKS / NEW YORK

Copyright © 1996 by Marilyn Sides

Published by Harmony Books, a division of Crown Publishers, Inc., 201 East 50th Street, New York, New York 10022.
Member of the Crown Publishing Group.

Random House, Inc. New York, Toronto, London, Sydney, Auckland

Harmony and colophon are trademarks of Crown Publishers, Inc.

Book design and illustrations by Cathryn Aison

Printed in the United States of America

Library of Congress Cataloging-in-Publication Data
Sides, Marilyn.
The island of the mapmaker's wife & other tales / Marilyn Sides.—
1st ed.
I. Title.
PS3569.I4449I82 1996
813'.54—dc20                    96-4012
CIP
ISBN 0-517-70395-5

1  3  5  7  9  10  8  6  4  2

FIRST EDITION

*For Carolyn Morley and Michel Dargent*

# Contents

"This is an imaginary Island, of Kin to that which is call'd the *Painters Wives Island,* placed in some unknown part of the Ocean, meerly at the Fancy of the Map-Maker."

—Jonathan Swift, *A Tale of a Tub,* 1710

# THE ISLAND

## OF THE

## MAPMAKER'S WIFE

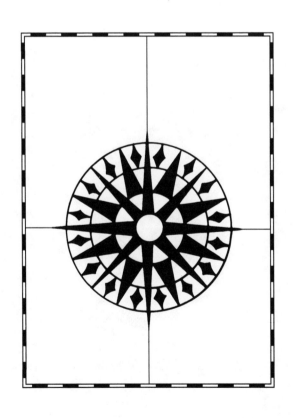

SHE TRADES IN ANTIQUE MAPS. Her small shop is on Congress Street, three blocks from Boston Harbor. Full of history, tourists drop in from Bunker Hill, Beacon Hill, and exclaim in surprise, "You're the owner?" They wonder, often aloud, Why does this rather young woman, only a few silver threads glinting in her hair, why does she spend her time behind the tarnished letters C. M. DESCOTES on the dusty window? What makes her hand linger so on the ancient sea charts as she smoothes out their creases? An unnatural woman they think, never out loud, to care about latitude and longitude.

The old map dealers, retired military men and historians in worn tweeds, know better, point out that Descotes is only too predictably a woman. For all her expert abilities—which they admit with grudging respect—to date any map, to attribute it to its designer, to price it for the market, Descotes betrays herself by her specialty. Her passion, the map she knows best and collects for herself, is the frivolous picture map prized three hundred years ago by fat Dutch housewives for the walls of their homes.

"Descotes," the dealers reproach her in dismal tones,

3

"merely interior decoration, you know." But it pleases her to think of thin light coming from a window, watery light falling on a white wall spread with a gaily colored map of Europe, Africa—it makes no difference, any annihilation of vast seas and continents to a rectangle will do—bleak light falling farther on a table spread with a rich red Turkey carpet, one corner lifted back like a raised skirt. Pure light falling on the woman reading there.

"Ah, Descotes, most unscientific, those maps. Truth? Progress?" But, like her map masters, Descotes would sink a newly discovered Alaska for a mermaid billowing her breast on a wave. Descotes would shrink Siberia for the long-whiskered sea monster rolling at his sea queen's side.

Among the map dealers, only one indulges her taste without raising an eyebrow. William taught her everything he knew about maps. She learned to love them as much as she loved to pore over his old skin, lined and loose, until the day, years ago, he decided that he was "Too old for you" and rolled himself up and away from her as she lay still in bed. Between them now, there is the cool comfort of shoptalk. One afternoon in January, William telephones her from his shop in Salem, a shop with something for people with all sorts of specialties: Indian medicine bags, Chinese chess sets, embroidered chasubles, grass masks with little saucer ears, and maps.

"Sweetheart, two of *your* maps are coming on the market. In Amsterdam, number four, Prinsengracht. Very fine maps, I hear. Now, the dealer's a strange bird, likes to talk out a deal. Won't deal over the telephone. Sweetheart, you're going to have to get up and go there, this time."

"Right now? But it's so inconvenient for me to go, right now. Right now, I'm expecting offers. Do you have his number? Maybe he'll talk to *me*. I'm good on the phone, you know."

"No number. My friend there says you have to show up. So, sweetheart, I've said you're on your way, and I've reserved a seat on the plane for tonight at nine-thirty."

4

"The maps are good ones, you say? Excellent ones? Very good, your friend says? *My* maps, you're sure?"

"Beautiful maps. You won't be disappointed. Good-bye, sweetheart. Good luck."

On a card she writes "Closed 'til Saturday" and tapes it right above her name on the front window. Three days, she tells her answering service. Three days should be enough. No need to loiter once the map is hers. There's nothing else in the world that interests her anymore. For several years, after losing William, before opening her shop, she traveled cheap drugstore map in hand to Italy, Mexico, India, anywhere, for months at a time, every chance she had, wide-eyed, ready to snap a picture, ready to exclaim, How strange, how beautiful to the man next to her, whether it was Stephen, Mark, or Bill, willing to stroke the flesh of Stephen, Bill, or Mark lit up by a tropical moon or the northern lights. One morning, however, New Delhi seemed like Paris, like Tokyo, all the same red dot on the maps, the hotels the same black blotches. Bill murmured the same dry crisscrossing sentences as Stephen or Mark.

Back in Boston, she "retired," as she likes to put it, and opened her map shop. Using her computer and her telephone, she manages to find the maps she wants without leaving the city, much less the country. A quiet day spent stroking the downy surface of the thick map paper, a long walk puffed up and down the harbor by fat-cheeked winds, and at last home alone with mad continents of color on the walls—this is a day filled with enough earthly glory for her.

That night, the plane cabin seems a prison and a hell. It is drab and smelly; plastic forks and passengers clatter. As the plane rushes past the last lighthouse on the coast and into the blind, shapeless night, she sweats with a fear that, bound to her seat, she can't walk off. She never used to be afraid to fly. What has made her afraid to die now? When her mind strays toward the black nothing outside the window—sleep is just as dark, just as much a dense dark fog—she tries to guide it home by sketching out on the airline napkins her favorite maps, so bright, so brimming with ships and flowers and the walls of perfect cities. She makes herself imagine the maps in Amsterdam, very fine maps, William says, very good maps, lovely maps to gaze upon.

In Amsterdam at last, exhausted, she takes a short nap in the hotel room before going to look at the maps. She sleeps too long.

Waking up in the dark, she angrily reminds herself that there is no time to waste on this trip, and now the shop will be closed. All she can do tonight is walk to the dealer's shop and make sure she knows the way. A good decision, she congratulates herself an hour later, as after several wrong turns in the maze of canals—it has been years since she used a map to find something, the small map so awkward in her hand, the tiny print a strain—she circles toward the shop.

Along Prinsengracht, tall, narrow houses stand stiffly up into the night, the light from their upper rooms blurred by drawn lace curtains in a hundred starry patterns. The maps had better be good, to get her away from home, where she, too, could be behind her curtains in a soft light. Number 4 is a house narrower and darker than all the others. Yet downstairs in the tiny ground-floor chamber, there glows a heavily shaded lamp. No one comes, however, when she taps, and taps again louder on the cold glass, a sound too loud in the empty street. A neighbor may look out the window and think she is a thief. The door is locked. Pressed against the window, she makes out the quite good things risked in the window—Renaissance globes, Islamic sextants—the maps will be fine ones. Startling her, a face looms up before her eyes, that of a huge cat, dusky yellow with a white tufted bib, stretched out between an astrolabe and an ancient tome. The cat shakes his head officiously, like an old clerk, as if to say, Closed. Go away.

A cold winter wind turns through the canals. She has to move on. Walking back down the street, she enters a pub for some dinner. The customers, mostly men, raise their heads to stare at her, but out of habit she looks only at the waiter, nods to him, and follows him to a table near the central stove that heats up the dark-paneled room. She orders, and the food comes promptly and properly hot. As the waiter sets the plate before her, she thinks how long it took to acquire the ability—self-taught—to enjoy eating alone. To make sure she is served well and courteously, to eat slowly, enjoying her meal, thinking her own thoughts.

A shout of laughter bursts from a group of men standing behind her in one corner. Startled, she turns to look at them, and a big, tall man, obviously the teller of the joke, catches her eye with his bright, curious glance. Of course, the laugh was raised to make her turn around. It always provokes men, as men, to see a woman alone, making her way without one of them. She must still be quite exhausted to have fallen for that. She knows better. Yet at one time, she suddenly recalls and it's like finding an old dress and thinking instantly of a certain night, at one time, when she used to travel, she would have looked back at this man, looked him in the eye and smiled, she would have let him join her for a drink. Now, it's a quiet triumph to have only business on her mind—the maps, her maps, fine maps—once they are in hand, she can go home, stay at home. She turns back around, finishes her dinner, pays, and nods good night to the waiter.

In widening circles, squinting at her map again and again, she returns to her hotel and goes to bed. Having slept too long that afternoon, she sleeps fitfully. Finally, she falls asleep and sleeps heavily. She wakes up late, again.

Rushing through her breakfast, hurrying past canals, she arrives at number 4 by eleven, only to find a note saying, "Back at 11:30" in Dutch and English. An unwilling tourist, she idles along the canal, glancing at shop windows. She finds a little pleasure after all. In one window, a painting with a map in it, her kind of map, is on display. A sign she will be successful, she tells herself, and begins to be more cheerful. In the picture, only the back of a painter, elegant in a slitted doublet, is visible as he sits before his easel. At the far right corner of the room, placed between a casement window and a heavily carved table, stands a model bedecked with pearls, ostrich plumes, and blue silk brocade. Her face turns slightly away from the artist's gaze. The rival beauty of the painting is a map of Spain, bordered with panoramic views of the principal cities. The map takes up almost all of the back wall. The artist has spent his best efforts on where the light falls from the leaded window: the shirt shining through the doublet on the painter's wide back, the averted cheek—pearl-pale—of the woman, the gleaming emptiness of sea on the map.

The picture keeps her standing so long enthralled before it that Descotes has attracted the attention of another idler. He has been strolling up and down the street, looking at windows, watching her. She has felt him there, behind her, she realizes. Now he moves closer. In a moment—she remembers how it goes —he will be so close that they will have to say something about the painting, then the weather, and then will come the invitation to coffee, to dinner, to bed, if she stands still for a few more seconds.

Her maps. With a quick glance at her watch, she sees it's time for the shop to be open. She turns away as he takes the last step toward her. She used to smile a polite, apologetic smile at moments like these. The practice comes back to her an instant too late now. The man frowns after her.

At number 4, the shop door opens with a grating scrape and shuts with a loud click. The room is as empty as last night, except for the big yellow cat. The cat rises, stretches, and jumps to Descotes's feet. Running at her ankles, he steers her to the desk at the back where the lamp still burns. From the ceiling to the wainscoting are shelves of calf-bound books whose spines glimmer with gold lettering, beneath the shelves wide cabinets of polished drawers—map drawers, she knows. A large table blackened with age takes up the rest of the room.

Steps come thumping down some hidden stairs. A big head topped with a shock of red hair ducks through the low door to the left, the heavy body that follows blocks up the doorway. How this body fills this narrow house, how it almost appears at this moment that he is some great hermit crab, bearing on his back this fragile shell house.

---

It is the joke teller from the pub. He recognizes her right away. A grin splits his wide round face. She can see how he could make people laugh. Just looking at him would make anyone laugh. His brown corduroy suit hangs flabbily around his thick body. His rumpled white shirt sticks out between the waistband of his pants and the thin belt he has hitched up too high and too tight. Part of his shirttail is even caught in his fly, the tuft of it unfurling like a gay white sail before him. She remembers the quick eyes, she sees they are a warm, rich chestnut, curious and direct. His long, thin nose, along with these eyes, gives him the look of a courtly bird. A very funny man, except, it strikes her sharply, for the lips. Lips almost too thin, too severe, the lips of an exacting man. Between the upper part of this face and these lips, there must run some invisible fault line, along which two characters, the clown and the master, strain.

She hands him her card. "You're expecting me, I think."

Throwing up his hands in exaggerated surprise, he exclaims, "Ah, the map lover. I should've guessed it was you last night. Loitering around the shop, hoping for even one little look at the maps? A little lovesick already? No? A good sign for the dealer. Yes? He can charge what he likes. He knows his customer must have the map."

So she's to be paid back for her coolness in the pub.

"I must say, my dear, that it's rare to encounter a young woman—oh yes, my dear, to a dilapidated, insomniac, old carcass like myself, I'm broken beyond my forty-five years—yes, yes, you're young, very young—it's rare to meet a young someone as fervent as you about their trade. Lingering in the cold night. Simply to be near the maps." He pauses, notes her annoyance with delight, and quickly turns mock-professional. "All right. Let's be very very serious. Let's have a look at my maps. The all-important maps."

He bustles over to the locked drawers, at the same time pulling a ring of keys from his pocket. The ring comes out, and along with it a thick ink pen, a crumpled handkerchief, and a leather change purse that falls to the floor, spilling coins all around. "See how clumsy I am—maybe the customer says to herself, The dealer is nervous, the advantage mine." He stops and bends over to pick up the coins. As he stoops over with his back to her, his jacket pulls up, his shirt pulls out of his trousers, and he is exposed down to the cleavage of his buttocks. How ridiculous, she says to herself, and at the same time she wants to place her hand there on that skin, it is so fine-grained, and luminous, as if the whiteness were some sheen of silver melted onto gold. She'd like to run her fingers down the ridge of the spine to where it ends. She'd like to feel under her palm the muscles playing there so smoothly and powerfully. This must be the center of power for that big body.

—

Her body tightens up, her thighs, her belly—it has been a long time since she longed so sharply to touch someone's flesh, to have the feel of it in her fingertips at that moment, knowing it will linger there like a soothing shock for days. Just as she becomes afraid that her hand will go out of its own accord, he straightens up, the clothes cover him in a clumsy bunching of fabric.

Descotes allows herself to smile. She shouldn't let such a silly thing distract her. The maps are all that count, the maps and going home. Luckily, he has noticed nothing and, unlocking the drawer, has drawn out a roll and pulled the desk lamp over to the big table. He smoothes out the map and with a click turns up the lamp to illuminate a beautiful—William was right—a beautiful piece of work.

And with one look at the map, she is completely back in her map world. Here the Netherlands of 1652 has been painted in as a blue heraldic lion rampant on the northern coast of Europe. She almost laughs, for the lion—despite his gold crown and elegant tufted tail—looks like a fat blue cat standing on his hind legs to bat at a fly. Perhaps the royal ancestor of this yellow cat staring at her from the desk. Turning professional, she admires the coloring, a fine wash of blue bice, names the probable date of the map and the mapmaking firm. The dealer cries, "Oh, very good, very good. Absolutely right. How I shall sigh when you are gone. Most people who come to see me are pretentious amateurs or ignorant tourists."

Descotes estimates what she thinks the map's price should be. Maybe she could afford it. The map of the Battle of Waterloo that she has been holding on to as the price climbed, she could let that go for this. Finishing the thought, she straightens up. He takes the hint, rolls up the map, and then, going back to the drawer, he brings out the second map.

Before her are unfurled all the fanciful figures of the East, quaint and funny as in a children's book. Ruling the Mongolian plain, the great Khan twirls his mustache in front of a golden-tasseled tent. Farther south, Mandarins bow beside their pagodas. A cannibal couple of Borneo, modest in their grass skirts, glance shyly at each other over the human elbows they nibble. In the reaches of the sea, fretted calligraphy, like a handwritten letter home, details the terrible marvels of the world.

As she looks the map over, Descotes almost hums. It's good.

It's what she had hoped to see. Her explorer's map of the Belgian Congo—she knows a small, rich museum that covets it. To the dealer, again, she names the date and the mapmaker. He is delighted. Of course she is right. Now to business, she thinks, and prepares her offers in her mind.

However, the dealer has one more map to show her. "A special map. Not a map for sale. But if you don't mind, I'd like you to see this map. It'll give me great pleasure to have you appreciate it—oh, I don't mean you should appraise the map, give it a price, no, no—simply see how beautiful it is. I'm rather proud of my new map. So, please, allow me to show off my good taste."

As he takes out the new map, he tells her that the circumstances of the map's purchase were quite curious. One day, an old woman had summoned him to come look at a map she had for sale. The map was kept in a locked cabinet in her room. Descotes should imagine a big, tall, white-haired woman with the smallest of keys on a blue scrap of ribbon, leading him to her bedroom, shutting the door behind them. The map, the old woman told him, was a gift she had made to herself years ago, with some money left to her by her grandmother, a gift she had kept all to herself all these years, until now when she needed the money—and the old woman laughed—to bury herself. Once he saw the map, he thought how well she had rewarded herself all those years of her life. "Another map mistress, she was"—he grins at Descotes—"though of only this one map." In fact, he felt very humble in front of her, as if she knew the map better than he, an expert, did. After one look at the map, he bought it.

Descotes is wary. Declaring the map not for sale, telling the odd story of its former owner—the map dealer must be setting her up for the map he really wants to sell today. She will cast a cold eye on this map.

Yet when he spreads out the map before her, she finds it impossible to do anything but gaze upon the map with absolute abandonment to pleasure. This map of South America would have seemed to anyone else a very plain map compared with the first two—but she sees right away it is as lavish, even more so in its own way. She has to admit to herself this map is the best of the three maps, truly a superb map, beyond comparison. The work could only have been done by the best illuminator of maps in the seventeenth century, Margarethe Blaeu, the wife of the master printer Willem Blaeu. The long spine of the Andes, Margarethe Blaeu has rendered in the finest golden tincture of myrrh, with the western slope reflecting the setting sun in a delicate pink wash of cochineal. Several stands of trees, in a thousand varying shades of green, play the vast rain forest of Brazil. Rivers thread through the continent in indigo banded with magenta. The southern pampas wave their bluish leaves and golden stalks. Red lead, the color of dried blood, shadows the double cathedral towers of Spanish settlements. Surrounding the land, showing off its gentle brightness, the sea is stippled like shot silk in dark indigo and a wash of lighter blue bice.

---

As she examines it, what strikes Descotes about the map is that its very perfection wants to be saying something, like a child perfectly composed at high tension to attract the attention of its mother. Taking her magnifying glass from her purse, she works down the Chilean coast, around the Horn, and up the Brazilian coast to the Caribbean. Everything, every inlet and spit of land, every island, is absolutely correct, and Margarethe Blaeu has blessed her husband's perfect outlines with her rare colors.

No, wait, here is an island out of place, just off the coast of Venezuela. No, not out of place, for it belongs nowhere else. An imaginary island, drawn in with quick strokes of a pen, not printed. This is what the map's perfection silently strains to tell —the error, the gratuitous island.

The dealer sees Descotes staring at the island and laughs in delight. "So, you have discovered the secret of the map. Frau Blaeu has sketched in her own paradise: 'Let there be an island, and an island appeared on the bosom of the sea.' "

The island *is* a lovely Eden, all for oneself. There are minute patches of greenish gold furze, tiny trees toss in a breeze, tender hillocks—and then Descotes gasps, looks again, narrows her eyes. She can hardly believe it. This exquisitely detailed landscape, its contours, take on the breathtakingly precise outline of a woman embracing a man. That faultless drawing of the upper coast, the taut single line is the woman's exposed neck, her back, the curve of her buttocks, the sweep of her legs superbly clean down to the graceful feet tapering off into the ocean. The arched lower coast is the lover's long back, stretched out and afloat on the Caribbean waves. He presses up against her breast and belly and thighs, his thighs and legs flail. His arms are outstretched above his head and grasped by her hands. The good Frau—oh, Margarethe!—must have found it unbearable to show them crying out in pleasure— her and her lover, her husband, some sailor?—golden hair falls over the woman's face, the lover's face, it flows into the sea, curling and rushing like foam against the rocky shore.

Staring at the island, Descotes's own breasts ache. Her face must glisten. Again a sharp and sudden excitement makes her almost tremble. It's not fair to be taken so unexpectedly with longing.

"Quite wonderful. No?"

Of course, he knows! He has set up this scene like a voyeur, forcing this upon her, so he could shock her, watch her. Angry, she cannot look at him. She won't give him satisfaction.

"You don't find the island delightful? Oh, you must! I'm so disappointed!" His voice is innocent of any smile. He seems genuinely puzzled by her silence.

Descotes can hardly believe he cannot see, truly see, the island. This island is so alive, so terrible a picture of possession. He sees only an island, an idiosyncratic island—not a seizure, a conquest, an establishing of rights. It is as if he were an amateur and hadn't recognized the signature or the distinguishing stamp that would make a valuable map, in fact, priceless. Will she be dishonest if she doesn't point out the true nature of the island to him? But she cannot bear to. That would be like making him aware of her own body pressing, it seems to, against the very walls of the room.

Why should she tell him, if he can't see it himself?

"Forgive me. I'm sorry. I was completely lost in it. This map is beautiful." Trying to control the tremor in her voice, she adds, "It's so beautiful. How much do you want for this map?"

━━━

He laughs in triumph. "I knew you would love my map. But, as I said, this map's not for sale. I simply wanted you to admire it. Now that your immense expertise has confirmed my own judgment, I'm very happy. I shall not regret the enormous sum I paid for it. So, the old woman knew what her map was worth."

Descotes, thinking she hears him working up the price, almost smiles and bites her lips. She sings to herself, He's going to sell, he's going to sell.

"We all," he continues, "must allow ourselves an extravagance once in a while. Don't you agree? And this is a beautiful extravagance. So beautiful." He looks back down at the map with unfeigned pleasure.

"A masterpiece, I agree. Name your price."

Surprised by her insistence, he stares at her. Then he laughs. "Oh, forgive me. Of course, you must think I'm bargaining with you. No, no. I don't make deals that way. With me, business is always very straightforward. I'm sorry, this map is not for sale. I tell you very honestly, I bought it for myself. It called out for someone who would admire the map as much as the old woman."

"What if I admire it more than you? As much as she did? Then, this map should be mine."

He thinks it over for several moments. As if testing her, he names a price. An immense sum. Almost humiliated to show him what the map means to her—but then, he doesn't know what she knows—she swallows and says she can raise the sum. If he will sell the map to her.

His silence is rather cruel, since he must know now that he has her, that she would probably give anything to have the map. Yet, when he finally speaks, it is in a serious, friendly tone—a tone that strikes her as only too much like that which William uses with her. "My dear. I'm older than you. I've been in the business longer than you. So I must protect you from yourself. Take one of the other maps. They are masterpieces, too, albeit gaudy compared with this one. I'll give you a very good deal on either of them. For this map, you would, I imagine, have to beggar yourself."

"That's my affair. It's my business. I would like to buy this map. All you have to do, it seems to me, is decide to sell it."

He gazes at the map again, stares at it intently, questioning it, searching for some answer to her. "It's a fine map, a very fine map. There's not another map like it. A map so quiet and calm in its mastery. So happy with its lovely island. Is this map really worth so much to you? Why, I must ask myself."

She manages a crooked smile. "You know women—we've got our fancies, our cravings. Mine is your map. That's all."

"A woman's weakness? You're that kind of woman, then? Not a map dealer?" Rolling up the map, he turns to put it away.

Oh, my island, gone, Descotes cries silently.

He turns back to her but doesn't look at her. "Go back to your hotel. Think it over carefully. Can you really get the money? Come back again at ten o'clock tomorrow. I have to think about it, too."

He has to sell to her. He has to give her his word *now*. She wants to argue more, badger him. With difficulty, though, she reminds herself that she has already passed the limit of what is considered civil bargaining among dealers. She consoles herself, with difficulty, that at least she's made him consider selling. Forcing herself to nod, to smile, she turns and leaves the shop.

Spinning out canal by canal, she hurries back to the hotel. She places her telephone calls as if she were raising a ransom—quick, it's a matter of life and death. She lies to the manager of her bank and gets a loan. From William, she demands money. She tells him the map is an invaluable map, that she has to have this map. When he argues that it is too expensive for her business, she argues back that if he hadn't taught her to prize maps, she wouldn't be in the business. For the first time in all these years, she makes him feel he owes her something for making her go away, and he has to pay her off with the map.

William promises her the money. There's his cold "Goodbye," and he hangs up.

Descotes doesn't waste one second feeling ashamed of herself. Adding up the figures, she finds she has the dealer's price. At first she is elated, the next moment frightened at the thought of throwing all this money away on one map. She hastily promises herself she'll work extrahard this coming spring. She'll move maps around. She'll deal in ways she's refused to before. Descotes is already thinking how she can strip her favorite maps from her own walls, maps she used to treasure as if they were her children. Now she'll sell those maps down the river—heartless.

At dinner, she is worried again. Is her map worth so much? She sketches and sketches her map on a scrap of paper. Her island comes out merely as an island every time. If the island was really that man bound to that woman, the map dealer would have seen it. It is only an island. Only an island. But the old woman knew it, Descotes argues back to her own doubts. The old woman kept the map secreted in her cabinet, an exquisite torment. That was the clue, wasn't it?

Descotes packs. There will not be much time tomorrow to close the deal—he has to sell it!—and make her flight. Trying to sleep, she finds her mind too busy adding up columns of figures, or sorting out the maps she will have to sell, or attempting to conjure up the island—but her island is always only an island. That makes her despair more than she ever has in her life, the very thought of that island being only an island, merely an island.

Only an island. Descotes gets out of bed, gets dressed. She must go back to look at the island, tonight. She has to know, tonight.

---

Once more, Descotes winds in and in to the shop. Now she has found her footing, she knows every landmark, every bridge, every house along the way. Here is Prinsengracht, number 4, cat, lamplight. The door is open, but at the loud click of its closing, no one comes. She walks to the back of the shop and sticks her head through the small door. Off to one side is a dark kitchen and on the other a narrow screw of white stairs. Up and up Descotes goes, up into this whelk. At the top is a large room, most of it in the dark except for a light on the table, where the dealer sits in a big wooden chair. His jacket is off, his shirtsleeves rolled up over massive forearms with gilt hairs glinting. He stares at the map, her map. Descotes walks into the room and over to the table. Looking down at the map, she sees instantly that she was right. Yes, two bodies taut as one arch in that sea.

"I have the money. I raised it." She has barely any voice.

His eyes are sharp and black, his lips tightened, as he stares up at her face. As if he would read it. "What do you see in my map?"

Her face is made as smooth and as white as thick paper, her eyes almost closed into thin brush strokes of black lashes.

Provoked by her silence, he pushes his chair back. He stands up and steps over to her, watching her closely. "Please tell me about my map."

Descotes stays perfectly still and says nothing. If she just waits and stays still, he'll have to give her the map. She says to herself over and over, Stay still, just wait. Let him find his way to giving me the map. It is inevitable that he will give her the map.

"I won't sell it to you."

Oh, mere defiance easily brushed aside, brushed aside with her hands, reaching out, brushing against that big chest, over across the shoulders, down the arms to take the thick forearms in her hands, to steady herself, to grasp the thick forearms, brushed with gold in the light, to steady him, to keep him on course. She holds fast to them, at the wrists, she wants the feel of them in her hands from the very first, she wants to know the sinews, the muscle, the bone, to feel the grace of flesh—her hands had almost forgotten such grace—she wants to promise herself with this grip, to make a claim with this grip, that she will close her lips over his, that she will unbutton his shirt and push him back to the bed she sees over his shoulder, there she will free him from that belt, pants, shoes, and socks, she will lay him out on that bed, his fine white legs, the knees knotted intricately like silk cording, the thighs, white and firm as ivory, furzed red-gold, she will smooth him out and then raise up with her hand the long thick spit of land from his bristling thicket of gold, raise it up very long and high, then mount it, dawn's light falling on her as she mounts him and holds the wrists down, hard, as she leans over to watch his face in exquisite dread, as she pulls herself up on him, then crashes back down, as he cries out sharp and hard against the white walls of that room, as she washes up gasping in the billowed sheets, the cat lolling in the shallows at their side.

# TEMPORARY TATTOOS

F ROM THE LAST TURN IN THE ROAD, a motel, a roller-coaster track, and a french-fry stand stood stiff as theater flats against the dark drape of ocean. A crowd edged around them. To the right stretched the beach. There kids staggered through the sand until stopped short by the water. That day, no one swam or splashed in the shallows, though it was a late-summer day and they wore bathing suits or shorts. From this far north, a hurricane in equatorial waters gathered its strength—television, radio warned that the undertow had pulled out six people, not swimmers, but waders swinging their shoes on two fingers, had pulled them out to sea, like the tentacle of a giant squid.

Bingham and Leth cried out at the same moment as they took this last turn in the road and chanced upon the tiny town of Salisbury Beach. Bingham parked the car, and they wandered along the boardwalk. Leth had come to work at Bingham's company in Boston for a year as part of a cultural exchange, and Bingham liked to think of herself, among other things, as Leth's guide to American life. On this Sunday drive north along the shore, as always, she took command. Yet Bingham, who had transferred to the company from a landlocked part of the country,

found this seashore life new to her, too. Before long, Leth's eager
questions exhausted the few facts Bingham had cribbed from a
guidebook. She started to make things up. Then she laughed and
admitted, "Got me. I don't know."

From then on, they were both foreigners. In Salisbury Beach,
they marveled at every detail of the quaint and tawdry life of the
town: clams tortured into fried curls and stuffed in buns, red
plastic lobsters trapped in toy lobster pots, and soon things that
might have been familiar even to Bingham—Skeeball and carny
games, "Oh You Lucky Winner" and "Easy to Win," where
boys shot at tin ducks for prizes to give their girls, the Wild Wave
roller coaster screaming down a rickety scaffold, the crowd in
their flapping shorts and sagging halter tops, their flip-flops slap-
ping the boards—all these things seemed as exotic to Bingham as
they did to Leth.

It took two trips up and down the boardwalk for Leth and
Bingham to tire of the wheeling colors. Then every greasy waft
from the food stands began to remind them too much of their
experiment in fried dough at Mr. Mike's. Passing up on Dr.
Blood's House of Horrors, they stepped down to the beach
strewn with cigarette butts and paper plates. As they walked past
the posted warnings, a lifeguard turned toward them, lifted his
arm, then let it fall, because they stopped. He turned back around
and Bingham heard him question his girlfriend. "Where were yah
last night? At yah sistah's, no lie?"

The girl dug her hand in the sand and looked at the sea.

Rollers swelled the glassy black water, thudded dully at Bingham's feet. The sky was livid. The air smelled sharp. Leth sniffed at
it and told Bingham about the time he had been lost at sea, his sail-
boat carried out by a riptide—he believed he would never get back
to shore. After that, he sold his boat, and although he sailed sometimes to make up a crew for friends, he was afraid of the sea, didn't
trust himself on it anymore. He put his arms around Bingham,
pulling her back until her shoulder blades pressed into his chest.

Bingham leaned against him. Soon Leth would have to go home, quite soon, across oceans. She didn't speak about his going home. She prided herself on never speaking about it. At the very beginning, as Bingham politely drew Leth out at a company cocktail party—"Where exactly are you from?" "First time in the States?" "What a nice picture of your two sons and their mother! That's your house?"—she promptly fell in love with him.

For the next month, in odd suspended moments, even sometimes as she lay in his arms, Bingham glanced down the length of the coming year to his departure and forced herself to imagine him gone. She would exorcise future suffering by provoking it prematurely.

Once the vertigo thus conjured up had passed, Bingham began to prepare practically for Leth's going away. She never told her friends that she and Leth were lovers. At the office, Bingham and Leth greeted and treated each other politely as colleagues—no one noticed their eyes. At the end of the day, they left work separately. They attended company parties alone. Bingham insisted that it be that way, their secret. When Leth left, there would be no inquiries into how she was doing, no reproaches that she should have known better. Everything would go on as before, as if nothing had happened.

Staring at the ocean this day a year later, Bingham took some satisfaction in the success of her plan. When his arms were no longer around her, the world of Leth and Bingham would dissolve into nothing. There was nothing to say. There would be nothing to say.

Rather than dodge again through the crowd, they made their way around the edge of the town back toward the car. Here they came across a summer shack straying from the others, with a curtain for a door and a sign above it: TEMPORARY TATTOOS.

Leth stopped. "We have to go in."

Bingham wanted to head back home. All they had done that day suddenly dragged on her now, she was so tired, and the drive home so long. They should get going. "Oh, it's some stupid thing for kids. They dab some paint on and call it a tattoo."

Leth teased her, "But what about my American education? You stand in the way?" Temporary tattoos must be very American. He had seen tattoo shops in many port towns, all over the world, but he had never seen a shop for temporary tattoos. So very American, he lectured Bingham, these temporary tattoos, just like American houses of stick and shingle, shack houses no better than this one that a good blow would collapse, just like the way Americans move from place to place—

Bingham abruptly pushed aside the curtain and stepped in.

A strange world swam before Bingham's eyes. Swelling octopi with reaching curving tentacles, dragons flying swiftly through fleeting clouds, flowers of botanical oddness and complication tacked up next to a flock of American eagles clutching in their talons the shield of the republic, anchors festooned, arrow-stricken hearts, elaborated alphabets, women's profiles with the wide blind gazes of figureheads, scowling pirates. Hundreds of these tattoo patterns papered the walls of the shack from ceiling to floor. There were photographs of tattoos, too. One life-size of a muscular back bearing upon it a crucifixion scene complete with cherubs drifting, weeping in the small of the back. Another advertised the latest breakthrough in tattooing, a photo-realistic effect of flesh ripped open to reveal a portrait of the sweetheart buried underneath.

Leth gazed with delight at the patterns.

A short blond girl stuck her head out from the back room. "Hi!"

Leth turned to Bingham and motioned for her, his guide, to speak. He was always shy at first about his foreignness.

"You do the temporary tattoos? Like these?" Bingham waved her hand at the walls.

"That's what the sign says," the girl said in a pleasing voice. "You interested?" A woman—not a girl, as it seemed at first—

between thirty and forty, with a bright young look, eyes lit up, skin fine and clear. Only up close showed the lines knitting under her eyes, dropping their net down onto her cheeks.

"Well, I think we're just looking. Do you mind?"

"Go ahead. Be with you in a sec." The woman disappeared again. There was a clatter of dishes, and a moment later she came out of the back and up to the makeshift counter.

"Sorry. Just finishing the dishes. Not much business today, thought I'd straighten up." She pointed to the patterns on the wall. "Actually, these're for real tattoos. But I try to make my temporaries look like the real thing. At least more real than those temporary tattoo transfers they sell in drugstores now. Real tattoos're my real business—I have a shop over in Saugus. I only come to the beach to make a little extra money doing temps on Sundays, in the summer. Most people don't like to get real tattoos on Sunday. Maybe's against their religion." The tattooist smiled.

Bingham turned her wrist slightly to glance at her watch.

Leth laughed.

Encouraged, the tattooist rattled on. "But just in case, I always keep my needles handy. Sometimes people get a temporary, like it, and want the real thing, right away. And, you know, nowadays, in fact, having a tattoo is not so strange. Lots of celebrities have tattoos." She reeled off names of movie stars and quarterbacks. "Still, on Sundays, I've got mostly kids and temporaries. Today, nobody. Weather's weird."

Leth forgot to be shy. He overflowed with questions about the tattooist and her art. Soon she was leaning toward him over the counter, flattered to be of so much interest, eager to help a foreigner to anything he wanted to know. "Once I got into tattooing, that was it. I really found myself. It's funny, I never liked school, but now—if you can believe it—me!—I actually study, you know, read up on designs and techniques. And I go down to an annual workshop in Virginia with tattooists from all over the world. You know, most people don't realize that tattooing is an ancient and a universal folk art.''

The tattooist stiffened—she caught Bingham's glance at Leth, Bingham's smile. Abruptly pulling out a sheet of paper, the tattooist started sketching a sharp-edged flower that seemed already etched on living skin, blooming with a nearly unremarkable heave of respiration.

Leth set out to soothe the offended artist. Thanks to his attentions, she was persuaded to invite them to the back room to see her tools. With the neat movements of a jeweler, she showed them how she would draw a design with a wax crayon on a plastic sheet, sprinkle black stencil powder on the wax, and press the powdery outline to the skin. She laid out on the drainboard of the old sink two tattooing needles with their trailing electrical cords. Each needle was, in fact, a cluster of needles: one of tiny needles for outlining, another of larger needles for coloring in. Handing Leth a tube of ink to look at, she held up her palette, as she called it, a plastic dish with many grooves. "It's just like painting. I pick up ink on the needles and then work on the skin, mixing the colors right as I go along. I mean, I really think of myself as a painter, in a way.'' Balancing the palette in one hand, a needle in the other, she bent over an imaginary client and gave power to the needle with her foot on a pedal.

To Bingham, peering over Leth's shoulder, the buzz of the needles moving in and out was more horrible than that of a dentist's drill. "Does it hurt?''

"Depends on where the tattoo's located. If it's on skin toughened by the sun, hurts less. If right on the bone, or where there're lots of nerves, it hurts more. I tell my clients to get the tattoo done all at once. After a while, the skin gets numb, so you don't feel the needles as much. Of course, if it's a large tattoo, that takes a couple of sessions. Can't be helped.''

The tattooist was replying to Bingham's question but looking at Leth. And Leth had many more questions. How many tattoos had she done? How many tattoos did she have herself? He admired the brilliant yellow flower on her shoulder that she pulled down her shirt to show him. The tattooist beamed. Designed it herself. And her teacher, who called himself Sailor Bill, Sailor Bill of Norfolk, Virginia, had done the work. She was the only woman Sailor had ever taken on as an apprentice.

Drifting around the room, Bingham stared at the tattoo patterns pinned on the walls here, too, and watched Leth as he talked to this woman. A woman about her own age, Bingham guessed. Probably a few years older.

Bingham started laughing to herself. Laughter pressed up into her mouth. She turned back to the tattooist and Leth. "Could I get a tattoo?" She hastened to add, "A temporary, of course. Sorry."

Both Leth and the tattooist looked at her. The tattooist quickly and politely assured her, "Oh, that's all right. It's all practice. I need all the practice I can get."

Bingham's joke was perfect—Leth would die laughing—a tattoo with Leth's first name, not his unpronounceable real name, but the American version of it that people used at work. What a joke. "I'd like MIKE." She pointed at Leth. "It's his name. Same as the fried-dough man, Mr. Mike." Bingham tried so hard not to grin that her face hurt. "And I want it right across my chest. And I want it just like a sailor's—you know, with anchors and flags."

The tattoo artist pursed her lips, considered Bingham's idea for a moment. "Well, MIKE's easy." She turned to Leth. "You know, I could do something really interesting instead. Look at some pattern books while I set up," and the tattooist led them back to the front room and began stacking loose-leaf binders on the counter. "You might get some ideas." She busied herself unfolding the two metal chairs that were leaned up against the wall. From the back, she brought out her tray of ink tubes, her palette, a jam jar with several brushes stuck in it, and arranged them on a small TV tray.

Bingham threw Leth a tough sailor look. "I want MIKE. Right across here," and she drew a curve above the rise of her breasts. Her joke of MIKE with flying pennants would get away from her in a second if she didn't insist on it.

Leth smiled, but he didn't catch her eye and laugh with her. He leafed through the binders, and not only to be polite to the tattoo artist. Bingham could tell.

Leth stopped at one page of designs.

The tattooist was instantly at his side. "I like those Maori ones a lot, myself. You know, I can do them if you want. I've done them before. The spirals're kind of abstract, but you see how they look like the curl of the waves or the tiny whirlpools between rocks when a wave drains back. We had a Maori guy come to our workshop and show us his technique. Maoris use needles now. But they used to carve the designs into the skin like you carve wood—sort of chisel it right in. You should have seen this big funnel he brought with him. A person bleeding from tattooing is taboo and can't touch food. So he has to be fed with the funnel. They pour some kind of soup down it."

Tattooing made you bleed. Of course it must, Bingham realized, and broke out in a faint sweat. Leth called her over to look at the designs. Bingham glanced at them and quickly looked away.

The tattooist made a suggestion. "I could do a MIKE in spirals. Hey, I'm no purist. You know, tattooists all over the world put new stuff in with their old patterns. Did you know that the minute Tahitians saw the white men's ships, they started tattooing anchors all over themselves? I see this as kind of a challenge."

The tattoo had been Bingham's idea. She couldn't back out now. Bingham said yes to the spirals as long as MIKE was there, too.

Leth decided not to watch; he would go for a walk on the beach. The tattoo would be more striking, he and the tattooist agreed, if he saw it all at once, finished. Bingham didn't like the idea of being left alone with the tattooist. Bingham wasn't very good at small talk. What would she talk about with this woman? Yet she couldn't get Leth alone and tell him to stay.

After he left, the tattoo artist invited Bingham to sit down in one of the folding chairs. She sat herself in the other and pulled the TV tray close. With deft and curiously dry, light fingers, she slipped off the straps of Bingham's shirt and pushed it down until the shirt just covered the nipples of the breasts. She touched Bingham's skin and looked at her finger. "Hm, moist, slightly oily. You can't imagine what a difference skin texture makes!" Dipping a sponge in witch hazel, she carefully wiped off the skin from the clavicle to the line of the shirt. With a disposable razor, she shaved the area and sponged it again. Then, for several minutes, she stared at Bingham's chest as if measuring the space, getting a good sense of the contours, the hollows on the inside of the shoulders, the rise and fall of the breasts.

Bingham shifted in her chair. "Outline comes first, doesn't it?"

"Not necessarily. Not this time. I've got such a strong picture in my head of how this is going to look, I don't need an outline." Selecting several tubes from her tray, she filled grooves on the palette with blue, black, white, and green ink. She tested several brushes against her fingertip and chose one.

"Even for a temporary tattoo?" Bingham struggled up a bit with her shoulders.

"Yes, of course," the tattooist said blandly. She gently pushed Bingham's shoulders down with the pads of her fingers, a light but firm touch. Bingham settled back stiffly, like at the dentist, or at the hairdresser.

"It'll be easier if you don't talk," the tattooist added. "Talking makes your skin jump around."

With the brush poised, its blunt tip flattened between her fingers and now glistening with ink, the tattoo artist paused an instant, then set to work. At the first prick of the brush, Bingham flinched. She remembered looking at the brushes before. They had appeared soft.

The tattooist drew back. "Sorry, but the bristles have to be kind of sharp to get the tattoo effect. Doesn't really hurt, does it? No worse than plucking your eyebrows, is it?"

"Oh, no, no," Bingham murmured, and she leaned back once more in the chair. The brush, as the tattooist worked, kept pricking, yet Bingham became used to it. The pricking even came to be rather pleasant, like a cat treading, flexing his claws on her chest. Bingham's earlier fatigue returned, and relieved of any obligation to entertain the tattooist, she abandoned herself to the brush, let herself be lulled into something like sleep. Footsteps came into the shack, maybe Leth's, maybe someone else's. Her eyelids were too heavy to lift. The steps went away.

The only unpleasant moment was a dream, snatched at the edge of sleep. Leth sat beside her in an unfamiliar house but did not look at her. Even when she shouted and sobbed, he showed the most polite disregard.

Bingham stirred and was comforted to find the faint nettle of the brush moving along in its tiny sweeps, the tattooist's curled fingers barely touching the skin, her wrists sometimes, but not often, brushing Bingham's breasts, her warm breath—smelling a bit like vanilla, how odd—coming in small gasps after she held it for long moments of concentration.

To stay awake, Bingham tried to follow the progress of the painting. The tattooist had a special way of going about her work. She did not outline the letters and then fill them in and decorate them with the swirls of the design pattern, as Bingham would have imagined. She worked instead with a method quite different and more complicated. She constructed successive bands of the elements of the design that, completely laid out, would bring together the shapes of the letters. Each element was composed of a swirl, curling into another, and that pouring out, only to be pulled into yet one more curve. And the tattooist worked the elements and thus the letters backward, from right to left, against their grain. Steadily, she moved across Bingham's chest, was now almost all the way across. Bingham could feel the letters spreading over her. She tried to tick them off, but it was strange telling them backward, and, too, where did one end, another begin?

At last, the tattoo was complete. Clutching her shirt to her breasts, for the tattooist warned her to wait a minute for the ink to dry before pulling up the straps, Bingham looked into the large mirror held up for her. Here were Leth's footsteps behind her. Here was Leth staring at her in the mirror from over her shoulder.

"Do you like it?" the tattooist asked Leth, before Bingham had a chance to open her mouth. His eyes must see what Bingham saw—the timid expression on her face, the weirdly alive MIKE over her breasts. She saw him narrow his eyes just as she had to do to make out the letters. Yes, there they were, twisting and turning, flowing in a channel of foaming sea across her skin.

"Fantastic!" Leth cried out.

The tattooist beamed at him.

"How long will it last?" Bingham asked, still staring at herself.

"A couple of days, at the most. It just kind of fades away."

The tattoo was dry now. Leth asked the tattooist how much he owed her. The tattooist said there was no charge. She liked having a chance to try out that design. Leth refused, no, no, and reached for his wallet.

But Bingham insisted on paying for the tattoo. The tattoo was her idea, after all. Bingham paid the tattooist twenty dollars, more than twice the price she named.

Bingham and Leth left the tattoo shack and continued along the margin of the town toward the car, Bingham turning in to Leth whenever anyone came toward them.

Still, people saw the tattoo, for what could she do, there were only the thin straps of her shirt and above it the all-too-bright tattoo. People stared. Men seemed particularly stunned by the tattoo. Men looked at her, showing their interest in Bingham in a way they never had before. Bingham's usual attractions were subtle. She could seem plain, boyish—sometimes she even played at being a young friend of Leth's. Decorated with the tattoo, she had become another creature, even more than a woman, and the men drew near to her without realizing what they were doing. Bingham hurried away from them toward the car, a headlong step ahead of Leth.

The drive home was endless, and, after night fell, difficult, as if Bingham's eyes had dilated and each pair of oncoming headlights penetrated into her brain. So fearful was she of steering into those lights, her shoulders and hands soon ached from gripping the wheel too tightly. Leth offered to drive, yet Bingham said no, she was determined to get them home herself.

At last, here was her small house. Inside, when she switched on the light, Leth exclaimed, "Sweetheart, you should have let me drive. You're so pale!"

The tattoo stood out even more vividly than before, Bingham could see for herself in the hall mirror. Her muscles, stiff and tense as wires threading her, collapsed. She hadn't been so tired since she was a child, so tired that she could hardly get herself ready for bed.

Leth ran a bath for her and helped her off with her clothes. She brushed her lips across his cheek in thanks—his skin smelled and tasted of salt—and then lowered herself into the water. But Leth didn't go away. Instead, he rolled up his sleeves, got down on his knees next to the deep tub, and soaped up his large hands. When he ran his hands over her, washing her, it was as if now she were his namesake, she belonged to him, his hands sculpting her, shaping her, smoothing her, abolishing the labor of her mother. She was so weary, she let the hands have her. As he poured the hot water over her shoulders to rinse them off, her skin stung where it had been pricked by the tattoo brush. She looked down. The letters were sharp and bright under the sheets of water.

They had faded a bit, she noticed, after he patted her dry.

They faded more overnight. When Bingham woke up the next morning, she looked down at Leth's arm thrown over her. Freeing her own hand from the covers, she ran it slowly down his arm, bristling softly the hairs, gripping gently for the feel of the big bone, the muscle there, then her hand closed over his. Her fingers stroked her grandmother's old quilt between his fingers, tracing out its bands of worn cotton print, and she found her fingers tracing, too, her own skin. The edge of the tattoo, which she could just see, was like one more band of faded fabric. She could still make out the letters, though they had sunk into her skin another fraction of a fathom.

Two days later, Leth was gone. He left for the airport. Bingham left for work as usual. Everything was the same at work, except for people saying all day long how much they already missed having Mike around the office. Bingham kept the tattoo hidden under her high-buttoned blouse.

After the first quick fading, Bingham found that the tattoo only faded infinitesimally. Every night, she examined it in her bathroom mirror, looking for any change in the intensity of color. One night, she rubbed her skin raw trying to scrub off the tattoo.

Finally, it was gone. All over and done with, Leth and the tattoo, the year coming to an end. The leaves would now turn red and purple and finally, the first of November, everything would be black wet roads, black wet tree trunks with the last large yellow leaves plastered against them and wet laundry limp in the rain. And there would be snow and ice and white skies.

A month or so later, Bingham decided that it would be good for her to seek out other men. She thought immediately of two men at work who had shown interest a year ago. Her best friend in the office pointed out that, just yesterday, in the lunchroom, they had both made an effort to talk to her. Bingham hadn't noticed. The next day and the next weeks, she paid attention. She smiled at them, leaned toward them when they talked. She listened to them, turned her mind on them, thought of what they needed to hear and gave it to them. Such encouragement she lavished on their dreams, their better selves. It was irresistible, and both men pursued her.

One of the men dropped her after a while. Bingham saw him looking sharply at her when her voice climbed too high, almost clanging. She knew he grew suspicious of her self-effacement —certainly it was flattering, at first, to be the only subject of conversation, but when he wanted to know more about her, she had to shunt him off. He found out nothing. In the corridors of the office, Bingham watched him shy away from her.

The other man, though, kept after her. Difficult to say, after awhile, which one of them pushed more toward a climax, he rushing to claim her, or Bingham rushing to obliterate the memory of Leth, at least confuse Leth's touch with another's. As she rushed along, Bingham was sure, she congratulated herself, that she had forgotten about Leth. Leth was gone. She was going to be with this new man. All her friends at work who watched the romance develop in the office, over lunch in the cafeteria, agreed they would be a good match. Be so nice to have a marriage within the company.

Still, even though both Bingham and the new man were intent on their mutual pursuit, still there was the finest of hesitations on both sides. He caressed her passionately in his car, when they came home from a dinner date, but let her go into her house alone. She responded with kisses and touches of her own, yet was always glad to escape inside.

At last this stall made Bingham nervous. She proposed a weekend trip together up the coast. A friend at work told her about a romantic inn, all crisp chintz, rose sachet, antique furniture, and flowered wallpaper. Right on the ocean, and even though it was too cold to swim, there would always be walks up and down the beach, tightly wrapped against the wind. A fire at night, a big warm bed, the friend promised her.

The drive north led them past the turnoff to Salisbury Beach. Staring at the sign, Bingham all at once pictured a small, dark, dingy motel there under the dripping roller-coaster track. The Beach Bound—she surprised herself by remembering the name of the motel, and as her thoughts hovered there another moment, she saw the tattooist at the front desk under a buggy light.

Turning to her lover, Bingham asked if he was tired. It's hard to drive a long time in such heavy rain. Would he like to let her take over the wheel?

They checked in and unpacked their bags. They sat down to dinner in the inn's restaurant, which overlooked the sea. A spectacular sunset broke through the storm clouds and for a moment turned the rough whitecaps pink as frosting. Maybe the rain would stop by tomorrow. Their dinner was showy, but good. They ate slowly and lingered over their coffee as if an old couple with years and years behind them. Underneath it all, they were both excited. They knew that the room upstairs was warm, the bed large.

At last, they mounted the stairs. He unlocked the door. She walked past him to switch on the rose-shaded lamp. He offered her the bathroom first. She protested no, it was all right, he should go ahead. He did, and while she waited, she unclasped her bracelet, took off her earrings, put the earrings back on. The room was very quiet. She opened a window, but had to shut it at once because of the stinging rain. She stared at the mute waves through the windowpane. It would have been so comforting to lie safe and warm in bed and listen to the sea crash below. What if it rained all weekend? Too bad to drive this far and because of the rain never get closer to the sea. She gathered up her new robe, a toothbrush, and even perfume, which she had never worn before, for her turn in the bathroom.

He came out of the bathroom, smiling. Their hands touched

accidentally as he headed toward the bed and she stepped quickly to the bathroom.

Shutting the door behind her, she found herself in a big shiny box of black tile with a marble sink and a thronelike toilet near the door. Over in the shadows, a Jacuzzi, a bidet, an entire wall of mirror black with the reflection of the tiles. Twisting the brass dolphin taps of the sink, she washed her hands, her face, under her arms and between her legs, dabbed on too much perfume and washed it off, only to dab on more. Reaching for her new robe, she drew it over her shoulders. Was the robe long enough? Should she tie it, so he could untie it? Or leave it flowing open around her body?

There must be a light for the wall mirror. Yes, here was a control panel of switches. She flipped the top three one by one and got a fan, a suntanning lamp, Vivaldi. The next switch, finally, turned on six hot footlights under the mirror. Too big, too bright a mirror, a mirror one could never have at home. It made her take account of herself with the thoroughness of a dealer in flesh. Wasn't she getting old! She leaned into the light. Too many wrinkles, more gray hairs. She lifted up her breasts. Didn't they used to be this high?

She let her breasts drop and they trembled and swayed. What if he didn't find her attractive? And, of course, what if she didn't find him attractive? Found his flesh repugnant to her hands? What if it wasn't smooth and alive, burnished and warm like Leth's arms, Leth's back?

She leaned even closer to the mirror. Didn't her skin used to be plumper, with a faint blush to it like the thick petals of certain flowers, as Leth once said? When did it become so thin and transparent, so stripped down a layer, letting her veins, black, greenish, show right through?

Veins twisting and curving. Whorls faintly livid under the skin. Traces of the tattoo still there? The name there and then dissolving, not there? Bingham stepped back from the mirror. She shut her eyes. How could she go out to the bedroom like this? As he raised himself above her, he would see everything. She had to lock the door, call out to him through the door, tell him to go away. Make some excuse. There was nothing else to do.

Bingham strained every sense before she opened her eyes. Bingham strained every sense and she could smell the sea, could hear the waves tearing at her feet.

# KITES!

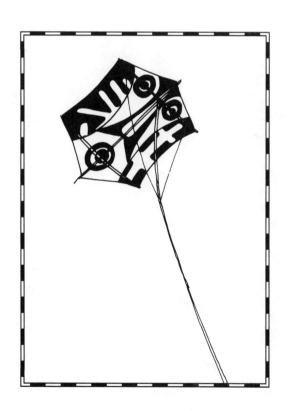

A BRILLIANT PINK BANNER CRACKED and snapped on top of a dune. I pulled the car over, and my wife and I staggered up through dune grass to see what was going on. CAPE COD HANG GLIDERS HANGIN' IN, the banner read, and under it a bunch of men and women stood staring down at a woman kneeling in the sand, a woman tied to a giant kite. Thick blue straps came down between her shoulder blades and fastened to thick blue straps reaching up from around her hips. Her hands gripped the side bars of an aluminum triangle attached to two long wings, curved, spined, pointy pterodactyl wings, wings barred blue purple yellow, wings lifting lightly in the wind.

"I can't," the woman cried.

My wife touched the wing of another giant kite tethered there, a giant kite rocking in the wind, pulling at its ropes.

Next to the woman, a man crouched on his hands and knees. "Now, remember what we talked about in class. Breathe. Remember, fear's there to make you focus. Breathe. Slowly. In and out. Breathe. Now let's stand up! Breathe. Now let's get ready to fly!"

Locks of the woman's hair stood up against the wind.

The instructor frowned and squatted back on his heels. "Okay." He looked around at the others. "Okay. Roger can go on and go."

Freed from the kite, the woman slunk away to the other side of the dune and sat down. The class turned their backs on her to help Roger get into harness. A low chant began: "Go, Roger, go!" I watched Roger go white, clinch his hands on the bars of the giant kite. A kick of sand and Roger is running across the dune, Roger's feet are treading air, Roger twists his head back to grin at us—

"Roger! Pay attention!" the instructor yells.

Roger sails slowly out, descends gently to the beach below. He's skimming the beach—oh no! skimming the waves, heading out for sea—

"Push out!" the whole class cries with the instructor.

My wife leans over the edge of the dune.

Roger pushes out. The glider stalls, drops him into the surf. The wings float flat on the water. But where's Roger? There's Roger, bobbing in the waves, waving to the cliff! Everyone cheers. I looked over my shoulder. The woman sitting on the sand put her head down on her knees.

Catching my wife's eye, I nodded, and we slid back down the dune. In the car, I scribbled out the details of the scene: the banner, Roger's flight, the giant hang-gliding kites, the weeping woman. Terrific—maybe?—opening for an article, exactly what I had come to the Cape for. Maybe I'd get two articles out of these kites, a newspaper feature about perilous sports on the Cape and a travel piece for a hang-gliding magazine—someone somewhere must put out a hang-gliding magazine. Hang gliders must want to know where to fly, where to eat, where to sleep on the Cape.

That day, instead of insisting, "You could put in that, but you should put in this. Didn't you see how he," my wife waited silently and looked out the window.

My wife and I had lunch in Chatham at the Sea-Inn, recommended to me by a friend. We ate outside on a deck overlooking the beach. We didn't talk much. We watched three kids hopping up and down around a man in baggy pants and rumpled sweater as he gassed up a model plane. The plane went up with a loud buzz, a smoke trail—one moonfaced girl shrieking, "Dad, Dad, it's too high"—then the plane turned and crashed into the sand. The kids screamed and went running after it, their father crying out to them in comical and desperate reassurance, "That happens! That happens!" Again and again, the father launched the plane, it crashed, and the screaming kids, tireless, fetched the plane. "That happens!" I heard the father still calling as we left.

Walking back to the car, my wife abruptly began, "I'm thinking about looking for a job. Something part-time. I'm—"

"But we agreed."

Three months before, my wife had been laid off. Her job was not a great job. From seven-thirty in the morning until seven at night, six days a week, she, by profession a structural engineer, made the palest of shady deals with the city: If they passed her on an ordinance, her company would plant trees along Boylston and hang holiday wreaths. On a good day, she got to inspect new employee cafeterias and bang food trays against the walls to test the paint. But her severance pay was generous, and I had just sold my latest big travel piece, "Ancient Monasteries of the World," so we agreed to get along without her working for a while. She would just rest for a while, let her body fill out. She had become so thin, her bones showed. Rest and boredom would be the richest breeding ground, we hoped. So we had agreed to be a little poorer for a while and then there would be riches beyond measure, our child.

"I'm tired of hanging around the house. I eat too much. I'm getting fat."

"Fat? Just fat?"

"One hundred percent pure grade-A fat. Just fat."

Before starting the car, I made a note: "The Sea-Inn's famous fish stew smelled like KitKat cat food, and I suspect that's what KitKat tastes like." I added an extra spurt of curare: *"Service slow."*

Back on the highway, I looked over at my wife. My wife had her arm out the window, hand out, curving palm riding the wind. My wife loves to feel the wind under the palm of her hand.

"If you wanted to, you could help me with this article. Here's your big chance to get in from the very beginning of a piece. We could even write it together if—" We had also agreed that I would stay closer to home, cultivating my own garden, as it were, try to do more local New England stories—though they don't pay as much—and not run all over the world in my usual style, pathological traveler—style. Helping me out with these local pieces, that would give my wife something to do.

To the road ahead, she said, "A part-time job won't hurt. Something fun. It'll be something I can quit on short notice."

Her shapely hand cleaves the air.

Is this breeding time a brooding time?

We stopped for gas before heading on to Truro. As I was paying, my wife, who had been prowling—aimlessly, yet still very much prowling—the aisles of the convenience store attached to the gas station (such an old-fashioned, polite word, *convenience*—marriage of convenience, apartment with all the conveniences, at your earliest convenience), my wife, I say, found that her convenience that day was a kite stuck in a cardboard stand. In the mirror angled to catch shoplifters, I saw her take it out, one of those old paper kites wound around sticks, stiff as a tightly furled leaf. A moment later, the kite lay on the counter and two fat balls of kite string came clumping down next to it.

At the restaurant where we ate dinner, I glimpsed our hang gliders in the bar. The gliding refusenik, sheepish but grinning, sat with them. Had she earned her wings at last?

That night, we went back to our "housekeeping cottage." I have always been attracted to the Cape's colonies of "housekeeping cottages," like the cottages of Leprechaun Cove scattered in a grove of slanting stunted pines, or like these Above Tide Cottages in Truro, tiny shack houses lined up in a prim peaked-roof row along the beach, all of them alike, white with trim of pink and green. Toy house, toy kitchen. We were setting up house in a housekeeping cottage, the thinnest shell of shelters. Would the sun show through chinks tomorrow morning? I thought I'd try to get the cottages into an article somehow.

Lying on the lumpy bed, I sorted out my notes. My wife had claimed the wooden table and was busily unrolling her kite. I looked up. She looked up. She grinned. "You can tell your readers the tables here are just right for making kites!"

Her happiness such an unexpected gift. I could breathe again —had I been holding my breath all day? I got up to take a look at the kite. I hadn't seen such a kite in years, but my fingers instantly remembered the soft, warm, smooth splinteriness of the balsawood spars, the thinness of the crackling paper. I wouldn't have guessed they still made these paper kites. Most kids' kites these days seem made of plastic, with cartoon characters on them, zoomorphic or extraterrestrial. I flew this exact paper kite when I was a kid, this plain white paper kite with thin red and blue stripes, *High Flyer* emblazoned across its face.

I lay back down on the creaking bed and flipped through my notes. Looked up again at my wife. Her long hair fell over her face, curtaining it off, cutting me off. I love it more when she wears her hair pulled back. The volumes of her face are displayed, the high-planed cheekbones—landing strips for my kisses, I used to tell her—the sheer drop, the hollow beneath them. The long winged eyebrows, the black eyes. The small potato knob on the end of her nose that makes her thuggish, with a riffraffishness that compels complicity, and at the same time she's like a young nun, sweet and young for all her thirty-five years, so easy to make blush. And when she blushes and beams at me, I know what it's like to be looked at with love, the simplest, plainest love.

Her face was hidden, but I could see her hands, long, pale, graceful hands gifted at corporeal benedictions—these hands now picked at a stubborn knot. My wife can swear most foully, too.

The kite is done. But what to do about a tail? My sister and I used to beg old sheets from my mother and tear them into strips. My wife, resourceful engineer, pulls out the plastic bag lining the wastebasket, cuts it into ribbons with her pocketknife, knots the ribbons. "Kite tail!" she proclaims, and ties her tail to the kite. Then she is at my side, laughing, tugging at my hair. "Let's go fly a kite!"

I hadn't quite finished with my notes, but she was laughing, I say, and we were only two steps from the beach, and outside a shiny dime moon rising, a wind blowing straight out to sea. Soon, I stood holding the kite to my chest, a faithful page holding his knight's shield.

My wife yelled, "Ready?"

I held the kite up by its spine.

"Let go," she cried, and the kite went up and up, then nosedived straight into the sand.

My wife moaned.

Yet the paper wasn't torn. The spine wasn't broken. We tried again.

"Ready?"

"Ready!"

The wind picked the kite up and the string spun out taut and alive. The kite shot up up so high, its plastic tail slick with light, a kite like a monster luna moth. My wife paid the string out, more and more string. The kite set out to sea, with that wind so steady, strong and steady. Our kite strolled down the path of rolled silver leading to the moon.

When I saw the ball of string coming to an end, I slogged

through the sand to the cottage for the second ball. "Hurry, hurry," she called as I came staggering back down the beach. I tied the second ball onto the straining end of the first, and my wife let the new string go singing out, burning her fingers, until we could barely see our shining kite far away against the faraway moon.

Suddenly, the string snapped. Our kite plummeted into the sea, fell into the sea, far out at sea.

"Oh no!" My wife held the limp string in her hand, so taut and alive one moment, limp and dead the next.

"Lost at sea, lost at sea," I intoned in funereal fashion.

She cried with laughter.

I lay in bed and my wife lay down next to me, turned over on her back, and said aloud to the ceiling, to me, "It was a beautiful day. We had such a beautiful day, even though we lost our kite, our beautiful kite—"

"Lost at sea, lost at sea—"

"I was so happy."

And I, convulsed with tenderness. Brooding breeding silence, now this sudden wind shear of joy. And she had confessed her happiness with such humility and joy, almost childish, her thankfulness for one day, her gratitude for one more day, snatched from death, stolen from sadness. I was in bed with a female Saint Francis of Assisi. A Saint Francis with an edible body, with the rear end of a queen, ample, perfectly designed, very lively.

As we drove on to Provincetown the next morning, a station wagon speeded past us. Two kids hanging from the windows pointed up at—my wife stuck her head out the window to see—a flotilla of hot-air balloons. On Cape Cod, everything seems up in the air. Good opening line—maybe?—for my piece.

---

A month later, I couldn't ever get my wife to look up at me from that sewing machine that whirred stop and go in the extra room, the would-be, should-be baby's room. The room taken over by the sewing machine, by the old Ping-Pong table she bought at a garage sale and used for cutting out not flannelette, but pieces of kites, kites for the kite store where she now worked.

Tatters of rip-stop nylon in kite-bright colors littered the floor. Yellow red blue pink at their brightest, purest pitch. Even a black bright like wet paint. As if there weren't any November colors in the world, like right outside the window now, brown leaves, gold grasses, black-red winterberries. Rip-stop nylon is a strange fabric, light and crackling, rustling like tissue paper but so strong, strong enough to withstand fierce winds and sharp branches. I've just become a partisan of paper kites: The art of flying should protect the kite, and if the kite fell, it fell apart, rotted, like us, our bodies. This frightening rip-stop, rot-stop material would last forever wadded up somewhere.

Early one morning, I watched her from the doorway. She is sewing, sitting on that old oak chair with two rungs hanging out of their sockets. Scissors knife up from a tackle-box sewing box. A drawer spills green fabric and loops of white nylon line that shimmer like spider threads in the sunlight. On the table, stacks of kiting magazines landslide. A needle raised in her hand, her head bent over a pink kite, my wife is naked, bare, smooth. The only uncluttered thing in the room. Demure, desirable.

Crouched on the kite scraps at her feet, his fur puffed full of light, the cat stares at me. But my wife doesn't look up at me.

I retreated to my study. I said to myself, When I hear her coming down the hall, I will come out of my study. I'll catch her and press her up against the wall, and ask her softly, Would you like to lie down with me, for just a while? I'll kiss her ear and breathe into it—my famous Spanish kiss, *la paloma del fuego,* "the dove of fire," I call it, she calls it the hot pigeon smooch. And if she fidgets and wants so very much to go back to her kites, I'll show her that I can be infinitely courteous. I'll say to her, Oh, you are such a good lover. You know how to make your man wait! Then kissing her softly, I'll release her.

Minutes later, I know, I'm sure she will appear, suddenly, take my book from under my beakish nose, and offer to impale herself on the sword of her Sardanapalus. If only I will let her, be so kind to her. She'll beg me humbly, all the while her quick hands descabbarding me.

Instead, my wife hurried down the hall, hurried off to work at the kite store.

The first day I stopped by to see my wife at work, I had just finished an article on a young woman, ex-hippie, long blond hair, mongrel dog with a bandanna kerchief, who had made herself into a local expert on sailing rope. For the one photo I was allowed, I had my rope lady stand up and I coiled around her her trademark orange rope, thick as an anaconda, coiled the rope around her from foot to chin, until she looked like a mummy, or a goddess of rope. To celebrate, I thought I'd take my wife out to lunch and tell her about the piece. We used to talk over my stories, but I hadn't really told her about this one, or the last one. She's too busy with her kites.

I walked down the hall of the mall where my wife worked, past a decorative decoys shop, a mineral-jewelry shop, a lingerie shop, and there around the corner was High as a Kite, a small shop with wind socks like dangling octopi draping the open door. Through the front window full of kites posed as if in flight, as if I'd scared up a flock of kites, I saw my wife. She was leaning back against a wall behind the glass counter, leaning there in her old black full skirt—worn soft as velvet, that old skirt, my favorite skirt of hers—a faded blue blouse, black sweater, black boots. Above her head played a video on kiting. Against a bright blue sky, yellow kites lift off, dart, swoop.

No customers. My wife was leaning back against the wall and listening to—it must be the owner, O'Caslin, a wiry, rusty-haired O'Caslin, with his hands full of kite line. A thick glass window and a wide glass counter between myself and my wife. Nothing came between my wife and her O'Caslin, O'Kasbah. I stared at her to make her turn her head, to make her look at me. She didn't look up at me. I was about to walk in, when the telephone rang, and my wife answered. O'Caslin, this rusty wire hanger of a man all angles, put down the line and mimed going out to get some lunch for them. For an obvious graduate of remedial mime, he rather cleverly enacted eating a sandwich, holding an invisible sandwich between his hands, biting into it with his small, repulsive baby teeth, then chewing. Cupping his hand, he guzzled an airy coffee, raised his eyebrows, and smirked.

To my shame, my wife grinned and nodded her head. As O'Caslin came out the door, I turned to study the bristling conic corsets and lacy but very tensile thongs for Lycra ladies mounted in the window of the lingerie store. My wife's plain black cotton underwear I instantly regretted and wanted to inspect, close up, live, in action. I turned back to the kite store. She had hung up the phone and was unpacking more line. I came up behind her. She turned, saw me—the telephone rang again.

"High as a Kite," she trilled, and waved me away. "Oh, yes, thanks for returning our call. We want to know if High Skyers would be part of the city kite festival in the spring?"

I knew all about this kite championship and kite festival planned jointly for the spring. At home, if her foot was off the sewing machine pedal, her hand was on the telephone, calling up other kite stores, other sponsors, teams of competitive kite fliers all over New England, public officials for the city park system, and vendors of food. "Hi, this is High as a Kite, and we're interested in your barbecue."

I fell in among kites, picked up a box kite, poked aside a bat kite left over from a Halloween display. Found a bookshelf of kite magazines, kite manuals, kite pattern books, and at last a history of kites, which I pulled out and flipped through. Big color photographs. Of a kite festival in Japan, with red, white, and blue kites sailing above the blue, blue sea. Of two kites trimmed in gold foil and tangling in India. Of an immense octagonal paper kite, many-colored paper patches, with pretty paper tassels, flying in Guatemala on the Day of the Dead, taking messages to the dead. Instantly, I could picture an article, an article with large color photographs, what we call a roundup article, a roundup of kite festivals around the world, including Boston, too. It would be a big article, like my best articles, big national magazine, lots of pictures of kites, talks with kite makers. I could go around the world to Japan, to India. Of course, it would mean traveling, going away, again, and we had, of course, agreed, but that agreement she had already broken, really, and the piece would be, after all, all about kites.

My wife hung up the telephone and came over to me. I put down my book, grasped her by the back of her neck, squeezed it to hold her still. I Spanish-kissed her ear—she squirmed and laughed—I whispered my kite tales to her: "Did you know that in Korea they write the name and birthday of their child on a kite, then let the kite fly away with all the evil spirits that might harm the child? And did you know that two hundred years ago in France, there were kite riots? In Indonesia—"

She laughed and, clenching her teeth, pushed me up against the counter with a sudden burst of energy. I slipped my hand up under her sweater—she never wears a brassiere, just a camisole, so sorry, corset store next door—up and over her breast, but it was not swollen, her belly, flat, too flat. She struggled, twisted out of my grasp. She gasped, "Oh, Stan, this is my husband. This is Stan. . . . This is Stan O'Caslin."

I bought the kite book. And at my wife's insistence, I bought a kite that day, a kite all ready to go, of rip-stop nylon striped pink red white yellow blue, a kite that packs up into a small pouch. She called it an emergency kite—when the wind is right and you just have to fly a kite.

═══

My flight from Singapore back to Boston took off at three o'clock in the morning. The taxi driver looked like a crew-cut hog. When I said, answering at last his brutal, relentless questioning, that I had been married ten years and had no children, he almost stopped his car. "But how can you live without kids?"

At two o'clock in the morning! I answered, *"I can't live,"* but was somehow still vaguely alive.

"Why?" he demanded to know with a sort of Chinese nosiness. "Because it is fashionable to live?"

I gave him a tentative "Perhaps."

He persisted. "Whose fault is it? Yours? Hers? Is it entirely medical?" We were in some suburb whose trees had thick leaves like glossy leather and waxlike fruits. "I know"—he fixed his eyes on mine in the rearview mirror—"get rid of her. Marry young Chinese girl with money. Or with computer diploma."

At the next stoplight, I took out my suitcase, my clumsy package of Japanese kites, which I should have mailed from Tokyo. I paid him and sat on the curb. Crushed by a sense of the utter, absolute failure of my life, I could hardly breathe. An aspiring seed planter, I had plowed my wife's furrow, moist and dark, but nothing sprang up. What use was this bulky body of mine, its hidden strength, if I couldn't wring out of it a child?

Thank God the next cabdriver only wanted to lament, endlessly, his fate, which kept him in puritanical Singapore. I should go to Bangkok, where they have brothels, great brothels where girls performed acts like The Living Soap and Tora Tora—"Kamikaze girls! You American battleship!"

Maybe the fault was mine. Back in Boston, I secretly made an appointment at a fertility clinic. The doctor unfurled a long list of procedures and eagerly began asking me how far I was prepared to go, how much I was prepared to spend. Couldn't we just begin with a sperm count? I asked him. A simple sperm count, just to see if the problem was with my male milk? I was turned over to a nurse, who shut me up in a bathroom.

My wife and I used to spend a fortune on home pregnancy-test kits with their ridiculous names, like First Response, a phrase that always made me think of nuclear war. We wanted to be so sure of getting the telegram our child was sending us that we bought three or four kits at a time—maybe this one was defective, maybe that one was not foolproof. And fumbling fools we were at first, yet soon expert enough with droppers, dippers, plastic vials. "I'm going to micturate now. Prepare for testing," my wife would announce, and I'd rush to the bathroom with the official cup, ready for her gush. Until it was no longer funny, but too sad. She started furtive testing alone behind the locked bathroom door. I saw the boxes in the trash. Finally, all testing seemed to have been abandoned.

Now I tried manning my pump in this pink bathroom, but nothing happened. How could it in this icy pink bathroom with faded instructions scotch-taped to the wall, with stacks of tattered magazines, their pleated and torn, worn centerfolds of superbosomic models? When I came out empty-handed, the lab nurse smiled in sympathy.

"Six-thirty? You know, the old hands hangin' down?"

She sent me home with a jar, "though any ol' jam jar will do," and instructed me that I had to get the sperm to the clinic within an hour of ejaculation. I turned away as another man came rushing in the door, exclaiming, "I have come to deposit my pollen."

I knew my wife would not be at home when I got home. That afternoon, after closing the kite store early, she had taken off for Martha's Vineyard to try out some new kites with O'Caslin and the stripling, O'Caslin's other assistant, a tall, thin, flaxen-haired youth. They would sleep over on the island and get an early start the next morning.

"Do you know where you're going to stay, exactly?"

"With Stan's friends. I don't know their name. On Chappy—"

"Chappaquiddick?"

"Well, Stan says Chappy."

"Well, do you know where you'll fly the kites?"

"Stan says it all depends on where the wind's up."

Her enthusiasm for the kites had come to seem so dangerous. She could fall in love with O'Caslin O'Kiteland because of the kites. He might become a pretext for the kites, and he might take advantage of that kite love. That was what I feared, the simplicity of this kite love, this love welling up, spilling over onto him, not me.

So I slept that night without my wife cupped in my hands, without her smell. Woke up in the morning without seeing her face half-asleep, almost a child's face again, sweet, her skin the color of quince blossoms, white flushed so slightly with pink. Hot soft skin.

The cat jumped up thumped up on my chest and stared at me accusingly. What had I done with her?

At breakfast, my wife used to chatterbox away, her half-open robe revealing one small breast, pointed, wolfish, a wolf mother's teat, while her hand slipped up my baggy shorts. She'd blush as if surprised to find something quite alive in there.

Now I sat in the kitchen, alone (the cat had gobbled up his food and gone out), drinking coffee made in our old pot that's big enough for a convent. *Caffè di convento,* I call it. I picture us as convent convict escapees, a renegade fat canon who likes his sausages, a nun with graceful praying hands and lively thighs and —I warm to my subject—a lovely quilted womb. For "Green Stone Cities," an article about Oaxaca, Mexico, and several other greenish cities on several continents, I visited the Church of Santo Domingo's rose chapel, whose pink Baroque ceiling is covered with gilt rose branches entwined in a latticed bower. I later made it a point to tell my wife (as I couldn't, unfortunately, my readers) that this chapel dedicated to the Virgin Mary is, in fact, an homage to a woman's womb, the squares bounded off by the branches an homage to the quilted lining of the womb, the soft but strong quilted flesh that grips the lover.

Thinking quiltiness, I ran to the bathroom for my jar. I think about my nun's chapel, and in a short while I had my jar of tadpoles, a thriving, crowded, I hoped, school of tadpoles. I jumped in the car to deliver them alive to the clinic, zigzagged through the narrow streets, then shot out on the highway, the road lifting under me and my tadpoles as we sailed up and on.

Twenty minutes later, those orange signs appeared: ROAD CONSTRUCTION—road destruction—1,000 FEET, no exit, 500 FEET, lightbulbed arrows pointing left, herding all cars over into one lane, before me bumper-to-bumper, behind me suddenly the same, and we slowed down, we crept, we stopped. Ahead, giant orange Caterpillar tractors jerked along in antediluvian pokiness. I shook the jar gently and whispered to it, "Stay awake, you guys!" Rolling down my window, I leaned out to ask a hard-hat worker sipping coffee how long—

"Long as it takes." He sipped again, his eyes half-closed, crocodilian.

"But my wife is— The hospital called!"

Hard hat, beetle-shiny hat, spat on the black tarred road. "The Mercedes's kids, *Siamese twins,* 're dying. The Honda's sister's dying."

I should have stuck my jar right in his face and yelled, All my sperm's about to die! Right now!

But I was too totally defeated. Ten minutes to go before my tadpoles' motility declined, before they expired. Across the highway, in a field, I saw that with so much rain, such mild temperatures, the weeds and wildflowers were not yet August scorched, the Queen Anne's lace not frizzled and brown, its silky green stems still lifting up tiny bouquets of white flowers. Beyond the field, the trees' leaves, too, were still the bright green of

June. Leaves rustling or leaves moving? My wife would appreciate the difference. She was always looking out our kitchen window at the neighbor's chestnut tree. Leaves moving—delta kites glide. Leaves rustling—bowed kites ride high. Good for something, kites are, make you look at the world, think about the wind. Good for something, when I was so obviously good for nothing.

I watched the clock on the dashboard. The tadpoles wiggling slowly, wriggling to a stop. The milky jam slowly turned into clear jelly.

Traffic, at last, started up again.

"Good luck to your wife!" Hard hat saluted me as I drove slowly by.

Several hours later, I walked off the ferry at Vineyard Haven, Martha's Vineyard, my binoculars strung around my neck, into the crowds waiting at the dock for the crowds on the boat. I, alone, was unmet. I rented a bike, an old boy's bike with a raveling reed basket and a *ring-ling-ling* postman's bell, brakes that kicked in only if you stomped hard on them. Pushing off, I headed east around the island, skidding in the sand at stop signs and stoplights, nearly hit by a car several times because I was always looking up, looking for kites in the sky. My wife was somewhere on this island, looking up at kites.

My wife looking at O'Caslin flying kites—but O'Caslin's so wiry and hairy—my wife looking at the stripling flying kites, this tall, tall, blond boy, white shining blond hair, graceful as a girl, smooth red lips, sweet face. But a man, I could tell, a man as sweet as a girl.

My wife thinks she's excited by the kites.

Bicycled through the ice cream cone–clutching crowds of Oak Bluffs and around the edge of the island, stopping and scanning the sky above the beaches and the interior with my binoculars. Nothing but birds and clouds. I pedaled into Edgartown, a town of the thickest white paint, viscous white paint on these wooden columns, clapboards, boxy steeples, white paint made for New England light in fall and winter, thick rich white paint. No kites above Edgartown.

I took the little ferry to Chappaquiddick, standing next to my rusty, spindly steed. I asked one of the hands, a longhaired, T-shirted, peeling young old man, "Seen any kites flying today? Heard about any?"

Nope, no kites.

On Chappaquiddick, I set off, but soon discovered that the main road only tunneled through woods, the snobby private beaches lay at the end of private roads. My binoculars were useless. I stopped two other cyclists, in their tight black shorts, clingy nylon shirts, helmets, their water bottles strapped to their elegant, efficient bike frames, and I demanded, "Have you seen anyone flying kites around here?" It seemed the most outlandish question in the world, asked by an equally outlandish figure in slacks, heavy wing tips, and a button-down collar, balancing fatly on a rickety bike. They stared and shook their heads.

Back across on the ferry and down around the south coast of the island, all beaches and dunes. I realized only then, of course, this would be the likely place to fly a kite. I bicycled hard, past cars parked for miles alongside the road, past families trudging coolers and bags and kids up from and down to the beaches. I was so tired, and hot. Even the wind was against me. Maybe I'd head back, take a swim and head back.

One more look through the binoculars. I scanned the sky in all directions and there, there was a bright red kite, bright in the sky, sailing high.

The kite seemed to be flown from behind the dunes. I had to take a road marked for four-wheel-drive vehicles. If I could have parked my bike at the bike rack by the public beach, it would have been easy, but I had forgotten to rent a lock. I began to wheel the bike down the road, and in two minutes, my shoes were full of sand, the bike up to its spokes in sand. Sweating like a pig, I dragged the bike through the sand. I even tried carrying it in my arms. People on top of the dunes stared and laughed. People in four-wheel-drive vehicles powered by and pointed and laughed.

Above me floated what looked like a kid's red air mattress tethered at either end and bowed out by the wind. It swayed back and forth, then took a sudden circular swoop down and up again, bright red against the brightest blue sky.

Trudging around the last dune, I saw it was O'Caslin O'Sandman flying the red kite, his left foot back, arms bent and tensed, pulling, yawing right hand, left hand on the two lines that controlled the kite. My wife held a triangular turquoise kite for the stripling, who was busy laying out the lines. At last, he took his stance, and the kite took off, flying straight up, now out at a right angle, and now diving down terrifically fast, with a ripping, tearing noise, as if the air were silk, and then up up again, climbing higher higher.

My wife spotted me and came over. My wife's brown hair gold-brown in the sun. Her squint against the bright sun made her cheekbones seem even higher. She grinned. "I can't believe you're here—"

"Of course I am here." I was curt and cold. She might recall that I *was* writing an article about kites, and that I *might* think it useful to talk to an expert, *like O'Caslin,* about kites.

My wife's face flattened. She went over to O'Caslin, who came back with her to talk to me about the kites they were flying that day. I nodded, I took notes, I made learned references to kites in Malaysia, "ancestral home of most kites, most kite historians believe. Do you agree?" O'Caslin looked blank. My wife stared up in the air at the stripling's kite.

When I could endure no more talk about their kites, about Peter Powell stunters, Phantoms, or even Speedwings, I thanked O'Caslin. I waved good-bye to my wife. With the tragic dignity of the circus clown, I began to haul my bike back between the dunes. Only to promptly sneak up the other side of one dune.

For two hours, I spied upon my wife, O'Caslin, and the stripling as they played with the kites.

They performed all sorts of maneuvers with the stunt kites. Pulled by larger kites, they skimmed over the water of a small lagoon. Through my binoculars, I see them speed along, leaving a lacy wake—if my wife were pregnant, she'd be like a clipper ship, sails big-bellying out, embarked for home, loaded with riches and contentment to last all our lives. My wife, however, steps from the water a slick and slim sea nymph, accompanied by two dripping Tritons.

Then the threesome took to the air. Stacking several of the largest kites one on top of the other for more lift, they took turns jumping off a dune, sporting in midair—my wife laughing, the stripling hooting, O'Caslin's pale face of a fanatic ecstatic in the air—and at last tumbling down in the soft sand. Everyone watching cheered. My wife trudged up the dune again and again, to jump, jump up in the air.

I could not bear it anymore and slipped away.

Pedaled back slowly, took a lonely swim in my underwear, my bike on its side at the surf line. I did not stay in the water long, for I might have drowned myself. So leaden with gloom and futility, I should sink beneath the waves to hide my shame.

That evening, the cat and I waited on the porch for my wife to come home. She drove up in her little car, rusty car—I should get the rust fixed. She had pink on her cheeks, her hair knotted with sun. There would be sand in her clothes, in the hair under her arms, black-and-white grit in the creases of her thighs, in the folds of her nymphae, her hidden lips. My prick lifted to play her a hornpipe welcome-home tune, but my heart hurt. Her shining face did not shine for me. It shone for O'Caslin, the stripling, the kites lifting her up, weightless. When I wanted her earthbound, gravity's creature, gravid.

I wanted to say to her how sad I was, tell her how much I hurt. Instead, I just sat there, a ball of silent suet. The screen door banged behind her. The fickle cat leapt from my lap and skipped in on the door's rebound. I stayed on the porch a few more minutes, then hid myself in my study and busied myself with sorting photos for my article. Later, when my wife passed by my door, I called her in. I began to pitch my kite talk at her: Do you know—guess how this *pakpao* kite is made? I always used to tell her the story of whatever article I was working on. Telling her the story out loud helped me get all the pieces in the right order. And when I finished a good draft, she was my reader, all readers implicit in her—a mother-muse, giving birth to the world of readers for me.

That evening, I had to make her listen to my kite story. She could not keep not seeing me, not paying attention to the matter at hand, her kites *and* my kites, our bodies, in conjunction, conjoining, here in this house. This house with a roof, a house with windows and doors fastenable tight.

That night, however, she sat right there, in my desk chair, very still, very polite, but her face had paled. She seemed to be paying attention, absolute attention, yet she was not there. I was looking at a memento of her propped up in the chair, a life-size dry-rot cardboard cutout of her. I tried my best to move her, quoting to her the Japanese poem about kites that I might use to end my piece:

> A kite—
> in the same place
> in yesterday's sky!

Yet she seemed preoccupied, absorbed in some other thought. Some thought at the end of a line she held concealed from my sight, but to whose every tug she was alive. Before she left, though, she did look at the three prints I had picked up in Japan. In one print, an old priest approaches a temple, while behind him fly two kites over the gray roofs of Edo. In another print, a boy lashed to a kite is flown by his father off the island on which they have been exiled. The last print is a black-and-white forest scene, with a red kite caught in the branches of a leafless tree.

Then my wife returned to her sewing machine, her whirr machine. The new kites she and O'Caslin had designed were selling well. She informed me she would soon need to hire an assistant to help with the cutting out and the filling of orders. When it was time to go to bed, we each spent a long time in the bathroom and by mutual mute consent each clung to his and her side of the bed.

Until I smelled the sea salt on her, dwelled upon in my mind the sparkling fine sand sure to lie between her breasts, in the curling hair between her thighs, and I turned her over, she turned over to me. We made love, fiercely, in the dark, out of our estrangement, as strangers. She was faceless to me, she closed her eyes and masked her face, made a mask out of it, so that she seemed any woman, nameless and multitude. And I knew she closed her eyes so that I was any man, in the dark, a man she used any way she liked, she held that man with her nails, thrusting up at him, pulling him into her wide, deep pelvic bowl.

It was like being visited secretly in the night by an unknown lover, a sign from whom you seek everywhere, in everyone's face, all the long day long.

Do others, I suddenly wondered, do others like O'Caslin, see us as almost "separated"? Where was that parallel set of footprints, leading back to that elusive two, the two of us? The two who used to walk together, side by side?

A week later, I went alone to the city's kite festival, Kites Over Boston, the big event my wife had helped organize and that I was to feature in my article.

As I came up from the train station, over a hill and into the park, I looked up and saw hundreds of kites in the air. Suddenly I was so happy, I began to grin and felt like crying. Families, couples, groups of old people, of kids, had brought their old paper kites, box kites, dragon kites with long whiplash red tails, fighter kites, so many kites! For my article, I took photographs of children assembling kites, becoming initiated into the tangled life of string, then launching the kites and promptly crashing them. One Muslim woman, like a walking laundry basket in her layers of veils, struggled to keep a plastic Superman kite up in the air. A man and his two kids flew a small homemade kite, octagonal, and painted in a bright design—Africana colors, Africana design, the father told me. When the kite came down, they posed for me with their pretty kite. The laughing boy, black eyes turned up with laughter, ducked behind his father the moment the shutter clicked. The girl looked straight at me, bright pink ribbons fluttering from her braids.

Up where the kite festival turned kite championship, the rigging of the kiting club banners pinged frantically. My wife sat at the High as a Kite table, command central for the official kiting events. Around her milled the teams in their nylon team uniforms emblazoned with their team names: SKYSAILORS in lime green hats, SQAIR DANCERS in pink, KAPITOL AIR KORPS in black hats and jackets.

My wife's voice crackled and spat over the loudspeaker, announcing the next event, the kite duo competition. The reigning champions, the DUODRONES, in blue, were ready to go.

My wife's voice, in bed, in the dark, is like granite water, the water that seeps through granite, pure cool stony-tasting water.

I went to tell my wife I was going home. Tapping the ground with her foot as she always does when she's excited, she's all kite talk with the others. They talk about kite ballet and kite skiing— "*Parapente,* in French," my wife informs the others, her pronunciation execrable.

"Good-bye"—all she had to say to me.

In bed that night, my wife lifted up to me in a quiver, but she was not my mare anymore. Not my dark-haired, handsome mare with her mare's croup, who used to nuzzle me, bend her head against my neck as I stroked her spine, two pools of perspiration in the hollows on either side of her spine, at the end of her spine, little lakes. I dipped the tip of my tongue in them.

My wife was a kite on a string—the string is taut. Then it snaps, falls limp in my hand.

———

That Sunday, a Sunday at the end of a long, long spring, I was still trying to finish my article on kites. I was almost finished, but overwhelmed by the despair, the doubt that often grips me right before I finish a big piece. I lose all my pleasure in the work, I sleep too much, wander around and around the neighborhood, come home, recline decline into the sofa. All this somehow necessary to deliver myself up to the finishing of the piece, to rise up and take it in hand, to look one more time at every word every sentence and say yes, that this has a bit of joy, that this is filled with the simple joy of looking up in the air and seeing a kite, yes, kites!

I sat at my desk. Unfortunately, I had already straightened my desk up, so that very useful bit of procrastination was gone.

Had already eaten lunch, drunk too much coffee.

I walked around my study on a small pilgrimage to the souvenirs of past articles. I rolled in my palm a Tibetan bone bead. I studied a reproduction of an old Spanish map. I even pulled out and inspected my emergency kite for the first time since my wife had made me buy it. Out of its pouch, the kite seemed not so small after all.

I lay down on my sofa. Somewhere in Japan, someone makes a kite as small as a postage stamp and flies it with a long strand of human hair. I couldn't find that tiny kite anywhere in Japan. If I had that tiny kite, I could fly it here in my study, lying down.

Chasing after kites in Japan, I had been strangely happy. *Tako* means "kite" in Japan, and *tako-kichi,* "kite-crazy." North of Tokyo, I saw the whole town of Shirone go *tako-kichi.* Two giant kites, each flown by dozens of men, meet over the waters of the canal dividing the town. Now the kites' lines entangle, and the fight begins. The kite with the fierce warrior's face tries to pull to its side of the canal the kite with the white cresting tidal wave. The wind turns sharply and both kites begin to fall. The men pull even harder on the line. The kites rise, hover a moment, then sink into the canal. The thick paper melts, and the bright colors bleed red and blue and black into the water. The bones—they call the bamboo frame the bones—free of their flesh, are pulled from the canal to live again, next spring, in another kite.

At the Hamamatsu festival, thousands of kites in the sky. Along the long beach of black sand, kite fliers in short black jackets, cigarettes drooping from their lips, attack an enemy's red-white-black kite. The kite lines saw away, one line snaps, and the defeated kite drifts out over the blue Pacific. "Lost at sea, lost at sea," I intoned, alone among the crowd picnicking on the black dunes.

At Hamamatsu, I learned, kites were first flown to celebrate the births of sons.

For my daughter, if I had a daughter, I would fly a kite. I would have liked so much a little girl, a girl like my wife. Corinna, I'd name my little girl, Corinna, such a ringing, tinkling, clinking name. I'd bedeck her with the jewelry my wife's stopped wearing now. I'd pin brooches on her, fasten bracelets around her wrists, slip rings on her ten fingers and tell her to make two fists so the rings don't slip off. Send her into the living room to surprise my wife, surprise her with herself. My wife would laugh. We would all laugh and be one with love. My wife always said— before we stopped saying these things—she hoped for a boy with a crooked front tooth like mine, a bookish, bespectacled boy like me. But I never wanted that. I couldn't bear to see my ugly self as in a living mirror. Yet she was, once, fierce on the subject, to have another me, a boy coming out of the womb laughing and woeful at the same time, telling her a ridiculous tale while still tethered to the umbilical cord.

A tiny Japanese kite. I only had an Edo kite, a large rectangular kite painted with the dark face of a green-eyed demon. The old, old maker of my kite told me that his father had loved making kites, that he himself loved making kites, but since kite makers are always poor, and now everyone in Japan wants to be rich, his son will not make kites. Soon no one will make kites anymore.

If I had a tiny kite, I could fly it here like a moth fluttering in this room. I could finish my piece, if I had a tiny kite.

I did have a sheet of Japanese paper somewhere around that I had bought to wrap a gift for my wife. I found it underneath a stack of magazines—I'd forgotten what a pretty piece of paper it was, busily printed with fans, butterflies, flowers and waves and whirlpools, a busy little world, in lovely worldly colors black and maroon, dark blue, olive green, and creamy white. The paper felt soft, like soft cloth. Clearing off my desk entirely, I cut out a rectangle the size of a regular playing card. For the frame, I went to the kitchen and broke off broom straws from the broom and trimmed them to the length and width of the paper. I had my own bones. I laid out the straws this way, that way, glued them together, glued the paper to them. From my wife's sewing box, I picked out the finest thread. My wife had had her hair cut short this winter, so no good going to her hairbrush. I attached thread lines to the two top corners of my little kite, to the middle of its face, tied them to a long line coming off the spool. Attached streamers of thread at the lower corners to steady her.

Up from the basement came a dusty fan. On Hi the kite spun wildly, but on Lo the kite lifted. My tiny kite lifted and hovered steady as a hummingbird. What a pleasure the gentle tug of the thread at my fingers! I laughed out loud to no one. No one here to see I had gone *tako-kichi,* flying this tiny kite all my own.

I flew the kite from my sofa, and I began to think about my wife. In the last months, we had come to live peaceably enough with the strangerliness between us. I sat in my study. She sat at her sewing machine or in the kitchen, packing up mail-order kites with her new assistant, long and lanky Liz—Liz Lizard, I call her, because she always looks like she's sunning herself. The best was when I had the house to myself, like that day, my wife off at the kite store, or off kiting with Liz, with the rest of her kite friends, I assumed—I didn't ask anymore. The sewing machine quiet, Lizard's loud laugh long gone, and I didn't have to listen to the maddening rustle of their rip-stop nylon pants and jackets.

With my tiny kite sailing on high, suddenly I pictured my wife stepping from the shower that morning, wet and sleek as an otter. My flagpole idly stirred. I wondered, Could I fly the kite with an erection? So I worked on it, poring over my wife's body as I had seen it that morning. Round brown-tipped breasts. Behind, the sacred spheres. Yet something was different about my wife that morning. Was it that her face seemed browner than usual with sun, those scraped elbows and a knee, or her waist so curiously chafed a rashy red? This was my wife, whom I used to know like the back of my hand, my wife, whom I had held in the palm of my hand.

I saw her again, in detail, this morning, stepping from the shower, her breasts surely filling, her belly swelling, an indefinable but certain welling-up. Maybe. It wasn't fat, I'm sure. Her face still lean, her arms still firm. Maybe.

I heard the front door open, shut. My wife was at my study door, watching my little kite fly back and forth. I had forgotten how she could grin, all teeth, gums, a grin like a holiday. What could I say to her? She lingered there. Did she have something to say to me? Something important to say to me? Almost shyly, she turned away. It was as if we hadn't yet been formally introduced, and we couldn't find the right words, the right moment, to begin the conversation, to stop being strangers.

But, then, my wife turned back to me. She asked me nervously, bravely in a rush, my wife asked me if I would help her go kiting. She wanted to go kiting, but O'Caslin couldn't go, and Liz at the last minute couldn't go, but Liz had lent her her truck. And she wanted to go while—she looked at the tiny fluttering kite—while the weather was perfect.

From out of nowhere, the cat leapt at the kite, batted it down, pounced on it, and rolled back and forth, clutching the kite to its belly, shredding the paper with its hind claws.

"Bad, bad cat!" my wife scolded, and got her hand scratched trying to get my tiny kite back, all in all making a big fuss.

All in all, it was finally so easy for me to give in.

Up north of Boston to Plum Island we drove and then down the island's narrow road between the dunes and the marshes where the birds flitter. We parked and from the back of the truck my wife picked up a pile of folded kites, line, and a harness. I lifted out a winch with a reel of orange rope. We wound around the dunes to the long, curving, deserted beach.

I helped my wife fasten the winch to the concrete pylon of a lifeguard's station. We checked the teeth and the mechanism for reeling out, for stopping the rope and cranking it back up. I took some time to make sure the teeth caught, did not slip.

When I looked up, I saw my wife poking her head into a Styrofoam bike helmet. Next, she clasped the harness around her waist—swelling waist. Yes she had her jeans safety-pinned at the zipper a bit down, as if she could not fasten the top button anymore. To the rings of the harness, she clipped the rope coming from the winch. She tested the clip, pulling at it, standing on the rope and tugging at the clip again. She attached to the harness the two lines that linked the limp kites lying on the sand.

I stand by. My wife comes to me and quietly explains. Now I stand by the winch, though I'm afraid. One more time, I tell myself, I'll let her go just one more time. Picking up the first kite, she angles them one after another toward the wind, the wind fills the channels sewn into the kites, and suddenly, she has a red kite, a yellow, a green, two orange, a pink kite, like large air mattresses, all rigged together, rustling and bumping on the sand, coltish restless and ready. She grabs for the two handles attached to the kite lines. The kites roil, buck, they lift higher and higher, they line up six kites one on top of another, the lines tighten. My wife tenses her arms.

Now my wife is up, too, lifting up, the loose rope snaking up behind her, and now she is moving toward the dunes. The rope straightens out, is taut. I unlatch the catch on the handle of the winch and begin to let out more rope slowly, slowly. My wife hovers in midair, flying the kites. She pulls at the kites and flies to the left, then to the right. She goes up and then down, all in midair.

And I, with one hand on the winch crank, one hand on the rope, I am flying my wife.

The crinkled white soles of her tennis shoes dangle over my head and fill me with terror.

At the same time, I begin to see that her sweetness and her thuggishness, which I had always prized and had sorely missed and had finally almost forgotten, seem the lowest next-to-nothings of her compared to this discovery of her. She is no longer my mare, my riffraffish girl, my Saint Francis. She is a swan queen taken mortal form. She is—with my help—empress of her element, air.

Slipping off my jacket to free up my arms, I tied it to the pylon as high as I could, away from the teeth of the winch. In the sharp breeze, the jacket snaps out like a blue banner.

Here came three tugs, one tug two tugs three tugs—meaning, let out more rope, and I let the rope reel off up into the air. Breathing slowly, in and out, I was terrified, I was excited, but had to stay perfectly calm. I was in charge of the rope.

Two tugs—put the catch on—and I did. The kites so bright floating almost over the dunes, I had to trust in them. I told myself that they were the best kites, that she was an expert now, that she knew what she was doing. I had to trust in her knowledge of the wind and of rip-stop nylon and nylon rope and winches and hopefully of her husband, some knowledge of him, some confidence in his equipment.

One tug two tugs three tugs. I let out more rope.

She was right over the dunes, the wind steady, remarkably steady, a straight blow in from the ocean. It has to keep blowing and blowing.

The rope quivering—one tug—reel in—or two tugs—put the catch on—or three tugs—more rope? More rope, I was sure it was three tugs—yes, give her more rope.

Think of all she was seeing now! Think of all she would have to tell our child! The birds lifting off from their nests, the soft-furred does bedded in the dunes. The early hay greenish silver, which later in the summer would be gathered into giant wheels standing singly in the field. Rusting tractors and cars a bit of mirror glinting, white farmhouses behind a line of leafing trees. Rivers and streams emptying into the sea, highways, maybe the skyscrapers of Boston. To the east the gigantic Atlantic and to the west the hills and ranges of the continent lifting.

When my wife flew in front of the sun, it was hard to look at her, hard to see her for all the glory obscuring her outline. Yet I exulted, I had that light, too, on the end of my rope. The whole bright world was pulling my rope taut.

One tug—reel in.

I felt her tug again. But not yet! I couldn't help myself—I loosened the winch, I let the rope out. Let her out just a little bit farther, past the sun, beyond the dunes, out of sight, or maybe swing her out over the sea. Let her out to see even more of the world. I had to let the rope out to show my wife my child the whole world.

Thinking, all the time thinking, I'll let them out and then reel the whole world back to me.

# THE BEAD TRADE

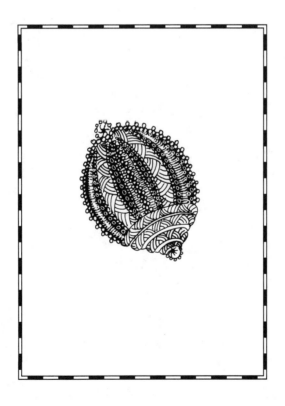

I

## *The Bead Trader*

HE UNCURLED HIS FINGERS.

On the bead trader's palm sat a bead of yellow bone carved all around as an old man with a bald head and whiskers, an old man leaning on a rock, sleeping like a rock, his cloak bunched up around him, around the bead in craggy folds.

The bead trader called the class to order: "Ladies! Ladies!"

The bead trader used to begin the bead class with this big speech: "Once, beads were sown in temple grounds for good luck. Bartered for continents, for slaves. Beads still buy wives in Borneo. Who knows, perhaps one of these beads right here"— he flung his hand toward a glittering spill of beads on the table before him—"is a bead unearthed from the oldest of graves. Ladies! Tonight you will hold bits of history in your hands! Beads, the small change of civilization!"

But the ladies had always been good for only a minute or two of his speechifying. The eyes outlined in black flatten, the heads of wispy hair bob, the spectacles wink at him—come on, enough preaching, let's get on with it, let us at the beads and wire and string.

These days, the bead trader merely and mildly welcomed the ladies to his shop, The Bead Trader, in this fashion: "We've got a world of beads for you tonight—like this *ojime* bead in my hand here, a beautiful bone bead from Japan. Now I'll turn you over to my daughter to begin with. She's better at explaining the how-to than her old dad. But I'll still be poking my nose in from time to time, so if you have any questions, jusk ask me."

He pocketed the old man bead, too expensive a bead to let the ladies play with.

The bead class was good for business. The ladies paid thirty dollars for two sessions. One class on how to string beads and how to handle a pair of needle-nose pliers with the special bead wire and clasps. The second class on bead design tips. They also received a ten-dollar credit toward beads bought in the shop. Once the ladies had handled a bead, ten dollars never got them nearly enough beads, never as many beads as they just had to have. His knack for business had made the bead trader successful in his previous line of work, a start-up business manager for new churches, turning a profit on raffles, combination Sunday school–crafts classes, summer day camps for kids, and—one of his brainstorms—day camps for senior citizens. So successful, that four years ago, at the age of forty-six, two years after picking up his first bead and cradling it in his palm, he could turn to the bead trade to try his luck.

Teaching the bead class himself had been the bead trader's single miscalculation. Something about the beads made him run on. He taught the class as a geography lesson, a history lesson, a little bit of art, sharing all the things he had come to know about beads, from all the books he'd read, maps he'd looked at, places he'd been to buy beads. Soon enough, though, he found out that the ladies never cared where his beads came from, didn't even know where Guatemala was, or Prague, or Java. They never even remembered the names of beads—it was always, "Do you have some more of those bitty seed beads?" "Any more of the stripy ones—you know the ones I mean?"

Tonight, as he stood in the doorway watching his daughter teach the class, he saw why the ladies preferred it this way. Without him, the class seemed more cozy, like a knitting circle. The ladies cooed to one another: "That's so pretty." "That will look so good on!" "Won't that look just right on a teenager?"

Strangely enough, the bead trader admitted to himself, giving up the class had come as a great relief. Sometimes, he had become suddenly frightened as he looked around the table with the bare lightbulb hanging over it and saw these women, mostly old women, older than himself, gathered half in the light, half in the darkness of the room, intent on stringing their beads, stringing together worlds, planetary systems, without regard, without plan —except, "I don't know. Just like it like that."

Now, once his daughter started up, the bead trader retreated to the front of the shop, to the boxes of beads that needed sorting. He liked being alone with the beads, picking them up between his thumb and forefinger, rolling them in his hands, weighing them in his palm, tumbling them into their clear plastic boxes, arranging the boxes in groups for orderly shelving. Never cared for stringing beads himself. He preferred them one by one. This *ojime* bead (was it an old man leaning on a rock or an old man shaped as a rock?), this Egyptian eye bead studded with knobby eyeballs, the black pupils alert in all directions against the evil eye. This Venetian glass millefiori bead, like Christmas candy the sugary brilliance of yellow and red and blue flowers fused onto a white core. This Chinese boxwood sphere carved with twining vines, that Islamic filigree bead, tiny silver wires joined by tiny grains of silver into something like an exquisite birdcage. All the world of beads passing through his hands, as if his dusty shop, this shack of a shop, in this suburb of Boston, were a grand bazaar at the confluence of mighty rivers or some great port of empire.

In the back room, his daughter had just finished her demonstration and her encouraging words. The squeak of folding chairs meant that each woman was settling down to her first string of beads. He walked over to the door to look in, to smile. The ladies did like the bead trader, the owner of the shop, to show himself now and then. And, besides, he had to keep an eye on things, see what beads they liked, so he could order more. Little trends turned up in the classes—one season, it might be mermaid beads from Oaxaca, the next, porcelain beads from China.

The same thing always happened in the first class. A few ladies rushed to get their pick of the loose beads lying on the table. The rest fumbled with the pliers, turning them around and around in their grasp, trying to get a grip, trying to twist the bead wire onto the clasps, often twisting the wire too much and breaking it off. His daughter walked around the table, showing them how to hold the pliers, how to make a neat tuck of the end of the wire.

One woman, without lifting her head, without disturbing the crown of light shining on her brown hair, started in with questions. What kind of wire was this? What were the beads strung on in the lands they came from? Cotton or wool thread, fishing line, sinews, braided grasses? She asked these questions of his daughter as if there were something important to know, all the while slipping beads one at a time onto the bead wire, holding the wire up to see how the different beads hung, comparing the wide angle between two cylindrical African trade beads to the narrow angle made by a couple of round Czech beads. Then with her pliers, she twisted the end of the wire onto a clasp—expert, here was someone used to tools.

As she listened to the few answers his daughter could supply, the woman rapidly picked out some heavy cloisonné beads, hardly looking at them, choosing more by touch than sight, rolled them between her palms, and, lining them up precisely before her, quickly strung them and tied them off. She did the same with the light Saudi silver beads on a thin silver wire. Now with her three strings of beads in hand, she let them fall one at a time against the table, *clack-clack*. She picked up the necklaces and did it again, as if she were throwing dice, or bones, or I Ching coins, studying each necklace as a fortune-teller might for the chance pattern scribbled out on the table.

The other women stared at her and made faces at one another. Who did she think she was? Talking up all the time, taking up all the time, making such a racket? Yet the bead trader waited until his daughter caught his eye and made a face herself, shaking her head slightly at the woman. Smiling, he walked into the room and started working his way around the table, a word to this lady with her dark scalp looming through thin white hair, that lady upholstered in a beige that matched her makeup, so that you couldn't really find her face, showing them how to hold the wire in the pliers—he knew the ladies liked the touch of his hands over theirs on the tools. Soon he came around to the woman about to cast another string of beads.

"Taking them for a test-drive?" He spoke in a low, deliberate voice, a voice perfected in parish halls. The other ladies laughed.

Without surprise or offense, she looked up at him—she was younger than the rest and her eyebrows stretched long and dark across a pale face. "Oh. I just like to see which way they fall."

The bead trader smiled, began talking about the beads she had put together on one string, the most peculiar combination of beads, yet curiously belonging together. She listened to him, asked questions about this bead, that bead, and he watched her pick up a string of beads, this time letting it pour slowly from her hand onto the table. Then another string. It was true that there was something different if the beads were all the same size and weight; then the curve was simple and smooth. If the string was a mix of heavy and light, large and small beads, it made a broken curve, like a dislocated arm.

The other ladies sighed out loud.

The bead trader suggested to the troublemaker that she come with him into the shop. There he'd be happy to show her many more beads and answer all her questions. His daughter smiled at him gratefully.

For the next hour, the bead trader took this woman on his world tour of the shop, through the European room, the African room, the Asian room, the Americas room, four shallow rooms lined with shelves and crowded with counters. She gratified the bead trader by going through every case with him, through every box, one by one, looking, fingering all the quick bright things. She asked about these silver disk beads, that cinnabar bead, where he got those yellow gourd-shaped beads. From a locked case, he took out his Egyptian treasures, the sky blue faience beads, which he was sure came from a pharaoh's tomb, and the fertility beads, glass beads in the shape of a right hand cupping a breast. She listened to the stories of his bead-buying trips, and although he himself later reflected that so many mishaps and discoveries were scarcely credible, she didn't question them at all as she rolled his beads in her hands.

They arrived last in the Americas room. He showed her the glass beads white traders had bartered for furs and food with the Indians. What caught her eye were some stone beads lying in a dusty plastic bag at the back of the case.

He had forgotten them, *las piedras,* "the stones," stone beads. The bead vendors in the Taxco marketplace had urged him to take *las piedras*—special beads, old, old beads, they said. He bought the stone beads only as a favor, to keep the vendors happy so that they would get more clay fish beads for him; those were what he really wanted. He didn't like the stone beads. Stone, cold bead, the barest bead of all. Pebbles almost straight from the streambed—human work hardly showed on the stone beads, at best beads scratched with a few lines, and so dull even in color, dusty black, faint green, and grayish blue. Probably the lowliest woman of the tribe put to the task of drilling the hole, the tribe itself the poorest in skill, in love of beautiful things.

These stone beads belonged to the earth, more to the earth than to people. All his other beads showed the quick hand, the careful eye. All his other beads were made of warm, workable wood or clay or glass or metal, their animal or human shapes, their flower patterns hymns of delight offered to the world. Even turquoise beads, though technically stone, were almost always carved by the Chinese with detailed scenes. Even seed beads, like his cinnamon brown *rudraksha* seeds from Java, were prized, surely, because they appeared naturally to be intricately carved.

No other customer had ever picked out these stone beads. Just looking at them, they seemed too heavy ever to wear as a necklace. Why had people consented to wear these lumps of stone, to be so weighed down, to have to bend forward, to turn slowly?

Yet the stone beads excited this woman. She ticked off the names of the dull stones: soapstone, greenstone, serpentine. "Look here, this was probably bored with a reed or bone. Probably used sand to act like the diamond chips on a drill bit." She picked up the largest bead and ran her thumb fondly around the opening of its hole. "See how the lip of the hole has been worn down by the string rubbing against the edge—for hundreds of years, I bet. You know, I've got some of these stone beads myself. Of all 'the world of beads,' I think I like them the best."

Her quote from his speech embarrassed him. He quickly looked up to see if she laughed at him. But absorbed by the stone beads, she was weighing them each in her hands, turning them over and over, all the time humming faintly, tapping her foot. He could feel this unexpected, sudden veering away of her attention, away from the other beads, away from him, strangely as if he weren't standing there in his very own shop.

The back door opened and the bead class came out, chatting,

holding the plastic bags filled with spools of wire and loose beads to their breasts. He lifted his hand in farewell. They nodded to him, stared at her, and filed out the front door. His daughter was so good with the ladies, walking them out to the parking lot down the block, talking to this one, that one, calling good night to them all, and reminding them that the second class was in two weeks. Good night, good night.

"Good night," the woman said abruptly to the bead trader, looking down at her watch. "I've got to get home, too." She disappeared into the backroom, returned with her purse and jacket, and headed out the door.

He tried to keep her talking on the doorstep, under the brightly lettered sign, THE BEAD TRADER, that creaked in this first autumn wind, a September wind still mild, idling down the street. However, quickly, she was gone. His daughter came back up the sidewalk, raised her eyebrows at him, smiled.

Two weeks later, the class meets again, but the woman doesn't come. The bead trader sorts his beads, looks up at the clock every few minutes. Maybe she is running late. An hour later, he thinks maybe she will come to the second class in the next round of classes. His circular for the bead class promised that if anyone missed a session, they could make it up the next time the class was given.

October, November go by, two more groups of ladies, and she never shows up. During the day, he finds himself in Africa more than usual, near the front door—she might come back for the stone beads—and he glances up every time the bell tied to the door rings in a customer.

As he perches on his stool, staring at his inventory of beads on the computer screen, the bead trader tries to remember when he had first noticed her, really noticed her as she sat next to him, what she looked like. Was she even attractive? He imagines she is at his side, very near him. He glances at her slantwise while she studies the black stone bead, and he sees suddenly she is handsome in her own way. The shape of her head is neat and round. He'd like to hold her cranium in his hands, feel its shape. And her face so alive when she talks, yet then so still, its polished plains shining as if washed with rain, like a stone now, it strikes him, but a stone alive, outside, in a field with green grass growing around it or bright in a pretty rushing stream—he tries to redeem her from sheer stone.

He notices her hands, long fingers tracing a line incised into a bead, nice-shaped nails, but hands hard with muscles and sinews, scarred, the nails short and cracked. On the middle finger of one hand a larger knuckle, as if at one time broken and never set properly. His fingers want to gently work that knuckle.

This discovery of her, in his memory, stirs him, thrills him to be in the presence of this woman. For a few days, this thrill hovers above him like a high cloud, even as the autumn lowers in with rain, rivulets of water draining everywhere from rainspouts, down gutters. Soon, however, he can't help but notice that the birds are all gone, so silent outside. Time for him to go south, looking for more beads, for the beads promised to him, for all the beads that might be waiting for him.

Yet he can't make himself think about the trip. He hasn't ever talked to anyone like he talked to her, about what he loves. Not to his daughter, who is kind but more comfortable with practical talk about the shop, and never to his former wife. Of course he had had only ordinary, old, and tired things to say to his wife, but that was before he turned to beads and everything changed. Before he discovered he had so much to say.

Now he finds himself full of things to tell this woman about the beads, about the world of beads, things he is sure she will be interested in.

Until, finally, in a dream he sees her, only for a second, silent, dark, turned away from him.

The bead trader woke up angry. She won't come back.

MARILYN SIDES

## 11
## *Stone Beads*

THE BEAD TRADER LOOKED UP HER ADDRESS on the class
registration form. One afternoon, he set out to pay her back for
the class she had missed. He had the money ready in his pocket.
It was coming to her—he didn't want somebody's money for
nothing. On his way out the door, he stopped and picked up the
stone beads, weighed the beads curiously a moment in his palm,
then wrapped them in a paper towel, put them in his pocket with
the money. Why not? He would never sell these beads, anyway.

Turning his truck down Winnicott Court, a street dead-ended
by the train tracks, the bead trader parked in front of number 9.
This old brick building, next to an ink plant, had probably been
only a warehouse, yet it sported a fancy facade, rows of brick
rosettes. The snow blew in around the rose petals and filled up
the letters carved on a sandstone plaque: PETROSE & CO. 1911.
On the ground floor, the windows were boarded up and mesh
grills nailed over the boards. Light shone from the second-floor
windows, and on the roof of the building he saw mobiles whirling
silently, mobiles made out of a sort of iridescent glass or maybe
metal or plastic, in clusters of cubes each with three sides cut
away, the icy breeze catching the hollows, spinning the cubes and
the snowflakes.

By the doorbell, stick-on letters spelled out THE SCULPTORS
STUDIO. Her name and another name were written on two strips
of tape. He rang. He rang again, a long ring. The door opened
and a man with wire-rim glasses and a white beard, Father Time
on a New Year's card, stuck his head out. The bead trader asked
for her. Father Time nodded, turned back in. The bead trader
followed him across a cement floor, dusty, gritting under his feet,
along a path between several machines on one side and a long
curtain of opaque plastic sheeting. At the back wall, they climbed
rough wooden stairs to the next floor, one large room stacked

84

with sheets and sheets of the prismatic stuff, glinting cobalt blue, orange, pink. Father Time sat himself down at a workbench and motioned the bead trader toward another set of stairs.

The bead trader went up the narrow plank stairs and into a dark room, empty except for several flat stones placed on the floor and one tall column of stone standing guard against the back wall. There was some light from somewhere near the ceiling.

He called out, "Hello?"

"Who is it?"

Her voice, rather high-pitched—he recognized it—came from above him. She was bending over the balcony of a loft.

"Remember me, from The Bead Trader, the bead shop?"

"Oh, sure. Come on up."

He tried to find a door in the gloom. Overhead, he heard a man laugh, say, "Ah-ha, that's where you got the idea," and her quick, sharp denial: "No, no. I already knew what I was going to do. I just wanted to see what he had. Just a way of thinking about beads."

What idea, and whatever it was, was there only enough at his shop, in him, for one night, all to be found out in one night?

The bead trader discovered a small door behind the guardian stone and climbed the stairs tucked in the wall. He came upon her and two men sitting around a table, a lamp shining on a deck of cards, coffee cups, a crumbling cake, orange peelings, and a pear. Behind them, a sink and a counter with clean dishes stacked neatly in a drainer, a telephone. The balcony railing on this side had been turned into shelves, filled with books, some rocks, and several figurines. On the wall hung a pen-and-wash drawing, of what looked to him like a ruin.

She introduced the bead trader to the two men. He would always think of the short, compact one as Sandy, because of his yellow-red hair, tufty eyebrows, and freckles, and the tall one as Handsome, with his dark, finely modeled face. They were younger than he was, even if Sandy was balding and Handsome had deep lines in his face. The men politely tried to talk to the bead trader. They asked about his beads. He told them about his bead-buying trips. Sandy asked him if he had ever seen some of her sculpture work, the piece up at Lowell, the one at Porter Square. He said no. Handsome inquired if the bead trader had seen the several crafts shows in town right now—beads were crafts, of course they were—the furniture show at the museum, the ceramics at the gallery downtown. The bead trader said he went to museums only to look at beads.

Handsome turned abruptly to the others. "Doesn't it just kill you how everything's crafts now, and it's only because a chair's easier for people to get than real art. There's a hook, so they buy it." He glanced at the bead trader. "I'm sorry. But real art comes after furniture and food. It's the numinous, the abstract! It's— it's about grace!"

The bead trader thought Handsome got away with talking in big terms because he knew he was good-looking.

Sandy jumped in, complaining that all the reviews were going to those craft shows. With his new sculpture installed already a month ago this week, he had been afraid of a bad review, but it was worse having no review at all.

While they talked, the bead trader watched her. Picking up the pear, she ate it as she listened to the other two. Which one was her lover? She treated them both the same. When either one turned to her, she answered him with a word or two, nodding pleasantly, laughing, but really saying nothing.

Reaching into his pocket, the bead trader pulled out the money, laid a ten-, a five-dollar bill on the table. He looked straight at her. "Here's your refund."

"Oh, no, what's this for?"

Handsome and Sandy stopped talking.

"You didn't make it to the second class. I don't take people's money for nothing."

"Come on, you showed me all your beads that night. That

was like a second class." She picked up the money and held it out to him. "Here. Take it back."

The bead trader didn't take the bills, and after a few moments, she dropped them on the table. The bead trader had won. He made the most of this moment by reaching in his pocket again, digging out and then unwrapping the stone beads.

Her face came alive like that night at the shop, the bead trader noted with satisfaction. Putting down the pear, she wiped her fingers and took up the beads with delight: "You know, I meant to go back and get these beads. Just didn't get around to it." She made Sandy and Handsome look at the beads, told them everything about the beads, as if she had owned them for years, had held these beads in her hands for years. Leaning back to a shelf, she took out from a box three more stone beads, like the bead trader's, rounded lumps of stone hardly worked at all. Pushing aside the money, she spread out the paper towel, placed all the beads on it. She picked them up and put them down again at different angles to one another, her long fingers arranging, rearranging the beads until something obscurely satisfied her.

In her delight she seemed to come to a decision, a sudden decision. She laughed and said to the bead trader, "All right. I've got a few more stone beads to show you. Want to see them?"

Sandy and Handsome grinned. The bead trader didn't get the joke, but he didn't care—he had won some ground, even if it meant only seeing more stone beads. They all filed back downstairs, past Father Time working at his workbench and ignoring them, down to the first floor. Handsome drew aside the plastic curtain with a flourish, Sandy flipped on an intensely bright light, and she walked in, the bead trader right behind her.

Three huge stone beads. Three huge stone beads sat on the cement floor. A blocky green bead about six feet high. A round white bead seven feet high. And a blue-gray bead towering over the other two. Much taller than the bead trader—he didn't have to stand next to the blue bead to know that. Sandy stepped over to the blue bead and, reaching out, ran his fingers along a hollow carved into it. How did she get this polish? Did she start with sixty-grit sandpaper and then move to four hundred, wet disk, yes?

"Well, I'm still working on that." She went over to the bead, stroked it lovingly—the bead dwarfed her. Handsome followed.

The bead trader was left staring at the beads. They are beads. Each has a hole bored into it, all the way through it, through the massive stone, showing off the massive stone, and at the same time, the hole makes each bead improbably airy, open. Light pours through the hole.

Now the bead trader knows absolutely that the beads are not carved into recognizable shapes. But in a panic, his mind has to make them out as shapes of familiar things. So the green one is a great cube with rounded corners and hollows cut into each side, making the corners flare, the highly polished hollows quite shallow but giving the impression of depth, and with the hole running right through the center, yes, it seems the vertebra of a monstrous prehistoric creature, the bone fossilized to this dark greenish color. Above it rises the blue bead, at least eight feet high, triangular and curved like an animal's tooth, a blue-gray horn or tusk, with its large hole carefully worked in the upper part of the horn, and the three long, curved hollows halfway down seem ridges of bone or folds of thick flesh. The enormous white bead appears almost perfectly rounded. Can it roll away? Roll over him, crush him? Several incised lines curve over it, long, graceful, living lines. The hole is not as wide as in the other beads, and not cut straight through. Instead, it burrows between what the lines sketch out, what looks like the belly and the limbs of a body, an animal body. A white rabbit, or a snow monkey, sitting curled up over its haunches. The surface of the stone lightly pitted, not polished, an animal's winter coat fluffed up in a ball, the down underneath standing straight up against a storm, the very stone must feel warm.

When he touched the bead, of course, it was cold. Cold as granite, so cold and so hard.

"They're granite?" he heard himself ask out loud, interrupting the others.

She turned to him. "Right, that's a dark Quincy—the bluest I could find, and this is a Labrador green. That's a light Barre granite over there. They get their names from where they're quarried."

How awful to make beads in granite. What a horrible joke. His beads had come to this? Beads were made to roll around in the hand, slip around the neck. They were light, portable. Granite was a flat slab squared off and stuck in a cemetery to weigh a dead man down. Nothing alive about granite, nothing so unlike his bright, beautiful beads.

The bead trader, lifting his arm, touches the smooth rim of the blue bead's hole with his fingers. Then he sticks his hand down the funneling hole, feeling along the grainy inside of the narrower channel. Cold, cold. He drew his arm out quickly.

She was telling Sandy and Handsome about the snow-monkey bead. Decided not to use the flame—the newest method of stone carving, she explained to the bead trader, including him, at last, with the others. Didn't really like the scalloped effect it left on the surface. Still, it might be right for one of the other beads.

"How many more?" The bead trader couldn't help himself.

Two beads left to do. She pulled back another plastic curtain, revealing two huge rough blocks. "Had all these stones for a long time," she said, "but not 'til I came up with the bead idea did holding on to them make some sense. I must have been saving them up for this project without knowing it."

"Belle Marie red, right?" Sandy put a hand on the dark pink stone.

"Right, and the black is Bonnie Brook."

Handsome wanted to know how she got hold of the black granite. The bead trader touched the immense pink rock—that rough word *rock* fitted the craggy chunk, so raw that it tore at his fingertips as he tried to run his hand over it. So massive—without the hole for the bead, it sat impenetrable.

Sandy had more questions for her. While she talked, she drifted back to the white monkey bead, and her fingers began plucking at the strap of the safety glasses on the workbench by its side. Obviously, time for them to go. She wanted to work.

The three men moved slowly to the door. Swinging the safety glasses by the strap, she walked quickly ahead to open the door, to hurry them up. Sandy and Handsome lingered for a couple more minutes with some gossip about a friend. The bead trader waited until they left to take his leave.

Standing in the doorway next to her, close to her, he could hear the tires squeaking on the snow as the others pulled away. The sand between her feet, was it the sand used on the icy sidewalks outside, or grit from the beads? "Thanks for showing me your beads. And I'm glad you liked the ones I brought."

"Oh yes, thank you. Sorry, I forgot to thank you." She wanted him to go.

"Maybe I'll find you some more stone beads, if you want me to. I'm off on a bead trip, soon, I guess. Off to Peru, Paraguay, and back up through Guatemala, Belize, then to Mexico. I buy up whatever I see that looks interesting. There're even some villages making beads especially for me. This friend of mine was a missionary down there—well, it was more like the Peace Corps than a mission—and he arranged a deal for me couple of years back. Need to get down there, though. The people down there don't really believe I'll come back, so they sell when they can. I don't blame them."

Suddenly, it was as if he had inadvertently tapped some secret spring that opened a secret panel concealed in the plainest of surfaces. She stopped swinging the glasses and looked at him. "You know, I haven't taken a trip for so long. I've been thinking, as soon as I finish off my beads, the studio'll be empty, so maybe I'll rent it and go away for a long trip. I don't know where yet. I guess anywhere else'll be fine, as long as I get away. You like Mexico? I hadn't thought about Mexico." She paused and then looked straight at him, looking very young for a moment and almost sad. "You know, sometimes you just have to change everything. Sometimes it's like you have to strip yourself down. When my beads are done, it will all be over and I'll go away. I tell myself, Just get the beads done and you're free, you can go. Mexico. Maybe."

The bead trader hesitated, not sure what to say. Had he even been invited to say anything?

The secret panel slid back into place. She turned away from him. "Well, have a good trip to Mexico. Get lots of beads."

The bead trader didn't move. He couldn't be dismissed just like that. "If you don't mind, I'd like to drop by to see how your beads are doing when I get back. Tell you about Mexico, too." At that moment, he told himself he would never come back here. Since she's going away, no use thinking about her. And that's good—he can forget about these monstrous beads, think about his own beads, real beads.

"Sure, but if I'm working, I'll have to say so and throw you out. Okay? You're lucky you found me just talking today."

"A deal."

"Would you mind pulling the door shut behind you? You have to pull it hard."

Yet the stones are beads. They have something to do with him. Yes, he is an expert of sorts. He can tell her a thing or two more about beads, although already he knows better than to say that to her. The bead trader still hears her voice ringing from the loft, denying him.

## III
# *Cenote*

THE BEAD TRADER FINISHED UP HIS TRIP in the Yucatán. It was April, the hot, dry season. Scraggly trees, rattling-dry, shot up by the road like a wall. Here and there, paths cut into the jungle, and along them stood the thatched huts of the Mayans in clusters of four, squarely facing one another. He had spent two months in villages of huts like these, bargaining for beads in his hit-and-miss Spanish.

On his way to Mérida, he stopped at a hand-lettered sign, CENOTE DZITNUP, and an arrow pointing to a clearing with a covered stand. His guidebook recommended a dip in this sacred well, now a swimming hole for tourists. He swung the car in, parked, and got out.

A thin little girl ran up to him. "Swim?" she demanded, and pushed her arms into a breaststroke, making her necklace of plastic pop beads bounce on her bony collarbone.

He nodded. *"Sí. Nado. Quiero nado."*

She pointed to herself. "Benita." Taking him by the sleeve with one hand, Benita pulled him over to the stand, where an old man, motionless priest in the shade of a temple, sold him a ticket torn off a big wheel of tickets, a ticket printed in faded black ink, on the thinnest paper.

Benita pulled him along a path into the forest and down a gully to a pile of boulders. There the path headed between the boulders. He hesitated, but Benita called, "Swim!" and steps, anciently worn in the middle, appeared leading into a mouth of rock. Benita first—she ducked, though she didn't need to; it was a gentle courtesy to indicate to him he should stoop and step down into the rock. He followed her down a passageway, narrow, yet with a fresh feel to the air and light filtering from somewhere. Down they went, twisting and turning with the path—was that writing on the stone walls, those faint red and black lines?—

then suddenly there opened up a large chamber of stone, domed completely by rock except for a small hole draped in trailing vines and framing the disk of bright sky. A beam of sunlight slanted down to the clear pool of water below.

He had read that Benita's ancestors had come here for water, came to throw offerings to their gods: jade necklaces, balls of incense, men, women, and children, husbands and wives, sons and daughters, captured in war. He offered his ticket to a boy standing silent against the wall, ticket taker and guard of sorts, tender of the floodlamps that shone on the water, making it a turquoise blue against the brown and white of the rock walls.

"Swim!" Benita pointed to the pool and flailed her arms in a clumsy backstroke.

The bead trader took off his shoes, his pants and shirt, waded in in his shorts. Benita squatted near his clothes to guard them and kept calling, "Swim! Swim!" The water was clear and fresh. For Benita, he did the backstroke, then the breaststroke. He dove, shot back up, breached the water with a smack for Benita. Her high-pitched laugh rang against the walls, and she was so excited, she flapped her dress up and down as he remembered his own daughter doing when she was young. Benita had the longest white cotton underpants he had ever seen.

By now, he was breathing heavily. He is almost an old man, he had to remember. He paddled over to the farthest wall, stopped to rest up for the next show. Treading water, he could sense the gentle rush of current pushing against his legs, the current that kept the water clean, the current that had carved out this chamber and, beyond, the many adjoining chambers he could see from here, one after another, until they turned out of sight or were swallowed up in darkness.

Here he was inside rock, but defeated rock, a fragile shell of rock above him, with its thin skin of dirt and scrub trees. Putting his face down in the water, he let his legs and arms drift to the surface. He tried to listen to the water coursing through the rock, carving it away. Water, master of rock, flowing, seeping, lively, gentle water insisting its way through veins and channels underground. Or wild ocean banging through that wall of rock on the western coast, surf spuming through, drenching him.

He turned and floated on his back. But the dripping of that same water brought back rock, hung these frozen veils, still waterfalls of stalactites from the roof of the cavern above him. Of course, below him there was harder rock that defeated water, and below that, in the earth's innards, molten rock, heavy, sluggish, spewing up through vents and cracks in the softer rock, erupting, catching fire, petrifying into frozen flows of rock.

Here inside rock, if she were here. For the first time in two months, he thought of her, for the first and only time named her, *la piedra*, "the stone," La Piedra. He must be thinking in Spanish after all these weeks of trying to speak it. La Piedra, the stone woman. Or was naming her, and in Spanish, a necessary evasion, a flimsy substitution, a cover for the stone, as if a storybook name like this would help. If she were here, if they had come on the trip together. If she were here, he wondered what she'd think of being inside rock like this. She belonged inside rock, like a seashell embedded in rock. He tried to think of her that way. What if she had come with him? They would be floating together—

Would she float, or maybe sink like a stone, that old test for witches?

Her granite probably harder than this rock here, this limestone, he believed it was, which appears to him frail, gentle by comparison. Now he can't hear the water, he hears the ring of a hammer in the frozen air up north, the ring of the hammer on granite, doubly cold, enameled with ice and snow and underneath so hard already. That woman hammering on the pink block. What kind of bead will she make of it?

A bead nothing like the light, sweet beads he was sending back home.

This had been his best trip ever. In Peru, despite the warnings the consulate issued about the Maoist guerrillas, the bead trader rode buses into the countryside, edging along the mountain ravines to get the tiny beads painted with elegant silhouettes of llamas and eagles.

In Guatemala, he busily went from village to village, the villages with churches painted bright greens and pinks, in the plaza basketball hoops on posts plastered and painted the same pink and green, under the hoops the local members of the civil patrol loitering in their black ponchos and straw hats, their rifles almost at ease. In San Mateo Ixtatán, the bead trader found Doña Victoria Ixtamazic again, ready with the beads he had commissioned. Kids there had always first learned to handle pottery clay by making *animalitos,* small bits they fashioned into birds, dogs, jaguars. For him, Doña Victoria taught the kids to take more care in modeling the *animalitos* and to make other beads, whatever shape appealed to them. She fired them lovely colors, a combination of hot and cold colors, she told him, malachite green, coral pink, a blue-green so alive, the tiny sphere it graced reminded the bead trader of the earth, as the astronauts have seen it. Next time, the bead trader suggested, showing her his Peruvian beads, they might try making some tube beads and painting them with the scorpion designs he noticed woven into the girls' belts.

From Paraguay came more of the *animalitos,* especially armadillos, very plain, glazed, not painted. He didn't know why he liked them except that the shape of the animal was so vivid even in such a small slug of clay. There was the touch of the fingertips still on them in faint whorls.

All the beads in the mail going up north, except for the samples he kept with him as a record of what he had already bought and to show other bead makers—he liked to think of himself as a fat bumblebee busily cross-pollinating styles. He kept samples, too, to pour out on his bed every night, or on his handkerchief in his lap as he swung in a hammock, to roll them around, sort them over and over again.

Up north, too, granite beads, a granite woman. The bead trader is frightened. That coldness—could her hands, her breasts be that cold? That coldness, that hardness might be contagious. He might petrify, prove to be granite, too, rock, too, if he thinks too much about her, if he keeps on not forgetting her.

He had stopped dead in the water, merely floating.

Benita cried out, "Swim? Swim! Swim!"

That afternoon, he walked around the Mayan ruins at Nohpat, the buildings still mostly obscured by brush, trees teetering on their terraces. In an open place bordered by four pyramid mounds were sculptured monuments, fallen, shattered, half-buried. Massive heads of bleached stone lay faceup in the grass, the carving blurred by the rain of centuries. Maybe six hundred years from now, someday, someone up north would come across in a ruined town, among summer-thick trees, a group of granite beads, bits scaled off by rain getting in and freezing, cracking the stone, five beads spotted with orange and green-gray lichens, birds nesting in the holes, or the holes silted up with soil carried by the wind, grass stalks growing out sideways like feathers stuck in a hat.

This future explorer wouldn't find them in the ruins of her studio. Where would the finished beads go? The bead trader now has so many questions to ask her. Why didn't he think to ask them before? He finds himself talking to her on the road as he drives toward Mérida.

She doesn't answer, though, one way or the other.

IV

## Quarry

ON THE FIRST OF MAY, the bead trader came home to cold spring rains, most trees still gray and black, hardly a shimmer of green yet. His daughter had been quite worried about him, for he hadn't kept in touch as he usually did on trips, although when the boxes of beads showed up, she had known, at least, he was still among the living. More boxes kept coming during the next weeks. He cataloged and shelved. His daughter strung display necklaces to show off the new beads.

Two weeks later, he had nothing left to do at the shop. The new beads were put away. They were between classes. Business was good, but steady, nothing that would count as a rush.

Several times in one week, the bead trader drove out of his way to pass by The Sculptors' Studio. He didn't know which of the parked cars belonged to her, never saw her go in or out, although lights burned there late at night.

The rains stopped. The days grew warmer, although the nights stayed cool. Early one morning, he left his house to go to the shop and saw that the pitch pines had thrown their pollen, pollen sulfur bright, lying like light sulfurous snow on the new grass, the sidewalks, the windshield of his truck. The windshield wipers smeared the pollen into wide yellow streaks. The world through that glass instantly wonderful, as vision must be. He drove to her studio.

The door was open, so he slipped in. It was quite cold in there. The smell of stone dust in the air. He would have never thought stones had a smell, but they did, a dank odor, flatter than the smell of soil. He looked first behind the plastic sheet. There were five beads. The green vertebra, the blue tusk, the snow monkey about to turn a somersault. Now an even bigger bead, a pink oval worked like—it must be like a thick flower bud, with thick petals lapping at the bottom where the hole begins, petals slightly swelling, lifting around the other hole. The fifth bead low and wide, black bulging coils, a snake coiled up around a clutch of eggs, except the clutch was the hole. The black stone highly polished. The bead trader reached out to touch it—silky as scales.

"If she keeps leaving that door open, someday, somebody's going to steal a piece of hers."

Father Time's beard was sticking through the curtain. He pointed the bead trader up to the loft.

The bead trader slowly climbed the first flight of stairs, Father Time right behind him. He rushed up the second flight, the third, up to the loft. She stood at the counter, stuffing things into a knapsack. Catching sight of him, she needed a moment to place him. Oh, yes—she lifted her hand and smiled.

Before he could say anything, the telephone rang. She picked it up. "Yes, I'm leaving right now. Oh damn. I'd forgotten that. Yes, fix that, all right? Good-bye. I'll be back as soon as I can, probably later than dinner. Don't wait."

While she talked, the bead trader moved over to the table and fixed his eyes on the stone beads still there on his white paper towel, now a dusty field of snow. He had forgotten to look for some more stone beads in Mexico.

"Yes. Good-bye." She hung up. "Oh Christ. Just been reminded of a dentist's appointment that I've missed. Or will miss —I've got some other business to attend to this afternoon." She cinched up the knapsack. "And so you're back? Have a good trip? Get lots of beads?"

"Where are you going?" The bead trader kept himself from asking who that was on the telephone. Her husband? Her lover?

"Oh, up to Rockport and then a quarry at Pigeon Cove for my last bead, I hope. I've used up all my own stones, but I've got an idea for one more bead. Even going to spend my own money on it, my 'capital.' Of course I'm crazy." She swung the knapsack up on her shoulder. "Sorry, but I've got to go. I'm kind of late already." Feeling for her keys among the papers and tools on the counter, she asked again, out of politeness, "Did you have a good trip?"

How white she was, though it was nearly summer. She must stay indoors all the time. How dark he was, had become on his trip, how dark and warm the people he had met on his trip, and here she was, in spite of her dark hair and dark eyebrows, so pale. If he were to lay his hand on her arm—well, how dark his hand would look on her arm.

"I could help you with your accounts. I've got lots of experience with small businesses."

"Oh Jesus, that's all I need, somebody else to tell me what I don't have to spend." She flipped a switch, and the overhead light went out, leaving the table lamp shining on the beads.

If she were leaving soon—no, not today, but leaving Boston soon for a long time, in spite of or because of whoever was at the other end of the telephone line—the bead trader knew he had to stick close to her now, make the most of the time left. He looked at her. "Do you need some help at the quarry?"

She moved toward the door, moving out of the light. He could not read her face. "Thanks, but no. I'm fine."

"I've got nothing else to do," he assured her. "Wouldn't mind going up to Rockport at all."

"You'll be bored. There's really nothing for you to do." She was waiting for him in the shadows by the head of the stairs, waiting for him to leave. "Could you get the lamp?"

The bead trader didn't move from the table. Picking up one of the stone beads in front of him, he made himself finger it. "Look, we have a lot in common. I mean, you're making beads out of granite. And I'm a bead man, sort of a bead consultant even."

As if he could read her mind, the bead trader knew how she came to make her decision. She didn't want him to go, yet finally it didn't seem to matter enough to her to say no. Strange, this sense of being dismissed, blanked out not by anger but by a fundamental indifference. Still, indifference he could take advantage of, at least for a little while. So the bead trader knew he could go to the quarry, if he waited and said nothing.

The next moment felt as if he were taking a step closer to her, a step noticed by her, yet registered as insignificant, then forgotten.

"If we're going to go, let's go. Get the lamp, okay?"

Father Time, spinning a diamond-shaped sheet of colors on a rod, didn't look up as they went by. Throwing her knapsack among the wooden blocks and the tools that littered the back of her station wagon, she reached over to unlock the door for him. Her windshield, too, was coated with pollen, it lay thick along the rubber seals of the windows.

She took the expressway north, then another highway northeast, and after that they were spun off by rotaries more and more east.

In the car, she said nothing. Maybe she was nervous. Here he sat so close to her, within reach. He could put out a hand, put it quietly, surely on her thigh. Fine, let her be nervous for a change.

Or, maybe, she simply had nothing to say to him. For the whole trip, she would keep her eyes on the road, drive slowly, not change lanes or pass, think her own thoughts.

The bead trader told her about his trip. But she must have forgotten that she had wanted to go to Mexico.

They drove in silence, again.

Then he told her that he had been thinking about her beads, that he had lots of questions to ask her, about her beads, in the interest of work, her work, his work. He had even written them down. He drew out a folded sheet from his billfold, some sheet stuffed in there with the address of a bead distributor scribbled on it.

Taking her eyes off the road for a second, she glanced at the sheet of paper, at him, and she laughed.

He protested. "Don't laugh. I'm an old man. Everything leaves my head if I don't write it down."

"All right."

"All right." He cleared his throat. "Let's get down to business. First, why did you make the beads out of granite?"

She sat up a bit at the wheel. "Well, look around you. See this road cut up ahead—that's granite. Glaciers stripped the whole coast here down to the granite. It's the stone of this part of the country.''

It amused the bead trader to be lectured like this, reminded him of himself in front of his bead class.

She glanced over at him. "You know, people spend all their lives in a city that has been quarried from some small hole nearby, one small hole, and all their lives they are shaped by this stone. Denver's got this red, red sandstone. Other places totally out of limestone. Around here, towns are mainly granite. It'd seem strange to use anything else.''

Again, abruptly, silence.

He looked out his window, and he saw the great outcroppings of granite, granite raw in the road cuts. He saw the main street of every town they passed through was a narrow, twisting, tiny canyon of granite blocks—the banks, the schools, the town hall, the courthouse, and the paving stones. Outside the towns, low stone walls trailed off into the woods or bounded a worn orchard. Granite, too? At least today the stone was gilded, softened by this yellow pollen. He could bear to look at it.

The bead trader made a show of consulting his sheet of paper again. "All right, second question. Where do the beads go when you're finished?''

Turning to him, taking a hand off the wheel, waving it, she instantly came alive, almost violently alive, with a pent-up energy that exploded into a rush of words.

"I didn't tell you?" She acted as if she couldn't believe she hadn't told him about it, as if of course he must know about it. "I didn't tell you? You won't believe it. I still don't believe it— that I'm doing it.''

She sat forward now, her left knee drawn up. "Oh, it's a funny story." Two years ago, a small town on Cape Ann, Manchester-by-the-Sea, elected a woman mayor. The newly elected city council members, too, were women, the mayor's bridge club, whom she had encouraged to run. They had entered the race late, run without a prayer, but after a door-to-door campaign, they won as write-in candidates. The mayor and her council decided to commemorate their victory. They pulled together some town money, some private donations, state and federal grants, and set out to make a small park right on the sea cliff in honor of a famous Boston suffragette who summered in Manchester-by-the-Sea a hundred years ago.

As she told this story, she kept turning and looking at the bead trader, and he looked at her, at her blue-jeaned hips rather large, thighs muscular and splayed a bit on the car seat, the dusty work boots, a bit of lipstick, some vanity there.

Their suffragette, the mayor and the council ladies discovered, had had her heart set on becoming a preacher, of course the real New England thing to do, then. But impossible, then. So instead, she had marched for the vote; she gave speeches, wrote books about women's rights. In one of these books, the mayor found something about how in the future women would be preachers and sculptors.

"Who knows why sculptors?" She laughed out loud and lifted up her right palm.

This quote put the ladies on the track of a "sculptress," as the mayor quaintly phrased it. They requested a list of "sculptresses" from the state arts council. Most of the artists invited to apply for the commission didn't, not enough money, not enough prestige. She went to see the site, the suffragette's estate on the cliffs, because she had always wanted to put something next to the sea, and she thought about the stones she had saved up. A good way to clean out her studio before leaving Boston.

When she showed them a sketch of the site with the beads, the mayor and the council murmured something about how they were thinking about a statue of a goddess, or of the suffragette herself. Something noble. She told them it had to be the beads. Well, she didn't say it quite that way, but she persuaded them anyhow—and they were grateful someone wanted to have the commission. The beads would be granite, she kept reminding them, such a dignified stone, the one stone for monuments.

She looked over at the bead trader and laughed.

The bead trader had only one more question to ask. Where would she go when she was finished with the beads?

But they had just arrived in Rockport. "Entering granite city," she said, alerting him with a last wave of her hand.

Rockport. Granite Great Arch over Granite Street, Granite Pier, blocky stores and houses of granite, piles of granite rubble, the arm of the unfinished granite breakwater stretching out to sea.

She pulled into the parking lot of a diner, The Rock Pile. Sandy and Handsome lounged inside, drinking coffee with a young woman. Sandy and Handsome, sure, they remembered the bead trader. Handsome introduced his assistant, who sat still as an idol, her angular face and narrow eyes averted.

The bead trader tried to explain his presence, that he had some extra time, was curious, thought he might help out. He felt foolish, of course, saying this, as if she needed help, hadn't done this a hundred times or more. Sandy and Handsome didn't seem to notice; they started teasing Idol, the assistant, about her latest tattoo, which she refused to show them.

After a round of coffee, they all took off. Sandy, Handsome, and Idol in Sandy's car followed her station wagon. Swinging north and west of the town, to Pigeon Cove, they turned in at the sign JOHNSON QUARRY. At first, it looked like they had happened upon a junkyard. Rusting machinery once painted blue, caving-in sheds covered with spray-paint graffiti, grass stalks thick between narrow train tracks. There were signs of life closer to the pit—a tall derrick lowering a boom, stacks of granite blocks. A couple of men standing in front of a shed waved at them. She, along with Sandy, Handsome, and Idol, who had come to look at stones for themselves, headed over to the shed to check in with the supervisor.

The bead trader walked on to the edge of the pit and looked in. The drop was ninety feet to the bottom of the pit. He almost sank to the ground from dizziness. He grabbed at the trunk of a tree straggling on the brink there. Sheer cliff faces falling straight down from narrow, terraced ledges. Ladders reached from ledge to ledge, like the ladders in adobe pueblos, but these ledges and cliffs weren't of hand-patted adobe. They were rock, immense walls of rock, dwarfing the ladders and the few men scaling them, the rock making the men its creatures, their hard hats, their masks, their clothes gray like the pool at the bottom of the pit, scummed gray with grit the same gray as the rock. The sulfur shower of pollen had not scattered its softness down there.

It was like coming upon some terrible accident, seeing the raw, open body of the earth cut all the way down to the bone, only stone.

She and the others came from the office wearing hard hats and carrying small cans of spray paint.

"We're going down to look at stones. You'll have to stay here. All right?"

The sculptors descended into the pit, stepping down the ladders, becoming smaller and smaller, but their voices still ringing up to him, echoing on the rock.

Fanning out at the bottom of the pit, each one looked for a stone. She headed for the far side of the pit, straight into what looked like a city of stone rising from a plain of stone.

Not once did she glance up at the bead trader. Swinging her knapsack from her shoulder, she took out a hammer. Crouching by a stone, a long, flat block, she tapped it with her hammer and seemed to listen for some sound, perhaps for some flaw. She stood up, walked around the stone, and then reached out to mark it with the spray paint, a vivid green initial.

The bead trader watched her intently. He had her in sight, at last. He has been too close-up to her; he has let himself think that she is merely a woman who likes stone, when she is stone, at home with stone around her, stone here not shaded with green leaves, or brushed by grasses, brightened by running water. Simply pure stone that you cannot talk to, hardly talk about.

A stonecutter came and stood beside the bead trader. Together they watched her climbing back up the ladders.

"Not seen you here before. One of her artist friends?"

The bead trader shook his head. "Not really. Just kind of looking. Sort of a spectator."

The two men didn't say anything more. Without stone in common, they had nothing to talk about. Soon she was there speaking to the stonecutter, who turned out to be the foreman. They discussed the stone. The foreman signed her form, told her to make sure and have her rig here ready on Friday, ten o'clock sharp.

On the way back to her car, she told the bead trader that once she's picked out a stone and they've brought it up, the quarry wants it moved out as fast as possible. Partly because the quarry would have to replace it if they accidentally damaged it. Yet there was something more to their rush than that, almost a superstition. The stone has to be cast out from their world because a shape has been seen in it. The stone is already something other than sheer rock, something almost human.

They drove back to Boston in silence, the bead trader thinking on this odd interchange of state, the stone become human, the woman revealed as stone. Then the motion of the slow-moving car lulled him into a doze, and he slumped over sideways against the window. She woke him only as she was pulling up in front of the studio.


v

# Shrapnel


THE BEAD TRADER MISSED THE DELIVERY of the stone. The block came a day early, and she didn't call to let him know.

When he showed up on Friday, he did arrive in time to see her making the first cuts into the block. No one had answered the bell, so he tried the door and found it unlocked. From behind the plastic curtain came a deafening noise, and on the other side of the room, an engine roared. The bead trader slipped inside the curtain. The large gray slab of granite was set upright in a wooden frame, the bottom of the stone sandbagged. She stood on a ladder, her face made strange by safety glasses, dust mask, headphones. With some tool connected to hoses and wires, fitted with a drill, she drove into the stone off-center, in the upper left of the slab. Her body leaned into the stone. When the drill disappeared in the stone, she stopped and held still a moment, steadying herself against the block. Then, reaching around for a hose behind her and turning on the water with a twist, she flushed stone grit from the hole, pausing several times to dig it out with a file.

Setting the drill back in the hole, her body really a part of the drill itself, she pushed once more against the stone. How hard the stone was, how resistant. What must it be like to come to stone again and again, with no sense of conquering it, merely of shaping its fate in the slightest fashion?

Only when she stopped for a moment and came down the ladder did she notice the bead trader. He stiffened, ready to be asked to leave. Lifting her hand in a brief greeting, she fitted what looked like an extension onto the drill and went back to work.

Until she could no longer hold the drill, it was the same actions over and over: drill, flush the hole, drill again.

Under the stone grit, she was pale. When she rested for a moment, he saw the muscles trembling in her legs and arms.

The next day, he found she had set up the ladder on the other side of the stone. The cut into the rock from that side demanded the same patient ritual. Then the drill went through, and it surprised him how tense he was until that moment—the drill exactly hitting the hole from the other side and spinning free with a shrill screech. She turned off the drill and for a moment stood still, then came down the ladder, shaking all over but elated. She confessed to him that she had been afraid to not hit right on, and, even more, that she would find a flaw, a crack hidden in the rock, that going right in with the hole was the test. You had to find out, but you pray for the stone to be whole, perfect.

That day when the bead trader left the studio, he went straight to a building-supply store. He bought himself a pair of safety glasses, a package of dust masks, and a set of headphones. Every day, upon arriving at the studio, he slipped in the door, put on his safety glasses, adjusted his mask, tightened his headphones, and sat suited up to watch her work.

When he told his daughter that The Bead Trader would have to get along without him for a while, his daughter wanted to know what he did at the studio. "Sculptor's assistant," he entitled himself on the spot. And he had moved the ladder, rearranged the sandbags, helped reposition the stone with the electric hoist. But most of the time, the bead trader sat on an old sawed-off tree stump there and watched her work.

At first, he had tried to be attentive, to show his interest. They had lowered the stone. Now, she needed to take off the extra length of it. The basic tools for stonecutting, she explained, hadn't changed since the Egyptians carved the statues of the pharaohs along the Nile. The pneumatic carving tools were practically the same hand tools, only fitted to a compressor. Showing him a thick, blunt-handled metal chisel with a long, flat edge—the hand tracer, she called it—she set it against the stone and with a series of sharp taps of the hammer she carved a line where she wanted to cut the stone off. Fitting a handset—a tool like the hand tracer, but with a thicker edge—squarely into the traced line, with her hammer she hit off big chunks of stone along the line until it became the new edge. The square stone she had as a result, she rounded off with the point, a thick stake-shaped tool, until the stone looked something like a millstone.

That was early on in the carving of the bead. Very soon, the bead trader gave up trying to pay attention. He sank into merely sitting there. Sitting there became so restful—how had he ever become so tired, so dead tired, so in need of rest?

He might fall asleep as he sits there, barely aware of her except as constant, patient movement in front of him. She sets the point against the stone, lifts up the hammer, and then surrenders to the weight of the hammer, letting it do the work as it falls, the motion a whipping action, the rhythm of the stroke the crack of a whip, again and again, always on target, never missing. She, too, might fall asleep and the hammer would still lift, would fall, clang on the point, the point bite into the stone, the sparks fly, a shower of shooting stars.

This crack of the stone, the patter of stone chips, the roar of the yellow vacuum arm she pulls up close to her to take off the stone dust, the splash of water on stone, these have the effect of a blessed silence. Never has he rested so fully, as if every joint in his body, every strain in his soul were loosened, and that loosening more welcome than he ever would have guessed. He is loosened into a floundering, without direction, but in floundering he discovers the simplest, the deepest of pleasures. He listens to himself breathe in and out. He takes from his pocket the chunk of granite he picked up from the floor, he rubs his thumb across its face, explores the nubby crystals, considers the flecks of white and black and gray.

Once in a while, they were interrupted. Father Time stopped in to say a word or stare. Sandy, Handsome, and Idol came by. The bead trader didn't care. He sat there in his corner, waved, shuffled his feet until they were gone, obscurely aware and grateful to her that she made it so they never questioned him, disturbed him.

Both of them were the same species now, looking curiously alike with their safety glasses, masks, headphones, their coating of silver stone dust.

Days and days passed. He didn't pay too much attention to

time. It became all one time, the time he spent there. When he left in the evening, it was as if for a few minutes, for he went straight home, ate something quick, and lay down on his sofa— he found himself unable to sleep in his bed—until the next morning when he left for the studio.

All this time, the bead progressed. She carved down the outside edge of the millstone so that it sloped from a rounded, swelling center. Four rippling lines traced from the hole to the edge gave the bead the look of a round Aztec stone calendar he had seen in Mexico City, with the sun's rays radiating out from the center. She hammered the stone into a pitted surface and in several places she marked it with a claw chisel, tracing small parallel scratches that curved into one another. Turning the stone over, she looked at it a long while, began to polish some of the surface, then left some of it rough, even jagged. So at last it seemed both bright and shadowy like the disk of a full moon, or was it the smooth and troubled surfaces of a pond as a cat's-paw plays over it? His mind played over the stone with these pictures, not wedded to any one of them, and content, at moments, to see the stone as stone.

Next, she returned to the hole of the bead and chiseled out a wide, shallow funnel mouth on the side of the moon disk. Sprawled on the face of the wide, round bead, she polished the funnel with the grinder, finishing it by hand with grindstones. He remembered what she had said about the oldest beads, how their holes were worn down by the rubbing of the cord. The slow work of years, she performed here in hours of intense concentration, but wasn't that, this time rushed up, as good as time at its usual rate? On the other side, the Aztec calendar side, she carved away the stone two inches back from the hole, until she had left a lip around it, which she shaped into a smooth coil, very elegant, very formal. It struck him that no cord could wear away that lip. That hole would mock time.

One day, she walked up to the bead, put out her hands, and

took hold of the lip of the hole for a long moment. Then instead of buffing it again, she turned on the hose and washed the stone for the last time, rubbing off the muddy grit with her fingers until the water ran clean.

Staring at the stone gleaming with water, she told him, "You know, when you see it underwater, the polish that it has, you want it to look just like that when it's dry. It shines so, it's perfect. But that's impossible to get. I've tried. I just have to remember that it rains a lot here. The stone'll look its best on those days."

Tired and happy, they climbed up to the loft and sitting side by side—as lovers sit, he fondly noted—they drank a cup of coffee. How freely she talked to him, about how good it was to finish the bead, how she hoped the installation of the beads in Manchester would go all right.

Looking down at herself, covered in a paste of grit and sweat, she grinned. "I can't wait to go home tonight and get clean."

Sometimes when she got home, she told him, if everyone else was asleep in the house, she washed and put on this old satin robe she had found in a junk shop long ago. It is heavy, but so soft and smooth, and she sits quietly. Oh, she likes the grit—she laughed as she rubbed her forearm—and she doesn't mind finding it in her hair, under her fingernails. Even so, it is a pleasure to wash the grit off at night, to be smooth again—that's a pleasure, the contrast. Though there are things you can never scrub off. She held out her arm to show him several blue spots. "See here. And here." Sometimes, she said, when you hold the point to the stone and hit the point with the hammer, the metal of the point's head mushrooms—that is, its edges flatten out and then curl under like a mushroom cap. If you don't grind the mushrooms down immediately, bits of metal shear off sooner or later while you're carving, fly like shrapnel at an incredible speed right into your left arm, your shoulder. "See, they're under the skin." The bits of metal are so small, though, it's not worth having them dug out.

Later that night, in the dark, lying on his sofa and staring out the window, the bead trader saw her arm, her shoulder, her body defined by the bits of metal as constellations are defined by stars, a celestial dot-to-dot, an armature that imagination clothes with flesh. He would be sitting with her some night. He would reach over, lift back the robe to look, pull aside the satin robe of night —he is sure the robe is black or midnight blue—and on her pale flesh find the stars buried in the skin. He would pore over her, seeking them, finding them one by one, touching them, gently, not probing. He would trace the lines imaginable from one to the other, reading her differently again and again, her body, a new body with each way he realigns the stars.

He takes hold of his prick now, circles his upright flesh with his thumb and index finger, pulls down the skin. His body stiffens and stretches with a long-forgotten delight, as if that stretching is the body giving up, not to death, but to once more being alive. He pulls up and then down, hard, again, then stops. What if maybe she will one day soon be here with him, so he can enter her with this flesh, her flesh? Maybe she might accept him. If he presses her, or shows her his interest. He has held back too long, played the old man. When now here his body is ready, not young, but full, powerful, aching with joy, it couldn't go to waste, it would not be fair for this to go to waste. He would hope. He would sweep all before him. He is a man. He is still a man. He would go to her when all was over, the beads all gone. He would present himself to her, she would be in her robe, he would come before this woman who in her robe has deemed herself of high rank, a self-crowned queen in her coronation robe. He lay on his sofa, watching the planes of light on windowpanes just catching the dawn, his body still, alone—and brimming with life. It would be wrong, unjust, a waste.

## VI
### *Dressing Table*

THE SMALL MUSEUM AT MANCHESTER-BY-THE-SEA had been slow in taking shape. Funds promised by the state were frozen in the recent budget, but luckily, she had her money already. The installation of the beads on the park grounds could go ahead. Early on a Saturday morning, her friends showed up at the studio. Sandy and Handsome came, Idol brought along two women and two men, and several others turned up with Father Time. The bead trader had been the first to arrive. So he had the satisfaction of knowing that the others would see how close he had come to her and to the beads.

The rigger and his sons drove up in their trucks. She unlocked the garage door, Sandy raised it, and the rigger backed up the first truck. The blue bead, the pink, the black, the white, the green, the silver bead, one at a time the beads so alive and docile were brought forward and readied to be loaded. Again and again, men and women busied themselves around a bead, laying out the straps, then hitching the stone, making sure the sling wouldn't slide off. Once it was hitched, everything happened so fast: the stone was choked with the sling, hoisted and set down on the truck bed, padded and secured.

The last bead loaded, the riggers took off for Manchester-by-the-Sea. Everyone else jumped into their cars, and they formed a convoy behind the trucks. The bead trader drove alone in his truck, with only his sleeping bag in the seat beside him. He did manage to get in line right behind her station wagon, which was piled high with extra slings and wooden blocks. Ahead of her rode the beads, padded three-quarters of the way up, the crisp colors showing at the top, the crystals glittering in the sun.

They pass reed beds silver-plumed with midsummer, then the Mystic River flanked with gleaming white storage tanks of oil. They move up through the rocky cuts along the highway; coming closer to the coast, he notices the thinning out of the underbrush, the trees growing farther apart, their trunks and branches bent westward, though it is a windless day. The convoy leaves the highway, takes the local road, and makes the right-angle turn down into Manchester center, by the harbor still bristling with tethered sailboats. The people busy with their Saturday shopping stare at the caravan as at some circus passing through.

The trucks turn off onto a rutted Sea Avenue. Light from what must be the water slants through the scrubby trees. They roll past outcrops of shingled condos, a tract of new cardboard-cutout frame houses, wind past the older clapboard houses faded pink, yellow, and gray set right on the road. The light from the sea grows brighter, and he can smell and taste salt in the air. They must be near. Here at last, a turn into a drive walled with a low stone wall, the wall tipped with sharp-pointed chevrons of rough granite, blocks with the drill markings still on them, past banks of rhododendron, past stunted pines, through a wooden gate swung back forever into lilac hedges, the hedges growing through the gate. And ahead, a craggy point with a large house perched on it, the most peculiar house the bead trader has ever seen. It resembles nothing more than a weathered silvery brown wooden basket perched on a pile of boulders polished by the sea. Of course it is a house. There are all the signs of a house—glass windows that reflect the sunshine, doors with knobs—but the glass only glints through wooden shutters, the doorknobs are buried deep in the shade of verandas enclosed by batten lattices woven in a Japanese style with a round moonlike space in the center. Beyond the house stretches the sky. Below must be the sea.

The rigger's trucks with the beads headed right, down along the cliff, and disappeared among some pines. The cars and the bead trader's truck pulled under a shingled round arch to a court-yard and parked. Everyone tumbled out. She unlocked the front door, they unloaded coolers and sleeping bags and carried them inside the house. The house was empty except for a few pieces of furniture, old summer furniture, wooden rockers, rattan ottomans, folding chairs, battered low tables clustered companionably before windows that gave out onto the cliff edge, and at last the ocean, huge and forever, all the way to the horizon without haze or cloud or ship.

Next to the fireplace, on the far side of the long, wide entry hall, stood a worktable covered with plans for the renovation of the interior as a museum. Among them, in pencil and watercolor wash, an architect's sketch of the front door and its carved lintel: "But in a few years it will not be thought strange that women should be preachers and sculptors," Harriet Hosmer, *Daughters of America,* 1883. A layer of dust covered the plans, the bead trader noticed.

To work. Everyone very excited, talking and laughing as they followed her down a path by a stone wall, through a pine grove of black slightly twisting trunks, to an open stretch along the cliff's edge. It was a fantastic site. There the Atlantic, green below and blue-black beyond, the stretch of ground grassy as a meadow and haphazardly paved with smooth, flat patches of the cliff rock that had worn through the soil. A crane had been set up. The trucks were parked next to it. She and the rigger spoke a few words to each other. Then the work began.

They readied each bead in the sling. Then the bead was up and hovering in the air, twisting a bit, disporting itself for an instant, almost frivolous, until the crane turned and lowered the bead precisely at the place she indicated, where she waited, motioning as the bead came down, standing back as it bumped down and took its place with regained gravity. It was a friendly and courtly ceremony, in which they freed granite, swung earthbound granite free of its nature momentarily, denatured rock in order to reinitiate, reseat it.

The first bead ordered forth was the blue tusk, or rather, that day, it seemed to the bead trader a small mountain, with handholds and footholds carved in its side like those he had seen once on the canyon wall at Mesa Verde. She made sure its large hole was lined up with the lighthouse, white, erect, on another point of land down the coast. The other beads were slung and swung over, set into place. One by one they took their seat, the green vertebra, the snow monkey, the pink bud, the silver moon disk set upright, the black coiled snake. As the crane lifted free of the black bead, everyone cheered and clapped. Someone popped open a champagne bottle, presented the bottle to her. Grabbing it, she took a long, long drink and passed the bottle on.

The bead trader kept staring at the beads, at these huge beads scattered along the cliff several yards apart from one another. This loose arrangement of the beads on the cliff was deceptive. The hole of each bead had been aligned in such a way to the bead before and the bead after it that, although there was no chain or cord to string them together, the bead trader sees a cord stringing them together into one necklace, a bead necklace scrawling across the tiles of stone.

All at once, it strikes him that the meadow is the top of a fabulous dressing table. And the bead necklace spilling across it belongs to some titaness, some gigantic woman, majestic, ample, equal to and proportionate, who stands right now before her dressing table, starting to undress by taking off her beads, the string of beads slipping from her hand onto the table, and who holds still there a moment, fingering the beads, gazing into her mirror, the reflective sea, contemplating her reflection in the waves sometimes rolling, sometimes crashing, as perhaps she sees herself in the water, sometimes tranquil and sometimes violent.

Vanity of vanities, all is vanity. But what kind of vanity is this, to look for your reflection in the sea, to delight in a string of stone beads?

He swung around to the others, who were all laughing and talking. Did no one else sense that presence? Would no one else acknowledge the visitation? Grinning, nodding her head, cutting at the air with her hand, "the sculptress" stood there and talked to the riggers. At this moment, for the first time, she seems vulnerable, now that she has been separated from the beads, now that they belong to this other woman. She has been merely the jeweler, a court craftswoman, the maker of the necklace that has invoked the presence, summoned it with this tribute, certainly, but now not the same as that presence itself. She has diminished into nothing but, merely, a woman.

Is this what it means to be free of the beads?

## VII
## *One More Bead*

THE RIGGERS DROVE OFF IN THEIR TRUCKS. Father Time and his friends left, too. Everyone else walked back to the house for a party. They broke out food and beer from the coolers. Someone turned on a radio, and some people danced. The artists drank, and they talked their projects to death, complained about not getting grants, about the commissions that always went to New York artists. They traded inside information on this gallery, that gallery, who was the person to see.

The bead trader wandered about the edge of the group, lurking in doorways, always only looking on, looking at her. Unlike that afternoon, now she was not laughing, not celebrating. She sat among the others, silent, withdrawn, almost sullen. She must feel uneasy. She knows that she has lost something with the finished beads. None of the others took notice. He notices, yet she doesn't look up, invite him over. She leaves him to his own devices.

Angry and bored, tired, too, the bead trader picked up his sleeping bag and a flashlight, climbed up the stairs without saying anything to anyone—no one said anything to him. He threw down the bag in an empty room. The bag still smelled of the south, a green, peppery smell from, it seemed, so long ago. He got in and went to sleep.

The bead trader dreams he is in a dark room; he knows she lies in the next room. Then she comes in to him, naked from the waist up, or at least that is all he can see of her in the dream's dim light. He stands up and takes a few steps toward her. She reaches out and touches him on the shoulders, her hands, her strong hands, press his shoulders—no, she places her hands at the joints between his arms and his shoulders as in a ritual gesture. Although it is clear that the touch is meant to restrain him, keep him where he is—how clear that is—the bead trader feels, too, how warm and strong her hands are. He leans into her hands.

The bead trader woke up, wide awake. The beat of the surf boomed through the cliff rock and up into the house, the single sound.

Where was she? Rising from the sleeping bag, he padded out of his room to look for her. It is all over. She cannot hide herself. There is no retreat. Her time is come. Her hands cannot, will not, keep him back. Now is the time to sweep everything aside and insist with that power a man has that it is inevitable that he take her, lay hold of her. He is certain she will give way to him.

Shading the flashlight with his hand, he gazed at the face of each sleeper. They were so tired or so drunk, they slept soundly. Or was his mastery of this moment something prepared from a long time back? Was it fated that he wouldn't awaken them? On the veranda, he found one sleeping bag by itself. Triumphant, he slipped up to it. When the light fell on it, he saw it was empty.

The bead trader thrusts his hand in the bag—still warm. He turns. The screen door stands ajar. Now all is simply pure pursuit. She must have gone out, she sits in the meadow by the cliff, with the beads. How it will unfold is quite clear, all the steps shining with the certainty of their unfolding. When he finds her there, he will grab her up by her hair and take her in the grass, among the stalks, in the shadows of the beads, on the smooth rock, prove her a woman of flesh, make her cry out, to him.

Along the low wall through the pine grove, he passes silently, swiftly. Here are the beads, white and gray and black in the light reflected up by the sea. Patches of pink, blue, green as he plays his flashlight over them. She is not among them.

Quick, down the cliff path to the beach below—maybe she has gone to look at the sea. There on the beach he will work her into the sand, working a hollow in the sand, their bodies crusting with sand, tiny shells.

In the beam of the flashlight, footprints, faint, then crisp closer to the water and leading down the strand to the rocky point crumbling into the ocean. There, the footprints disappeared where the water washed in, drained out. He stared at the sea, among the flecks of light, no swimmer to be seen, and he could see far enough. He flashed his light several times. No call came.

He stood there as long as he could bear it. And he suddenly hoped she had drowned. Whether by accident or by intention, she swam out until she grew tired and sank. She will wash back in only when she has been carved down to bone by fish, rocks, sand, and water. Maybe—he laughed to himself—he could get a piece of that bone and carve it into a small bead, the way Tibetan monks fashioned the bones of their holy men into rosaries. He'd take her hair, her hair would be floating on the waves, curling with the waves the day they found her. He'd wind his hands in that, it slipping chilly through his fingers. He'd braid it for a brown silk cord.

The bead trader walked back up the beach, climbed back up the cliff path. Calm, supremely calm, he passed among the beads, touching each one. He will come here often and be with the beads like this, look at them in the rain. He will sight, from the hole in a bead, the lighthouse down the shore. As self-appointed guardian of the shrine, he will pull weeds, talk a bit with the tourists who stop off to visit the beads, simply another item on their list of curiosities to see along the coast. After they leave, he'll dig out the trash they inevitably stuff up the holes of the beads. Then when he is dead, the weeds grow over the beads. In several hundred years, the sea undermines the cliff, until one by one the beads slide off, crash into the waves below.

The bead trader made his way back to the house and went right to sleep. He slept soundly.

Voices calling. Must be morning, although the sky was still quite black. The others must be looking for her or asking one another where she is. He waited. Let them discover the accident themselves. Later on, he would explain away his footprints in the sand, tell them how he looked for her, didn't find her, assumed she would come back later in her own good time.

Dressing slowly, he finally went downstairs and found them huddled on the porch—around her. She stood there, her hair slicked back, her clothes sopping wet, water pooling round her feet. He almost cried out.

Tremendously excited, she says there's one more bead she has to get. Yesterday, after the beads were installed, she realized that something was wrong somehow, unfinished. She got up in the middle of the night, stared at them, went for a walk, ended up crawling over the rocks at the base of the point, and has found on a neighboring beach her last bead—a perfectly wonderful granite sea boulder.

Handsome reminded her that last year he had been arrested for trying to take a sea boulder for one of his pieces. But Sandy and the rest of them only got more excited: Let's go get the bead, before the sun comes up, no one will see.

They loaded the bead trader's truck with straps, wooden blocks, and all their sleeping bags to use as pads. After telling the others how to get around the cliff from below, she and Sandy climbed into the truck with the bead trader. The bead trader was glad Sandy sat there between them, for he couldn't bear to sit next to her, this apparition smelling of the sea. They drove down Sea Avenue about a half mile, until she ordered him to stop and turn off his lights. She and Sandy jumped out to help the bead trader back the truck down onto the beach and up to the barrier of boulders there.

The bead trader turned off the engine, got out, and went over to the boulder. Shining his flashlight on the stone, he watched her hands caress her boulder, smoothing it with her palms, stroking it. It was the perfect bead. A slightly asymmetrical sphere not as large as the sculpted beads, this bead rolled back and forth into shape by the sea was of human size. In the stone's smooth black surface were suspended large white crystals, some square, some rectangular, block letters on a blackboard—here is a Rosetta stone from the interior of the planet, these hieroglyphs the mind is almost always about to read, and then cannot. The bead trader sees it is the right stone, a wonderful stone. He can already see the hole, a very plain hole sunk softly into it, a hole so plain, so narrow, you would hardly notice it.

The others had rounded the point. They came up from the sea wet and ready for adventure. In whispers, they tried to figure out how to get the stone into the truck. Sandy suggested that since the stone's perch on the other boulders was already at the same level as the truck bed, if the smaller rocks in front of it were cleared out, the bead trader could back his truck right up to the boulder and the bead could be tipped in.

They set to work clearing the way to the boulder. When they were finished, he returned to his truck, put it in four-wheel drive. Handsome and Sandy guiding him with hand motions, he backed up to the stone. The moment he turned off the engine, a light flicked on in a nearby beach house. They all froze. Then it blinked off. They laughed like teenagers stealing street signs. Half an hour later, at the cost of several bruised fingers, aching backs, and sore shoulders, the bead was pushed onto the truck bed. They packed it in with the wooden blocks, padded it with sleeping bags. Straps secured it to the cab.

Everyone bowed to her, to one another. They mimed applause. Waving, she was headed for the door of the truck when Handsome called her back in a loud whisper. "C'mon with us. We're going swimming."

She hesitated, then glanced over at the bead trader and asked him if he would be all right driving back alone to the house.

The bead trader looked at her. He saw the beads were now, at last, over for her, finished, completed. Having cast off the weight of the beads, given up their gravity, she wants to float on the midsummer sweet breeze, free at last to enjoy the waves against her legs, the night sky, the morning sun, the entire world new and alive for her again.

He looked at the bead. It is the perfect bead. "You go on. I'll take care of the bead."

She touched the bead, spoke to the bead. "Don't try to unload it yourself. We'll take care of it later, when we get back."

In his rearview mirror, he saw that she waited as he slowly pulled out toward the road. When his tires screeched softly on the asphalt and he switched on his headlights, she turned and followed the others to the sea.

The bead trader took Sea Avenue back toward the house, drove past the driveway, drove through the silent town of Manchester-by-the-Sea. Only a light on here and there this Sunday morning, but it's good to get an early start, even on a Sunday. The bead trader drove straight on toward Boston.

The stone rides well in his truck. He will keep it at the bead shop, in that corner between Asia and the Americas. The bead will take up too much room, he might even have to knock out part of a wall to fit it in, his daughter will think he's gone crazy, but that is where the stone bead belongs, right there within reach. He sticks his left arm out the truck window, reaches back around to touch the bead, a bead so smooth and cool to his touch.

# THE MASTER

## OF THE

## PINK GLYPHS

# I
## A Two–Time Zone Watch

MORLEY PULLED THE BOOK OFF THE BOOKSTORE SHELF and flipped it open to the first page.

"Why are there so few guides for women traveling alone?"

Morley put the book back. What did she need with this travel book? She used to travel alone, years ago. It would all come back to her the moment she started her trip to Central America. Surely, Morley didn't need to travel by the book. She left the bookstore.

The next day, Morley went back and bought the book. She had to have the book—it seemed suddenly of the utmost necessity. Perhaps the book would help, help her get over the fear of taking the trip, this unaccountable fear. Oh, there were all sorts of accounting for it, but those accounts did not yet add up to the fear that kept her at home when she was so, so restless to get going, while her mind and body still have some force, still have a need to live, while she's still not so sure that she has had enough.

She would go.

December 24. A week of school vacation already wasted. Only three more weeks of a teacher's dearly bought dream time, fertile with boredom, a restless time still left to go before she would have to start teaching again. Morley could still go. She had to go.

Morley turned into the gate of her house, checked the mailbox, climbed the stairs to her third-floor apartment, pushed off her wet boots. She would not go. Yet she would not visit family or friends, either. She would stay home. Take the book on solitary and female travel back this very moment, unread, full of unwanted advice, while the receipt for it was crisply new—proof that she had thought about it and thought better of it.

But to take the book back, she would have to pull her boots back on.

Morley dropped the book on her desk. Maybe the day after Christmas she would take it back. Maybe she'd keep it, anyway. Maybe she'd go on the trip, anyway.

The bang of the porch door, two stories down, the tread of the mailman's boots, the bang one, two, three of the mailboxes open and shut. Bang of the door again.

The red cat walked in from the bedroom and brushed against her ankles, once for love, once for food. Feed the cat first, then eat lunch, and only then go down and check the mail.

The very next instant, Morley was down the steps, opening the mailbox. No letter from him. Morley slowly climbed back up the steps and sat at the kitchen table. She picked up the latest letter from her stack of his letters. The winter light white, the street outside silent, all the house so still. The red cat sitting there, watching her.

—————

*November 11, Madras*

Dear Parvati,

In India, what I like is the many gods, Krishna, dancing Shiva, his wife, Parvati, Ganesha with his elephant head. There's not the one-on-one of Christianity. And I like the animal presence of gods. All the beauty comes from the animal nudity of the gods.

Here, you see anuses everywhere, those of little girls and old men as they shit while waiting for the bus. Violet anus, tight as a sonnet. The vulva more sinuous, like a novel. The shit smells like curry, not this stink of death, of assassination we have in our Western shit, the stink of carnivores, hunters, winners.

At a bus stop near Madras, I saw a woman in a sari (everyone here is draped, it makes the hands and feet so moving, the skin becomes a trap for light) approach a traveler waiting for the bus. She opens his eyelids one at a time, revealing the white globe finely veined of his eye, and with the point of her tongue, she cleans the ocular orb. Then she wipes the point of her tongue on an old Kleenex and reaches out her hand to show the particles of dust she has removed. The traveler gives her a rupee. All the other travelers line up to have their eyes washed with the tip of her tongue. So that when they come to the office, their boss will say, "What bright eyes! What vision!"

In India, the towns are impregnated by millions of particles of dust. I have bought gray postcards as gray as the hands of the children who sold them to me on the street.

Here, everywhere, at any moment, fights break out between Hindus and Muslims. "Just a little knife play, pilgrim," the desk clerk at my hotel assures me. I am more afraid of my own collapse.

I count on the monotonous, sterile days that I pass here to protect me, protect this humble loser.

Your pilgrim cum dust

P.S. Indians love the latin word *cum:* "Does the gentleman want his spaghetti cum sauce?"

Morley reread the page—only one page—again and again, until the cat cried three times and walked over to his bowl. She put the letter down, fed the cat, then sat again at the kitchen table.

Looking around the apartment, she saw that the traces of his life here had disappeared. The spill of her life by herself was taking over. A few clues to his former existence were now and then discovered, remains to which she was terribly alive when she happened upon them. Underneath the sofa cushions, she found three of the German toothpicks he favored. Six silver-foiled suppositories—a minischool of minnows—glinted inside an old briefcase of hers he had used.

In the back of the closet was a suit, the plain rough cloth hanging limply like his flayed skin, or was it a shed skin, a snake's skin you see abandoned on a path, transparent, weightless, but still ghostly alive with the shape of the flesh? Where now was that new flesh, glistening flesh, gone out new shining upon the world?

And in the bottom drawer, a pair of cotton undershorts. The fabric of the crotch worn by the friction of his testicles—those heavy balls, like two huge grapes, she had weighed in her palm, impossible to have had the weight of his balls in her palm and not to have it there anymore. The fabric so worn that it had torn and been clumsily mended by him—he insisted upon her teaching him to sew.

Morley had sketched these things to take note of them. She used to keep a journal, but lately words had turned into drawings. First in the margins of her written record appeared more and more drawings, really illustrations, then words shrunk to captions in the margins of drawings, then there were only drawings. Now it was more accurate to say she kept a notebook of dated drawings for her record. She sketched a button he had sewed back on his suit, the flat face of the button tilting on a fat lump of thread wound round and round, knotted and loopy. She piled up the toothpicks into a cross-hatching to sketch them. Her pen scratched on the rough paper, until the cat at her side switched his tail, scattering toothpicks to the floor. She had enough of a sketch, though. The drawings affected her strongly when she looked at them. Accurate to the object, they were at the same time compressions of unsaid, unsayable things.

He hadn't precisely left her. The situation wasn't like that at all. September, a year from last September already, his mother had fallen ill. His mother was very old. He knew she was dying. He took leave indefinitely from his job and went home to France.

So one moment, he had been sitting there with Morley at the kitchen table, looking at her. The next moment, they were at the airport, at the boarding gate. She pushed him up against the wall, held his wrists against the wall, held him there to look at him one more time. Until he gently loosened himself from her hands, and he folded her to him, held her head in his hands, against his chest, tightly. A last moment, he was gone.

At first, they talked often on the telephone.

He told her about a trip to the sea with his mother—once an excellent swimmer, an expert diver. He waded into the sea, holding his mother in his arms to let her feel the sea on her skin once more, old, slack, shiny skin. The plastic sack for her excretions got loose and bumped up under her clothes.

He cataloged his mother's grievances against her children: their indifference, their ingratitude, their wasted lives that had wasted her life.

He paid tribute to his mother's politeness. She ate alone in her room, not letting anyone see and worry about how little she could eat.

He described his mother lying in a refrigerated drawer, her yellow flesh like church candles, her impossibly sharp cheekbones.

After burying his mother and settling her affairs, when all that was over, still he hadn't come home. The telephone calls stopped. Part of the money his mother had left him, he sent to Morley to help keep the apartment going. With the rest of the money, he started to travel, traveling east—to Greece, to Turkey, to Iran. No word about when he might come back home.

At first, Morley had been angry. Next, she had cried, all night long, every night, every morning, stopping only to teach, every afternoon cried in her office, cried to her cat, in bed, all night long, every night.

After a while, though, Morley came to understand that she couldn't take this abandonment personally. His flight came to seem to Morley something that had had to be done, something that she told herself she had to allow. Clearly, she could not help. He had not asked her for her help.

Morley's family and her friends thought it clear that he had abandoned her. The money was a payoff. And there must be more to this strange, sudden disaffection and prolonged disappearance than merely grief. "It's been over a year now," her mother dared to say to her recently, to remind Morley of time passing, that she should turn her back on the past and start over.

But by now, Morley lived for his letters that came, every week, every two weeks, from so far away. It was difficult, though, in the beginning to read those long descriptions of wher- ever he stopped. The letters too much like his face turned away from her, averted, looking at something else. Slowly, however, those same long descriptions became readable. To be with him, she had to read every single word of those passages as the world began spilling into the space of their separation. She had to look at the world he looked at to bridge the widening distance between them as this traveler drifted along from airport to airport, con- ducted by psychopomps disguised as smiling travel agents, as soothing air hostesses who poured out, then came back with their carts to pour out again the waters of forgetfulness: "Coffee, tea, juice, or Pepsi?"

Morley had many sketches of her stack of letters. She sketched the stack again after its small landslide.

The letter from India slid and hung halfway down the slope. Was it possible to be so stripped-down—it felt like layers and layers of skin, down to the thinnest last membrane—and still live?

Morley abruptly stood up, walked into the other room, and threw open her atlas. In Madras, India, she calculated the time to be 10:30 P.M. She checked her watch. Of course, she had the right time already. She didn't need to reset it.

A year ago, after the letters began to arrive, Morley spotted in the window of a watch store a watch with a peculiar face. No Mickey Mouse waving his arms, no moon revolving through its phases. Simply a small rectangular white face, with two dials the same size, one with tiny black Arabic numerals, the other tiny black Roman numerals.

The showroom closed around her like a gray velvet jewelry coffer. Elegant salespeople, each with discreetly clinking keys attached to his or her belt by a long chain, padded behind their showcases. A short, dark man in a fine suit approached her, glanced at Morley's rumpled clothes, at her heavy boots for the slick sidewalks, and welcomed her to Alpha and Omega, offering his assistance in courteous, clipped subcontinental.

Morley claimed to be "just looking, really," but she said she'd like to look at one of the watches in the window.

Instantly, the dapper salesman produced his key, unlocking and sliding the window open.

"Pick it out. That's right, miss. Just pick it right out."

Morley plucked out the watch and held it up to the salesman. "I don't understand. Is the second dial a seconds dial?"

"No, no. You see, miss, this watch is a two–time zone watch —for people who must keep track of London time and New York time, Tokyo time and Los Angeles time. An international businessman, or rather, a businesswoman—this is a woman's watch." He leaned closer to her, stage-whispered, "For people who lead a double life." Pulling back, he added with a most perfunctory salesman smile, "The man's watch has four dials."

"What time is it right now in Turkey?" Morley inquired.

The ritual of setting the watch followed upon the arrival of each letter. A glance at the watch at work, at the grocery store, waiting for a friend was to be aware of two different times, at the same time.

In the sketchbook, the watch appeared encircling a wrist.

Two dials on one face. Morley became acutely aware of him as a double, as a twin would—that was more exact—a twin brother and sister who do not look alike, yet in a photograph, the two faces in one frame, there is this third presence, their implicit resemblance, their complicit selves overlapped. Morley began to recognize his hand in her hand's particular caress of the cat right at the base of its spine. And sometimes she saw him, in her mind's eye, waiting in some airport, heard him in her head talking to some Americans and coming out with some phrase of hers. Some plain old American phrase like "What a joke!" came out and surprised him.

An odd assessment of the situation. Even Morley knew that. Yet the thought kept running on in her mind, and soon she knew that as his twin, she, too, had to set out on a journey. That was what the restlessness was: her other half was in motion, while she remained immobile. This immobility affected her as a physical discomfort, like that of a muscle atrophying, aching with the lack of exercise. Set out on a trip—that was how to be with him, now. If he came home and she hadn't set out on her own trip, wouldn't she always be lagging behind, out of step?

Of course Morley wouldn't set out after him. If he were moving east, she would go in a different direction. North or south. Traveling west, she might meet him.

Morley didn't have much money to travel. So someplace not too far away, although out of the country, but not expensive.

One afternoon, waiting almost naked in a freezing pink examining cubicle for a nurse to give her a physical, a desperate Morley grabbed from the magazine rack an issue of *National Geographic*.

The lead article called for an entertainment park–preserve in Central America. An artist's vision of the future, "Mayaland" featured a monorail skimming through the jungle canopy among monkeys and toucans, above gleaming white ruins curiously intact. Tourists wandered about villages of deluxe thatched huts.

More reassuring to Morley were the photographs of the rain forest, of the people who lived there, of ruins still overgrown. There were pictures of sculpted facades, details from painted vases. On one vase, two Maya figures, a man and a jaguar, danced together, heels raised, the colors a rosy pink, orange, and black, the figures so alive, such a celebration of the grace of flesh, full curved arms and thighs, seeming to her so familiar.

Morley finished the article in the waiting room. She had decided: she would go to the Yucatán or to Belize or to Guatemala to see the ruins.

First, though, she must study the situation. Soon she had piles of books edifying into columns around her, new columns springing up all at once after a short period of deciding not to go, then deciding to go—but only after researching the trip a bit more.

So, throughout the summer, instead of taking the trip, Morley read widely and wildly. Soon she had assembled many bits and pieces of knowledge into a crazy quilt Central America of toucans and manatees, women's weaving, so many different Maya, so many wars among the Maya, against the Maya, lineages of Maya kings and Spanish conquistadors, the affiliations of Guatemalan death squads and the CIA.

An absurd coincidence—a famous archaeologist, one of the first great Mayanists, was a Morley, one Sylvanus Morley, no relation.

Her eyes raw from reading, Morley read one last thing, a conquistador's account of Botello, the astrologer, a member of Cortés's expedition, who cast fortunes for Cortés and the Spanish soldiers. On the night of June 30, 1520, the famous and infamous "la noche triste," the Spaniards and their allies, the Tlascalans, stole out of Tenochtitlán, the Aztec capital, along the causeways that connected this city built on the lake to the shore. The Aztecs shouted and whistled to one another to come quickly and destroy the fleeing foreigners. They threw spears from canoes, hurled stones from their roofs. The Spaniards were soon treading on dead comrades weighed down by the gold they were taking from the city, on sorrel mares dying from spears thrust in their bellies. Captured soldiers were led to the top of the tallest pyramid, adorned with plumes, prodded with spears and made to dance, then their hearts ripped out, their bodies hurled down the steep stairs, dismembered, and later eaten with chilies and tomatoes.

In Botello's box, the surviving Spaniards found Botello's calculations of his own fate scribbled in a book of necromancy: "Whether I shall die in this wretched war, murdered by the Indians?" followed by these answers: "You will die" and "You will not die." Botello asked about his horse: "Whether they will kill my horse?" "They will kill him."

Morley took up from her desk the eight ball, a black plastic ball like the billiard ball, a kid's fortune-telling toy she had bought for a joke. With not a little trepidation, Morley asked the eight ball, "Will I go to the Yucatán?" She turned over the ball and waited for an answer to appear in the little transparent window set in its base. Floating up out of the darkness came the message: "Signs point to yes." She asked again to make sure. "Very doubtful." A third time. "Hazy, ask again later."

Morley sketched the eight ball.

Morley went to the archaeological exhibit at the University Museum. Inside this redbrick Victorian vault, this famous center of Maya studies, she hoped to be helped to see, as in a vision, the bright white buildings of limestone overgrown with towering trees, some sort of a picture where everything fit. However, she found only a dusky room of dusty fragments, their yellowed labels askew, and old plaster dioramas of Maya cities with nicked corners like kids' school projects. It was too dark to sketch anything there.

Morley told all her friends, her family that she was going south to the Yucatán or maybe to Guatemala. Although, as she said the words, she knew that she listened to herself, to hear for herself whether the trip had acquired some reality.

Morley tried being practical about her trip. She laid in supplies of pink medicine for her bowels. Cassette tapes, *Speak Like a Diplomat in Days,* clacked on her kitchen table. When, in late August, it seemed her country might soon engage in a small war halfway around the world, a friend found for her a Spanish textbook from World War II, *Wartime Spanish,* with chapters entitled, "Un paraíso tropical y armado" and "Bombardos nocturnos."

Then it was too late to take the trip. School started again. Night fell too early, too soon. Morley hated to come home after dark to a house where the windows were always dark.

December 25. This Christmas Day, the sun shone, the streets were bright with white light on salt-bleached asphalt and empty when she went for a walk.

December 26. The red cat bounded up on the bed, skidded across her chest. Morley looked at the window to see what time it was by the light. The sky softly shone an opaline pink, a low sky, a snow sky. Yellow-gray-pink sky dropping softly soon snow on the town. She had identified snow skies for him, when he was first a foreigner to these skies.

Alone in bed. How horrible not to have that wall of back to lean against in her bed, that thick, strong wall of bones, spine and shoulder-blade bones, of firm flesh furzed like an apricot. Alone in this bed, what a poor, thin, negligible thing her body was, lying still out of habit on her side, carving out a single bed from a double bed.

A fear stood double to Morley's fear that he would never come back: her fear that missing him would never, never end.

If she could fall back asleep, right now, she wouldn't cry.

Two hours later, when Morley woke up, she had had a dream. At a party, Morley met this tall young man. She recognized his name from her studies; it was Michael Paddler, a leading Maya archaeologist. In the dream, Morley had become excited and said to this young man, "I have so much to talk to you about. Can we talk sometime?" She had spoken purely and simply out of enthusiasm, yet when he smiled and suggested they have lunch, his smile was sweet, and she was attracted, she could tell, and, worst of all, she felt like this, this is what it would be like to fall in love again, to come to life again. So sweet, happens in a moment, and through this traitorous act, the whole world might be lost.

While eating breakfast, Morley felt ashamed and yet excited. She laughed at herself. In real life, she knew Michael Paddler to be at least seventy years old.

Washing up the dishes, she wondered, though, if maybe the dream was a sign she should go. That sweetness promised in the dream. A sign of another life?

Over the radio came news of the preparations for the little war in the desert so far away, soldiers flying off, setting up camps, on maneuvers. Of course she shouldn't travel now.

In the mail, finally, another letter:

---

*December 14, Rangoon*

Dear Huckleberry Finn,

Burma, this newfangled Myanmar, is a Marxist-Buddhist-military dictatorship, absurd and out-of-date like myself.

You can't buy maps of Burma in Burma, Myanmar in Myanmar. They've taken them out of circulation. You can't buy field glasses, or rather, you can buy them, but they've all been fixed so that you can see things only close-up. Faraway objects are hazy, blurry, no matter how you turn and turn the dial to focus.

At least they can't change the course of the Irrawaddy River.

I did two hundred kilometers on a bus boat full of chickens, families, and Buddhist monks in thick-soled running shoes and wraparound black sunglasses sent by their colleagues in Thailand. The river is lemon-colored. A man at the prow calls out the soundings to the pilot (Myanmarese Mark Twain), who steers us around big islands of sand, islands pointed keen as arrows. On these islands, fires burn with sharp, thin flames, bright, dry flames, without smoke. Passing us are huge rafts as large as shopping malls, with gas stations and stores.

I travel like a sick person. No place interests me, only moving.

And moving from city to city, I begin to see that death is like a city, beginning well before the countryside comes to an end. The straggling shops and houses, the full suburbs, make you anticipate the city. You'll see when your mother dies, your father dies, and there is no one left between you and that city. I see death everywhere, the seed of death born in all bodies at birth, a hidden tumor even in the most desirable bodies. I am afraid to see the tumor in your body, seedlike, flowering in the deep swell between your hips.

I might go on to New Caledonia, where there's a fitful revolution going on against the mother country. I hear they speak a mangofied French. And there are islands and islands—I can move on and on, from island to island for a long time.

Your old river rat Jim and aspiring island-hopper

---

In Burma—Myanmar—the time was 9:25 P.M.

If Morley didn't go on her trip, what would she do with the rest of this vacation? She could not bear to read anymore. She should start preparing her classes for the next quarter. She might rewrite the assignments.

Morley could go on her trip. Get rid of the ache in her legs, the restlessness, set out, journey, move on and on.

That afternoon, the snow fell lightly. The red cat sat curled up on the kitchen table by the window. Red cat and snowy sky, why leave behind this peace, this silence?

December 27. Morley set out to take the single woman's travel guide back to the bookstore. That day, the wind was wet but fresh, almost inviting, almost like spring. She felt an absurd joy—the weather at least could change, even if she remained so frozen, so immobile. Summer would come soon. Blue skies, green leaves. "Blue-green plate, blue-green bowl," the ancient Maya called the earth and the sky.

A panic for change came over Morley, to do something to make a change—to stay alive, it is so urgent to make a change. Maybe a change-of-life haircut, a short, shorn haircut might do the trick—not a trip. Save lots of money.

Morley passed a jewelry shop with a sign in the window advertising a sale on earrings and free ear piercing. In an instant, Morley was sitting stiffly in the chair. The thin, wiry man assured her, "Don't worry, there have been fifteen thousand ears pierced in this shop. Done fourteen thousand of them myself." He grinned at her in the mirror. "Personally. Personal guarantee."

Morley raised her eyebrows. "How many have you lost?"

He laughed, with nicely practiced self-deprecation, picked up a small punch, and shot an earring through each ear. He handed her a mirror. The sight of blunt, thick wires stuck in her poor pink earlobes made her slightly ill. Packing Morley off with a bottle of antiseptic, he reminded her of other available piercing services, for tongue, nose, nipple, labia, foreskin—for her friends, of course, unless perhaps, you never know—he had done one hundred foreskins this last year, without losing a one.

Morley hurried out and ran right into two colleagues from work, Mina and Tina, two round balls in their puffy quilted jackets, both bespectacled. Mina short, with short curly hair. Tina tall, with limp hair and heavy dangling earrings. Morley pulled up the collar of her jacket to hide her wounded ears.

"Oh, hello, Morley. Thought you'd be in Mexico?"

"I probably won't go right now. Maybe next summer."

"Oh, no." Mina laughed. "I can't stand another round of 'Should I go, I should go' every day at lunch."

Tina tried to help Morley. "Well, this war off in the desert may start any day. So, not the best time to go on a trip."

Morley nodded. "They're talking about terrorists at big airports. And the trip itself's a little dangerous. For women traveling alone, this book says." Morley pulled out the single female's travel book and held it up as evidence. "You have to be too careful. I think I'm too old to be too careful. I should stay home and clean my house. Prepare my classes. And there's my cat, too."

"Doesn't your neighbor always watch your cat when you go away?"

"At least you've made a decision," Tina offered.

Morley couldn't help it—she brought him up. "I've heard from him. He's been in Burma."

Mina glanced at Tina. Morley knows they think it's crazy for her to go on about him like this.

Now Tina frowned. "Burma's—I mean, Myanmar's dangerous. My human-rights group writes letters to Myanmar all the time about their political prisoners. Why would anyone want to go there? We think it's like abetting the military regime."

Morley argued, "These places have to be seen, too."

"They should be boycotted by right-thinking tourists."

Morley had nothing to say to this. She fingered an earlobe. It hurt more than she had ever imagined it would.

"What a strange watch," Mina said.

"It's ten to three, A.M., Burmese time." On the river. Morley added, "I might go to Guatemala, instead of Mexico."

Tina was indignant. "Guatemala's one of the worst human-rights offenders."

Two blocks up the street at a travel agency, Morley asked for the cheapest flight south, as soon as possible. Lucky for her, many people had caught a case of war jitters and canceled their trips. The cheapest flight, nonrefundable, turned out to be to Cancún, the resort on the easternmost tip of the Yucatán Peninsula, a resort site selected by computer to be the queen of Mexican resorts, a computer not programmed with the information that the reef running along the coastline of the Yucatán Peninsula was one of the great shark habitats in the world.

## II
## *Ruination ("to fall, crumble, into ruin")*

MORLEY WROTE LETTERS HOME from the Yucatán:

*January 4, Cancún*

Dear Homing Homer,

I suddenly thought, What if you come home and don't find me at home? I should write, let you know I'm in the Yucatán for a week. So, maybe, in a few days, you'll be sitting at home at the kitchen table reading this letter, my travelogue.

Dave, my neighbor during the flight—big black glasses, white skin opaque and moist like a slice of raw potato, ragged mustache, and worn backpack—claims to be an old Yucatán hand. Eats like a horse down here, swears he's never been sick, "never danced the Toltec two-step." Doesn't swim—he's read about the sharks lurking in the reef. Mostly picks up American girls on the beach and shows them around. His finesse with women, he lets on, he acquired in California while hanging out with famous movie stars, whose cars he "detailed" for a living. "Detailing," I learned, means an elaborate cleaning of a car by hand, even under the fenders, and polishing with a chamois cloth until not one smudge remains. "Detail Dave," they called him.

Dave finally drifted off. Looked over and saw he was drooling in his sleep. At that moment, I became almost fond of Dave. A month ago, at the Kamakuras', as I scratched the chin of their white cat, Nijo, she drooled on my fingers. Kyoko apologized: "Nijo's so old, she drools all the time now." Immediately, I wanted to testify that I have known delightful droolers, meaning you, of course, that every small thing the beloved does, even drooling, is delightful. You do drool often when you talk, and I am so moved. Your liquid diamond dripping, spitting, is just you spilling over. Which makes perfect sense—your element is water. When you take a bath or a shower, you must splash water everywhere, as if you will not be satisfied until the world is splashed with water, life-giving water, water from underground streams, called forth by the diviner. You divined me—I was waters called forth, a spring, an urn overturned and flowing. I couldn't say this out loud. Everyone disapproves. But with my caresses, I tried to tell Nijo—instantly your familiar—this old cat, getting old like you, drooling dodderer. If I'm blessed, I'll soon come to drooling myself.

(Writing you this long letter, I begin to spill over, or is it leak? Yes, that's it—I'm brimming, threatening to spill over. Let's hope not onto Dave. Ugh.)

From the air, the Gulf is very blue, Cuba very green, the Yucatán very flat, endless forest with a few bald spots—I think of the clearing on top of your head and laugh. At the Cancún airport, billboards feature blond and pink-fleshed gringos frolicking with beach balls, but gringos with short, compact Maya bodies, the bodies of the vendors at the airport, the cabdriver, probably the artist. The taxi bus dropped off the other tourists at the great white cliffs of beach hotels. Dave knew of a cheap hotel for eight bucks a night in the town of Cancún, where the hotel workers live. A ramshackle hotel next to a car junkyard. We ate across the street under a thatched roof over a cement floor. I took a prophylactic swig of pink medicine and tried a shredded-pork dish, with a chili relish, searing-hot and very good. Dave, it turns out, eats only eggs down here, huevos rancheros—"Always ask them to cook the huevos hard," he advised me. No wonder he doesn't get sick.

I looked at my plate like a condemned woman.

During dinner, Dave flirted with me, in his potatoish way. I wondered, in my detached way, what it would be like to make love with him. We all now know what to do with bodies, have mastered so many techniques. What would you like me to do? Dave might ask, as if I were ordering from a menu. Suddenly, I had an awful vision of being detailed, like a car, Dave's hand wrapped in a chamois cloth, running inside the lips between my thighs.

But, as you say, the real pleasure lies in finding out.

My room is quite bare, a bed, a toilet that may become my close companion very soon, this table and chair where I sit and write to you under a twenty-watt light. A ceiling fan cranks, cranks.

To write to you is to be in touch with you again, even though I am ashamed at how plain my talk is, all talk about the plainest tourist things. And at how stiffly I write to you—I'm out of practice talking with you.

Your very own Toltec Penelope

P.S. Looking at your Java postcard (which came right before I left) of the Buddhist temple at Borobudur with its gray stone floors, stone platforms, stone domes, the stony range of mountain rising behind it. I can picture you sitting at Borobudur. You've come on a pilgrimage to this world of stone, scoured stone, and you do your best to look stony, pious, in a state of Buddhist renunciation of all desires, because desire leads to suffering. Yet your body gives the lie to renunciation. You sit there advertising your ample flesh, the world incarnation of desire, my desire rasping over you like a cat's tongue, your desire lifting its head, just by me looking at your serpent, not even thinking about it. Lifts its head and nods at me and I start to laugh.

These seven days, I won't know where you are, so you'll be in Java for a while, at Borobudur. I'll have you marooned there. Or maybe you're home and will get this letter from me.

———

*January 5, Still in Cancún*

Dear Borobudur,

Touristing doesn't come easily to me anymore, I make myself make a plan of the things I know a good tourist should do. Today's plan: change money, visit the market, take a taxi to the hotel beaches to swim out beyond the surf and the people hopping over waves—then I think about the sharks. Instead, I wade in only up to my knees.

You'd have your swimming suit instantly on, that suit you always carry with you. Who knows, a stream, a lake, a river, a sea, an ocean may appear. That bathing suit, gray-green like snot, balloons up pearly gray in the water as you swim facedown, eyes open to the sea, your tonsure slick pink. The suit puffs up like a pearly Portuguese man-of-war riding the waters, and I know your sting—one long, dangerous, and delicious sting. Then, protean, you dive and come up mammalian, slick seal head bobbing in the water, with dark, friendly, curious eyes. There's a flip and a show of slick, shiny flesh, a muscular thrust, and the obvious sheer pleasure of gliding through the water.

Beach wrack at the edge of the small surf: flat silver fish, driftwood, a rusty can, cockle shells, scallop shells, and a paper white conch shell, large as my fist. A perfect white conch shell wound round six times with major ridges, the whole surface ridged subtly, except for the mouth of the shell, where the animal had been alive and left a kind of white plaster coating that effaced the ridges, smoothed them over. The ancient Maya used large conchs with rosy pink inner lips and brown-mottled exteriors as trumpets. These paper white conches, they cut in half lengthwise, to expose the hidden chambers, and used as paint pots. The conch fits perfectly in my palm. Sometimes they incised glyphs on white conch shells, filled in the glyphs with red paint. This shell is still a blank sheet. I put it carefully in my bag.

Visited my first Maya ruin up on a hill above the beach—a tumble of stones. Down below on the beach, spotted Dave at work on two American girls.

Your beachcomber, washed up on the beach

—

*January 6, Tizimín*
*Feast of the Three Kings, los Tres Reyes*

Dear Fellow Traveler,

This morning I spent waiting for the bus to Cobá, a ruin still half-lost in the jungle south of Cancún. At the bus terminal, I sipped boiling-hot, weak coffee, heavily sugared, dipped from a large kettle by a woman at a stand. The bus station altar stars a framed picture of the Virgin of Guadalupe. That red-gold pod of light in which the dark lady manifests herself resembles nothing so much as the open lips of the vulva. All light and power emanates from the vulva—bleaching the paper flowers crammed in the Coke bottles surrounding her.

The bus is late. I read one guide, a second guide, a third guide about what to see at Cobá—if the bus ever comes. The first guide again, and I discover in small print, in a section where I never would have looked unless I was waiting for a bus that didn't come, the information that the Cancún-Cobá bus sometimes does not run.

There's a bus to Chichén. On to the ruins of Chichén Itzá.

As soon as I sat down, I took a slug of pink medicine to plug up my bowels for the bus ride. Next to me sat a boy holding hands across the aisle with a girl. Too awful not to let them sit together. My Spanish is poor, so I grin at them, make stupid gestures with my hands. At last, they understood and—*gracias, gracias*—we switched around. For the next two hours, they whispered to each other, arms around each other, fingers furtively probing, untucking, tucking.

The bus rolls between walls of dry trees. Once in a while, a village suddenly appears, the bus slows down for the speed breaks, and with lumbering care takes them *bump bump* coming into town and *bump bump* leaving town. We roll past the chickens scratching, the pigs lying in the shade, the kids staring at me staring. After each village comes a square-walled cemetery, such a formal little city compared to the straggling village.

The church towers of Valladolid, the big town on the way to Chichén Itzá, are visible for miles over the treetops. Lunch stop in Valladolid, lunch in a courtyard with pots of red flowers and a blue parrot chained to a perch—*click click* he paces his perch. I looked inside the cathedral of San Bernardino. Impossibly high yellow-plastered walls guard the cool emptiness within. Like a seashell. I walked up and down the several streets. The stuccoed walls of houses almost flush with the street give it the look of a narrow river channel with high banks carved out by rushing water, flash flood.

I'd forgotten that when I'm traveling alone, eating takes two seconds, a walk maybe three, and then there's all the time in the world, too much time. In the plaza, I sat in half of a cement love seat, a thick S-shaped seat, an instant implication of two. A guidebook calls them *confidentiales*. Two people sit side by side, face-to-face, gazing into each other's eyes, leaning toward, whispering to each other.

What would I confide in you if we were face-to-face?

The other round cup of my S is empty.

I put my bag in the empty seat and pulled out the guides to read up on the ruins at Chichén Itzá. Ruining is the thing I expected to do, the expected thing.

Instead, I see that an hour north of here, in Tizimín, there's a great festival today, January 6, the feast of the Three Kings, *los Tres Reyes.* Maybe put off Chichén Itzá for two hours?

The crowded bus to Tizimín stopped every ten minutes and every time more people materialized from what seemed an empty forest. Near Tizimín, the bus got stuck in a big knot of trucks, Volkswagen Bugs, old Dodge Darts, and people walking in between the cars. All the bus passengers demanded to be let off, so I got off, too, and followed the crowd to the plaza crowded with long rows of stalls. Stalls of sweets—limes stuffed with coconut, wasps clinging in buzzing clumps to nougat, stalls with women sitting behind the counters, their quick fingers picking picking the flesh from cooked turkeys. Stalls with hairbrushes, with underwear, with dishes. Nothing for tourists.

I bought pineapple chunks on a stick, sprinkled with cinnamon, took a bite—not cinnamon, chili powder.

Behind the stalls, a tiny Ferris wheel turned, its buckets empty. Small empty race cars rumbled around in a circle. From a tent painted with a huge yellow-tusked rat—LA RATA GIGANTA— came a shaky rat roar summoning the crowd, but no one lined up. A kid dozed over the roll of tickets.

Back across the plaza, people carrying green branches were lining up. The line moved toward the church, through its front doors. I edged my way among some crowded stalls to the church's side door, and a priest standing there at a worn velvet barrier gestured for me to come closer. The procession snaked around from the back of the church to the front in tightly packed S-coils, the worshipers inching forward, children, women, men, their dark faces turned curiously on me as they waited to go forward, then turned away as they moved forward again, and finally passed before three statues, the Three Magi, the Three Kings, *los Tres Reyes,* three short statues with white Spanish faces, dressed in Spanish Renaissance robes of brocade, velvet, and satin, with gilt crowns. Three Kings bagged in plastic bags by someone practical, for each person in the procession brushed the kings with their branches—the statues would have been bright green by the end of the day. The walls above the black heads were bare and very high, shell-like, like the church in Valladolid, with faded frescoes green and red and blue high up on the walls.

I leaned against the door and watched for a long time, not watching anything in particular, not staring, barely conscious of the feet stepping forward, the kids straying from the line and pulled back in. Very soothing, the slight smell of the candles—or was it the branches?—a pine smell, and the *swish swish* of the branches brushing the plastic.

At last, though, I had to go. I thanked the priest and made my way back through a cluster of religious stalls selling tapers large and small, rosaries, green branches.

One young woman presided over a table spread with tiny silvery arms, legs, buses, pairs of eyes, houses, hands, and sheep. These must be amulets, charms to be hung by their loop of pink or green yarn on a cradle, in a stable, from the rearview mirror of a car. Protection for our bodies and our animals, and our precious cars. They are also called *milagros,* or ex-votos, and are hung on the altars of saints or the Virgin in fulfillment of a vow. Thank you for healing my broken arm, for my daughter's safe bus trip. Amulets, *milagros,* help coming, going. Ounce of prevention to be spared, ounce of gratitude for being spared this time.

Eyes, arms, legs, feet, hands—bodies dismembered and scattered over a green cloth.

Remember that small cheap hotel right in the middle of Paris, that quiet hotel at the end of a covered arcade? Remember the wax museum next to the arcade? As we went in and out of the hotel, we had to pass by a waxen woman lying in a glass case, dressed in a feather-trimmed nightgown, with dust on her face and eyelashes, every twenty seconds, her chest pumped up and down, stirring the feathers. Our bathroom had a window opening up on an inner court, all gray-white walls. I remember standing at that window brushing my teeth, listening to the cries of children playing in a nearby schoolyard. Other windows looked in on the court, some closed, some open and with flowerpots. To the left, one floor up, was a long bank of windows, like a studio, and sitting there a woman in a white smock coat, her head bent over her sewing, so absorbed in her task.

Then I saw that around the woman hung, in neat bunches, human legs and human arms. On shelves above her head were orderly rows of human heads. She was sewing together—all of a sudden I knew—bodies. For the wax museum, of course.

Such a vision of dismemberment, of bodies fragmented, dispersed, and now calmly and painstakingly sewn back together by this woman. At once, I thought of your body, on the other side of the bathroom door, sprawling heavy on the bed as you read the newspaper. Your beloved body so wonderfully knit together, the huge hands that cover my hands, the legs very shapely, knees strong, so intricately bundled that with my fingers I always tried to feel out the fine mechanism. A whole body, a compression of the whole world and its riches, a whole world so rich in its ordinariness all knit together. At once, I was afraid of your death, that your body would be fragmented, scattered all over the world, lost. I would instantly set out to gather the fragments up, piece by piece, and collect them, and in this kind of light, in this silence, stitch them back together.

Sew back up that little seam that holds your testicles in their baglet, remake you, remake the world, have you then sit up and look at me, again.

These tiny silvery ex-votos here before me, pieces of the body, hand and heart, and pieces of the world, bus and house, all these precious things. I want to link them into one necklace, with a pair of needle-nose pliers link them all together again.

I bought three tarnished amulets. A bus for the buses I'm riding. An arm—my bag is heavy with books and bottles of medicine. A pair of eyes—to help me see what I've come to see.

At the Tres Reyes restaurant, where I'm writing this, I just ate *pavo negro,* a black turkey stew. In the toilet, as I sat on the throne, I was puzzled at first by a circle of small droppings two feet from and around the porcelain seat—then I realized—of course, the droppings of small children attending their mother. I know this would move you, the kids flocking near the mother, keeping her company. Reporting these details to you makes me sharpen my look at the world for you.

Your seamstress

P.S. My favorite Christmas carol in a minor key.

> We three kings of Orient are,
> Bearing gifts we traverse afar
> Field and fountain, moor and mountain
> Following yonder star.

—

*January 6, Chichén Itzá*

Dear Milagro,

On the road to Chichén Itzá, a sign pointed down a dirt track: LAS RUINAS—ICHMUL DE MORLEY. A ruin in the family.

Got to Chichén after the ruins closed. Found another of my genre of rooms, what the guidebook calls a "basic room, rec." —*rec.* short for *recommended*—basic bed, basic ceiling fan, basic cement walls, basic pine table, basic dim light, a stripped-down convent room, room for weary pilgrims. At La Bocadita, a thatched-roof restaurant open to the road, I ordered coffee and a plate of little tacos, *taquitos.* Coffee in the Yucatán is always a cup of hot water, a spoon, and a sticky bottle of powdered coffee.

People were coming home from the fields, kids gathering to greet them, pigs trotting along. Then everyone stopped. All heads turned to watch two American joggers. A man with a leonine mane of golden hair jogged shirtless, his broad, deep chest leading him forward, trim hips keeping up in clingy neon blue nylon shorts, the thickest-cushioned running shoes, like platform shoes, bouncing him along the dirt road. At his side, a stick-thin woman, muscled, too, her veins standing out on her muscles. Her runner's shirt clung to her chest and showed off her sports brassiere. Clingy tiny pink shorts, a visored headband, sweatbands on her wrists, white running shoes with sock pom-oms bobbling in back. The couple ran the length of the village, turned and ran back toward the fancy tourist hotel near the ruins.

Back to my basic rec. room, sketched my conch shell, read again your Java postcard, and now am finishing this letter to you. Then I have to clean my ears. I had them pierced before I came —I'm not sure why. It makes me queasy to thread the wires through my earlobes. Odd how this little thing fills me with such repugnance. And I'm always afraid my earrings are going to be ripped out by accident or by a thief, although I wear nothing of value. Ear piercing is a permanent mark on your body. The hole can grow back, but you can't erase the mark. What will you think of me with torn ears?

You have left no physical mark on my body, no token of your touch. Only now do I fully understand my entire body to be that token. But amulet or *milagro*—importuning or offering?

Sometimes I worry that I might seem changed to you—my body cells replaced in your absence have not been under your penetrative influence. I might have a different taste, or a taste-lessness like tomatoes ripened under fluorescent light. Will you be able to tell when you taste me again? Or, in the split second I see you again, will my cells turn back to you again as into my sphere you move celestially large, radiant, irradiating, all my cells like sunflowers turning in that same motion as plants turn and grow so quickly, yet one can never see them do it. All of me subtly turning toward you, all readiness, all ripeness.

Your token friend

*January 7, Chichén*

Dear Ruiner,

Ruins and ruins. Less and less sure why I stare at ruins, yet I visit ruins ruinously.

At Chichén Itzá, up early and out to ruin. Visiting ruins I find a loose occupation. Reading a guide, you walk around the grassy park from ruin to ruin, looking at the ruins as if you might understand something. I climbed the steep front staircase of the main pyramid, El Castillo, holding tightly to the iron chain bolted to the middle of the stairs, counting out the ninety-one tiny steps to keep myself from being scared (I keep seeing sacrificed bodies hurled down these gray stone steps, bodies bouncing, limbs flopping). At the top, I avoid looking down—so I looked out at the flat plain of gray-green forest stretching for miles. Rising above it, the jagged, shrubby tip of another pyramid, breaking out of the forest like an outcropping of stone. Are all the breaks in the forest ceiling more temples? Or merely taller trees?

Saw the famous red jaguar of Chichén (surely our red cat's noble ancestor), rather a dull red, with green jade spots and eyes. Square, stiff, doglike jaguar, his back a flat throne, his teeth real jaguar teeth and not grinning and goofy like the copies sold to tourists at the gate. I looked and looked at the jaguar, trying to impress it on my mind. There was something I wanted to see in it. The guard motioned me on. (I hope the red cat is all right, not feeling too abandoned.)

I stared long and hard at the stone relief of the ballplayers in the ball court. Squinting, I could make out the big rubber ball, the two figures on either side, one player with his head cut off, six thick plumes of blood shooting out of his trunk, the other player holds the head and the ax with which he cut it off. I walked away, came back, stared until my eyes hurt.

In the older part of the site, in front of the Observatory—they call it El Caracol because of its spiral shell shape—I sat for an hour. I got out my sketchbook and, looking up, looking down, tried to get the rounded shape right, the smooth surfaces of the beautifully worked stone, precisely fitted blocks, and where that stone facade had fallen off, the rubble that lay beneath it. I like the blinding-white rounded surface with the blackness of the rect-angular door. I like knowing about the snail-like spiral staircase that winds up inside. The rest of Chichén Itzá is too angular—the squared, sharp-cornered Castillo, the columns in the Temple of the Warriors, squared off, too, their reliefs of warriors so angular in their plumaged armor like scales, their stacked headdresses, their posture hardly human, crammed inside the squared-off face of those columns. Maybe it's the later Toltec or Itzá styles influ-encing the Maya, but it's not like the earlier art that I saw in the books. It's not exactly what I've come to see.

When I had seen all I could, my eyes hurting in spite of this sense of not having seen something, except maybe my Caracol, I walked back to the hotel. To see everything here would take another day, but my days slip away and I'm restless. So, West-ward ho! On to the ruins of Uxmal.

Your package dealer

---

*January 8, Uxmal*

Dear Caracol,

At Uxmal, again too late to see the site. Again I found a basic room, rec. Again my joggers tripped up and down the road. Again up early to ruin, guides in hand. I climb a steep pyramid with the rounded base, the Pyramid of the Magician, and see the same gray-green flat plain stretching out all around me, the same flat blue sky. I stare at the fretted patterning of the stone facade on a long, low building, at the stone turtles on the House of

Turtles. If I close my eyes, I still see walls of gray-white stone, bright in the sun, with a small black rectangular doorway.

Caught a bus to Kabah, another site nearby. There's something I'm not seeing, that I've come to see. One wonderful thing at Kabah. I spent the afternoon sketching the Palace of Masks, the facade covered with carved masks of the rain god Chac—two goggling eyes, curved-up, thick, scrolly eyebrows, teeth like a skull, what's left of a beak or nose that's been broken off. There are rows and rows of Chac masks, the same mask in "ludicrous profusion," an example of "demented decoration," the guidebooks exclaim. Why ludicrous? The infinite repetition of this mask, each with its innumerable carved details, is the quintessence of excess. No surface unmasked, un-Chaced. What if I were to decorate our house with your face over and over again? Your mask, for sometimes your face sets in a mask, severe, impenetrable, the blade of the nose, the bones there high under your eyes, the large forehead, the big skull, almost a death mask. Or shall I use your face when it's most alive, the eyebrows lifted, the fleshy jowls shaking, the crooked smile, the wrinkles raying out around the eyes, this face a thousand times over and over, my own demented excess of you?

These guidebooks—they'll say almost anything. You realize it's often just talk, no real knowledge or taste. For example, they prefer to Chac-Chac the plain freestanding arch at the entrance to Kabah. It looks triumphantly Roman to them.

Back at the basic hotel near Uxmal. The joggers are back, too, recognize me, spare a bit of energy on a smile. We are all going to ruin on the same tour, a most congenial tour because I don't have to talk to my traveling companions. As if I have taken a vow of silence. Maybe this silence is the guarantee of all these words for you, the source of this flood.

Still, I do like saying the simplest things in Spanish—like, *¿Cuánto cuesta esta carta gorda?*

Only two days left. I should head back to Cancún—I can't miss the plane. I have to start teaching again. Yet I keep feeling I'm not seeing what I came to see, as if I knew, had some dim memory that I keep checking these ruins against and saying, That's not it, that's not it. On my way back, I'll stop off again at Chichén. I didn't see it all, at all.

Your basic traveler, not rec.

---

*January 9, Palenque, the town*
Dear Chac-Chac-Chac-Chac-Chac-Chac-Chac-Chac-Chac-Chac,

The guides say Palenque, ruins far to the south, is a *must*. I remember certain photographs of Palenque in my books at home. I calculated the time for going there and getting back to Cancún for my flight until I got the calculation to come out right—if the buses run on time.

I took a night bus, not rec. to women traveling alone, and sometimes robberies. I am scared, I said out loud to myself. But I start to like being scared. I like the hurtling to catch the bus. There was an empty seat next to a woman and her baby. So I'll be Joseph with Mary and Jesus on the Flight into Egypt.

The night was pitch-black in the forest. A hundred times I touched the bulge between my breasts where I stashed my money.

About midnight, the bus stopped in front of a restaurant lit up by a few bulbs. Everyone got off. I sat at the end of a trestle table near my mother and her baby. Two girls took orders, ducked under a counter, and came out quickly with platters of food. I ate chicken stewed in a tomato and chili sauce. Back on the bus, off again into the night.

The tomatoes and chilies burned pleasantly in my belly. The Aztec cooked an arm or a thigh of their sacrificial victims with tomatoes and chilies. What if I were to stew you? Yes, sometimes I want terribly to eat you, incorporate you, have you in me, turning into me. Then I would always have you near. I would have all that I'm afraid of losing, losing you. If I ate you, I would be content. You would burn pleasantly in my stomach, make me pleasantly gassy, for I would cook you very nicely with very ripe red tomatoes and very hot green chilies. I have not eaten enough of you yet, not all of you.

In the first light, I saw that we were climbing slowly from the flat plain at last, climbing up and between hills, the forest thicker, darker green, though still a gray-green. Even the jungle must have a dry season. At six, the bus pulled into the town of Palenque. I saw Mary and Jesus safely off the bus, and as the guides advised, I bought my return ticket for that afternoon.

The *collectivo*—the minivan that runs to the ruins—makes its first run in an hour. Once more, I sit in a bus station, drinking a thin, sweet, hot coffee. So desperate and foolish to have come this far. I'll miss my flight from Cancún, I'm so tired, I'm crying.

Palenque, the ruins.

Palenque—lovely, lovely buildings of creamy white stone set against green foothills. As you enter, a large pyramid to the right, a palace with a four-story tower in the middle, two pyramids on terraced hills behind that, and two pyramids to the left on the other side of the lawn. The buildings are not massive. Palenque is more human in size than the other monumental sites, simpler, and graceful, so graceful. Instead of a white wall with a little black door set in it, there are many doors, so that the walls seem like columns of a gallery. And the roof of every building curves in above the eaves, like a hipped roof. This openness, this lightness makes the buildings graceful, not monolithic and geo-metric as at Chichén Itzá, not so decorated as at Uxmal and Kabah —though I liked my Caracol, my Chac very much.

Made my tour of the ruins, now a familiar routine, yet I was more alive to something here.

Stood for an hour and stared at nine stone panels that line the palace courtyard. In each panel, a man carved in relief is kneeling, facing to his left, his left arm crossed over his chest in a salute.

Portraits of individual men—one has a fleshier nose, one higher, rounded cheekbones, another a bigger chin, this man's jowls sag, this man compresses his lips, this one holds his lips slightly open. All have rounded, fleshy shoulders and thighs, rich, heavy, sloping flesh. The kilts they wear around their hips drape the flesh, showing off the flesh. A sense of weight, too, in the heavy belt that hangs down to their knees, the heavy earrings. The plumes of their headdresses fall over with their own weight. I suddenly feel the specific weight of things, so real, so full, so much the weight of the world. I mean that in a wholly other way than it is usually meant. I mean the specific lovely weight things have, our bodies have. How precious it is really, how these portraits remind me of that.

Remind me of you, your bulky body, firm and fleshy majesty, large and yet graceful, quick. Except I am afraid of stone. Stone is monumental even in these panels, dead somehow, cold like bone. While you are warm life, rosy, golden flesh, so sweet.

I climbed up and down the other temples. All are haunted by bodies raised from the stone in relief, so detailed—the world of bodies in detail. In the museum, I stared at the modeled stucco heads, the beautiful arch of the long noses, the open mouths, the prominent eyes. A face, lifted, revealed, looking forward in a sort of wonder. Your face lifted to me, unguarded, the face of anyone in the world lifted, unguarded. I stared until my eyes hurt. I could blind myself with these faces.

The best came last. Climbed up the tallest pyramid, the Temple of Inscriptions, up a steep flight of stairs again, but I'm getting used to heights, I think. Inside the little room at the top, I looked at a stone tablet of carved hieroglyphs, which I liked very much, the letters shaped with human and animal faces and set in rows, rounded and nubby like kernels of corn in their rows.

Climbed down inside the pyramid, down a steep diagonal stairway to a landing. The stairway then cut back and down in the opposite direction to a burial chamber. The stone walls clammy to the touch and the stone stairs slippery underfoot. An iron grate set in a stone arch was the doorway to the tomb. I pressed against the grate to see a huge rectangular stone slab, the sarcophagus cover.

The stone is carved with a large tree, a bird sitting at the top of the tree, a man falling down the tree—the ruler Pacal, the glyphs name him. Pacal is falling down the tree, his knees his arms gently bent as he falls backward down the tree, those limbs wonderfully rounded, such flesh, another body not encased in the crocodile armor I had seen at Chichén. Wonderful, too, the way the tasseled ends of his necklace float up, lift up, swinging up as he falls. He's falling into the underworld, this ruler, this Pacal, the guides say. They never said how poignant this body is that is falling, how alive this dead body still is, how much the joy of flesh can be celebrated even in the moment of death. I stared. Walking away, I walked back to peer into the tomb again. The guard finally motioned me to move on.

Back on top of the temple, I sat down to make a record of this place between the hills and the plain. I sketched the nubby cornrow glyph panel. I sketched the towered palace. I sketched the vast flat plain of the Yucatán before me, where I had been riding the buses and which I have to cross again so quickly. How far I had come, what I had come to, to this place between plain and mountains.

Walking down the hill back toward the entrance, I watched my feet on the path to keep from tripping on the rocks embedded in the ground and scattered in the grass, rocks the same creamy limestone rock as the buildings. One bit of stone had a polish, and lines, not cracks or scorings. I picked it up, the lines *were* carved, the lines part of a feline face with rounded, heavy jowls, the face part of a glyph. The stone a chunk maybe off a tablet of glyphs, like those I had seen at the temples. A bit of written flesh, fitting right into my hand. My fingers, clasped inward, traced the lines of relief.

I pocketed it quickly and in fear. Signs everywhere warn me

DO NOT REMOVE ARCHAEOLOGICAL PROPERTY and threaten big fines and jail. Still I kept my hand wrapped around this fragment, which probably only names the year, the day some king came to the throne or died—what was so important? I held fast to it. I couldn't bear to return it to rubble.

Hurried past the guards, who didn't give me a second look. Past ten silent Indians outside the entrance, with their long hair and bangs, their loose white robes and bare feet, their gold watches glinting on arms holding up handmade bows and arrows for sale.

While waiting for my bus, I am writing from a restaurant back in the town of Palenque. My joggers just jogged by and waved. When I get home, I'll show you my glyph, my white conch shell, tarnished *milagros*—bus and eye and arm, my sketches.

I look at my sketches of ruins. Ruin now seems a most natural state, a pleasant, livable state. The first time you touched me, we were walking around the lake and you put your heavy arm around my shoulders as we walked. You declared your love and promised to be a wall for me, protect me like a garden wall protects the fruit trees and the flowers. And I—after all the stories you had been telling me of all your failures in the finely honed rhetoric of despair which is the way you talk, I had to laugh out loud—asked you how could a crumbling wall, a ruined wall, protect anyone? But now I know how to live in ruin. When I get back, and you get back, we'll live peaceably in ruin, ruined for each other.

I will take buses one after another without a stop through the night back to Cancún. If you are home—I can see you at home, sitting at the kitchen table by the window, reading a letter, the cat basking in the lamplight next to you. I know you may not be home, but I'm sure maybe you are at home. I shall be back home before you get this letter. If you are there—I'll reach out and grasp your shoulders.

Your thief

Morley folded up this her last letter, sealed it carefully in an envelope, addressed the envelope, and put the right postage on it. Her trip was not for nothing—in just one week, she had mastered Mexican postage. She ran over to a mailbox across the street, dropped the letter in, ran back to her seat in the little restaurant where her bag waited.

So the trip was over. She had done what she set out to do, yet she felt curiously incompleted.

Two more hours until her bus came—the bus better come on time. No one was watching her so she took the glyph from her pocket and began sketching it, very carefully. Yes, she saw the carved line of a feline face.

"Hey, where'd you get the glyph?"

Morley jerked her head around. Two young men were leaning over her shoulders, staring at her drawing and grinning at her. She put her pencil down across the drawing and covered the glyph fragment with her other hand. Would she be arrested? At the same time, she was eager to hear the rock was really a glyph.

The two young men pulled up chairs, one on either side of her, and introduced themselves. An odd pair now bookended her at her little table. There was Eddie—short, slim like a garden snake, and pretty with his brown skin, bright blue eyes, long dark blond hair pulled back by a rubber band, one toothy earring, faded bandanna tied round his head in piratical fashion, woven cotton bracelets, some bright in color, some faded, banded the muscular arms emerging from the sleeveless sweatshirt. And there was Michael—very tall and lanky, white T-shirt, blue jeans, wire-rim glasses, very black curly hair, very black whiskers, although it was clear he had shaved that morning, black eyebrows, black eyes, black hair softly bristling on the forearms tanned a light brown, and full lips.

They both were archaeology students, Eddie still vaguely in college and Michael a graduate student.

Morley confessed her sin, "I stole this from Palenque."

"Stole it?"

"Picked it up off the ground. Will I get arrested?"

Eddie laughed. Michael smiled and shook his head. "There's so much rubble on every site, right on the surface, rubble the diggers already know about. Besides, this's broken, half a cat."

Eddie waved to the waiter and ordered three beers. The two started talking about their dig down near Tikal in Guatemala, their bus ride up from Guatemala to Palenque, how great a town San Cristóbal de las Casas was. They were off to Palenque now —well, whenever the next *collectivo* came. Then they were head- ing back south, stopping off again at San Cristóbal and nearby Toniná, a big dig run by the French.

Michael began leafing through Morley's sketches. "These're real good. Real good. You do drafting for a living? You could."

No, no, Morley assured him, she just drew to take notes for herself.

Already, though, Michael had a great idea—she should come down to their dig with them, she could do some drawing for them, they always needed someone to draw their finds. Eddie joined in, said no one on the dig could draw "worth shit."

How strange to be talking after a week of silence, in English at least. Her tongue heavy and unused to words, she almost hesitated before every word, not sure what would come out of her mouth. Words probably in the wrong order, like after spend- ing a whole day reading and someone telephones—at first it is so odd to talk.

One thing Morley learned from her two experts—that Pa- lenque is older than the other sites she had seen. It belongs more to the same period and culture as sites in Guatemala, like Tikal and Dos Pilas. Same style of art. Those rounded bodies, those faces, so particular, faces lifted up.

The *collectivo* for the ruins came. Eddie and Michael had to go. They drained their beers, said good-bye to Morley. Michael pressed her again to come on down to their dig. He was serious, really. When Michael spoke, he had that southern manner— slow, polite, seemingly diffident, but subtly insistent. He had— funny to say, but true—rosy red lips, a large, mobile, lovely mouth. Morley found herself laughing at him and told him she almost believed him. To Morley, the boys suddenly seemed so sweet, so young, so young. They made her feel old, so old. Maybe they flirted with her because she was old—there was no danger—it was only for fun.

Eddie and Michael took off. She felt even more alone.

Morley's bus finally came, two hours late. Tired to death, she arrived at the last minute at Cancún airport. Tourists clutching their stuffed red jaguars of Chichén were talking about the little war so far away, which finally had been declared. In the air, the captain announced the precautions taken against terrorism at the Boston airport. Under straw hats with woven bands proclaiming MEXICO or COZUMEL, tanned faces paled. Morley stared out the window. First there were blue waters, then brown hills, then white fields, then night fell. Boston's lights, a swing over the black ocean, except for the lighthouses in the harbor blinking, and the plane was on the ground.

Airport police stared at the passengers getting off the plane. In shops full of stuffed red lobsters, baseball caps, and postcards, the war flickered on tiny televisions.

A few minutes after midnight, Morley stood in an icy rain in front of her house, the windows dark.

Her neighbors had dumped her mail in a box on the kitchen table. She put down her bag, stroked the angry and affectionate cat. Still in her dripping jacket, she dug layer by layer through bills, advertisements, official communiqués from work. Her own letters were layered in between.

At the bottom of the box, a letter mailed from New Caledonia, postmarked before she left for her trip, so that all the time that Morley had been on Java time had been the wrong time.

**III**

## *A Guided Tour*

MORLEY HARDLY RECOGNIZED HIS HANDWRITING, the strokes fragile and angular as grasshopper legs. There was no greeting.

━━━

*December 27, Km. 8*

Here in la Nouvelle-Calédonie, they are very excited by the prospect of war. They follow the news about the war sucked in by their satellite dishes. Talking about the war makes them feel international. All a farce, their interest, this war itself will be a farce. Last night, I watched a special broadcast from Marseille— this already shows you the level. An old ratlike general leans over a map in some filthy back studio in Marseille. He bares his ratlike front teeth, certainly false, as he points to the positions of the British Desert Rats, these positions he marks with crusts of Gruyère cheese. Then a rat, a real rat, runs across the map, snatches a piece of cheese, and the general and the camera crew throw themselves into the chase.

Living here on Kilometer 8 (Kilometer 8 is the name of the island— *"Bonjour, je m'appelle Marie. J'habite Kilomètre Huit,"*— one of many tiny islands too many for these languid lotus-eaters to name), I find I can hardly sit up straight, so forgive me for not writing very often. At night, I push my fingers against my eyelids so that the night will be more night. I swallow handfuls of barbiturates, for nothing—I cannot sleep. During the day, I take fitful gloom baths in my room or nod over a book in the small public library here. When I have to walk somewhere, I'm a ruin ambling through a white town smelling of frangipani and old anuses. People smile at you with orange mango strings dangling from their teeth. The sea is shallow, you have to wade out quite far to get your kneecaps wet. If you squat down, out of fatigue, lassitude, you risk being pinched in the balls by a hassled crab. When I sit on the café terrace by the sea, I sometimes hear the cries of the other victims, but most of the time I'm too enthralled by the faces of my dead.

The idea comes to me often to make a dinner for all my dead, my mother, my father, my operatic aunt, my grandfather the grafting maniac whose grafts never produced a single fruit, my great-uncle who owned a failing marbles factory, my friend the publisher who died in the Himalayas, all those others whose companionship keeps me occupied while orienting me quietly toward their country. I dream so often of death, always, and at the same time to have a child with you. These subjects are, of course, very close. A child is a barrier against the night, the annihilation. My dart springs up at the idea of making a child with you. I want to deform you, disfigure your belly, make you ugly and sublimely beautiful before everyone, to see your thighs bloody, open, and the small, viscous crown passing through your lips, making you a mother, different for eternity from what you have been before. Yet I am too old for this, too tired. I would have to come back from the shadows, and the journey back is too far a journey for this old, flabby shadow.

A shady brambler

Folding up this letter, tucking it back into its envelope, Morley's fingers performed these operations in needlelike movements. She stood up to find the atlas, to reset her watch for New Caledonia —instead, Morley sat right back down.

It came to Morley, with all sudden conviction. The phrase rose to her lips, she said it out loud, "He's dead." There could be more letters, but "He's dead." Morley was quite sure, yet she needed still to declare it one more time, out loud, "He's dead." The phrase had a faint echoing quality, "He's dead. He's dead."

Spring would come and Morley would go south again, beyond the green mountains at Palenque, deeper, deeper. She had to go much deeper than she had before, to see—what? She had no idea at all what she would do except go beyond the mountains and into Guatemala. She would go there.

This trip Morley planned with a ruthless efficiency. Her request, a demand at such short notice, to take the spring quarter off as an unpaid leave of absence was granted, grudgingly and only because she never asked for anything. She sold their car and ran out their savings for cash to take with her. A student would sublet the apartment for two months and watch the cat. The ticket was purchased. She would go in late March.

In the meantime, Morley taught her classes, and she turned on her television like everyone else to watch the war against "naked aggression," the phrase repeated over and over with a childish pleasure of getting to say a nasty word in public by the thin gray president heading for his helicopter or his golf cart. She listened to retired generals, military experts, and economists, predicting rashly, predicting cautiously, anything and everything about the war, the loss of life, the outcome, the troops' morale, the progress that, with the news blackout, no one could see. She saw demonstrators against the war. A man shouted into a microphone, "The world is collapsing, collapsing"—his face contorts in the anguish of expression—"to the point of collapse!" Morley held the glyph in her hand, rubbing its smooth face, tracing the curved lines. She rolled the conch shell from hand to hand or spilled the ex-votos, arm, eyes, bus, on the table. She picked up the eight ball, yet hard to know what to ask about the future, so she simply turned the ball over. Floating up from the dark came the phrase: "It is undoubtedly so."

The little desert war sputtered to a version of an end. There was rejoicing. There was self-congratulation, even ticker-tape parades. There was growing knowledge of the costs—the number of dead, the destruction of cities. A new round of experts turned up on the television demanding to know what this war had accomplished. Morley listened while she read accounts of the history of Guatemala, accounts of, it seemed, a four-hundred-year-long war still going on, against the *indígenas* and the poor and those North Americans and others who attached themselves to their cause, wars of dispersion and annihilation. Oh, the number of dead in the world hurried on before their time. And the number of walking dead, still in this world but dead, dead.

All through February, fear rose in Morley. During the night, she often could not sleep, and when she slept, she dreamed of deserted mountain villages, with cooking pots smashed, looms broken, and brightly patterned cloth ripped into shreds. Skulls and bones litter the site, brush taking over. During the day, small yet alarming things happened to her. She left umbrellas and gloves and her purse behind in stores and waiting rooms, she locked herself out of her house several times, she got a speeding ticket on a road she drove every day to work. Holding a glass too tightly, she shattered it and a shard dug into her hand. Blood ran everywhere. Washing the deep wound, she saw layers and layers of skin. A scar formed that she would have forever and ever.

No more letters arrived.

The first week of March, Morley's red cat became very sick. Morley was with him when he died, stroking his fur, calling him by all his secret names one more time. Afterward, she furtively buried him in a local park, in a grove of trees she had often admired. With a shovel, she dug a hole, all the time afraid of being caught by the groundspeople, afraid of being heard by pedestrians dawdling down a nearby sidewalk. The turf was so netted with roots difficult to unravel or sever, and there were so many stones, the shovel clanged so against the stones. Tears running down her face and yet laughing, too, Morley swore to herself that if she ever killed anyone, she would shred or burn them, never, ever bury them—for now she understood why murder victims were always found in "shallow graves." At last, the hole was deep enough, she hoped. Lining the grave with pine fronds, Morley laid down an old shawl matted over the years with his fur, tucked the cat in, rounded him, his head between his paws, his tail curled around. She gave a last stroke to the soft, rich fur—how alive it still looked, how alive it still felt—then tied up the shawl. A layer of dried catnip from her garden, then with her hands Morley pulled soil and stones down into the hole, replaced the clumps of turf on top, strewed dead leaves on the grave to disguise it. Last, she placed on the grave four large stones taken from an old farm wall now running through wild woods, four large stones so she'd know exactly where he was. Four stones as a memorial—one stone for the red cat, one for herself, one for him, one for the time the three of them had spent together.

The last stone in place, Morley felt terribly satisfied.

Returning to her house almost impossible, however, now that both its presiding dignitaries had gone.

The third week of March, Morley left for Guatemala City. The plane stopped over in Miami. Listening to the Spanish spoken everywhere in the airport, Morley already felt safely under way. Then across the Caribbean, over Cuba, over the Yucatán, and hills and high mountains, the plane dipped down at a steep angle and came into a dusky valley, for night was falling in Guatemala City. A long wait at immigration, standing in line behind an American evangelical church group—their luggage stickers read THE FAITHFUL OF A FEATHER FLOCK TOGETHER. The line suddenly moving fast, her passport was stamped and she was on the other side of the door, among many people pressing, pressing, looking for their relatives, taxi drivers shouting at her and grabbing at her luggage. One wins, and she's on her way.

From her taxi, the city appeared very dark except for a white glow from a soccer stadium, a few streetlights now and then, some faint lights from behind shutters. Even most traffic lights were out. A city like a far-flung suburb, the darkness, the buildings all earthquake-afraid and low, and long stretches of walls, walls along which no one walked. The smell of this city a particular smell, the smell of diesel exhaust, yes, but under that, more powerfully, the smell of wood burning. And now she saw, as they drove more into the city, on every corner a brazier with roasting corn ears. Behind every brazier, on a stoop, against a wall, in a doorway, sat an Indian woman, bundled round in a shawl, her head piled with a knotted cloth headdress, sitting still, one black-headed child or two bundled in with her.

At a stop sign, Morley watched a man carefully piling up his charcoal on the sidewalk, he had no brazier. The little pile was built most expertly—it seemed the moment she watched him was an hour long. Was she so tired that she could be thus mesmerized?

The room at the Hotel Lito, the very inexpensive hotel near the center of the city that a tourist guide at the airport had found for her, seemed very quiet, very clean.

Morley planned to start where she had left off, with what was most familiar to her now, ruins. Start with the ruins of Kaminaljuyú, which meant, the guidebook said, the Hills of the Dead, a vast early Maya site taken over slowly by the suburbs, the *colonias,* off in the southwest sector of Guatemala City.

Bus after bus roared down the 4 Avenida. She would step close to the curb to see the number, every number but the number 17 Terminal Kaminaljuyú bus, then the black exhaust would make her step back and turn her face away. The sun was out, its outline curiously distinct in a sky white with smog. She knew the valley was ringed by high mountains, but could not make them out.

At last, a number 17 bus. She waved it down, blurted out *"¿Kaminaljuyú, las ruinas?"* with one foot on the step to hold up the bus from its mad dash down the avenue. The driver nodded yes, she stepped in, and they were off. The bus headed south past miles and miles of gas stations, small grocery stores, tire stores, everywhere Indians lining the road, standing, waiting. Finally, the bus wound through a development of North American ranch-style houses. Small cars parked in front of small houses, campers in the driveways, statues of elves in the gardens.

At the terminal, a shack with a bus official checking in the driver's fare box, Morley, the only remaining passenger, got off. Across the street, a chain-link fence fenced in the Kaminaljuyú park, a park of lumpy, worn hills, dusty gray, a few graced with tall, airy pines.

An old man with an ice cream cart on one side of the front gate talked to an old man with a soda cart on the other side. They paused a moment to see if she would buy something.

The gate stood wide open, no guard, no admission charge. Morley walked in.

Paths led around the several small hills, hills strangely top-heavy, their sides rough and flat. Of course, these hills must be ancient mounds. Morley went up to one mound fenced off with a straggling strand of barbed wire. In the exposed side of the mound, she could see rows of blocks the color of dirt and tufted with weeds, still, distinct rows and rows of blocks. Morley climbed to the top of one of the unfenced mounds. The ground was a dusty gray-brown, the weeds rasped under her feet. Crickets leapt up and away as she brushed by. This is what is meant by the dry season, everything rattling, whispering with dryness, a white-gray brown the color of dryness. From the top of this mound, Morley spotted, as the guides promised, two sheds built over excavations.

Morley also saw lovers lying in a pine's shade, two boys kicking a soccer ball back and forth, a woman walking her dog.

Edging down the dusty path, sliding in the dry dirt, Morley headed for the closest shed. Near it was a stela, the oblong stone set up straight and about five feet high. The only carving visible on the stone was a row of glyphs along the back, large, nicely plumped-up glyphs as if made out of lightly stuffed cushions, the relief not deep at all, but rather very fine, so slightly raised. She looked around—no one saw, probably no one cared—and traced the glyphs with her fingers. So fine, so smooth, so simple. She walked up to the shed, walked around it, looking for an entrance in the chain-link fence surrounding the excavation, didn't find one. So she ducked under the low eaves of corrugated tin and pressed against the fence to look in.

The archaeologists had opened up the hill. They had exposed steps and walls built with big blocks of what looked like white stone. It was hard to see clearly from where she stood. The shadows fell too much into the trenches that cut across centuries. What she could make out looked like living spaces, small rooms. Stooping, Morley circled around the fence, but she found no better vantage point from which to picture what had once been here. Disappointed, her back aching, she felt she had had more a sense of the ancient city from the unexcavated hills, those hills she could see and draw as a city. Under this roof was something exposed, probably pedagogical, but unless you knew the mound from its outer skin and got to the bottom of the trench, the lesson didn't take.

Morley stepped back out into the sun and trudged toward the other shed, two hills over. She passed the caretaker's fenced compound, with plants in tin cans, lumber and fencing rolled up, a dog that came slowly to its feet and barked twice. Maybe the caretaker worked as a guide of sorts, could show her around, open up the fence. The sound of a movement attracted her attention. Someone was in the outhouse, the little appended shack, relieving himself or herself. Morley hurried on.

The boys ran by, kicking the soccer ball up and over the hills. The shaded lovers reclined on their sides, talking in low voices, a radio playing three feet away. Morley, a dusty wraith, walked through this dusty park.

The other excavation shed looked larger. When she came nearer, she saw that it, too, was fenced in and, worse, buried in the side of the hill, so that the eaves of the shed rested on the ground. She wouldn't be able to get close enough to see anything. Circling around, though, she found that the fence funneled into the mound. The fence door stood open.

Inside, finally, Morley could see something. The trench was quite deep. Fifteen feet straight down stood a terraced building in the shadow. She knelt down on the edge of the trench to look. Then she heard a voice, a low, soft man's voice, almost diffident, a North American voice. That soft falling off at the end of sentences wasn't Spanish. The voice coming closer.

Stepping back, Morley fitted herself into the corner between the door and the fence. Down below, two couples came around the corner and into view, both couples well-off, probably Americans, around fifty-five, the women clad in batik blouses and white pants, looking rather like Maya stelae figures in full regalia, their ears flanged with dangling, clinking silver earrings, their breasts loaded with chunks of amber and silver and turquoise. The men presented themselves in military chic, aviator sunglasses and brown-splashed khakis—"desert camouflage"—the fashion colors of the war. Following them was a tall young man swinging a flashlight, the young man, lanky and at ease in a plain white shirt and blue jeans, a black baseball hat pulled way down over his glasses. He herded his group to stand right in front of the terraces, right below Morley's feet.

It was one of the young archaeologists from Palenque. The tall one. Morley had forgotten his name. He had probably forgotten about her.

Morley clung to the chain link behind her, her fingers weaving into it, gripping it to hold herself as still as possible.

"Now, we're going to go in this tunnel here that cuts right through the different phases of the mound. Like I said, the Maya always built new mounds over old mounds. By the way, these terraces here were painted red. You can still see a kind of pink tint." He clicked on his flashlight and led the way into a tunnel cut into one side of the terraced steps.

Morley let go of the fence, edged around the trench to some wooden stairs, crept down them to the bottom of the trench. Being down inside the excavation felt much more satisfying. Here you could see the temple, really, temples—one had been cut away to show the earlier temple inside, rising stepped platform upon platform. She slipped into the tunnel and followed the wavering light of the flashlight as the guide took the others into the center of the mound. He stopped in a large chamber. Morley peered around the corner of the tunnel.

"The mounds're used as tombs. There're some bodies here —well, just skeletons when they found 'em. Up on this bank here was probably the main guy. They found him buried with a bunch of stingray spines, beads, pots, and a big turtle shell." Morley leaned her head in a bit more. The flashlight played over several raised areas of dirt. "On these lower ledges, they found what they think were sacrifices, a kid, another man, probably both peasants. We can tell by the teeth who didn't get much to eat and who did. We can tell by the wear on the bones who had to work a lot and who didn't."

One of the women frowned, whispered to her husband. She finally spoke up. "Are you sure? Everything I've read about the Maya"—her voice was fraught with expertise—"certainly everything I've ever heard about the Maya, says they were peaceful. They were not at all like the Aztec, killing and sacrificing everybody."

The guide paused only a second. "Well, ma'am, a while ago some people—archaeologists, I mean—liked to think that this might be the one place on earth without wars. They sort of pictured Maya cities as run by professors, or, actually, astronomer priests, who, of course, ruled over the peasants, but in a real nice way. But when you look at the murals at Bonampak, at the sculpture, at paintings on pots, it's pretty clear they had wars, and they took captives and later sacrificed them." The guide laughed. "You know, I know these two archaeologists—they had a big debate about whether it was better to be sacrificed by the Aztec or the Maya. They finally agreed they'd rather be sacrificed by the old Aztec—who'd just cut out your heart. Whereas the Maya liked to bleed you for a long time, off and on for years sometimes, 'til a real big holiday come up and then they cut off your head. After skinning you a bit." Morley could hear the swell of a tall tale in the guide's voice.

The group was very quiet for a moment. Earrings jangled. "A sacrifice right here?"

"Yes, ma'am. Now, let's move on here to the next phase of KJ." The guide shepherded his group to an adjoining chamber. Morley stepped into the tomb. There was just enough light from the flashlight flickering next door to look at the bare dirt room. Nothing rich, alive about this room at all, a stripped grave, desecrated, all the belongings, all the bones, taken away, scattered or sitting in a box somewhere.

He's dead. He's dead.

Morley quickly backed out, turned, and began feeling her way through the darkness back the way she had come, along the blocks of the inner mound. Outside once more by the terraced steps, she squatted down and stared at the tint of pink still visible on the flare of the terrace.

On the other side of the excavation, the guide was speaking. She couldn't hear much, only the high pitches his voice sometimes climbed to and the low murmur of the tourists. She should get out now, but she didn't move. Still crouched down on her haunches, she stared around the hole she was in. The ditch quality of the trench, with ice cream wrappers blown in by the wind, attracted her along with something about the terraces, not built with perfectly shaped blocks, but lumpy and smooth at the same time.

"Hi, ¿habla español, inglés?" The guide was standing on the ledge high above her, looking down at her.

Morley stood up slowly, her legs stiff. She looked up at him. Of course he had forgotten her. "Inglés—English, I mean. I'm American."

He grinned. "Hey, so you're here. Hi, again. Morley, right?"

"Sorry, I just found the door open and came in."

"That's all right. Listen, we've got to move on from here and so I've got to lock up now. Guess you got to git, too. Would you—"

"I'm sorry. I didn't mean to bother you."

His gold-rimmed glasses caught a bit of sun and glinted. He said softly, "That's all right."

Morley moved slowly around the terrace and up the wooden steps, her legs still stiff. She knew he was watching her.

They walked to the door together. He looked down at Morley. He was very tall. "I was going to ask you if you wanted to come along with us? We'll just be walking on over to another mound a little ways outside the park. Why don't you come along?" Behind him, right outside the door, the tourists were staring at her. The women hunched up their shoulders, both hands holding on to the white shoulder bags slung across their chests for safety. The men stood with hands on their hips, like colonels waiting for orders.

"You're really sure you don't mind?" Morley wanted badly to be in someone's company.

"It's all right. Come on." He told the others, "You'll not mind?"

As he drew the door shut, looped the padlock back through the chain link, and turned the key, Morley introduced herself to the two couples. Just a teacher, she said, had read a bit about the Maya and was traveling through Guatemala. For a moment, her countrymen and countrywomen were a bit awkward with her. After all, she hadn't paid to be on this tour, and besides that, she had been caught trespassing. Then the women unbent and introduced themselves and their husbands. They were the Shruves and the Bilgers, from San Francisco, the men two lawyers, the wives two friends on the art museum board. The couples always traveled together. The women asked her if she was traveling alone and clucked, Wasn't she afraid? Was she really all right at a local hotel, not the Sheraton?

The guide rejoined them. "Let's get going." They trailed after him out of the park and down a couple of blocks. Small dogs yapped at them. The people out in their yards stopped and watched the procession go past.

In a vacant lot between two streets, they came upon another mound behind a high fence of barbed wire, which the guide unlocked. "Where these houses are now was a whole city of mounds. They just bulldozed 'em flat for the development. This is one of the few mounds left outside the park. They call it the Jaguar Mound"—and he led them up to the side of the mound —"you see there are these flat chunks of obsidian stuck in the adobe. Obsidian mine's not far from here. Obsidian seems to have been a big trade item of KJ. We think these hunks of obsidian are supposed to be like the spots of the jaguar, a sacred animal for most of the native peoples of Central and South America."

"*The* most sacred animal." It was the same woman who had spoken before. "I went to a lecture and the speaker said the jaguar was *the* sacred animal. They believed the sun turned into a jaguar at night, that somehow the jaguar spots were like the stars, or something like that."

"Yes, ma'am."

Morley spit on her finger and cleaned one of the dusty pieces of rock to see its bright, glassy black surface. Her guide let her linger, holding up the tour for her. At the base of the mound, more traces of red paint. Were these mounds all painted red once? Bright iron red. Fantastic red temple platforms. Especially in this dry season, against the gray-white dirt, the bleached grass.

The group climbed up the temple stairs. "Used to be some clay sculptures along these stairs, but the kids broke 'em off playing here before they fenced it in."

From the top, everyone looked around. A khaki colonel asked his wife, the expert, "So all these dumpy hills are mounds?"

The guide spoke almost entirely for Morley now. "On this top platform would have been four posts holding up a wooden hut with a thatched roof. They find these postholes on the top of most early temple mounds. Later on, the Maya made these temple huts out of stone or adobe, but they still kind of looked like a thatched hut. Supposed to represent a temple on top of a mountain. That's what some think the mounds represent, sacred mountains. The stelae, those carved flat stones set up—did you see the other excavated mound?" he asked Morley. "Lots of 'em at Tikal —you should go to Tikal if you can. Well, they think the stelae are sacred trees—'tree stones,' they call them. Again, that's what some think, but they'll be guessing, of course."

Then suddenly, he had run out of things to say. Yet he made no move to go. He kept looking at Morley, smiling. Finally, the men conspicuously looked at their watches, and he looked at his watch. "Time to get y'all back to the hotel, I guess." Speaking to Morley: "You want a ride? I think we can make some room."

Morley walked them to their minivan. The guide unlocked the doors. One of the colonels quickly jumped into the front seat; the other three started climbing in the back. The guide and Morley were alone for a moment in this dusty suburb. He pulled at the bill of his baseball cap, pulled off the cap, stuffed it in his back pocket. Crossed his arms over his chest and laughed. "I bet you don't remember my name, do you? It's Michael, Michael Draw."

Morley blushed. "I'm sorry. I'm getting old. My memory's failing."

"Not so old as that."

Michael Draw was very tall, and with an uprightness that made him seem taller. There was an ease about him, too, as if he were always leaning against an invisible wall.

Morley decided to stay a little while longer at Kaminaljuyú. Not knowing what else to do, she bowed to Draw and thanked him for the tour. "I think I'll just stick around here a little longer. I hope you didn't mind me listening in—I mean, I wanted to see things here. Listening to you, I'm starting to see a bit, I think."

"That's good, I guess, then. That's okay." He began kicking at the ground, digging at it, his toe conducting a small excavation right there on its own. "You staying in town?"

"But not for long."

"I'll be leaving tomorrow, myself. In the evening." His foot filled in the hole. "But in the morning and afternoon, we'll be looking at stuff in the National History Museum and the Popol-Vuh Museum. Shouldn't miss it. Want to come along?"

"I'm not sure yet what I'll be doing tomorrow. Maybe I'll run into you, I don't know. Anyway, I don't want to impose myself on your tour again—"

"Don't worry. I say it's all right, and I'm in charge here."

"Well, then, maybe. I guess I'll say good-bye here, anyway. Thanks again."

Draw retrieved his cap from his back pocket and stuck it on his head again. "Well, bye, I guess." He jumped into the van and took off.

Morley walked back to the park, bought an ice cream bar and a soda, to be fair, from the old men at their carts, sat underneath a pine tree, in plain sight of others so she wouldn't be afraid. She ate the ice cream, which tasted like sawdust, and she cursed her sticky fingers and rinsed them with the soda. Back at the first shed, she sketched as best she could the excavation, trying to get the shadowy quality of the deep trenches. Morley shivered. In this bright, serene air, among these lovely hills. She walked back to the Jaguar Mound and sketched it, this mound coming right up between the suburban houses like a lonely island. She was very precise with the jaguar spots. Under her pen, the mound became too alive, a big crouched jaguar. She stopped. Walked around the park again, to make sure she hadn't missed something. Looked hard at the loafish mounds, the straggling pines. Took the bus back to the center of town, walked home to the Hotel Lito.

That evening, Morley watched television down in the lobby. She watched the local news, a beauty contest, a soap opera called *Pobre Diabla,* and saw not one Maya on the screen for the entire hour, only creamy-skinned European descendants lived in Guatemalan television land. With the owner of the hotel, who was very nice and seemed very bored with his hotel, she practiced speaking Spanish. Her Spanish came out sounding like French to the owner, so he began telling her about his French friend who lived up in Antigua, about how much he, the owner, would like someday to go to Paris, but he was too poor to go. Morley asked him if many foreign tourists came to his hotel. He sighed. No, the people who stayed at this hotel were usually the families of the sick and dying at the big city hospital around the corner.

## IV

# A Fat Cacique, a Jaguar Priest, and the Master of the Pink Glyphs

THE NEXT DAY, Morley set out to see the modern city built on the site of the ancient city.

Morley walked from the central plaza, flanked by the crumbling cathedral, and down the crowded 6 Avenida, signs for clothing stores—MIAMI, KOOL WORLD, SUPERMUNDO—strung out over the street, past a McDonald's with an armed security guard leaning against a wall and its spray-painted graffiti message: A LA BUENA A LA MALA YANKY FUERA DE GUATEMALA ECONÓMICA. She walked past the Parque Concordia, a square of dusty trees and straggling bushes, a crowd of taxis, loiterers, beggars, women wrapped in their shawls, selling food, combs, the black head and bright eyes of a child peering out of the shawl's folds, evangelical soapbox preachers, pickpockets—according to the guides, they spray mustard on your shirt or trip you while a partner robs you. Morley kept tapping her breast pocket for her passport, feeling at her waist for her money belt. In an alley, as she passed, she saw the police gathered around a dusty and barefoot child backed against a wall. On a corner, she saw people gather around a stand, buying roasted ears of corn.

Morley walked through the financial district, past skyscrapers with enormous neo-Maya reliefs stamped into the gray cement, a small cast-iron Eiffelesque tower, the Sheraton Hotel with its red-suited porters, white mall cubes of elegant dress boutiques, beauty salons, and glassed-in cafés, security guards resting their arms on machine guns, leaning with one foot up against the walls of restaurants that displayed the sign: POR FAVOR, LEAVE YOUR ARMS AT HOME. GRACIAS.

Now the city opened up into parks and hills. Faint, faint outlines of the mountains. Odd to remember she was up high in the mountains.

The sun quite hot, the air thick with black exhaust, the charcoal smell she would never forget.

Morley walked on. Moving two blocks over onto the Avenida de la Reforma, she passed into a wealthy residential section of town. Shaded houses set in walled gardens, and sleek, gleaming cars parked a few steps from the front door. Inside the gates, Indian gardeners working. Outside the gates, Indian women balancing great baskets of vegetables on their heads, knocking, calling out at the locked grill gates.

Morley walked on.

Walking came back to her. She hadn't walked like this for years, it seemed. Walking for hours like this, going nowhere in a sense, except for having determined one distant point to get to.

Not for the sake so much of getting there, but only to be headed in some direction that allows her to walk for a long time, not lost, and to spend every second looking at the shops, the houses, the sidewalks, the people, how they wait for a bus, the food stands with their red- and black-coaled braziers. Walking, at first her back always aches right at the bend of her waist, as if the top half of her wobbles off balance, her vertebrae not hitting just right. Then her body adjusts itself and she is walking, almost loping, in a way incongruous with the dress she has on. She is loping along, all pure walking, the easy settled pace of an animal in the forest, running a territory, alert to all sounds and smells, walking, *that* pleasure of walking.

He had been a great walker—all the places he had walked— in New York, back and forth across bridges, downtown, uptown, in Paris, navigating his way through all the old arcades, in the steam-bath streets of Jakarta, walking all over the city with his peculiar grace, the big body and the fine, strong legs. When he thrust open her thighs with both hands and entered her, he walked into her, treading, treading, one foot treading the sheet, then the other, the knees pushing up and down, setting a good pace. Did he notice the smells, note places to visit later? She is like a road, a sidewalk unleveled by tree roots. For him, too, there is somewhere to get to, but the walk is what matters, the stretching of limbs, setting a pace. She is a winding road, a road curling up and opening before him, an open road, open for development, or a lost road, an old wagon track, overgrown after he passes, its trace seen only from the air by an archaeologist in an airplane looking for ancient overland trade routes, a road trod so well, so many times, for generations, its trace forever ineffaceable even under centuries of plowing. Or a road in a small western town, a road lined with houses and then suddenly leading to nothing, disappearing into foothills, dropping off toward a mesa, vast and trackless.

She is interstate, freeway, highway, boulevard, avenue, road, street, lane, terrace, court, place, dirt road, graded road, unimproved road, path, deer trail, rocky streambed wash, road washed out.

Morley walked on.

Morley walked until she saw the sign MUSEO POPOL-VUH. She went into the steel and glass office building; the elevator let Morley out right in the museum. She paid and walked in.

Funerary urns lined the first room, enormous lidded pots mounted on tall stands, so that Morley was face-to-face with their great masks of staring gods. Fierce-looking gods, the barbels of a catfish curving out from a mouth, another beaked like a bird. Thick, lowering eyebrows and curling mustaches, great flanges attached to the sides of the urns to show off huge earplug earrings. Most of the urns had been returned by time to a pink-orange clay color, though some still bore traces of bright blue, white, black, or red paint. Morley liked best the lid of a Quiché urn from the western highlands of Guatemala. On the domed top sprawled a jaguar cub, its legs splayed out, its claws unsheathed and lifted, ears pricked up, baby snarl, sharp baby fangs.

Lining the next rooms were glass cases glittering with sun from the large windows and filled with shelves and shelves of ceramic vases, so many different vases. A covered vase whose lid handle transformed marvelously into the raised head of a duck. A vase shaped like a turtle, complete with turtle webbed flippers sticking out, and a turtle-man head peering forward, lifted in turtlelike attention.

The plainest vases were cylindrical, hardly even the slightest flaring to the top part of the vase. But upon some of these vases, elaborate care of another sort had been expended. They were wonderfully painted. Here an armadillo saunters along on his hind legs, smoking a fat cigar. A portly woman draped in a netted dress offers the bladder used for "the enema rite" (Morley read the caption twice) to a seated man. Two men in jaguar suits, two funny plump men in skintight jaguar suits, stare at each other.

Glittering glass cases of vases. Morley walked slowly through them, staring at the vases, so complicated, so simple, just clay, not even thrown on a wheel, but built up slowly by hand, coil upon coil, or slabs pressed into slab, seams smoothed over with slip, a slurry of water and clay. A thousand vases, each an object for the hand, to be taken in hand, a vertigo of vases, glittering glass cases—Morley escaped into another room.

Here the light was softer. Morley sat next to a broken-off stone stela, with carved glyphs rounded and raised in slight relief. It looked like what she had seen at Kaminaljuyú, that same rounded, plumped-up carving, and yes, there was the note saying it was from Kaminaljuyú—maybe she starts to recognize, know for herself a particular style, a distinctive trait. On her other side was a coiled snake in black basalt, its head lifted in a slightly ironic smile. Since no one was looking, Morley touched the snake. The stone was cool and smooth, polished without a formal polish, just rubbing and weather and years.

She roused herself. What do the vases feel like? She would like to get her hands on a vase.

That one vase, in particular, the one with the fat men in cat suits, she wanted to hold it up, look at it more closely, sketch it. Her eyes burned a bit, her feet hurt, she was tired. She might leave now, but if she left now, she would have missed that vase, and so, curiously, missed everything. She needed to make a note of that one vase.

One more moment of rest, sunk in herself, then Morley walked back to the right room—she knew it automatically.

Because the vase was on a shelf against the wall, Morley couldn't see all the way around it. The other figures, besides the fat jaguar men, one to each side of that pair, weren't entirely visible. So she would draw only the two larger figures facing each other across the front of the vase, the two very plump, short men dressed in jaguar suits, like jaguar tights with all four of the paws attached. Morley started to laugh. These very fat cats take themselves so seriously, their faces so fierce and intent.

Morley positioned herself on a pink cushion. The museum was a hushed place, perfect. She took out her sketchbook and pen.

The second Morley had settled herself, she felt excited. She could feel the excitement between her legs, the engagement so pleasurable, she might liquefy. Morley emptied out her mind of everything else and gazed at the vase.

Because the two figures face each other across an open space, the center of the vase, the curve of the surface allows only half of their bodies to be visible at the same time. To see one figure entirely, Morley had to shift over to one side of the cushioned bench. The other figure disappeared.

Morley thought at first to draw the jaguar men together in a single sketch, flattening the vase's surface into a rectangle that would include both figures. Yet that seemed wrong. The vase was made for the hand to turn in order to see the figures; the hand turned the vase to set a motionless scene in motion. To be as true to that as possible, she would draw three pictures, one of each figure and then one of the space in between them, with the faces of the figures staring across that space. For that, it struck her, was the truth of this vase. The two were always two separate jaguar men, but also always one, both part of one fierce gaze, the drama of the vase the scene of their shared look, to which the other two figures seem the ritual attendants, solemn and attentive, stiff with ceremony.

Morley placed herself before the right-front figure first. She began to draw.

How much she wanted the sense of the vase itself as an object in the drawing, to defeat her flat paper, to make the vase spring up, re-created whole and round. She drew the contour of the vase, a plain cylinder about nine inches tall, probably four in diameter, and slightly flared from the base up to the rim. You could see the coils almost, feel it built up in coils. One side of the vase dipped down slightly.

Now she turned to the painting of the vase. The base was

defined by a dark band of brown-black painted around it, the paint even running underneath the curved edge of the bottom of the vase. The band was a pretty steady brush line, but sometimes dipping ever so slightly, sometimes a bit thicker, then thinner, ever so slightly. At the top of the vase, there was another band of brown-black, thin, barely visible, worn off in places, and running right beneath it a line of hieroglyphs drawn in that pinkish rose-rust color that had drawn her so much to this vase, a different red from that of the other vases, whose reds were browner or more orange. Each glyph washed in a light pink, a thinned-out tint of the same pinkish red the lines of the glyphs were drawn in. She copied the glyphs as best she could, though some were worn, the paint flaked off, and some were obscured by the plumage of the masks that curled up over them, as if the figures stood in front of the glyph band.

Morley couldn't read the letters, so all her pleasure lay in copying them, like a child first learning to write her alphabet, whistling under her breath as she worked. Some glyphs or parts of a single glyph had rounded animal shapes—yes, here was a cat face like her stone glyph, here a fish shape maybe. Some glyphs were like several-celled beings, the big circles plumped up with smaller ones. And in every line of the glyphs, the feel of handwriting, a certain slant to the right, an ease.

On to the fat jaguar man. The floor on which he stood was established. The text, perhaps the auspices under which he appeared, was in place.

How very nice, very good, the very fine outline of the figure, a thin line—her fine pen could make this line. It came up from the floor band in one wonderful line emphasizing the plumpness of the short legs, the chunky thighs and the waist, a roll of fat, the incurve of the right arm of the figure—the arm in midgesture, slightly raised—and the other arm, the figure's left arm, lifted a third of the way up and held out to his side. The curve of the hand—or, rather, the paw, with its plump pads and the tufts of fur, she remembered from an examination of her own cat's foot. So the two arms acted in concert, raised, gracefully pointing away from the direction the figure is facing, giving emphasis to that direction. A gesture of action arrested, like one is either getting ready to do something or is caught by surprise, arms raised, on the alert.

The big heavy body so planted there on these two big feet in their jaguar socks and yet graceful, alert. The tail, a spotted jaguar tail, is shown falling behind the figure. It lies behind the left foot, flat on the floor, a true tail, again pointing in the opposite direction from which the figure is facing, underlining the gaze again, the thrust of his attention. No, no, correct the tail. It's not quite limp, but painted here as about to be swished around. There is such an alertness to the entire figure, Morley notices, that the jaguar suit serves as comic relief, as a comically ironic turn to the scene.

Around the neck of the fat jaguar hangs a big scarf, like a muffler, tied in a large knot on his chest, the two ends falling straight down to his knees. The scarf is dyed red except for the ends, the white ends, to emphasize the soaked-in quality of the red. Above the scarf, hanging from his thick neck on thick shoulders, two strands of round pebble-size beads.

Now the profile. A plump jowl jaw, again drawn in outline with the fine, thin black line, the slightly open, thick lips. Again that look of alertness, full attention. The fleshy nose, a small dip above the knob on it—this is a personal portrait, Morley's hand knows it—the nose slanting back, the almond-shaped eye, rounded, with a sharp black dot for the pupil at the inner corner, the rest of the eye slanted up fiercely. Sloping forehead, sloping back in almost one line from the nose, the skull sloping up and back at an angle shown clearly by the white-fringed cloth that tightly wraps the head. Drop earrings. And the whole head framed in the round hole cut into a huge monster-head mask, sort of like a huge old-fashioned diving helmet with a small glass window. The mask is covered with jaguar skin, but it is not a jaguar head.

There's that long muzzle, like a deer's, fitted with two curled-in tusks, and two long, straight reddish plumes, a large flower bud bobbling on top of the head, a jaguar ear pricked up toward the back of the mask. From under the ear, five long black plumes shoot out and then fall behind.

Morley took her time filling in all the jaguar spots—on the vase not drawn as dots and filled in, they are blots large and small, some dark, some light, cloudy, like Chinese or Japanese ink drawings. She'd have to get a brush and ink to really copy this piece. The pen was all right for a sketch, but not at all the right tool to do these blots, spots not perfectly rounded, but rather, like rosettes. Rosettes seemingly blotted on at random, but upon inspection they give you such a sense of flesh as they curve around a fat haunch.

Sitting there making spots on jaguar tights—no one could ever imagine how peaceful, how delightful.

Absorbed in her work, conscious only of the sound of the pen hissing on the paper, still Morley was at the same time aware of other people passing by, murmuring, rustling behind her, looking over her shoulder. Then she heard a voice in English—yes, she was listening after all—a familiar voice, and there, ambling into the room, his lecture rambling on, was Michael Draw, his two couples in tow. There was Michael Draw standing next to her, looking down at her, staring at the drawing, so that she, too, had to stop and look at it herself. The fat jaguar man so alive—she was taken aback. She wanted to cover it with her hand.

"Hey, this is so real," Michael Draw finally said. "I've looked at this vase a lot, but the drawing makes me see it more powerfully than just looking at it behind the glass there. This jaguar guy—it's like he moves."

The American couples crowded in to look and were silent for a long moment. Morley could see herself that the vase stood off the page, almost as an object itself, with its own power.

Michael Draw then found his guide voice again and spoke to

his charges, to Morley. "This vase here, people think it's one of a series of vases in the same style, with the same figures. They're called the Pink Glyphs series, because see this wash of pink over the band of glyphs?" Draw pointed to the vase on the shelf. "The guy that painted them's called the Master of the Pink Glyphs. We don't know his name. Those same two guys appear on most of the vases, the Fat Cacique and the Jaguar Priest. It's hard to tell on this one which is which, 'cause they're wearing the same suit. On the others, it's clear one guy is the cacique, meaning chief, headman, and the other guy is some sort of head priest. We think the vases commemorate some event or series of events important for the cacique."

One of the American men—Morley had forgotten their names—pushed up his sunglasses onto his bald head, looked down at the drawing and then up at the vase on the shelf. "I don't get these cutout places where we see their faces."

"It's one of the special things about these vases—I think there are only one or two other examples of this cutaway mask. They think the cutaway is to make sure anybody looking at the vase knows these guys aren't gods, though they're dressed up for some ritual as jaguar gods. Those scarves're special to one of the jaguar gods, seem to be a sign of sacrifice, decapitation sacrifice. This might could be some warm-up to a sacrifice, but we don't really know."

Draw paused, looked down at Morley's drawing again, then spoke to Morley. "This is real good."

Morley saw the Americans glance at one another. Draw followed her glance and recovered himself. He grinned at Morley. "I guess we have to go on and look at the rest of the rooms. How long you going to be here? You want to come along?"

"I've already been through—"

"Well, will you be here, say, another hour? I have to get these folks back to their hotel to pack. We'll be taking the flight to Tikal tonight. But I really want to talk to you." He saw Morley was about to say something, so he hurried on: "I kind of need to talk to you. How about four, then?"

Yes, she'd meet him at four, say in the bookshop. She'd be poking around there. Draw bobbed his head and began herding his charges on to the next room. The couples nodded good-bye to Morley.

Morley needed a minute or two to get back to her work. She had liked Draw to talk to her, to see her drawing. When he saw something, he became alert, and she had more of a sense of his body—again in the shirt and jeans, the old felt baseball cap now stuck in the back pocket—tall and solid, beautiful like a tree, flexible, upright.

She looked at the drawing again. It wasn't perfect, yet she had caught what attracted her, and that was a thread somehow she had picked out, a thread to follow. She repositioned herself to draw the other figure.

Here was the other fat man, even fatter, full flesh, powerful flesh. In the same jaguar suit, except that instead of a tail, the figure wore a jaguar-skin cape, like a square, with two paws dangling, almost lifting in motion—had he just stopped moving a second ago? His arms were raised like a hula dancer, chest high in the opposite direction of his gaze. Wears the same jaguar spotted mask, with a floppy ear, bud, long muzzle, tusked and plumed, although the plumes on the back curl up over the pink glyph band, the same knotted red and white scarf. She draws the face framed in the cutout hole. Again, her hand knows these are portraits, both faces so different. Here the chin thrusts forward and up, there's a line of scarification following the upper lip, the eyes slant fiercely above an arched nose with a small bump at the brow bone, the white kerchief is smaller and worn back on the crown of the head. He wears a necklace of flat plaquelike beads.

His alert gaze is equally fixed, however, locked in the gaze of the other jaguar.

Once more, Morley took delight in shading in the rosettes on the jaguar suit, but she did need a brush and ink.

Two jaguar men, the Fat Cacique and the Jaguar Priest, two twin jaguar suits, twins not looking exactly alike, fraternal, not identical, twins, but likeness in their glance, the same body almost, the almost identical dress. They were two, but each one's attention held completely by the other, one look.

Tired suddenly, Morley could have lain down on the cushioned bench and gone right to sleep. However, there was one more thing to draw before she gave up—the space in between the two figures. Morley saw right this moment that the space was important, the empty space crossed by the two plumes of the muzzle of each mask, plumes almost touching, one stiffly straight out, the other gracefully drooping ever so slightly so as not to touch, the plumes an extension of that shared look. Right below the plumes were three glyphs in a column written in that dark reddish pink, and washed in with the lighter tint. What did they name? Whom did they name?

Morley closed her notebook, closed her eyes, and dozed sitting straight up.

Someone tapped her shoulder. "Like to let you sleep, but it'll be closing time here soon. C'mon, you want to get a beer, or a cup of coffee?"

She dropped her pen. Michael Draw bent down and picked up the pen gracefully. He moved powerfully, easily.

They walked out into the lobby. Morley needed a moment to wake herself up entirely, still dazed with sleep and feeling so foolish and exposed. How long had Draw been watching her? She said she wanted to look at the postcards. Picked up one card, put it down, picked up another—a postcard of a jaguar up to his neck in water, cooling off, nice rosettes on his fur, exactly like the ones on the vase. She bought it.

Out on the avenue, Draw said, "I've only got an hour and a half before I pick up my group at the Sheraton. The plane to Tikal leaves at seven. But I want to talk to you. I need to talk to you. You staying near the center?"

He drove the van too fast, parked it at his hotel. He led Morley to a Burger King, quickly, almost belligerently informing her, "I always go to these places, Pizza Hut, McDonald's, too. They're the fastest, even here, and the cleanest. After you've been here awhile, you'll see—you'll not want to feed like a tourist anymore." They walked past the uniformed security guard with his machine gun. The restaurant was crowded with well-dressed, clean-cut Guatemalan teenagers.

They went through the line and found a small table. Draw was silent a moment, stirring his coffee as he wound himself up. "What I wanted to know was if I could get you to do some drawing for me back in the States, for my thesis?" He started leafing through Morley's sketchbook. He stopped at the drawings of the jaguar men. "You know, what I like here is the way you get the vase to be a thing. Usually, we take roll-out photos or make roll-out drawings, so the whole picture ends up one rectangle, just like a Western drawing. These make you see each figure one at a time."

Morley was startled. Here was someone who pays attention, who sees things. She watched him more intently. She could almost feel her look sharpening with interest. She watched the head of black curly hair, so black, thick, bent over the notebook.

Draw closed her sketchbook. "I could really use some good drawings of my important pieces. I can take photographs, of course, but drawings show a lot more, if they're really good. Like I said, the drawings of the Pink Glyphs vase are real good. I'm real interested in that vase. I think it might just come from the site I'm at right now. 'Course, all the Pink Glyphs vases are looted vases, so we don't know where they come from exactly. So they're really no good to us, since we can't see 'em in relation to other stuff found with them. There is, though, on the other side of this vase, a glyph like a capital *T*, sort of. That's the Ik glyph, wind glyph, and we think it's the emblem for Motul, my site. But this's just based on an assumption about the emblem glyph.''

''Where's your site, exactly?''

Only then did Draw discover that he had her complete attention. He took off his glasses and polished them with a faded blue handkerchief.

''Motul's up in the Petén, on Lake Petén, across the lake from Flores—where you stay to go see the ruins at Tikal. Right outside a little town called San José de Motul. As soon as I get rid of my tour group, I can get back to work. They're just some relatives of my adviser. He kind of asked me to do this as a favor, but of course, 'cause I'm his student, I have to do it, have to listen to them talk about things they don't know anything about. I'm not even getting any money for it—you'd be surprised at how many big-time archaeologists do package tours for the money these days.'' Draw looked grim. ''But when I'm famous, you can bet I won't play tour guide. When I'm famous, I'll teach as little as possible, be down here as much as possible, out in the field digging, with no one to bug me.''

''You're actually digging in Motul, right now?''

''Yeah, last year we surveyed the whole site, every last little building. This year, we're excavating two mounds.''

''And the vase?''

''Well, like I said, there's that emblem glyph on the vase.'' He blushed and added quickly, ''I really didn't want to keep on going around the museum at all. I liked watching you draw.''

Morley was looking at his large scarred hands, the nails cracked, stained by dirt. His forearms long, muscled, the silky black hairs all smoothed down. Riffling them up with her palm, they would feel very silky. Just to grasp those forearms, hold on to them.

Draw said, ''I was hoping you'd be at one of the museums.''

''I really wasn't trying to get another tour.''

''I don't care about that.''

Why didn't he ask her again to come to this site, Motul, and draw for him? Can I come? she wanted to ask, but couldn't.

Instead, she inquired, formally, "How long before you get to go back to your dig?"

"We'll be just a day at Tikal. Then my tour group's gone for good." Draw looked at his watch. "Speaking of that, I'll have to be going." He got Morley to write out her address in the States on a paper napkin. She repeated she would be happy to do some work for him, if he wanted, to pay him back for the tour.

As she wrote out the information, she paused and looked up at Draw. "How's Eddie? He still on the dig?"

"Eddie's fine. He's romancing all the local girls. Smoking lots of dope. Up and decided not to go back for his spring semester. Think he's going native. It happens."

As they walked out the door, Draw asked Morley, "Just how long were you at the mound yesterday before I saw you?"

Morley admitted that she had followed him into the tomb.

"Funny to think you were right there all that time. Should have said something." He paused for a moment. "Maybe you heard me going on about the sacrifices and all that. Weird how people want to know about the sacrifices. It kind of thrills them, even though they act like they're disgusted. They act like they can't believe other people could be so primitive, so cruel, but they themselves can't wait to hear about it."

Morley and Draw walked through the streets loud with buses rushing by. He kept drifting toward her as they walked, almost bumping into her. They stopped at a drugstore. Draw said he had to buy some clear fingernail polish for the field lab; they used it in labeling potsherds. Morley knew that he wanted to keep her with him as long as possible and that it was for her benefit that he flirted with the salesgirl in his twangy Spanish, the girl teasing him about buying nail polish, trying to sell him a hot-pink color.

Morley and Draw parted in front of a restaurant disco, under its large banner proclaiming that week Mexican Mariachi Week.

The sounds of the mariachi band practicing blared out into the street. Leaning on a car were a man and two women. Three kids danced on the sidewalk.

Draw asked Morley where she would go after Guatemala City.

"Probably go see the usual sights, Antigua, Lake Atitlán, maybe Copán," she said.

"Think you'll get to Tikal? Plane's tonight at seven."

How surprising it is when someone looks at you. That they dare look right at you with their black eyes. Morley looked away. "I don't know. Maybe I'll show up there sometime."

"All right. Well, if I don't see you again down here, I've got your address. So I know where to find you. I'll be in touch. Like I said, I can really use your help. Anyway, it's been real nice talking to you."

They stood close together. Everything sheared around. Michael Draw might touch her. She sensed he wanted to. But Morley couldn't do a thing to help him out. It was as if her body were still not her own, and she was ashamed not to be in control of her body. Michael Draw, did he sense her shame? She was helpless to hide it. "Maybe I'll get to Tikal. And maybe—what's the name of your site again?"

"Motul. Across the lake from Flores. Go see Tikal and then come on over."

Then Michael Draw left it alone. He seemed suddenly aware —or did she imagine this, hope for this?—of her as exhausted, therefore not to be pushed or forced. Perhaps he had risked enough of his pride.

Draw almost smiled. "Well. Come or don't come."

He turned and walked away.

Morley felt so alone.

Still, there was something exciting to think about, and she touched the notebook with the pictures of the vase, of the Fat Cacique, of the Jaguar Priest. Morley said out loud, "The Master of the Pink Glyphs.'' And Morley smiled to herself. It was like the title of an old mystery story, a girl-detective mystery story she had read long ago.

V

# Corazón Viajero

"COME OR DON'T COME."

Morley sat in a *comedor,* a bright empty room with its doors open to the dark empty street. A woman served Morley her dinner and took several bottles of beer to some back room where men laughed and talked. In the light thrown out onto the sidewalk, two girls watched a baby toddle headlong toward the street and stopped him just in time, every time.

While she ate, Morley studied her guidebooks. She was in a bit of a stall, a wheel-spinning that might quietly, alarmingly, go on too long, on and on. Taking out her jaguar postcard, Morley turned it over to write home. "But he's dead," she heard herself say, and slipped it back into its neat-fitting paper sack.

There were day excursions from Guatemala City. To Antigua, the colonial capital. To Chichicastenango, the Maya market town. There were the ruins of Tikal, of course. Perhaps go look at Motul. Tall Michael Draw, and temple mounds, and trenches cut deep into the earth.

"Come or don't come."

Back to ruin, ruins.

The airplane to Tikal, too expensive, too direct. The bus a long day trip, but let her take her time. She needs a little more lovely drifting time, looking at the landscape, seeing things she can't see from an airplane.

At six the next morning, Morley once more found herself at a bus station. In the tent restaurant, she drank thin, sweet coffee, she ordered eggs and beans hot off the griddle, complete with a chunk of crumbling yellow-white cheese and small tortillas. She sat on a stool and ate, as contemplative as any single person in a railroad restaurant, an airport cafeteria, any traveler, ready to set out, isolate, intent.

Now it was time to go. Morley walked over to a gathering of buses. "Flores? Tikal?" she asked.

"¡Barrio—Barrio—Puerto Barrios!" Men waving thick ticket books charged Morley. Take my bus, *Corazón Viajero,* with red crocheted fringe draping the window. Take mine, *Amor en Silencio,* with gilt-paper cutout flowers spangling the windshield. No, take my *Tigre Feroz,* spelled out in shiny reflector capital letters. *¡Barrio —Barrio—Puerto Barrios!*

A quick glance at her guidebook assures Morley she could get off the Puerto Barrios bus at the Ruidosa junction to get a bus north to Flores. In an instant, she was ticketed and installed in a reclining seat on a bus like a Greyhound bus. In another five minutes, all the seats were filled. Men in white short-sleeved shirts with tiny tucks sat next to women in T-shirts and shorts, children in sunsuits lolled on their parents' laps or stood wedged between their knees, looking out the window. The sweaty conductor tucks his ticket book into a back pocket and starts the engine. Now the driver comes aboard in his starched shirt, sits down, and releases the brake. The conductor honks the loud horn and calls out the door, *"¡Barrio—Barrio—Puerto Barrios!"*

Morley was instantly happy with a simple tourist happiness, happy to be headed for the next sight.

The bus rushed through low-walled streets, walls white and gray, turquoise and pink, the conductor honking the horn at every intersection, the gears rumbling back and forth. The city's outskirts were dry knobby foothills overlooking deep ravines. Looking out her window straight down into the ravines, Morley feared to topple in at any moment. Balancing huge burdens on their heads, men and women climbed up tiny steps cut into the dirt of the steep slopes to shanties of corrugated iron, cardboard, car doors, old car tires piled up, with the address painted on whatever sort of door there was.

Farther out, farms—with names like Finca Gloria, Finca Luz —were terraced up the foothills. They passed acres of scorched land, stubbled with stumps, and in the distance, from a cleft in the mountains, smoke drifted as farmers burned off the brush to clear more fields. Except for the dusty dusty pines, all the trees were leafless or dead-leaved in this dry season. Yet, miraculously, a few leafless trees flowered in high clouds of bright yellow and lavender blossoms.

Every twenty-five kilometers, the white asphalt highway widened at a military checkpoint. The bus stopped, the driver talked to the soldier who approached, and the bus continued on. At first, Morley felt afraid, but everyone else seemed to sleep right on through these stops.

In every small town, the conductor swings out the open door and calls, *"¡Barrio—Barrio—Puerto Barrios!"*

Foothills dwindled into mere hills. The forest turned green with more and more palm trees. Morley sketched the palms in her notebook. How beautiful palms were, their embossed or latticed bark, their trunks, some lithe and graceful, some heavier, sturdy, planted so firmly—as men's bodies were so different, his body big and thick like a wall, and Draw, Draw so upright, like a young palm shooting up, flexible tall and lithe, well probably— she didn't know, she didn't know at all—and the immense fan of the leaves fanning out in so many brilliant greens. Morley liked the palms whose fans of leaves rise up and spill over, fanning, elegantly fanning. The cluster of fat yellow nuts at the base of the fan.

Through the open windows, the smell of burning wood.

Forest thickened into jungle. Jungle gave way to banana plantation. The blue sky hazed with humidity, and everyone on the bus fanned themselves with newspapers. From her window, Morley saw the old banana train that still ran from Guatemala City to

Bananera, the old banana center. Its wooden seats were crowded with people infinitely less prosperous than those on her bus, mostly Indian, clutching woven bags and bundles, migrant workers gathering for some harvest here. The people sagged in the heat. The train had broken down. As the bus passed by, Morley saw men working on the track.

The Ruidosa junction. A bustling collection of food stand after food stand, gas stations. The moment the bus stopped, an army of young girls invaded the bus, waving languorously in each passenger's face tortillas wrapped around hard-boiled eggs sprinkled with red chili powder, fruit drinks and sodas— *"Aguas, aguas, tamarinda, tamarinda, coca, coca."* Morley pushed her way off the bus. "Flores?" Another conductor ran up to her—such swift uptake, as if she were being handed over from one to another. "Flores! Flores!" She nodded and he grabbed her bag, climbed up a metal ladder to the top of the bus, fastened the bag —tightly, she hoped—slid back down, opened the back door of the bus. She stepped up and the door slammed behind her, pushing her into the crowded bus, no empty seats at all. She barely had time to settle her small bag in the luggage rack, next to bundles wrapped in striped cloths and tied with fraying string, before the bus lurched off.

This bus was the old Bluebird yellow school bus of her childhood, complete with its name plaque bolted above the windshield. Everyone sat as she had sat years ago, crowded three to the green vinyl seats with so little padding, the third person clinging to the curved handlebar with white knuckles, with only half her or his rear end on the seat's edge and always shifting for some advantage against those who shared the same seat, against the person standing up in the aisle, like Morley, wedged between two three-seaters, her feet apart, facing sideways, hands apart, holding fast to the luggage rack, knees locked and everything else surrendered to the sway of the bus as it lumbered over the rutted road, took the curves, stopped and started. As more passengers crammed through the rear door, the conductor climbed over Morley to ticket them. The vending girls pushed their way down the aisle —*"Aguas, aguas, tamarinda, tamarinda"*—and jumped out the back door at the next stop.

Standing up, Morley could see only the weeds at the edge of the road, spectral with silvery dust.

Hour after hour, Morley stood there, hardly aware of standing anymore, no thought in her head, given in looking at the weeds, at the streams when the driver, afraid to take a rotting bridge, turned off the road, plowed down into the stream, and lurched up the other side. Sometimes there were women and children in the stream washing themselves, the children in shorts and shirts, the women in cotton shifts, scooping water over themselves, their long black hair clinging to their arms.

Everyone else on the bus gave in, too, babies sprawling across their sleeping mothers' laps, an old old man perched on the edge of a seat, nodding off, two lovers kissing, murmuring, turning on each other their blissful gaze, wonderfully stupefied by the hours behind them and before them of lovely lovely dozing together. As if to make literal that spell, the back window of the bus fell out as it bumped over a particularly deep rut and the dust churned up by the wheels sifted in, gray-white dust, clouds of dust, dusted them for hours, until they all were the same fine-grained frosty white. People in blue or red shirts got on the bus, white ghosts got off the bus. A young woman came on in a pretty flowered dress with a white linen lace collar. An hour later, her dark hair turned prematurely white, her dress and collar one plain shroud of gray.

This slow trip so like a dream for Morley had its waking moments of almost terror.

Once soldiers stopped the bus in the middle of the forest. They climbed on top of the bus. Morley could hear them above her head, poking through the luggage, looking for weapons, Morley knew, weapons smuggled to the guerrillas in the Petén, who were fighting the government over land rights and civil rights. Then the soldiers ordered all the men and boys to get off and present their papers. The women looked furtively out the windows at their men. The papers were being checked for a record of their military service and their birth date. A man or a boy could be conscripted right then and there into the army. To fight against the guerrillas, to kill the Indians, often Indians themselves conscripted into regiments given the names of ancient Maya war gods. All these men were allowed to board again.

And at Poptún, while the bus filled up on gas, Morley suddenly remembered that a North American farmer and innkeeper here had been found decapitated just last year. The government blamed the guerrillas, the military accused the man of drug trafficking, and everyone knew the killing was carried out by the battalion stationed nearby. Now, outside her bus window, German tourists—that pale skin, those pale spectacles, short, wavy white hair, had to be Germans, too pale even for Americans —poured off their luxury air-conditioned Turismo bus to take photographs of Morley's bus with the vendors climbing on, the hands reaching out the windows to buy tortillas, corn on the cob, fruit, *aguas* from vendors standing alongside the bus dressed in Maya costume, *huipiles* and long skirts.

Morley was very very far from home. Was she really going somewhere? Was she lost?

At last, the bus came nearer to Flores. More passengers got off than got on. Morley and the woman in the nice dress finally could sit down. They sat down and began to laugh at each other. Each one, everyone was like a hill of dust. The slightest movement started tiny landslides from their shoulders. Morley passed around her bottle of water. The woman with the dusty dress spoke some English. She had been up north, *el norte,* to work, and now she had come back home with her money. She had liked *el norte,* but it was also good to be home—she had to say it. Please excuse her. Up north, the vegetables and the meat, too, looked so good but tasted like nothing, like this dust. *Las ruinas* at Tikal were very interesting she had heard. No, she had never been there.

There was no political talk, and Morley felt guilty. Her colleagues would, in her place, be interviewing the woman about Guatemalan massacres of the Indians and the fate of the disappeared. But for Morley, in this friendly, dusty conversation, that would be deeply impolite, too dangerous, too theatrical for their fatigue. It would start up their fear and her fear and disturb the mildness of them sitting there dusty and tired, spoil the unexpected mildness of this ride.

The bus passed through low ranges of hills divided by savanna. Her heart beat fast—are all those hills unexcavated temple mounds?—but then there would be thousands of mounds. She laughed to herself. They must be hills, merely hills. Cattle grazed on the savannas that were once forest: future Big Macs and Whopper burgers, her guidebook said. Blue sky and white sailing clouds, trees scraggly in this their dead season, but once in a while, again, a burst of lavender flowering, an exquisite pleasure to try to distinguish it, almost indistinguishable, from the azure sky.

Flores at last. Morley's bag tossed down to her, she was clapped into a taxi and crossing a causeway to the island town of Flores, a cluster of stucco houses, churches, shops, and hotels all gleaming pink and cool in the sunset taking color now. Soon Morley had her swimming suit on and was gliding into the lake off the terrace of her hotel, diving underwater to rinse off all the dust, then lying on her back, floating as the pink sky and the pink lake shimmered in one pearly sheet. Later in the evening, she walked along the causeway that linked Flores with the mainland. She stopped and watched the town come to wash, men, women, children, washing themselves, their hair, their clothes. The soapsuds floated on the water like light snow and drifted into, clung to the rocks that lined the causeway. She stood absolutely still and watched.

Across the lake was Motul.

But at 6:30 A.M., the hotel minibus set off with Morley for the ruins of Tikal.

At the ruins, Morley consulted the map in her guidebook. But she ended up taking the first path that offered itself.

A small plaza appeared in the turn of the path. Two low pyramids faced each other across the plaza, twin pyramids, strangely alike, both faceless. One did have five stelae in front of its stairs. The uncarved upright stones each had a round stone altar before it. On one side of the plaza was an enclosure; inside, another stela, this one carved. So much attention paid to the intricate detail of the warrior's regalia, the grotesque mask on his pectoral, the high sandals, the tight-fitting wrist decorations, the headdress a huge stacked crown of god faces, and finally the long fall of quetzal plumes, like a waterfall to the ground. Morley could hardly make out the man's body there. There were not the sloping shoulders of the reliefs at Palenque, not the thick, power-ful neck, the muscular legs, the particular portrait, the lifted, unguarded face.

Morley climbed one of the two most famous pyramids of Tikal, pictured everywhere on the cover of guidebooks, on post-cards, on posters in the airport. The two towering pyramids, cleaned of brush and trees, restored, faced each other across a green lawn. Unlike the pyramids at Chichén Itzá, or Kabah, which were more massive, wider at the base, these shot straight up 125 feet from a narrow base, the very quintessence of steepness, vertiginous in their verticality. A morning mist drifted up over their broken roof combs.

Gripping the tiny stone steps on her way up as if she were climbing a sheer rock face, Morley at last reached the top and clung to the doorway of the small temple there, out of breath and almost nauseated with dizziness when she looked back down the steps. To help her heart stop beating so hard, Morley tried to take note of everything. The acropolis was to her left, tier upon tier of buildings that had gradually grown together, as plazas and courts and walkways were built up between them. She tried to imagine what the city must have looked like. The grass plaza—now so green and soft, like a cemetery lawn—would be a plastered surface, the buildings painted red and white and maybe green, the roof combs alive with huge images of rulers or gods, like figures on giant billboards. It would be like looking at the President up there in color, his false dignity lowering on his bony face.

Roof combs of other pyramids bristled above the trees.

At last, Morley felt she was up to coming down the steps, step by step—concentrate—one step at a time—down the steep gray granite steps, soon so afraid of toppling over, tumbling, arms and legs flailing, skull bumping down the steps. Morley burst out crying. What if she died here, so far away from home? Why was she so far away from home? What if she died here and no one knew, ever knew, he never knew?

After this, Morley sat on a bench and watched tourists, laughing and screaming, shinny up and slide down ladders clamped to the slope of an unrestored temple mound. Morley liked looking at the trees and bushes on this still-unexcavated mound, the thick trees shooting up off its mass, their roots gripping the stones. But she felt the rest of Tikal resisted her. Tikal was so restored, finished off—thus, closed off to her.

Before the minibus came back, Morley visited the little museum in a flaking stucco villa veined with vines, shadowy and cool. Morley pressed up to thick plate glass to see a tomb reconstructed for pedagogical purposes, but it was so dimly lit, as if pedantically to preserve the twilight of the grave. She could barely make out a spill of beads, several seashells, what looked like leg bones, and two stacks of dusty pots, one tumbled.

A painted vase on display attracted Morley. A band of animals danced in a procession. A spider monkey, beach-ball belly and thin arms, stepped forward, his tail curled up in the air, his plumed headdress dancing, too. In front of him, a black cat—big body and haunches, the long red scarf worn like a muffler, his arms raised above his head, one leg stepped forward, bent at the knee. A swollen-bellied deer with flared ears standing straight up, playing what looked like a tall conga drum, one hoof stepped forward in the dance step, his tail lifted behind him. What Morley liked so much more than the stony blocks outside was the plainness of the vases, only baked clay, yet this exquisite sense of bodies depicted, the incline of the neck drawn out.

Morley spent a long time sketching a bloodletter (whose blood?) fashioned out of a femur (deer or human femur?). Incised on it, the incised lines filled with red, was the most graceful of all hands, a hand holding the long stem of a paintbrush, the brush itself plumped up with paint. A hand, its thumb and index finger grasping the brush, the other fingers ever so lightly crooked. The hand and paintbrush emerging, like a tongue, from the spread, fanged jaws of a serpent.

At last, Morley gave up on Tikal and sat in the shade by the Visitor Center until it was time to go. Two tapirs, like black pigs with their curved hindquarters, trotted down the path to the ruins. Up above in the trees, Morley spotted several loud-calling black birds—grackles? And a toucan—against the sunlit sky, she could see the outline of the enormous bill. She almost wished she had seen a jaguar. Two ocellated turkeys stepped across the lawn in front of her, their bright blue-skinned heads, beaded with scarlet bumps, poking ahead of their fat, waddling bodies. One turkey stopped to preen the blue and gold markings like eyes on the tips of its tail feathers. Their plumpness, like that of the plump animals on the vase and so many plump men and women on so many vases, proclaimed everyone should eat, be full, be fat, all animals love to eat, to have a big belly. She flipped through her journal to the sketches of those two fat men in jaguar suits and laughed.

At the hotel, Morley floated in the lake and stared at the pink sky. At the restaurant, stuffed ocelots and tapirs stared glassy-eyed at her from the walls—these animals stuffed but still painfully thin. Mangy jaguar fur trimmed the menu.

The next morning, Morley sat on the terrace of the hotel and unfolded her map. On to Belize? Back to Guatemala City? Mist rose from the lake as the sun heated up the day. Again, Morley felt very far from home. But to come so far and see so much—and feel so numb, dead to it. The only moments of being alive were when she sketched the vase of the Master—"The Master of the Pink Glyphs," she said out loud, and laughed—and the hand holding the brush. Alive, too, the deep trench at Kaminaljuyú with a voice coming out of it. The fat tapirs, fat toucans, fat turkeys. Palm trees shooting up, fanning. And the bus ride, silent and side by side with the others, all one in dust. The vase of the Master, two fat men in jaguar suits, Fat Cacique, Jaguar Priest.

Michael Draw, his young laugh a sharp bark escaping him. Present herself. Simply present herself.

At the travel agency run by the hotel, Morley asked how to get to San José and to *las ruinas* at Motul. The young woman agent seemed puzzled. San José was not for tourists. San José is only a village on the lake—it doesn't even have postcards! And *las ruinas, sí,* she had jeep tours going to the famous *ruinas* of Uaxactún, Yaxchilán buried deep in the jungle. Or was the lady interested in shamans? There was a famous shaman at Uaxactún who turned into a jaguar!

Five minutes later, Morley was putting out across the lake to San José in a lake taxi, along with an old woman and her big basket and two young men with machetes in leather cases.

The blue lake was larger than she had imagined. There was much activity—water taxis plying back and forth, fishing boats. Here was San Benito, then San Andrés, and finally, San José, a cluster of plastered buildings, white and cream and pink, red-tiled roofs, palm trees, fringed fronded palm trees again.

At a small café on the lake, Morley ordered coffee and got directions to *las ruinas.* "¿Arqueóloga?" the woman asked. Morley hesitated, shook her head.

Walking up the road, she passed the tall white-spired Catholic church and four evangelical churches squat and square, turquoise and pink, a stationery store—no postcards in the window. The pavement gave way to a dirt road with a few dogs lying in the sun, thatched-roof houses with thicket fences, in and out of which wandered chickens, a washing station with its thatched roof over a cistern and surrounding it a line of flat washing slabs slanted toward the water. Children playing in the shadows of palms stopped and stared at her.

The road became deeply rutted and steep as it left the town. Insects sang in the weeds, the trees grew thicker, hills rose higher on each side, tiny steps cut into the hills.

At last, a newly cut road into the jungle. Really an old path widened with machetes.

Morley looked back and saw a bit of glittering lake framed by palm fronds.

Then she was in shadow, walking through tall trees, tall palms, thick brush. Roots snaked along the ground, vines trailed in her face, invisible birds trilled. At her feet, slick things darted into the brush.

As Morley walked on, she became afraid in this forest shadowy as a tunnel. She began struggling for breath. She began to weep in her fear, wanting to cry out for him. If she were going to die, she would call out to him, for him, and in this instant she was sure she was going to die—someone would come along and kill her, or a snake would bite her and kill her, a jaguar would leap on her, sink his claws into her, drag her down and kill her, or she would die of panic or fear, of loss, of loss of him. She would die of his death. She struggled to breathe, weeping. She had never been so afraid in her life, of her death, so alone, when they had been such good companions. Companionless, she was terribly afraid. Weeping, she stumbled, tripped, and scraped her knee, barely, but it scared her, made her cry the more, and she wept and wept, suffocated by her weeping.

She walked on and on, weeping and fearful and struggling to

breathe, alone, no companion. She walked on and on, horribly attentive to every crack of a twig. Every noise meant her death, but now, consoling herself, still weeping, at least all would be over when she died, and she would lie here insensible in the shadows. She was sorry for her mother and for friends who might miss her, but really she was companionless, twinless. There was nothing but death, and she'd prefer it here.

A hot wind swept down the road, licked her face.

## VI
## *"It's Always Rewarding to See Unrestored Ruins"*
### *(The Real Guide to Guatemala and Belize 1991)*

MORLEY WALKED ON AND ON, until at last even her weeping was outwalked. She was still alive, and she was still walking, that steady action of the legs. How simple and horrible to be restored to life, still to look again at things with a bit of interest.

She took interest in the shapes of different trees, one in particular, a tall tall tree with great flanged roots angling off. Floating high above the tall, straight, smooth trunk were thick purplish-furry-caterpillarish epiphytes bunched along the leafless branches.

She found herself watching, with interest, the road beneath her feet. The road had been built up. On either side, the ground dipped down. Perhaps this was an ancient causeway, the ancient road to Motul.

The road abruptly left the forest and emptied into a large cornfield. Scattered here and there in the field were low mounds covered with brush and trees. Mounds, not hills—she could see they had a different shape from the hills.

The roar of a vehicle behind her made Morley move to the side of the road. A white pickup truck, the back bristling with shovels and picks, passed her but then pulled over a few yards ahead of her. Should she run? She must be near the site. If she shouted, would someone from the site hear her?

Michael Draw jumped from the cab, work boots, long blue-jeaned legs, white T-shirt, baseball cap. His spectacles glittered.

Present herself.

" 'Come or don't come.' " Morley could even laugh a bit as she sketched a bow.

"That's good." He ducked his head, a bow of sorts in return, then taking off his baseball cap, he put it back on backward so that the bill sloped down over his neck. His entire face, at last exposed, lifted like a kid's and beamed sweet satisfaction. "Hey, I was pretty sure you'd come. Want a tour? Jump on in."

They climbed in the truck, and at once Morley was at home, sitting in the truck with her elbow out the window, driving with someone she knows. Michael Draw counted as her one acquaintance in this part of the world.

The truck followed the road through the field of cornstalks and mounds. Then, rounding a clump of trees, they came upon a busy scene. North Americans and Guatemalans, all in khakis, jeans, bandannas, work boots, or running shoes, bustled about a group of thatched huts. Draw parked the truck, said to Morley, "Wait here a minute." Several people came over to help him unload the shovels and picks. They stared at Morley. She heard Draw tell them, "Going to take my friend here up from Guate for a little tour." He swung himself back into the truck, gunned the engine, and they were off.

Morley apologized. "You know, I don't want to interrupt your work or get you into trouble with your adviser. Are you sure this is all right?"

Draw waved his hand. "I'm in charge. At least I'm in charge of this truck right now. I just tell 'em what I'm going to do and then take off real fast with the truck before they get to thinking whether that'll be what I'm supposed to be doing or not. And anyway, my adviser's not here right now. Of course, even if he were, well, he may not know it, but I'd still be in charge.''

The truck jolted down the road, Draw stopping every once in awhile to edge prettily around the deeper ruts. A strand of tiny colored-glass beads bounced lightly on his T-shirt.

Draw fell back on the site for conversation.

"I'll show you around the mounds we're working on now. What we hope to find out is—our question's this: how did life in the small city of Motul, which'd always lived in the shadow of the big city of Tikal, change when Motul got a little power at the end of the eighth century? Right as Tikal was starting to lose power. Lots of small mounds here got real big then. And all these emblem glyphs from Motul start appearing from seven hundred fifty on, showing up like crazy on stelae and on pots in places like Tikal, like Yaxchilán, all the powerful city-states of the Petén. The theory being that the more the important towns mention you, the more important you are. Of course, that's just the theory. We don't really know for sure.''

Draw took his eyes off the road. He saw Morley listened intently, so he settled back in his seat, started driving with one hand. The other hand came to rest on his thigh.

"We did find some defensive fortifications dating to that period—I might take you out there if we've got some time. It's pretty neat. These fortifications might mean that the little lords of Motul decided they were strong enough to go to war for their own glory, not Tikal's, and expected to get attacked in return. My adviser's making a big deal of this. He thinks this period was all about war, a Maya arms race. His idea is that the expansion of the military drained all the resources of these cities and that's what brought on the famous, mysterious Maya collapse—which some other people think probably was just a transformation, not a collapse. 'Course, there was a collapse of elite stuff, end of big building projects, stuff like that. But the people, the peasants, didn't just disappear. They kept on living here. Maybe they just said, Forget this building and art shit. Not doing us any good.''

Again Draw glanced over at Morley.

Morley nodded. She thought of two short, fat men in twin jaguar suits, monster masks, plumes. Far from home. Homeless. She quickly looked away and out the window.

Up ahead, she saw a long mound, taller than any of the others she had passed, a mound with two wedge-flat towers at either end. Draw pulled over, and they got out. The towers of the mound seemed in good shape. She could see how the stones were fitted together. The base from which they rose, though, was a shapeless mass of stones, partly covered with gray soil and dry brush. A few wiry trees still rose from the slope of the mound.

''They're not clearing this side. Let's go round here.''

They walked to the front of the mound, marked by three staircases, one in front of each tower and one larger staircase in the middle, leading up to the platform between the towers. The brush had been cleared away here. A group of workers, Guatemalan and North American, were sweeping up the dirt. A man trundling a wheelbarrow wound down from the top of the mound.

''You been to Tikal?''

''Yesterday.'' Yesterday seemed a long time ago.

''Then you can tell that this—this is the main mound complex of Motul here—is real different-looking. These twin towers'll not be even half as tall as the main temples of Tikal.''

''I nearly fell off one.'' Morley's tears brimmed again. She really would have died, and so far away from home, and so alone.

''Those stairs *are* kind of scary for us big-foot gringos. Now see, the stairs in front of these towers aren't real stairs, just made to *look like* the stairs at places like Tikal. The temple at the top of each pyramid is not a real temple with a small room or rooms, just a wall of stone with a false door. The crest on top's not really a roof comb, just looks like one. The only functional structure's the little temple between the towers. It has a couple of real rooms and the real staircase leads to it. It's pretty clear the rulers of Motul wanted to use the grand style of the great Tikal but didn't really have the resources—translation: workers—to do it. Instead, they made quick knockoffs of Tikal. This is an important mound, we think, because all of a sudden they tried to make it look important. There's another mound like this up at Río Bec."

Morley smiled. "Motul. Motel. Small and cheap, but with a flashy sign."

"Motel, that's pretty good. I'll have to tell them back at camp. They'll like that." Draw stuck out his right foot and with the toe of his boot began to work at the mound, working away the soil down to the stone. "See here, even the stone they used to face the mound isn't really cut stone. Mostly piled rocks up and plastered them over to give it a surface. And we haven't found much in the way of decoration, stone or stucco, in the rubble of this main mound. Again, maybe that means Motul—motel—wasn't a really rich place, and that's what's interesting."

While Draw was talking, he kept working away at a stone with his foot. "This mound here's my adviser's baby—they're getting it ready for him to come supervise the excavation. Right now, he's off getting himself a Golden Jaguar Award from the Guatemalan government for his contribution to the greater glory of Guatemalan history. He hopes he'll be finding a tomb in here —which he probably will. Temple mounds're almost always burial places." Draw's toe had worked the stone free. He bent down and picked it up. "And he'll be hoping like hell that the tomb's not looted, that the goodies are here—jade, vases and such. If he's lucky, there'll be some good glyphs naming the ruler here."

He turned the stone over and over in his hand. "About fifteen years ago, my adviser wrote that the decipherment of the glyphs would never, never happen, and even if it did, glyphs wouldn't tell us much. Now, he's hot on glyphs because glyphs're the hot thing—glyphers are getting all those genius grants you hear about. It's true that now people're able to read more and more glyphs, and it's pretty clear glyphs can tell us some stuff, all what rulers and nobles wanted to say about how wonderful they were and how everything belonged to them." Draw frowned and tossed the stone away. "But when you get right down to it, glyphs'll not give you the whole picture. They'll not tell you how the people lived. Only good old dirt archaeology tells you that. I hate it when the glyphers act like, Wow, now we'll get real history. As if history only begins with written stuff."

A worker came around the base of the mound, spotted Draw, and waved his machete. *"¡Hola!"*

Draw excused himself for a minute and walked over. Morley looked at the mound, this rock pile rising from the middle of a field. The ruin was about thirty-five feet high. The towers at either end looked about fifteen feet higher. Twin towers.

Draw stumbled back across the stones and weeds. "Let's go." Soon they were bumping along among the mounds again.

"Roberto"—Draw laughed and tapped a tattoo on the steering wheel—"was just telling me how, yesterday, seems like a couple of Guatemalan workers made this figurine out of mud, see, and let it dry in the sun. Then they salted it in one of the sections where the Globetrotters are working."

"Globetrotters?"

"Sounds like a jet-set club for retirees, don't it? But Globetrotters're just these people who pay to come help dig on their vacations, pretty normal people, though you might consider paying nearly two thousand dollars to go work for somebody on your vacation not too normal. Of course it'd be great for my adviser —he makes money, and sometimes the Globetrotters'll be pretty good. In fact, we've got a couple of pretty good amateur archaeologists here right now. Most, though, come here dying to dig up a jade mask or discover a tomb and get bored real fast with real plain old digging, finding nothing, finding potsherds. Then, they get kinda mean. Anyway, so a Globetrotter—a guy who's been specially sarcastic lately—finds this figurine, runs it over to the field supervisor real excited like. The supervisor dates it to around eleven—'B.C. or A.D.?' this Globetrotter asks, his tongue hanging out—'A.M.,' the guy tells him.''

Draw laughed and drove fast, too fast, through the cornfield. Morley held on tight.

At a group of mounds, where two men sat on some stones, whittling rough stakes, Draw parked the truck. "This here'll be my project."

They got out and he introduced her to Francisco and Xavier. "I'm real lucky to have these guys," Draw added. "They worked over at the excavation of Tikal for years. I learn a lot from them. I made sure they'd be working with me—see, I'm in charge, remember?" He recounted to the men, in his soft Kentucky Spanish, almost a murmur, the "discovery" of the figurine. They all laughed. Francisco and Xavier glanced at her several times during the telling of the story. Draw, Morley could tell, liked having them see her with him, standing next to him, watching him perform.

Draw then turned to her. "C'mon." The other two men went to the truck to get out some equipment. Morley and Draw started up the largest mound, picking their way up the rough stony slope.

"We think this is an elite residential compound. Our proposal about Motul says we're supposed to 'excavate a representative sample of residential complexes, from the simplest to the most complex,' so we can see what's been going on for everyone at Motul over the course of about two hundred years. But my adviser knows he's not going to get grants doing low-mound commoner stuff—no goodies, no glyphs—so that's all bullshit. So in addition to his dig at the big mound, he's got me concentrating on what we're pretty sure is an elite structure with, he hopes, some good finds."

The buildings on each side of the little plaza were long and narrow. Three of them were connected to one another at not quite right angles. The other building stood alone. The buildings had been cleared of rubble to reveal the ruined walls.

Draw climbed up a low terrace and Morley followed. "Farmers have never plowed here, too much work for them to clear all the rubble. So nothing's been disturbed really. These buildings were only buried under the plaster and stone of the collapsed roofs and facade—it was literally like peeling off a thin layer to find the stuff underneath pretty well preserved. Turns out when Motul became a big-fish city, the nobles lived in, actually, not much more space than commoners. This house was probably built on top of a rock platform that once supported a hut with a thatched roof like everyone else had. The elites just put in more work on it. The 'energetic differentials'—that's the fancy term for more work, and you can't believe how dumb you feel when you write stuff like that in a report—went up. The building was better built, had a vaulted arch holding up a stone roof, and a painted facade. And the rich guys had bigger benches like these and probably better pots and pans.''

Morley could see the remains of plastered walls, niches set into the walls, and wide benches built out from the back walls. In one room, the floor had been dug down to expose a rough layer of rocks. How simple habitations were really—walls, floor, ceiling, palaces and huts all the same.

Draw pointed over to the separate building. "That may be a shrine or family temple. See, it's got a round altar stone in front of it—which usually comes with a stela, but who knows where that is, some museum, some living room in New York City. We'll excavate to see if there's a burial under the structure, another sign of it being a temple.''

He looked down and pointed out with the toe of his boot a round burn mark on the floor. "They put a brazier here to keep themselves warm.''

Draw talked on, talking, talking, Morley realized, to keep her at Motul. Morley wanted to stay, too, a few hours more, to see as much as possible, to remember it. She interrupted him. "Could I just sit and watch while you work today? I'll stay out of your way."

"Yeah, well, I guess that's all right." Draw relaxed. "That's good. We'll knock off at three, 'cause Francisco and Xavier have to go tend their fields. Then I can find some excuse to drive back to San José and drop you off there."

"I can walk back. I don't want to get you into trouble."

"Remember, I'm in charge. I'll get you back. And you'll not want to walk all the way back again through the jungle. 'Only liars and damn fools say they like the jungle.' Old Sylvanus Morley said that, years ago." Draw laughed. "You a Morley relation? He was one of the big guys in Maya stuff years ago."

Morley said she didn't think so.

Draw hesitated, then he looked at his watch and announced, "Guess it's time to get started."

She sat herself on the terrace of a cleared mound.

Draw set up a tripod and Xavier took a surveying rod and went to stand in front of a terrace. Draw sighted him through the instrument on top of the tripod, then called out to Xavier, who picked up the rod and moved with it quite formally—a king's staff, a priest's stave—from position to position in a pageant of measurement as Draw directed him around that area and another flat area off to the side.

For the next several hours, Morley sat there almost motionless, just watching the men work. She stirred only when Draw walked over to offer her a drink or just to ask, "All right?"

"Fine, just fine." However, Morley had begun to feel very tired. Coming to Motul seemed, at this moment, overwhelming. That so poor a sight, these mounds, this cornfield, could make her feel so much, could so exhaust her.

But there was Michael Draw. She watched him hunch over his notebook as he recorded his information. Later, he knelt down with the other men to hammer in the whittled stakes at the corners of what became two large squares bounded off by a cord wound around the stakes. Sometimes the three men talked and laughed. Sometimes they would be quiet, so quiet.

Draw had a gangling grace, the kind of tallness that can slouch and then stand as straight as the trunk of a palm tree. Yes, that was it—there was something supple like the young palms she had come to know from the bus window. Every once in a while, he looked up from his work and grinned, but almost to himself, and then looked away immediately. He, of course, noticed her watching him, and she didn't mind, for she watched him with, she told herself, nothing but mere appreciation, as if she were enjoying looking at a tree, an upright fine living thing.

Morley also watched the mound being readied for excavation, Draw preparing the surface, taking his time, but getting ready to go in, to lay back the layers, to penetrate, to show what had happened: come look at this.

Quitting time. They piled the survey equipment back into the truck. Draw and Morley got into the cab. Francisco and Xavier climbed in the back—a bang on the roof—ready to go! Draw turned off down a road and about ten minutes later stopped the truck at a village of small huts with children and women sitting in hammocks, chickens scratching around the yards. Francisco and Xavier jumped out, waved to Draw and Morley as the truck turned around.

Back at the camp, Draw and Morley unloaded the equipment. Several North Americans came up to the truck and asked Draw for a ride to the team's house headquarters in San José. Draw introduced them as Globetrotters: there was May, a thin, grizzled woman in her fifties; Ross, about seventeen and barely whiskered; and Glen, Ross's grandfather, short, dapper in a plaid shirt, about sixty, sharp-eyed. Ross and May wanted to rough it in the back of the truck. Glen sat in the cab with Morley and Draw.

Back through the forest, through the shadowy tunnel of trees.

Draw bumped along the streets of San José, dodging dozing dogs, and dropped off Ross and May at a grill gate in front of a small house where the Globetrotters were quartered. Glen went with Draw and Morley on to a bar by the lake. As they walked in, Draw announced, "This here's the bark bar." The walls of the bar, in fact, were just tree trunks lashed together, with the bark left on. Inside the bar, a girl stood behind a counter, leaning over it, and leaning toward her from the other side was Eddie, murmuring—tanner and blonder—his head close to hers. When Draw, Morley, and Glen sat down, the girl primly assumed a businesslike attitude. Glancing over her suitor's shoulder, she called out, "*¿Buenas?*"

"*Tres cervezas por los arqueó-locos,*" Draw called back, and then Eddie looked around at last, the toothy earring swinging back and forth.

"*¡Hola!*" He looked at Morley, puzzled, then recognized her. "Our artist." Since his girl was busy for the moment, he strolled over to talk to Morley. Draw teased Eddie. "Going back to school sometime soon?"

"Nah. I'm in *love.*"

The girl served the beer, smiling at Draw, knowing Eddie watched her; then she resumed her position behind the counter. Eddie drifted back to her and they were again gazing into each other's eyes, murmuring. Draw interrupted once more, asking what time the girl thought the lake taxi would come by. Twenty minutes. Morley bent down to stroke a small gray cat that stretched and stretched out its full short length on the cool cement floor.

Glen asked Draw about when he thought they'd open up the double-tower mound. Glen explained to Morley that his Globetrotter team was there for only two weeks. After that another team would come. Glen wanted desperately to see something big happen at the double-tower pyramid. He had guessed they'd be looking for a tomb there. Draw could only tell him that as far as he knew, his adviser would be coming any day. Then the three of them were silent, sipping their beers. Draw seemed tongue-tied, not knowing what next to say to Morley in front of Glen.

The lake taxi was coming, the girl announced, looking past Eddie's shoulder to the water. Draw walked Morley down to the dock.

Morley thanked Draw for the tour of Motul.

"Oh, that's all right. But you missed seeing the fortifications. If you come back tomorrow afternoon, I'll take you over there."

Morley hesitated, then quickly and coolly said, "I guess I can't see everything. There're too many things to see."

Draw kicked at a rotting piling. "That's true."

The boat pulled up to the dock.

Morley took a step toward the boat, stopped, and turned around. Suddenly, Morley's words began to tumble out so quickly: "Could I work here? I'll work for free." She had to be able to stay. There was no place else to go.

"Work for free?" He paused, as if thinking about it. Now he would make her wait for an answer.

"I mean it, I'll come over here every day—I'll stay in Flores. I'll bring my own lunch."

Draw looked at her. Again, how surprising, odd to be looked at, looked straight at, a curious and direct look. "I guess a Morley's always welcome," Draw quickly, easily said.


## VII
### *Another Digger*

EARLY THE NEXT MORNING, at the market in Flores, Morley bought a straw hat and a cotton scarf, some bread and small cans of fruit juice. She took the boat around the lake to San José, she walked through the jungle again, this time with a quick, determined step. A man on a rusty bicycle with a rusty rifle slung over his shoulder crossed her path. She froze, then nodded, a gesture of sheer bravado. He nodded and disappeared into the forest.

Reaching the camp, she spotted Michael Draw leaning against the truck, talking to several North Americans. Morley lingered near by, and Draw noticed her, yet took his time to finish what he was saying. Then he strolled over and stood quite near her. She felt, rather than saw, the others standing behind him, watching them.

"Are you sure you won't get in trouble? Don't you need to check with someone?" She heard herself treating him like a student.

"You keep forgetting—I'm in charge." He looked down at her and grinned. "I'll say I can use an extra hand at my site. That's true. And I'll get you to do some drawing for me. That'll be real valuable."

Time to go to work. Everyone tied on their bandannas, adjusted their hats—dashing safari hats, droopy canvas hats, battered straw cowboy hats, baseball caps—picked up the handles of the coolers, and began to file down different paths to the different sites. Draw picked up a cooler and arranged it in the back of the truck. "So let's git goin', if we're goin' to go." He laughed. Morley laughed, too. They climbed in the truck. Gears grinding, they were off.

It seemed so natural to be sitting with Draw in the cab. Everything fell so easily into place. In a very short time, the pattern of her days was set. Every morning, she rose early, took the lake taxi to San José, had a cup of coffee at the bark bar, and waited for Eddie to swing by in a van with the Globetrotters. From the camp at Motul, Draw and Morley headed off in the truck to meet Francisco and Xavier at the site.

The four of them worked first on the middens, the garbage dumps at the edge of the interior patio. Inside one of the large squares corded off, Xavier and Draw broke up the top layer of soil with picks and then began the careful centimeter-by-centimeter carving away at the soil with trowels. Draw lent Morley his trowel, such a plain tool, a rounded wooden handle, a diamond-shaped, flat forged-iron blade bent down from an inch-long neck. Odd that this tool made for plastering, for building, had been appropriated for the undoing of buildings, for prying into the crevices of walls, for scraping away floors. Draw's trowel was quite short, worn down by many sharpenings. Two small crosses cut into its handle marked it as his. Xavier showed her how to use the trowel, to scrape at the layer of soil, breaking up clumps of dirt with the trowel's point, to cut through the small roots that still clung to the earth, to keep the vertical wall of the trench a perfect right angle so that the layers of earth were plainly visible.

The other tools were of the plainest sort, too. With small hand brooms, they carefully swept up the scraped soil into pink and yellow plastic dustpans so familiar to her, any housewife's tool. The dustpans were emptied into tin buckets, the buckets hauled over to a rough box fitted with a wire screen, the box set up on a waist-high rack of four wooden stakes shaped by machete. Francisco and Morley would pull the box back and forth over two roller stakes, the sieved soil sifting down onto a fine hill of gray dirt, the clumps left in the screen broken up by hand, sorted through. Morley would hold up a small find to Francisco and ask *"¿Sí o no?"* Yes or no, something or nothing, sometimes *sí,* a fragment of a pot, or a flake of obsidian, a small animal bone, which they would put into the small muslin bag that hung on the rack and was marked with the date and the identifying numbers of the site. Often *no,* just a rock or piece of root, a piece of— Draw laughed—*"leaverite*—leave 'er right there!"* to toss over her shoulder. Once the clumps had been picked over, they lifted the screen, and, *"¡Uno, dos, tres!"* dumped what was left on the heap of dirt next to the rack. At the end of each level of ten centimeters, Draw tied off the lumpy muslin bag, recorded it in his notebook, filled out a printed card, and hung up another clean, limp bag.

The sun came up hot, the hours passed by slowly, and the work was hard and monotonous, much of it spent on her knees in the dirt at the side of or in the trench. Yet the tedium of the work proved to be of the greatest solace to Morley. She didn't have to think about a thing, just keep a sharp eye out for a potsherd, a chunk of a grinding stone, a change in the color of the dirt as she scraped away at it, a change that might indicate some change in the way this bit of ground was used hundreds and hundreds of years ago.

Beyond that, Morley didn't have to think about where to go next, what to do next. There was no place else to go. Had she ever been anywhere else, done anything else?

Deeply comforting, too, the polite but quite intimate feel of working with the men on the mound, everyone working in the same rhythm. Right away, she learned when to lift the screen, when to pick up the pail, without a word being said. Sometimes they did talk. As Draw told her, ''There're two modes of diggin' —finding stuff or not finding stuff, and the second's kind of fun, 'cause you can just talk.'' Francisco, Xavier, and Draw talked about other seasons, other digs, *el norte,* the weather, made fun of the Globetrotters.

At noon, Draw and Morley ate their sandwiches. Francisco and Xavier's children would show up with their food wrapped in a cloth or tucked in a basket. The small boys and girls sat next to their fathers at lunch, eating a piece of the melon Draw always brought for everyone and watching him try to coax tarantulas out of their holes in the bank of the mound with some cheese tied to a string. When work started again, the kids headed off through the field, dawdling along, busily talking to one another, some-times stopping by the side of the road, looking for tarantula holes, poking at them with twigs.

At three, the field day was over. They stowed the tools in the truck. Francisco and Xavier were dropped off at their village.

In the late afternoon, back at camp, Draw and Morley worked in the lab. Draw showed Morley how to wash the finds, set them out to dry, and, when dry, sort and number them. He painted on them a small stroke of white paint—he used the small bottle of paint made for correcting typographical mistakes—and, when the white paint dried, wrote the lot numbers of the project on them in black ink. Tiny letters and tiny numbers on tiny sherds. When the ink dried, he coated the label with a brush of clear fingernail polish. The finds were cataloged and bundled back into clean bags, tagged, and stored in a box until Draw was ready to start sifting through all this evidence, to see what it could tell him.

The two of them sat on high stools at the lab table, a large piece of plywood on two sawhorses. Morley hunched over the potsherds with the silly fingernail-polish brush in her hand. Draw sat in front of a pile of his notebooks and drew maps of the site. Glen sometimes came to work with them, but he never did very much work, just watched them curiously with his pale blue eyes ringed with creases.

Morley knew Glen was watching them, but she didn't mind. In fact, she liked that Glen came around to the lab to be with them; it made her feel even closer to Draw to be seen together by someone else as she sat with Draw. Every day she came more and more to enjoy sitting side by side with Draw, right next to him, listening to him talk about the jungle of eastern Honduras, where he'd really like to be digging, where you have to go in by mule and camp out. About how he couldn't wait to finish graduate school and run his own dig down there. About his ''arrogant as heck'' grandfather, part Cherokee, part Appalachian miner and labor activist, about his father, a farmer and a civil rights lawyer. ''You can't imagine how hard it is coming from impressive folks,'' he confessed. ''You just want to be impressive yourself, but you're afraid you're not and never will be.'' He talked about his pretty, sweet sister, how pretty Kentucky was, about friends of his from high school and the things they did—at twenty-three, high school was still an important subject for him, for him to talk about to her, to show himself to her.

Morley felt a queer physical relief sitting there listening to him talk and talk, the plainest, simplest talk. She had to catch herself as she started to lean toward him, as if she would lean against him. Their companionship became—Morley was surprised at the word that came to her—exquisite, exquisite because solitary, mutual delight, unexpressed, almost unacknowledged.

In the camp, at first, Morley effaced herself, still worried that Draw might be reprimanded for her presence and that she would be asked to leave. She did not talk much, hanging back when the others had coffee together in the morning, she scrupulously brought her own lunch from Flores. The Globetrotters, except for Glen, did do some mumbling about her, Draw told her. They complained that she had not paid for the privilege of working like they had. However, once they realized that she stayed in a hotel at Flores, and Draw exaggerated its expense, they were satisfied. Working at the dig cost her something, and, too, she had to remain an outsider by not living close to the site.

With the rest of the dig team, Morley found an easy acceptance. They saw her as a digger, that peculiar subspecies of archaeological sites, neither local worker nor archaeologist, itinerant, weathered, wearing jeans with big holes and shoes flapping their soles, who fell in love with sites, fell out of love, moved in, moved on, sharing a quality with the work of movers, fruit pickers, waitresses, people who don't often last on a job, but each day of their body's labor is accepted and used up. Diggers were twenty going on thirty, looking forty, fifty. They had come down a year, two years before, during a summer, or had taken off a year from college, like Eddie, or strayed from a vacation, come to dig for fun or just happened to fall onto a dig, and never left. When one dig closed, they migrated to another, for a place to sling their hammocks. They kept the winter digs going when the student workers had to go back to their studies. Their knees hurt from kneeling in the damp year-round. Their wrists were sore from the repetitive scraping of the walls of a trench. They smoked and coughed. They drank *guaro,* the local rum, and the next day were white under their bronze skin, eyes veined with pink. They never seemed to eat, were thin and yet tensile as steel rods. Always on the verge of quitting, the next day, or the day after next, the end of this dig, they told Morley over drinks at the bark bar, yeah, there was a much bigger dig across the border in Belize and there was reggae in Belize, too, want to be a part of that.

Every evening, Morley returned to Flores and swam in the lake. Sometimes she met the tourists passing through. Simple tourists who came to climb Tikal's pyramids or buzz the ruins in light aircraft, despite the guidebook's terse warning: "Often crash." Questing tourists who came on pilgrimages to Tikal, the center of the ancient Maya world, the Jerusalem of the holistic world order, the hemispheric alternative to Western civilization.

Bill, the tattooist from Virginia, showed Morley his book on ancient Maya practices of tattooing, scarification, ritual bloodletting, illustrated by sculpture, ceramics, and photographs of the author's attempts to link his own body with that tradition. "Look." Bill rolled up his sleeve to show Morley the huge tattoo running down his arm of a jaguar polka-dotted with round black spots, red tongue lolling.

Morley liked best the specialist tourists who came to visit Tikal as a side trip from the job they were doing in Central America. Ethnobotanists sent by large pharmaceutical companies to look for new drugs in the rain forest, and folk-art entrepreneurs like the man buying up masks and baskets for his store in Santa Fé: Jackalope—Folk Art by the Truckload. These tourists, like the archaeologists, had an advantage over the other tourists: their absorption in their work down here required a monastic-military discipline that physically involved them in organizing teams of workers, locating provisions, getting trucks fixed, relentlessly repetitive tasks that bound them that much more to the region. Morley noted particularly that, even while in Guatemala, they schemed about how and when they could come back to Guatemala—she pictured them as a crowd of Persephones doomed to spend part of their year up in the hellish north, in academic meetings, bright offices, or malls, until at last they could return here, put on their work clothes, be transformed once more into their real selves by the smell of wood smoke and by the task.

Some of these tourists, though, seemed so fragile and exhausted. She met a team, "Young Christian Doctors," who ran a clinic for the thousands of scavengers living on Guatemala City's garbage dump. And a team of forensic anthropologists who worked in mass cemeteries all over the country with shovels and trowels and tweezers, exhuming the bodies of teachers, students, labor leaders, and peasants "disappeared" by the Guatemalan security forces, while relatives waited behind a rope, clutching photographs and dental records in gray folders.

Morley examined herself. She had been somewhat of a questing tourist, but she was now more of a specialist tourist as she scrabbled at the dusty earth, sifting it, thinking of nothing but dirt, potsherds, and broken metates, letting the digging, the screening, the cataloging do her thinking for her. On some days, though, she felt most like the exhausted tourists, one of their world, digging, digging down, among, and for the bones.

Thus Morley's routine: an early breakfast, the lake taxi, the ride into the jungle, work, the taxi back, a swim, dinner with other tourists. Then, dead tired, she passed over into sleep.

By mid-April, the two middens at Draw's mound were excavated.

The first midden yielded three intact pots—a small bowl and two plates, very plain, everyday ware—thousands of pieces of broken pots, broken stone metates for grinding corn, splinters of animal bone.

"So we know people ate here." Draw would say that much.

There were fragments of pots that had been plastered and painted with figures in several colors. Draw picked up and held out a shiny cream-colored sherd of fine-grained clay with a brown hand and a black plume painted on it. "Look, this kind of pot here—like your Pink Glyphs vase at the Popol-Vuh"—Morley wondered if a bit of jaguar-suited thigh might pass through her hands—"almost never turns up in commoner middens. It's elite ware, so we just might have an elite residence mound. And they're showing up at the latest phase of the mound. Right when we think Motul's going big-time."

Like the first, the second midden was full of potsherds, but there were, strangely, no grinding stones, no bones. Instead, they turned up lumps of earth different from the dirt around it. Rubbing a bit of one of these lumps between his fingers, Draw said, "See how it's clumpy? How it's lighter-colored than the other dirt? Feel how it's grittier? Maybe pottery clay mixed with something to make it stronger." With the tip of his trowel, Draw also pointed out traces of color in the dirt of the midden, iron red and charcoal black, white lime, a bit of powdery blue. "Maybe pigments. The blue'll be attagulpite blue, Maya blue. Though that's kind of rare in the Petén."

He sat back on his heels. "You know what? We just might be looking at the site of a pottery and painting workshop here, attached to an elite residence—we're pretty sure elites were the scribes, the painters. But—we'll not know anything about the midden, anything for sure, 'til we get back to the States and then try to sort it all out."

Morley almost smiled. Michael Draw's caution revealed a habit of precision—and an excitement that was difficult to suppress.

Only that day, at lunch, did Draw allow himself to express a certain satisfaction with the find. He told Morley, "It's so important to look at dirt. You know, it's always been easy to go in a tomb and walk out with jade necklaces and pretty pots. But looking at dirt tells you so much, about everybody, even the poorest people. A posthole and packed dirt tells you there was some sort of shelter here, a scorched area that they did their cooking here. Believe me, you cannot believe all the things people do to dirt. I love dirt. You can dig down in the dirt anywhere in the world and find out what's been happening for thousands of years. You just have to be real careful, so you don't skip a century or two.''

The last week of April, Draw decided he'd better hurry up and go to work on the structure he thought might be a temple, ''To see what's there, if anything.'' When the rains started in late May, most digging would become impossible.

First, Draw looked under the altar stone. The rounded stone had tracings of glyphs on its face, but glyphs too worn by rain and scaled by the fires farmers set to clear the fields. Draw wanted to see if there were glyphs on the other side and if a cached offering had been buried underneath the stone. He and Xavier cut down two young trees, stripped them of their branches, and, wedging them up under the stone, they pushed and pushed, raising the stone enough for Morley and Francisco to hitch a rope around it. Then Draw and Xavier levering the stone up, Morley and Francisco pulling on the rope, the stone teetered and fell over. Everyone crouched down to look at it. Draw carefully swept away the soil, the roots that clung to it like tiny webby veins, the ants legging it, and there was the stone face. A blank stone face, no glyphs. They spent the rest of the day digging several holes in the ground uncovered by the altar and the area around it. Nothing. Draw looked down at the altar and laughed. ''You find stuff and you don't find stuff.''

That afternoon, in the lab, Draw teased Morley, asking her if she wasn't tired of digging, tired of not finding a jade necklace. Wouldn't she really rather go down to Antigua? ''See the pretty streets, the pretty houses. It's all real pretty, they say, shouldn't be missed.''

Morley shook her head. No, she was happy to keep digging.

The next morning, Draw marked out a two-by-two-meter square on top of the platform. They began to excavate, going down ten centimeters at a time, hauling the dirt, the platform rocks, the fill away, screening it. Then there was nothing but dirt, just dirt.

Draw now knew something about the different phases of the mound. However, he didn't know yet if the structure was a temple, if there was a burial, "with goodies." Extending the trench toward the stairs, again they went down. At the upper end of the trench, the one closest to the stairs, about five feet down, Draw found something.

He motioned to Morley to come down into the trench with him. "Notice how it's kind of crumbly all the way down." He poked the soil with his trowel; it loosened and spilled. "But looky here, in the corner. Somebody packed this down." Extending the trench once more, they went straight down, until they had uncovered a large area of the packed dirt. Morley, sitting by the trench, waiting for a bucket to be handed up, heard a sound unlike the dry scraping sound the trowel usually made. This was more like a tap. She hadn't realized she was listening at all.

Draw probed the soil carefully now with the tip of the trowel. The top of a large, flat stone appeared. Draw found the edge of the stone and delicately followed its outline. Scraping away the dirt from around the stone, he finally uncovered the walls of small rocks on which the large, flat stone rested.

"Maybe a cache for offerings. *Maybe.*"

All work stopped. Draw photographed the find, plotted it on a grid map, took the elevation with the surveying equipment. Only then was the flat stone lifted, revealing the large broken pieces of some ceramic object, pieces painted red, pink, blue, black, and white—but not a pot, even Morley could tell that. This had sharply curved-in pieces with white knobs on them.

looked at the beads, looked at the smashed pots, looked at the bones lying there so fragile, dust-colored, porous like coral. For a long while, Morley and Draw were as silent as the bones.

Something occurred to Morley. "I have a question for you. Is that all right?"

"Sure, that's all right."

"Does it ever bother you to find skeletons?"

Draw kept on brushing at the bones. "You kinda get used to it. Anybody who's ever lived on a farm like me, done some plowing, has seen lots of bones turned up, bones from some old, forgotten graves. But then the bones're all jumbled up in the dirt, and the skull's crushed, so it'll not look too human."

Then Draw stopped for a moment and swiveled up his head at her. "What's weird sometimes is when you find a real tomb like this, the bones all laid out in a room. You clean up the skeleton and there it is staring at you. Depends on your mood, though, I guess. You want to know what I mostly say to myself when I discover a body? I say, Shit, oh shit. 'Cause now I got to do something with that body." Draw waved his brush in the air. "All I really want to know is that there is a burial at the site with good or not-so-good grave goods. That tells me something about the site. But then I've got to photograph the body, map it, clean it off, get out all the bones, do something with them. Shit, oh shit, is what I say."

He laughed and went back to work brushing, brushing. "Sometimes, though, people sure do need those bodies. I've got a friend, she was supposed to be doing a body count, 'population study,' as we say, at Yaxchilán. That's west of here. She could only find three bodies. I mean, she was pretty upset. She had this grant for a year, and after nine months she still didn't really have shit. I offered to lend her ten bodies from this site I was working in Roatán. She'd have to come get them herself, though."

Morley tried to think of herself and the skeletons as fellow loungers. She was lying here, all stretched out, and the skeletons were lying there extended on their backs, all of them lounging around while Draw worked. But that would not be for long. She'd have to go home eventually, and even sooner the bones would be bundled up, then later, perhaps, put behind glass, on view as at some sideshow, even though the sideshow was called a museum.

Yet, maybe, at least, one could say that the work of archaeologists was orderly, not a wild scattering about of bones, but in fact a reassembling of them, that these dry bones lived again in the museum, refleshed with knowledge. At least identified as either male or female bones. If female, perhaps she had borne children; there is a certain groove, a small shallow trench in a pelvic bone, that shows the woman has given birth. The age of the bones, twenty, or sixty, or Morley's age. The condition of the bones, broken bones or a withered arm. No signs of arthritis meant the person probably didn't ever have to work too hard. Bad teeth meant malnutrition. Behind glass, in a diorama in a museum, these bones might live again adorned in jewelry and surrounded once more by the grave goods stacked around them. Perhaps a glyph even named the bones. The sacrificed child's bones would be reclothed by the visitor's horror and pity—the visitor readily brooding over these small, inglorious bones.

So these bones lived again?

Morley looked out of the trench and across the mound. Right now, in Motul, she herself lay in total ruin. The mounds had been ruined already, and the excavation ruined them even more, by opening up the mounds, making them disgorge their past into heaps of exposed earth. It was a terrific scene for Morley. She had a painful sense of her own joints pulled apart, the bones broken, to be reset, restored, of course, but not yet, not yet. This state of unrestoration, of disarticulation, was horribly thrilling. And, necessary: it seemed to her that this morphology of dismemberment, disarticulation, had to be exposed, so that it could be learned from. Before the bonesetter could start to work.

There was still the steady brush, brush of Draw's work.

Morley had the muslin sacks ready when Draw finally said he was going to start handing the fragments of pottery out. He picked them up one by one, pieces of orange pots, black pots, no creamy white pot, a hundred pieces of pots, handed up to her. Then, as she was tying off a bag, she heard Draw whistle. She looked over the edge of the trench and down, but Draw was crouched, with his back to her. She couldn't see what he saw. "Jesus!" Draw paused, took a breath, then turned to look up at Morley. "Looks like there's a couple of intact pots here, underneath all that crap. Just like they were made yesterday. I can't believe it, they're perfect—well, as far as I can tell, I hope. Here, get ready."

Morley seemed to stir in herself. What if one of these vases down among the bones were one of the Master vases, the Master of the Pink Glyphs, with the two portly jaguar men dancing again, jaguar tails dancing up, dangling down? Morley felt more alert than in weeks. These few weeks had all been a rest, a settling in. Now she would return to attention. She saw her search had become vertical. She didn't have to move horizontally from place to place over the face of the earth. She could concentrate her motion here, go down, go down.

The first pots were two small bowls, slipped in reddish orange, but without decoration. There was a vase, in several pieces, with a band of red horseshoelike decoration repeated over and over near the rim.

"I saved the best stuff 'til last." He handed her up, one after another, three small barrel-shaped pieces, the plainest kind of cup, no decoration at all, but inside were chunks of rose-red chalky-looking material. "It's red paint, some kind of cinnabar or hematite. And look at this." Up came a bowl, wide, rather deep, with the sides flared out, several bands of red and black on a buff background. In the center of the bowl, the head, in profile, of a man, with some sort of monkey-head helmet perched on top of his head. From the mouth of the monkey stuck out two long stalks. "Maybe those long sticks are brushes? Monkey gods were scribe gods. So maybe we're in a scribe's tomb, a painter's tomb. Here's his paint. Here's his portrait or some scribe's portrait, maybe. Too bad, no glyphs on the plate."

Yes, the paint the same pinkish red color. Yes, maybe the same hand drew these fine lines and brushed in this rosy wash, the Master's hand. But Morley was surprised to find herself violently, so violently disappointed. Here maybe was the Master's hand, the Master's pink tints. But where were his two fat men in spotted suits?

She tried to make herself sound excited. "Well, this makes sense, doesn't it, what with the pottery workshop, the bits of paint. So we must have found an artist's compound."

Draw laughed. Then Morley started to laugh, and they both said at the same time, "But that's just what *we* think."

By evening, the contents of the cache and the tomb were all safely stowed away on racks in the camp's field lab.

The lab was now to be her home. Draw decided that Xavier and Francisco would finish up the few things left to do at the site before the rains came. Draw had to record all the information he could, as completely as possible, on the pots, the skeletons, the beads, the thousands of potsherds, bits of obsidian, the fragments of animal bone, grinding stones, lumps of clay, chunks of pigment, because none of it could be taken out of the country. At the end of the season, it all had to be sent to Guatemala City. "At the Institute, all these little bags here'll be piled up in some old room with a leaky roof." He would have only his notes and a few samples to work on back at school. And Morley's drawings of the major finds.

"Wait a minute." Morley looked up from the crate in which she was packing the muslin bags of sherds from the first midden. "If you can't take the finds out of the country, how could I have done any drawing for you back in the States?"

Draw didn't take his eyes off his notebook. "Well, I had to get your address, didn't I?"

At this time, the team of Globetrotters left. Glen was very disappointed to miss the excavation of the twin-towered mound, although he, along with the other Globetrotters, had hurried out to Draw's mound to look at the tomb when word spread of what they had found. After the Globetrotters had gone, Draw offered Morley a bed in one of the camp's thatched huts. When the next Globetrotters team arrived, they would take for granted that she was just part of the dig.

Morley gratefully accepted. She was almost broke. Checking out of the hotel in Flores, she moved into a hut with Suzanne— like Draw, another graduate student at the dig. Draw sat on Suzanne's bed and talked to Morley while she unpacked her bag. He watched her stack on the rough shelf a dress, three blouses, two skirts. "Not a whole lot of digging clothes there. And I've been kind of wondering how you work in those city shoes."

Morley placed the muddy and cracked leather shoes underneath her bed, a white canvas field cot held up by crossed wooden lathes. "My jeans are still in good shape, but pretty dirty," and she hung them on a nail pounded into a post.

That afternoon, Draw showed up with a pile of clothes and shoes the Globetrotters had left behind for the Guatemalan workers. Morley appeared the next day in a pair of old but clean jeans, a man's shirt she recognized as Glen's, running shoes with a hole in the left toe, perfect for her—she laughed and held up her left foot—"It's always been longer than my right foot." She still wore the straw hat she had bought earlier, its crown now crushed, the brim unraveling.

Draw squinted at her. "When I first met you, you were so pretty. So pretty, just a little while ago. You wore pretty red lipstick, nice swingy earrings, and a pretty little watch. And now —just look at yourself."

Morley looked down at her hands stripped of her rings, so

rough and dry, her fingernails broken. Her rolled-up sleeves showed two scratched brown arms. She peered into the truck's side-view mirror. With her hair pulled back under the hat, it wasn't clear whether she was a man or a woman. Eddie's older brother or older sister.

Draw sighed loudly. "You were so pretty, just a little while ago. Now you're a digger. A real digger."

## VIII
## *Pay Dirt!*

MORLEY SEEMED TO FORGET HER DISAPPOINTMENT with the vase from the tomb and subsided into the old peaceful feeling of work.

The big finds, the broken piece from the cache and several vessels from the tomb, were to be paid special attention. Together, Draw and Morley pieced together the cache fragments. They tried the bigger pieces of the same color together, tried to match their edges, a line of the design. Draw glued the matching pieces together with rubber cement and rested them in a basin of sand for support while they dried.

Slowly, the object took shape, fragment by fragment. From their hands, a large painted ceramic conch shell was reborn, complete with the knobby points of a conch shell's crown, the flaring lip at the base of the shell. The shell was about eight inches long and wonderfully curved around a rich empty space. The outer surface was painted red, with the knobs in white, and the lower half of the shell divided into two pink sections with bands of black and blue paint, each section framing what looked like a human profile, but the paint here was flaked off. At the top point of the shell was a hole with a small lip. Probably a mouthpiece— the shell might be a trumpet of sorts.

When the glue was dry, Morley told Draw to try blowing on the shell. "I did play trombone once, and pretty good, too," Draw boasted. He put his lips to the hole and blew. A low, hollow roar sounded in the lab. Morley shivered. It was like a summons. She made Draw do it again and again. "Just one more time!"

Next, Draw and Morley put together several broken pots from the tomb. There was a large vase with glyphs faintly incised into the clay—"Maybe a glypher can get some reading off this," Draw said—and two small wide-lipped bowls. Morley liked handling the pottery more than she could ever say to anyone. After looking for so long at pots behind museum glass, here in the lab she could hold them, cup them in her hands—she discovered they were made for the hand as well as the eye. The bowls were lighter than she had thought they would be, sturdy but light. What had given her the idea they would be so heavy, weighting down her hand? The surface was slick except for a fine grain in the slip.

Draw took photographs of these finds and the intact pots. However, he still wanted Morley to draw them for him. He found for her a manual on archaeological drawing but insisted that she should also simply draw the pieces, as she had the vase at the Popol-Vuh. "Especially the 'we think scribal-painter pots'— that'll be the direction of my report now."

They unwrapped and ate their sandwiches. When he finished, Draw balled up the wax paper and shot it into the wastebasket. He turned to Morley with a big smile. "Just think! There you were drawing in Guate and now you're here!"

After lunch, Morley began drawing. The camp was quiet, everyone asleep in their hammocks or off at the bark bar. Because the lab housed valuable finds, it had to be watched during the day, and Draw slept there at night on a folding cot. The lab felt like a fortress, both a threatened and a protected place.

Morley sat at one end of the table, drawing the pots, and Draw sat at the other, drawing a detailed plan of the site and writing up the notes he had taken.

For practice, Morley drew the plainest piece first. The small bowl with flaring sides had been finished in a solid reddish brown slip. She measured the bowl with instruments Draw had given her, several pairs of calipers and a funny comb whose many teeth could be retracted to capture the profile of the vessel's rim and body. As the manual advised, she drew the bowl's profile and the bowl in cross section. The technical drawing never, though, made her feel she knew the bowl.

Yet when Morley drew the bowl in her own way, even this plain piece lived for her. Placing the small bowl in the light from the window, a light she thought would hold for an hour or two, Morley looked at the bowl for a long moment. She decided to use stippling for the bowl, the accumulation of tiny dots made by holding the pen straight down. The edges of the bowl, where someone else would have drawn a line, an outline, would be rendered by massing dots to make a surface as textured, as gritty as the surface of the bowl. To place each dot, she had to look at the piece for indentations in the surface, a slight rise or hollow, the slight swelling on the right-hand side of the lip. She came to know the bowl's surface grain by grain.

Next, Morley turned her attention to the deep, wide bowl painted with the head of a scribe—"But we don't really know that," Morley sang to herself. Again she drew the vessel's profile and a cross section. Even these tasks became pleasurable in their own way, like the restless movements one makes before settling into work, shuffling around the room, sitting and standing, arranging things, these rituals that invoke the god.

Setting the bowl up on a low box so that she was looking directly at its side, Morley began to draw again, to draw the vase as she saw it. Although this was a finer piece, the red surface much smoother, the slip silkier, still the stippling was able to give its human shape, the small wobbles of the rim, the very slightly uneven flare of its sides, the slightly rolled lip. Only as she set the pot up on its rim so she could be face-to-face with the profiled head at the bottom of the bowl did Morley see a problem.

It seemed so wrong to stipple in the wide bands of red and black painted around the rim, and even more the lines of the profile head. Yet drawing the bands and the head carefully with strokes of her pen would not be right, either. Morley knew sharply the difference a brush would make, the brush stroke bold, quick, full, and where the red color was washed in, the brush could give that watercolor effect, lighter, darker clouds of color. She drew the bowl and the head as best she could with her pens, yet it was wrong, wrong. She couldn't render the living sense of the object, in fact, its most purely technical sense.

Never had Morley been so fussy about drawing. She begged a dig member running errands in Guatemala City to stop by an art store and pick up several brushes. He found some cheap brushes in a Chinese store. But good brushes, thick hair bound in bamboo.

She simply weighed them in her hand at first. Morley remembered the sketch she had made in the small museum at Tikal, of the incised drawing of a hand holding a brush, the hand emerging from the wide-open jaws of a serpent. Studying the sketch, she practiced holding the brush exactly the same way, between her thumb and forefinger. In the camp's small library, she searched for pictures of Maya scribes at work and pored over them. In one vase painting, a rabbit scribe in his crisp kilt of white sits with his legs crossed, bent over his book, a book of accordion-pleated paper bound in jaguar fur. The rabbit scribe scribbles furiously, while the old God of Death on the dais above him is entertained by young women, one of whom taps the foot of her friend and draws her attention to the event going on to their right: a young man is being decapitated. The rabbit scribe records that event. The rabbit scribe is bent over in terrific energy—he himself must have been painted so quickly.

In another vase scene, a scene curiously compressed by thick bands of black at the rim and at the base to show off the only figure, a man this time, the scribe is again seated cross-legged. He leans way over, his full, muscular arm held straight out. His right hand holds the brush straight down, its tip painting a vase held up by his left hand. The painter's eyes are fiercely concentrated, again the figure's energy so obviously underlined.

Cross-legged on the floor of the lab, Morley bent over her sketch pad, her brush held straight up in her hand. She practiced her brush strokes by drawing again and again the head on the vessel from the tomb, building up the strength in her hand, the steadiness to make the quick lines. To load up the brush with ink and run a line all the way around the outline of a figure, as the ancients did, all the way to the whiplash end stroke.

On the shelf above her head, the bones of the sacrificed child.

And the bones of the scribe, if he was the scribe, the painter. He who held his brush like this, he who dabbed at the red chunk of pigment, filled up the brush, and banded the plate, who dabbed black paint into pretty rosettes on the jaguar suits, who drew fat fierce-eyed jaguar men, Cacique and Priest, almost twins, staring at each other. Morley held her brush like him, imitated his stroke. However, his portrait did not fascinate her. That was only his singularity, only himself, by himself, like herself. What he had noted, had drawn, had put down on the wall of a vase, perhaps vases, turning each one slowly as he painted each figure in its place, the figures staring at each other, almost alike, almost twins —that was what Morley thought about, thought about all the time.

The more she looked at the scribe's portrait, the less she was convinced the Master had painted it. The Master who painted those fat jaguars would never have painted his own portrait or the portrait of another scribe. Only the twins interested him, their petty power—no, that power of a shared look.

And always above her, the bones of the child.

Draw spent all his time in the lab now, too. He, too, was absorbed, absorbed by the careful account of his work. Morley liked him sitting there, several feet away, so self-effacing in his concentration, facilitating her own concentration. So comforting to work in the presence of another—she was alone and yet not alone. Then she began to feel Draw watching her as she drew, especially as she began to work with the brush. Then Draw was pushing at the edges of her attention, pushing into its circle, coming into that quiet, that single-mindedness.

So surely did she feel Draw coming closer, closer, all this time she had been waiting for him to come closer, she was not really surprised at all when one night, as they walked back to the lab after dinner, Draw took her by the arm and drew her off into the darker shadows and began ever so lightly to kiss her. Still, it's always a surprise when someone dares to touch you, though you know it's inevitable, but nothing had happened before and now something startling has happened. He grasped her around the waist, moved his hands up her back to hold her shoulder blades, and pressed her to him, murmuring, "When I first saw you, I thought you were so pretty. I looked at your lips and thought how pretty they were. What would it be like to kiss them?"

Surprising, too, to Morley, incredible, it seemed, to be touched by another man. Caught off guard by that, she watched herself deliver herself into his hands, curious purely curious about what would happen, even though there was no doubt about what would happen. She began to touch him, too, curious about this young body, so pliant, and smooth, wonderfully shaped to her hands, falling into her hands, so that after a while it was not clear who had started this, him unbuttoning her shirt and holding her breasts in his hands, she unbuttoning his shirt, spreading her palms over his chest to span it. In the lab, they took off the rest of their clothes, and they carefully balanced themselves on Draw's clumsy cot, and they made love.

Morley wondered, So this, then, was what it was like to be

touched again? To touch again? So this, then, was a man's body again—she had forgotten that it could be so smooth. This, then, was what it was like to open yourself up and be penetrated, give yourself up to that. This is how you crumple up toward a man, and this is how you straighten out, become yourself again. This, then, was what it was like to make love again, but without being in love. Morley knew instantly it wasn't that kind of making love. This was without fear. There was no terror, no terrible delight, just affection and curiously curiosity, as if she had come back from the dead and suddenly remembered, Oh yes, this is how it was. Really, she had forgotten so much.

From then on, Morley and Draw worked together, as before, in the lab in almost complete silence, each absorbed in her, his task. They ate with the others, went out with the others to the bark bar in San José. Later in the evening, though, with hardly a look or a word exchanged between them, they drifted away and took off in the truck. Draw drove fast through the night, along rutted roads to the ancient fortifications. They walked along the high embankment built up over a deep, dry moat. Draw laughed. "We'll just say we're doing 'pedestrian reconnaissance,' if anybody asks." They sat up there in the moonlight, listening to the howls of animals, the monkeys and birds from the forest, the donkeys and dogs and roosters from the scattered hamlets, howling in a huge chorus of hellish suffering. Morley had never heard anything so loud and wild and infernal, all the wild sorrow in the world welling up in one roar.

"Animals," Draw said, "at least farm animals, I know, have got a lot to be sad about."

Sometimes they made love there in the stubble, paying for it with scraped backs and elbows and knees. Or they returned to the lab and made love.

Morley came to know his body very well. It was as if when she grasped him, she was conducting an anatomy lesson for herself, and he offered himself up to her hands. This particular muscle a thick rope across the hip joint, the arm muscle lying just under the flesh and wound round to the elbow (Draw informed her, "That muscle's from lifting weights. I know all you girls like that, don't you?" and Morley almost died laughing), the leg muscles tied to the knee, fastened neatly off there, the thick cords at the back of the neck, so taut under her flexed palm, the little bead necklace resting so lightly on the neck. The body was a history lesson, too. She touched the scar that split his eyebrow in two, the thick, long red scars on the side of his chest from an operation for a collapsed lung, a long silver scar on his belly from an appendicitis operation, a twisted dark scar almost a hole near his groin from the emergency operation for the subsequent infection. There were the scars from this accident on a bicycle, that on a tractor. Even a young body bore the traces of a history, the history of near escapes from death.

Someone so young. Morley did not think of herself as old, but here he was at least fifteen years younger than she. What did he want with her? She didn't imagine that he believed himself to be in love with her. Did he want to be her age, in some fashion, know something she knew, be allowed to skip those years between them? Morley noted that, as for herself, she held his youth in her hands, but never with any sense of thereby acquiring youth, again, for herself. It struck Morley immediately and with great clarity that youth was not transferrable, even though she could see how a person might fool herself about that. His youth would not save her from becoming older and older, from moving toward death. This thought made her that much more appreciative, even cherishing of him, as he lay next to her.

But, again, Morley knew that her feeling for Draw was never love. Or if it was, this was a sublunary love, nothing like what she knew to be love, love that miraculously welled up from nothing, brimmed brimmed, spilled over, flooded all the world, all the spheres above, the traces of its disaster ineffaceable. Morley knew this with hardly having to think about it.

These were idyllic days and days. Morley could be content for the moment. This, too, was the world. There must be times like this in it, too. Or, maybe the rest of her life would be like this, she said to herself, and it would not be tragic, or only a little bit tragic, as if life were over and still, somehow, went on and on. Yet if this were the afterlife, or some sort of limbo, it was a very pleasant, peaceful postlife.

One afternoon, Morley was working in the lab when she heard, faintly, a *whop whop whop,* then louder and louder, *whop whop whop.* She went outside. Everyone had risen from their hammocks, from their improvised desks and come outside to look up at the sky, hands shading their eyes. A couple of helicopters advanced toward the camp. In a big rush of noise and wind and dust, they landed, two army helicopters green and brown with camouflage paint. Four men and a woman, all in khaki and sunglasses, climbed out of the choppers.

Casque, the "principal investigator" of the site, Draw's adviser, had finally arrived.

"Here we go," Draw said, and walked over to talk to a short man, a plump man, with curly, longish red hair, bushy red mustache, dressed in khaki adventure style—the shirt with flapped and buttoned pockets and the pants with flapped and buttoned pockets in the back, at the waist, on the lower thighs.

Afraid of being dismissed, Morley immediately retired to the lab to keep out of sight. An hour later, Draw came to report. Casque had arrived covered in glory and laden with spoils. He had received his Golden Jaguar Award from the Guatemalan government; the helicopter ride was courtesy of the Guatemalan army. "Guatemalan colonels like ancient dead Mayas. Hate the living ones," Draw noted. And Casque had also been awarded, unexpectedly, a grant from a Swiss watchmaking company, who made an expensive "Adventure Watch," to film the excavation for public television.

Draw tipped his stool back until his head and shoulders rested against a post. "It'll be lights, camera, action, now. Real old-time archaeology for the folks out there, full of thrills and chills and tomb discoveries—Casque better hope he finds some good stuff." Draw smiled, brought the stool legs back down to the ground with a bump. "And I just happened to mention that we've picked up a new digger on the team, who is working out real well. So you're safe. You'll not have to keep hiding out in here."

"I just don't want to get you into trouble."

"You've still got lots of work to do for me. So I'm not lying. I really need you." He looked at her across the lab table, blushed, reached out to pick up the conch trumpet, and gave a good blow. The moaning roar made Morley shiver and laugh. Draw grinned at her, happy to make her laugh.

That night, at the end of dinner, Casque introduced the director of the film team, Susan, a woman with graying blond hair, and her crew of two young men in identical khaki vests. Susan stood up and smiled at the dig team. They were all one big fantastic team now, she said, all working together to really show how archaeology really worked. She really wanted to leave no stone, or bone, unfilmed. "So, fantastic. So, I gather, we're onto the big mound—what do you call it, Stuart?"

"The double *cuyo,* Susan." Casque's mustache twitched. Casque had his speech all ready for the camera. "*Cuyo* means 'tower,' so double *cuyo.* That's what Maler—the famous scholar and intrepid explorer who discovered Motul—called the double-towered mound. Maler's been"—he nodded at Susan—"a *fantastic* role model for me. Lucky for us, of course, we don't have to come in by pack animals like Maler!"

Morley slipped out, by herself, walked to the double mound, and stood there for a while. It was an obscure night, no moon. Morley played her flashlight over the tufts of weeds covering the lower half of the mound, the dry gray dirt crumbling off the rubble that showed through here and there, and the two flat-faced towers. Yes, two of them, two companions, double towers.

The next day, while Casque prepared to work on the main mound, Susan's assistant filmed several of the diggers half-heartedly whacking at trees with machetes while Susan improvised script on her tape recorder: "Into the mist-enshrouded jungle, where Maya cities disappeared into the shroud of history, a fantastic cloud of mystery, now comes an intrepid team of archaeologists in an all-out search for buried treasure." Out at Draw's site, Susan scrutinized the faces of Francisco and Xavier. Morley heard her ask her assistant, "Which one of them looks the most like a Maya to you?" Xavier was set up in front of the camera, and Susan asked Draw to tell him to hold his trowel up and talk for a while.

"About what?" Draw asked.

"Anything, just for two minutes. We've got a part all written out about how he feels about helping the archaeologists dig up his ancestors. We'll dub in someone else reading it for the film. We just need him to talk—no one'll ever know what he's saying, so it doesn't matter at all. So maybe just get him to talk about something that will make him look kind of sad. Yes, sad—fantastic. After all, we're talking the decline of his people."

Draw got Xavier going about women, Xavier's wife, the women Xavier wanted, did Xavier want Susan there?—"¿La vieja?" Xavier laughed, and they had to reshoot.

Susan filmed Draw hunched over his notebooks in the lab. He refused to look up, but he turned and crossed his eyes at Morley.

When a shower blew up suddenly, there were shots of the team inside their thatched huts, playing poker, smoking cigars. Draw muttered to Morley, "Here're the rains coming, and we're mostly pissing around with home movies."

That night, late into the night, Casque was filmed in the lab, telling the camera all about Motul. He had asked Draw to write up the history of Motul ("It's all conjecture, of course, but he'll act like it's true," Draw complained), the history of the people of Motul, its rulers and peasants ("You watch, he'll only talk about the rulers''), the big find of the ceramics compound, and a little bit about the different pots now in the lab. From Draw's notes, Casque worked up a script on large panels of cardboard for one of the graduate students to hold up.

Susan called, "Okay, Chief. You're on," and Casque turned from where he was positioned at the lab table, half-perched on a stool, in profile. Capping his pen, which he wasn't using at all, carefully clipping it to a khaki pocket, he then spoke very slowly, his phrases drifting through the air: "Archaeologists now can solve ancient *mysteries* . . . These pots can tell us about the noble artists who painted them . . . We now understand the ancient lifeways of the Maya."

"More like deathways," Draw whispered to Morley.

"And the *collapse* of the Maya . . . This military complex of mighty warrior kings . . ." He leaned back in his chair and looked off in the distance, as if contemplating the melancholy fate of all human things.

"Great. Fantastic. *¡Excellente!*" Susan cried out.

The next day, the excavation of the double *cuyo* finally began. Casque ordered all the teams working at the different sites to the double-pyramid mound. Every morning, there was a great bustle as the whole camp tramped off in the same direction. Only Morley didn't go. She stayed at the lab to finish her work for Draw. As she sat in the lab, drawing, the brush felt more and more natural in her hand, yet she was always thinking, too, at the same time—she could not help it—about the excavation at the twin towers. Sometimes she found herself gasping aloud.

When Draw stopped by the lab late every afternoon, she greeted him with, "So where are they now? What will they do next?" Draw popped open the cold sodas or beers he had brought with him, handed her one, and gave his report. Casque had everybody clearing off all the rubble from the platform that ran the length of the mound, in front of the two towers. Casque started trenching through the platform in front of the left tower.

Casque thought he had found a tunnel leading down into the mound, underneath the tower.

"Something strange about that tunnel, to me. Too rough and jumbled for a burial passageway. Roots down there're too deep, wouldn't be there when they sealed the tomb and passageway up. Casque's theory's that the mound partially collapsed much later and jumbled the passageway, let the trees send their roots down. He told the camera all about it. Well, we'll not really know for a while yet. But I reckon soon enough."

"Will they find something?"

"Oh, they'll probably find something somewhere in the mound, even if this tunnel's a bust," Draw replied, "because one thing we know is that the Maya tended to bury their nobles and kings in these main mounds. Casque's right mindful of that. Just how photogenic a burial it'll be is the real question."

Draw paused for a moment, took a pull of his beer, and then, sitting back against the wall, crossed his arms over his chest. "You know something that's always seemed kinda funny to me? We're pretty sure some tomb's in there, and we already know that if the tomb's not been looted, it'll be full of more bones, with some jade, some pots, maybe some glyphs, just the same old stuff that'll tell us only a few things, and even maybe a few somewhat important things. But everybody's so excited, like it's something that never happened before. Or that in this tomb we'll make this one crucial find that will solve some *big question*—like all the novels and movies about archaeology make you think." He rolled the cold beer bottle between his hands for a moment, then abruptly held the bottle still. "Now I *know* it's never like that— well, hardly ever—but I just can't help it, even I get excited. When I'm ready to open up a tomb, I'd almost kill anybody that got in my way. Then I'm in and all of a sudden, it's weird, just like for a moment, I'm in a different time zone, their time zone."

Morley felt ashamed that Draw had become most important to her as a source of information about the dig at the twin towers.

But now she only cared about the dig. She had absolutely returned her attention to . . . to—yes, it was like a return to something, something she had almost forgotten about—a return to the path she had started out on, so long ago. When Morley tried to think what this something was, she saw another vase—there might be another vase or maybe twin vases buried in the mound at its double heart. Two hearts, one body—the vases were deep, deep, inside the mound. She was so sure. She could feel them there, alive in there.

Morley even forgot at times that she and Draw had ever made love. Draw, too, was so busy trying to finish up the work on his own site while digging for Casque at the double mound that he seemed content just being with her whenever he had a chance, talking to her, lying close to her, at rest like a child, his head on her chest and shoulder, sometimes his bare toe nudging at her leg or foot, out of habit, as if she were a ruin and he would dislodge some sherd or stone. Morley rested her hand on his shoulder but brooded over the twin-towered mound. A queer elation quickened in her.

The Globetrotters talked endlessly about the dig at dinner.

"I bet it's a burial passageway."

" 'Fantastic!' " A Globetrotter grinned.

Draw laughed out loud.

"Professor Casque says tomorrow we'll find the tomb."

"Oh, god. I hope so. There's only six days left. I want to tell people back home I found something 'fantastic'."

The next day, Draw came to the lab dirty and tired.

He opened his beer, sat on a stool. "You know what they have there? One genuine, authentic looter's trench. That trench walked 'em right to a tomb—"

"They found the tomb? Looted?" Morley could hardly bear to ask.

"Yep. A tomb totally cleaned out, no bones, no pots, not even a bead, as far as I can tell. I think the tunnel's an old looter's trench from the 1920s or so. We always thought the site's been looted—there're those Master pots that might be from here. Whoever it was, they made a nice tunnel, even kind of filled it back in. That's what fooled Casque. You can bet he wasn't talking to the camera today. What's interesting to me is that we did get into the core of the mound. There's only one other real pyramid under the one you see, and it's really just a low platform temple. That's what Casque should be looking at. That tells us that 'Motel' was just like we thought—a pretty poky place, then suddenly got kind of rich, suddenly tried to look kind of powerful. But Casque doesn't care. He's just tearing the mound up to get at a burial.''

The Globetrotters swallowed their disappointment.

"Well, it was cool seeing that room. It must have been really cool when all that red paint was still on the walls.''

"Hey, you guys, at least I made it onto film today. Watch out, a star is born!''

" 'Excellent! Fantastic!' ''

"Ah, dream on. You're a nobody. You'll just end up on the cutting room floor.''

An empty room, once red-plastered, everything worse than in ruin, everything gone. Morley said to herself, There is the other end of the mound. Underneath the other tower, maybe there.

The next day, Draw reported that Casque had decided to follow his suggestion and look for another tomb, right under the other tower, in the same place as the looted tomb.

Morley quickly finished her drawing, put away her brushes.

The next morning, Morley set off with the team to the mound. She had to go tear the mound apart herself. With the others, she climbed up the mound, finding steps on the rubble, holding on to the roots and vines that had refused to give way when the mound was cleared. Then she climbed down to the deepest part of the trench, the deepest hole within holes that had been sunk into the mound. From there, Morley handed up chunks of stone to workers standing above her at a higher level of the trench. They tied a rope around the stones, one stone at a time, and set them on a slide of two saplings lashed together. Others at the mound's surface pulled the rocks up, untied and tumbled them into a pile. Morley also troweled at the dirt and rubble, sweeping it up with a hand brush into a dustpan, dumping that into a bucket. She took her turn carrying the buckets and dumping them into the wheelbarrows, took her turn bumping a wheelbarrow down the dirt incline. All day long, Morley found herself working in a panic.

Every night, she returned exhausted from the work. Hardly had a thing to say to Draw at dinner. He, too, was exhausted with working all day, staying up almost all night to write up his notes. Morley slept alone and slept without dreaming.

Casque had now trenched about ten feet into the mound, right under the second tower. No sign yet of a tomb.

A wall of the trench collapsed, the wall nearest the front of the mound, behind the false stairs. Stones and dirt filled the trench again. The rest of the day and the next they spent hauling out the rubble. Some of the Globetrotters were so frustrated, they heaved the rocks out of the trench and the rocks crashed down the face of the mound.

Susan was everywhere filming, and when the camera was off, she sat above the trench, talking to the recorder in her hand: "It's a frantic race against time. The rains're coming any day now. The team has to spend days digging out the rubble just to get back to where they were just yesterday."

On the third day following the collapse, Draw was crouched down, working where the wall had given way. He stopped, stood up and stood still, just looking at the rough wall of stone there. He poked at the wall with his boot. Then he bent over and picked at the stones with his hands. He called for Casque, who was up on the edge of the trench, talking to Susan. Casque and Susan clambered down. Morley, always alert, moved close to Draw.

Draw pointed at the side of the trench. "See these flatter stones going this way? Looks like some sort of vaulting. And see these larger rocks on the side, around these smaller stones? That's not just plain old fill." He picked at the smaller rocks, pulling them out, clearing away an opening. "Could be some sort of passageway, a tunnel, a tunnel *they* made. That might place the tomb or whatever's at the end of this tunnel right behind the stairs, like at my site. And we know people are finding burials tucked right behind stairs at other sites, like over at Pacbitún."

All work stopped for the rest of the afternoon. The opening was photographed, the elevation taken, the find plotted on the grid map. Susan's cameraman panned over the trench, Susan prowled the trench, recorder in hand: "But then! Suddenly, the absolutely unexpected happens. An opening has been revealed by the collapse, an opening that leads to the deep dark heart of the mound! Fantastic!"

Draw looked up and over at Morley. "We think."

Buckets of rubble came out of the passageway, pulled out by Draw and handed to Morley, right behind him.

When Draw came to a flat stone wall, he stopped. Casque was to be the discoverer of the tomb. Draw and Morley backed out of the passageway and Casque wriggled in, carrying with him a heavy flashlight. The cameraman followed with a big lamp fixed to his head. Casque narrated his every move loudly for the microphone. Everyone was hovering at the opening of the passage to listen to him: "I'm going along this ancient pathway deep within the temple. . . . Now I'm carefully removing the last stones. . . . The last stone is down. . . . Now I'm leaning into . . . into a tomb—yes, a tomb! Untouched, looks like, and it's beautiful, painted red—red like blood, like it's a big womb—and . . . and it looks like some glyphs. Fantastic! Okay, there are a bunch of pots placed around the body—they all look intact—and a plate placed on the chest of the body, some jade beads among the bones, the bones not in great shape. . . . Wait a minute—definitely not human bones. Yeah, not human at all—some animal bones, a big cat or deer, a jaguar! I mean, the ruler was probably killed somewhere else, in some big battle, and I bet they buried his totem animal here, maybe a deer, to take his place. I can't believe it. Now what'd be great is to find a *way* glyph here somewhere, the special glyph naming the deer and ruler as a co-essence, as one being.''

''It's so shamanistic! It's so mystical!'' Susan cried out.

Draw stuck his hands into his back pockets and leaned up against Morley to whisper, ''Hell, he wouldn't know a deer bone from the pork-chop bone he gnawed on last night, much less a human bone. This is a no-way theory.''

Morley would find some way to go in.

The interior of the tomb was photographed from every angle. The location of every object was carefully noted by the archaeologists. The tomb was then tidied up for the camera, the dust brushed off the pots and the bones and the beads. Susan filmed Casque inside the tomb, pointing out the finds. By now, the deer skeleton had become a human skeleton—Draw had quietly pointed out that the shape of the collarbone kind of made him think the bones might be human, and the shape of the hipbone, too. The sciatic notch showed that the person was probably male.

Later, at lunch, Draw remarked to Morley, ''Casque better hope that Susan leaves his totem deer discovery out of the film. Anybody who knows anything will die laughing.''

''Did you see any Master vase in there?'' Morley had to know.

''I thought you might go see for yourself, if you want. Casque's going to let the Globetrotters go in and take a look this afternoon before they take out all the stuff. Get in line.''

Through the rest of lunch, Morley was quiet. Her heart beat

very hard, almost hurt. She kept putting her hand to it, pressing on it, as if that would make her heart hurt less.

At three o'clock, the Globetrotters lined up at the mound. Eddie went in first to hold the light for them, point out the objects, and make sure nothing was touched. A Globetrotter scrambled in and out, another, another. "It's incredible! Fantastic!" they gasped in turn as they emerged from the mound. They had gotten their money's worth.

Morley was the last to go in. Draw volunteered to relieve Eddie, for he knew Morley would want more time. So Eddie scrambled out of the hole, and Draw went in. Now Morley crawled into the passageway and began to scoot herself forward toward the light. The stones cut long scratches in her arms. She would only notice them later that night.

At last, she reached the narrow room. Morley stood up. Draw stood at one end of the vaulted chamber, holding up a bright lamp. The air in the vault was hot, suffocating. Deliberately leaving the pots for last, Morley made herself look at everything else slowly. Draw followed her gaze with the light. The chamber had been plastered a deep rose-red. The plaster still mostly intact. The narrow, vaulted ceiling red, too. Draw played the light on the glyphs painted there, but Morley was barely able to make them out. Jade beads, bright green in the bright light, big fat beads, tiny beads, beads scattered among the bones of a skeleton.

Now Morley could look for her vase. She squatted down on her heels to look, deliberately, at last, carefully, at the pottery piled next to the skeleton. There were stacks of pots, nested one in the bowl of another. There were some red cylinder vases grouped together, and there was a vase, gleaming white, catching the light. Like the one in the museum, the pink shading of the hieroglyphs at the rim, the plump figures visible in their outline. She had known there would be one here.

Morley leaned over toward the gleaming vase. "Here—here the light," she croaked to Draw. And there was one of her two twins, a fat man in a jaguar suit, dancing, gazing at—Morley shifted herself to see the other side of the pot—the other twin, now in a kilt, but sitting on a jaguar, a jaguar with his feet up in the air, doing a handstand. Now Morley wobbles a moment on her toes and her hand goes down to steady herself, crunching, her hand crunching down on the bones.

"Watch out," she hears herself whisper.

"Watch out," Draw calls sharply to her.

Morley looks down and sees her hand among the bones. Her hand has crushed pale brown bones into fragments, pulverized brittle bones into powder.

The bones of one of the twins, the ruler or the priest, Morley is sure. This is what flesh comes to, his flesh has come to. He is dead, here is the proof. She has touched the bones, crushed the bone. It is over.

All of a sudden, it is over. He is dead. He is dead. Morley looks again at the gleaming vase. Bone white fired clay lasts so much longer than bone. Pots are a kind of bone, of fleshlike clay fired into bone.

Bone powder must have gotten up Morley's nose. For Morley sneezed, and sneezed again.

## IX

## *Restoration*

MORLEY BEGAN TO WRITE THINGS DOWN. She did not write letters. It is not a journal that she kept. She called it an account. She will keep an account of everything that happens next, because it goes so quickly, like doors are shutting behind her, one after another. It will all be over soon, and someday she will read this and it will seem a marvelous tale.

Morley found it odd and clumsy to write again. But now drawing is only to be used for one thing, the Master vases.

*May 30, Guatemala City*

Everything that has happened. I came out of the tomb. Two things. Bone grit ground into my palm. And I had seen the vase, the Master's vase.

I came out of the tomb, Michael right behind me. Outside, everyone gathered around Casque and a short man, dark, gray-haired, his khakis clean and pressed. Two soldiers nearby. Susan wasn't filming this. Michael told me the man was Castillo, head of the Guatemalan Institute of Anthropology and History. A few minutes later, Castillo turned and announced that the dig was over. Effective immediately. We had to pack up, clear out by the next day. The Guatemalan Institute would run the site.

Castillo learned about the discovery of the tomb not from Casque but from the *Washington Post,* which Casque had telephoned to announce his find. The *Post* gave major credit for the dig's funding to the "Adventure Watch" company; only in the last sentence did it mention the Institute. Castillo's deeply offended—*he* should have been notified about the find immediately, allowed to break the news. The team worked at *his* discretion, on *Guatemala's* cultural heritage. Everyone's visa is revoked, and they must leave the country. The finds go to the capital.

Michael's not too upset. He has his notes in order, his samples, and my drawings for him. The coming rains, he says, would have closed them down anyway. Michael even thinks that the expulsion is temporary, a slap on the wrist for Casque. They'll be back at the site next year.

My name's not on the dig's official list. I'm safe.

The vase from the tomb all I can think about. Have to see it again. Absolutely must draw it. Michael's given me a letter to an American archaeologist who he knows is down in Guatemala City right now. She's not, he says, a real dirt archaeologist. Just an art historian, the lowest of the low for Michael, with an obsession about decapitation—he says for her everything Maya is about decapitation. But she can get me in to see the vase.

The letter makes me out to be a gifted, aspiring Mayanist, studying the Master of the Pink Glyphs series of vases, my studies to be eventually summed up in a groundbreaking article. Even loftily predicts, in the usual way of these letters, that I will become *the* expert on Maya Late Classic vase painting. Michael got Casque to sign the letter. "See, I'm in charge."

Promotion: digger to archaeologist.

At noon today, everything from the site and everyone on the dig flew to Guatemala City. I went, too, on the old plane with threadbare seats, an ethnologist from California sat next to me and told us that planes and helicopters are of great use in locating shrines built on hilltops. The Maya don't like to tell where their shrines are, he said, but from up here you can see everything. He has just made a statistical count of the area's sacred places and a map of them for an upcoming article.

One thing. Michael and I stood in the airport at Guatemala City. I had to make an effort to remember—oh yes, we made love. It seems a long time ago, and my effort to remember is mental. Not like love's memory—instant physical memory of a smell, of the feel of flesh, the color of flesh, so instantly conjured up, so alive, so at hand. Still, I note one more time these scarred hands, these quick bright eyes, this proud upright body, a wonderful young palm tree shooting up. I'm moved, with great affection and admiration. A gift. The truth of that.

Immense gratitude, too, for letting me into this world of dirt and stones and bones, layer upon layer, of digging down. Another gift. Perhaps it might save me.

His plane to Miami was called. So when would I get home? he asked.

Not yet, but soon I have to go back home. I'm broke, and school will start eventually. Back home, back to that empty house, so strange an empty house. Maybe I'll come to like emptiness.

Michael said I might think about him sometimes. Maybe I might pay him a visit someday? Then he was embarrassed, but he recovered himself and laughed. We both said at exactly the same time, "Come or don't come."

I shall think about him. I think about him.

Tomorrow or the next day or the next day after that, I'll see the vase again, and I'll draw it. It's odd how the vase shines so.

Then, I'll go home.

---

*June 2, Guatemala City*

The rains have come. Outside, green shoots, flowers instantly everywhere. And at last I have seen how high the mountains are that ring the city. They appear in the washed, clean light of the morning, before the rain gathers again.

Back at the Hotel Lito. The owner is glad to see me. He looked up from the television, from *Happy Days* dubbed in Spanish, and greeted me in broken French. I tell him what I've been doing. He advises me to stick to just digging up ancient things. Turns out the forensics team I met at Tikal stayed here, to be next to the hospital around the corner. He says he thinks the team is doing a good thing, but a very dangerous thing. While they were here at the hotel, he was always afraid of the security forces coming to take them, take him. I should stick to digging up ancient things.

Wrote to my neighbor, asked her to get the key from the subletter, who is leaving, pick up the mail, use the apartment for overnight guests if she wants. Wrote I'd be home soon.

Everything happens quickly. I gave my letter from Casque to Sandra Spondy at the Institute. She arranged for me to work in a room with shelves and shelves of vases, plates, urns, *incensarios,* and statues big and small—the biggest, richest tomb of all. They set me up at a table near a window, with good light, and they brought the Master vase for me.

The vase is stuccoed in a rosy cream-colored plaster. The plaster gleams so. Like the vase at the Popol-Vuh, the glyphs are outlined in rose-red and washed with a lighter pink of the same color. Under the emblem glyph for Motul, the *T* glyph, dances, again, one of the jaguar monsters from the other vase. The plump, strong, spotted thighs lift, a heel lifts, behind him lift the ends of the long scarf knotted around his neck and hanging down to his ankles, dyed red, except for the dancing ends. There is the bit of jaguar tail dangling down, curling on the ground. One arm is held up chest-high, the other extended—this is the dance. There is the same wide plaque necklace, the same mask of jaguar skin pulled over some huge skull with black plumes curling up and falling down in the back, the long proboscis with exaggerated incisors, plumed snout curling down. Inside the mask cutout, the Priest's face, this time painted dark red, except for his cheekbones, nose, eyes, and forehead.

The Jaguar Priest slightly inclines forward, his plumes almost brush—I turn the vase—against the head of a real jaguar, not a particularly fierce jaguar, but a very lively jaguar, which stands on its front paws and kicks up its hindquarters and twists its legs and heels back into the glyph band along the top of the vessel. Its tail curls in midair, curls right at the tip. On this acrobatic jaguar, seated sideways as if on a throne, is the Fat Cacique, the same fat man as on the first vase. Not in his jaguar suit, but simply dressed in a white kilt. Still he wears jaguar paw mitts, as neat as a lady's white cotton mitts, and jaguar-fur cuffs tied on his ankles.

He is masked, too, but this time with the mask of a man, complete with buck teeth, wispy mustache and goatee, Maya sloped forehead crowned by a headdress of black plumes, stiff upright some and some curving, falling. Inside the mask, in the cutaway, is the Cacique's head, neck and face painted brownish red, except for his cheekbones, nose, eyes, and forehead. The Cacique holds out toward the Priest a circular fan of woven straw that he grasps by a femur handle. The fan is crossed with two strips of jaguar fur.

The Fat Cacique stares at the Jaguar Priest. The space across which the gaze travels nicely filled in, made alive by the plumes of the monstrous mask, the pretty woven fan. Again, like the first vase, that central space is framed by the faces of the Priest and the Cacique. That is the space upon which the Master wants us to look. It is the central event of the vase.

The ostensible occasion of the moment becomes clearer with a slight turn of the vase to the left. Behind and to the side of the Cacique, kneeling, one foot crossed elegantly over the other, is an attendant. He is not masked. He wears a knotted white kilt, a necklace with a counterweight that lies close to his spine all the way down showing off the curve of the body, a tall turban of white, a kerchief headdress starched and folded up like a fancy dinner napkin. The attendant holds a bowl or basket with strips in it, spotted pink. They are strips of paper soaked in blood, an offering. Who gives his or her blood?

Turn the vase again and here is a small cat dancer facing in the direction of the Cacique and the Priest. One arm lifted in front chest-high, one arm lifted behind, one foot forward, heel lifted, one foot back, he is dancing, too, like a cat stealing forward, infinitely graceful. Jaguar tail, jaguar mitts, ocelot markings on the white suit round pink circles enclosing jaguar rosettes. The mask is half jaguar—nose, forehead, soft ear—and half monkey—grotesque jaw with huge teeth, grinning like a skull. A plume of short feathers thrusts from the back of the mask and from them a fall of quetzal feathers arched and falling to his waist. Inside the cutaway, a head of a man, looking down, intent on his dance. Around his neck the long, knotted scarf dyed a deep red, and in front of it—didn't see this at first—a naked baby floats on its back in front of or on the scarf, its legs and arms limp and hanging in the abandonment of death. Black-haired baby, tiny baby, a large cleft in its chest.

One more turn, but not much of a turn, a last figure stands right behind the small cat dancer. This stiff, solemn figure is not in costume. He wears a white kilt, and he is painted black, except for his face in the cutaway mask, a mask again of a man, a man with a mustache and goatee. One hand holds a black-plumed standard that fans out like a feather duster over the final glyphs. The bottom of the standard seems to have attached to it a panel of woven and embroidered cloth. The other hand is outstretched, held a bit down, palm outward, index finger inexorably gesturing down. Stiff at attention, he looks straight ahead of him, at the Cacique at the Priest, at the moment they meet, look at each other. Not at the small child, an obscure side event, occasion of but not the object of the event depicted.

One thing. This child—I avert my look, too. Someday I'll have to look.

Today, taking up my position, I dipped my brush in the ink. Slowly, I began to draw, a fine, fine line at the top of the paper, the rim of the vase, and I was in the power of the vase.

As before, I drew one face of the vase at a time. I wanted to copy the figures, as I have come to believe the Master painted them, one at a time, although I don't know if this is true. If I photographed this vase, I would not know it as I have come to know it by drawing it. It's like copying a poem—when you reinscribe every line yourself, you submit to every line, no day-dreaming allowed, and new understandings unfurl before you. The reader of that poem merely passes over what she reads, as if in an airplane, leaving no footprints. The palm fronds of the jungle never quiver for her. She has never come that way.

Now I get to go home.

———

*June 4, Guatemala City*

Sandra Spondy—a tall, very thin, sun-faded lady in faded jeans, field boots, with frizzy pink hair, big blue glasses—invited

me to her hotel room to have a beer. Her room like a lair, boots
and jeans in piles, a backpack bulging with clothing, stacks of
Xeroxes and journals, next to the bed a pile of Agatha Christie
paperbacks. Michael's letter impressed her. She kept wanting to
talk about my new "vocation," which, of course I know but can't
tell her, is leading to anything but a career. Spondy became very
excited when she heard Motul was my first dig. Was it like a
conversion experience? What happened to me with the Pink
Glyphs vases? Was it like being born again? When she first saw
Tikal, she was just a tourist walking around, but it was as if she
felt a power coming from the place, like a Three Mile Island of
power (this is how she talks). She just had to know everything
about it, so she became an archaeologist. Did I suddenly feel the
power at Motul? She bets that's what happened to me.

How to ever say what has happened to me?

Aren't we all holding still, paying attention, copying, deci-
phering, coming to understand the vase, the stela, the row of
glyphs, a history of birth, accession, war, capture, sacrifice, death,
passage to the land of the dead, rebirth?

I learned from her that the cleft in the child's chest is a mark
of heart sacrifice—"in this instance not decapitation, because it's
a child," she lectured me—that the bowl or basket is filled with
strips of paper soaked in blood and to be burned in offering.
The Pink Glyphs vases probably a series commemorating rites
surrounding the accession of the Fat Cacique to the throne of
Motul. The glyphs around the top, a formula that appears on
most elite vases and plates. The formula names to whom the vase
belongs (the Maya apparently loved to name every object, his fan,
her comb, his mirror), the shape of the vessel, whether it is bowl,
plate, cylinder, names the glyphs, the contents, the vessel is made
for either a *cacao*—that is, chocolate—or an *atole*—that is, a
corn drink. The glyph on my vase is for chocolate. They think
that sometimes vases were signed by the scribe-painter, but they

aren't yet sure about this. The glyphs next to each figure probably name those figures. The rosy red, the pinkish tint of these glyphs comes from a special hematite, specular hematite, imported to the Petén from the western highlands of Guatemala, which says something about the trade between regions, and about the value of the vase. This rose-red seems to have been used only on prized pieces.

I like that the vase had a practical use, for drinking chocolate.

*June 6, Antigua*

Spondy knows about two other Pink Glyphs vases, one in Fort Worth, one in Cambridge. She's given me letters of introduction to both museums. A vase in Cambridge—so close to home all the time. Bought my ticket to Fort Worth, but the flight's not for four days. So, a return to touristing. When I'm so restless, so anxious to see the vases, draw the vases, go home.

Today stood in line for a bus, again. At last, off to Antigua, the old colonial capital in the mountains. Rode the curving mountain highways third on the seat, gripping the bar before me. The old city is laid out on a grid. Michael's right, it's pretty—cobbled streets lined with white stucco walls fitted with dark doors fitted with small, grated windows. To the south, the huge volcano Agua. You can see the jagged edges of Agua's crater. The still, blue presence terrifying above the pretty city. Tourists who climb Agua to look at the crater are often robbed and beaten.

One thing. At the ruined convent of Santa Clara, in a ruined chapel, the back wall fallen away, I stared at an oculi, the eight-sided opening in the wall above the altar, framing exactly, perfectly the cone of the volcano. The jagged cone, singled out in detail, to be kept an eye on, the volcano that brings earthquakes, the city-tumbling volcano. I walk all over the city, wander among the ruins of the Baroque churches built, tumbled by earthquakes, built again, tumbled, left tumbled. Their huge arches lie on their side, lie broken, wildflowers and wild grasses springing next to them. Bones of buildings.

North American students come to Antigua to learn Spanish, sit in cafés run by North Americans, and write in their journals. Spondy sometimes runs a glyph workshop for archaeologists and the descendants of the Maya themselves. They all sit cross-legged and practice writing glyphs on large sheets of butcher paper.

At the workshop, met a specialist in Maya history of the nineteenth and twentieth centuries. When I was introduced, he smiled and asked the now only too familiar question: "Any relation to Sylvanus Morley?"

"No relation," I said. "I wish."

"If you were, the Maya in the Yucatán might like to meet you. In the '30s, Morley used to go to their festivals and give them gifts. And promised them, they believed, help from the American government in their war with the Mexican government. Even now, still, every time I'm there, the Maya ask me if it's really true that Morley's dead—you know, he died in '48. Some of the old men, in their storytelling, still speak to Morley as if he were alive, reproaching him for not coming back, not fulfilling his promises." The historian grinned at me, struck a pose, and recited: " 'Señor Jefe'—that's Morley—'the time has passed.'

" 'Every time we come, every time we come,
    every time we come here, well, you don't say anything to us.
    We don't say anything, either.' "

In my own capacity as a Morley, what have I had to say to the Maya on this trip that is coming to its end? I have only watched them from taxi windows, sat silently beside them on buses, handled their bones, obscurely made their eternal life part of my eternal life. But to talk to them. To let them talk to me. That would have to be another trip. There will be another trip?

=====

*June 7, Guatemala City*

Took the bus up to Chichicastenango, the famous Indian market town, for the day. I walked around the marketplace, looking at the stalls of clothing, food, and flowers—there were bundles and bundles of calla lilies, creamy white open throats, long green stalks. At the front door of the cathedral of Santo Tomás, a Maya official in a wrapped headdress and an embroidered shirt burns incense, blesses the Maya before they enter to worship in the Christian church. Inside, around the neck of the saints are hung small mirrors for the faithful to breathe upon and see their soul. A woman knelt on the floor with her sick chicken at her side, lighting candles before a saint. I would have done the same for my cat.

Following the guidebook's directions, I found near the church a path that led out of town. On the path, I passed a few Maya, who looked at me from under the tump bands across their foreheads, the bands supporting the bundles of wood on their backs. Finally arrived at a shrine, a black stone image presiding over a rough circle of black and blackened stones, over offerings of thin white burning candles, bottles of alcohol, flowers, and sacrificed chickens.

And there was Eddie, with his gleaming toothy earring, passing a cotton-cloth bundle to jaguar man Bill, my tattooist from Virginia. With them was another long-haired kid all decked out in loose pants and a knapsack made of the fake ethnic Guatemalan fabric which floods the tourist markets here. Bill, with self-conscious ceremonial flourishes, unwrapped the bundle slowly and laid out the objects it contained. There were several obsidian blades that Eddie must have ripped off from the dig, there were strips of handmade paper, thick and fibrous, oblong packages of folded corn husks bound with ties of corn husk, and a shallow ceramic bowl. Eddie and Bill and their friend, each in turn, cut the index fingers of their left hands and pressed drops of blood out onto the paper strips in the bowl. The paper immediately soaked up the blood into rosettes of pink and red.

Then they burnt the paper on a small stone in front of the *idolo,* and while it burned, they threw into the fire small black clotted crystals from the unfolded husks, bits of copal, the resin used as incense by the Maya. As the sweet-smelling smoke rose from the altar—mixed with the smell of the joint they were soon passing around—Bill and the other kid swayed back and forth in a kind of exaggerated trance. Eddie turned away and saw me, winked and came over. Told me he'd slipped away from Casque's team at the airport. Went back to Motul, only to find out his girlfriend had a husband. Met up with Bill and Jack here at Panajachel—"Man, do they have some great dope there!"—and decided to head north with them to Huehuetenango and over into Mexico. See about getting some work at the Toniná dig near San Cristobál de las Casas. "Bill and Jack here think they'd like to do some digging." He offered me a hit on his joint—but it's not my ritual.

The few Maya who came by stared at us and turned away, went about their business.

Later, I walked off by myself to the quiet walled cemetery on a hill in back and above the town. There are gay pink and turquoise and yellow mausoleums like little houses along tiny streets lined with pine trees. There are graves with headstones, some graves simply covered in green pine needles. At the very back of the cemetery, overlooking the hills, a crumbling chapel houses the remains of a North American priest who ministered in Chichicastenango. I think he was, before his conversion, an accountant from Norman, Oklahoma. In front of the chapel on the paving stones, spread a great black scorched place. Little heaps of ashes of burned flowers.

I stood there and listened to the wind in the pine trees, the wind in the needles, sifting, whistling. I looked at the hills before me, prettily terraced with fields. The scent of the pine, the sifting wind, my ghosts whistling by me. I broke off a fan of pine needles and put it in my bag, slim green needles, black rough bark even on this twig, yellow-white crystal-crusted resin. My fingers sticky and smell so strongly.

Everything happens quickly.

━━━

*June 9, Fort Worth*

With only my drawings and worn clothes and broken shoes, I'm traveling north like an immigrant, although of course I could be said to be going home. Here's another room in a small, plain hotel, this time near a highway. This must be what flight is like, one small room after another. On the flight into Egypt did Mary, Joseph, the donkey, and the child put up at motel after motel? Walked down a street, looking for something to eat. Everyone stared at me from their car windows, rolled up for the air conditioning—as if I were a foreigner and didn't understand that no one walks in this country.

We'll have our ruined monuments, too. The people who wonder about us will excavate, restore, call the ruin of this art museum the Temple of the Rounded Vaults, because of its row of seven huge rounded concrete vaults. I presented myself.

The vase is not the Master's vase. There is the Fat Cacique, there is the Priest, and there are the pink glyphs—but the vase is not the same as the two I've seen. So many details wrong. The hands too tiny for the bodies, not like hands on the Master's vases. No masks. The eyes wider and longer. The figure of the Cacique is stiffer, and the fine line makes him lumpy and cartoonlike. The stucco background too light, too white, too powdery. The Master's are pinker, rosier, warmer—they shine.

The Priest's head is bowed, he's alone in his dance. The Cacique appraises the string of beads a woman holds up to him.

There's another vase, Pink Glyphs vase, going on sale in New York, the curator tells me. Hurry, hurry, home.

———

*June 11, New York City*

New York, monumental city center like Tikal, Chichén Itzá. Another basic room, old plumbing fixtures, a broken window, and peeling paint, a small Central American hotel, except expensive.

Yesterday to Sotheby's to see another Master of the Pink Glyphs vase. Stood in the exhibition room, staring at it in the case. Again the wrong vase. A Masters of the Pink Glyphs vase, but not the Master's vase. Pink glyphs, a fat king, several fat priests, but the figures' fingernails are very long, and the drawing too dry, too sharp. No human gods, no masking, no shared look, no sense of the extraordinary moment.

The next day, I witnessed the fate of the vase. The objects for sale began to appear one by one as their lot number was called out. Up on the stage, a revolving dais turns out as in a game show or a fashion show, and mounted on a draped box the statue, the urn, the necklace. When the object was unable to stand up by itself, one of the guards, every one a black man, appeared on the dais, sitting or standing next to the object, steadying it, his face either impassive or ironic, or grinning. In lot 49, the Pink Glyphs vase came out, a faint pink blur so far away. The auctioneer set the starting bid, and the bidders started bidding. Up the bids went, until the auctioneer cried, "Do I hear 65,000, 65,000 in the center, say 70,000, now at 65,000, fair warning against you at 65,000, here now at 65,000, and all done at 65,000, in the book at 65,000." *Bang!* The man next to me has bought the vase. He has the sharpest bright eyes, blue and green, behind wire-rimmed glasses with the small windows in windows of trifocals. As he bid, he sat up on the edge of his chair, the pointed tip of his tongue caught between his teeth. When he held his paddle up, I saw he wore on the fourth finger of his right hand an antique silver ring, its stone engraved with an elegant Hermes in his winged sandals and leaning on his tall staff twined with two serpents. Hermes, god of thieves, of messengers, of guides.

We talked. He lives in Boston, and he invited me to come see the vase again and all his other Maya pieces. I was instantly struck that once that door revolves, the Masters' vase, all the objects are gone, into the collection of, the gallery of, the museum of these men and women, so richly dressed in soft suits, leather jackets, hands and necks weighed down by huge silver and coral rings, Peruvian beads—"A.D. 250," I heard a woman boast, lifting up her beads.

A moment of panic. What if someone like me, someone in need, never gets to see and hold the vase? Any vase, or any statue, or anything they need to see and touch?

Perhaps everyone must take their chances among what is at that moment floating through the world. How sad, still, to lose these vases, to have had them in my hands, my hands full with them, and have to give them back. At least I have my drawings, and I have the feel of the vases in my hands. The vases are gone, but they are not gone.

One more Master vase—will it be the Master's vase? It matters terribly. It doesn't matter at all. Then I go home.

One thing. Last night, as I lay in bed, I suddenly had the strongest conviction about the afterlife. I who have never given a single thought to heaven since I was a child at Sunday school. In the next life, I will see him and my red cat, and there in paradise he will make me laugh, paradisal laughter. My cat will arch his spine for the long, hard caress down the spine, the pull on his tail to stretch the spine.

X

# The Master of the Pink Glyphs

IT IS THE MASTER'S VASE.

It is about eight inches high, a little more than six inches in diameter, a low, wide cylinder vase. The vase is stuccoed a rosy, creamy white, though some of the stucco has flaked off, with the paint of the picture. The vase has been broken and glued back together, but the cracks are visible on the outside, not repainted. There are traces of the tiny networks of roots that netted it for centuries.

A thin band of rose-red encircles the rim of the vase. Below it, a band of glyphs in black, the band is washed pink. There are also glyphs by each figure on the vase. Around the base is a wider band of rose-red. Above this are several black lines that seem to indicate low steps. Other than these steps, like the other two Master vases, there is no architecture, simply event. One scene, one moment that all the figures concentrate on.

A procession comes to a halt. The Fat Cacique has arrived. Two kneeling men in white kilts and white-wrapped headdresses have just this moment lowered their lord's sedan chair to the ground—their hands still grasp the poles. Another attendant, in a yellow kilt and a wrapped headdress with a femur sticking straight up out of it, comes to help the Cacique from the chair. But he needs no help. The Fat Cacique has grasped the front of the sedan chair with one hand to steady himself, the other is stiffly outstretched, the fingers held straight out. One foot out on the ground, he rises from his seat in the sedan chair, the seat covered with a rosetted jaguar pelt. The fat lord's body, his thick, rounded torso, his thick knees and calves, his thick neck, firm and thick, solid, tensed, is painted red. He is dressed rather plainly, no necklace, a red kilt edged in black, red ankle cuffs, and white wrist cuffs, a tall headdress of plumes—although the paint has flaked off, the outline remains—which falls down his back. He wears a mask. This time, again, the mask is of a human face, carved very much in the outline of his own, the curve of the forehead, of the lumpy nose, the protruding lips. It is a mask, though. The cutaway shows you his human face, his eye slanted up, fierce, looking intently, fixed straight ahead.

Across again that central space of the vase, as you turn the vase to the right, he stares at his Priest. The Priest stands in front of the Cacique, erect, holding a red rattle, a round gourd fixed on a handle of some sort. The Priest's big body, firm and standing erect, leans a bit forward but from the feet up with the readiness of all that body's strength. His body, too, is painted red. His kilt is red, edged in black. His wrist and ankle cuffs are red. He wears a towering headdress, plumes towering right into the glyph band —from it, too, the paint has flaked away, but the outline remains —and plumes falling down his back to his knees. This time, the Priest also wears a human face mask, attached to it a small cord that he holds in his left hand—here's something new—a cord that seems to operate the lower jaw of the mask. Is he calling the ruler, the Fat Cacique, to come forward? Inside the mask, you see the Priest's face, the jutting nose, the eyes fixed in the gaze of the Fat Cacique.

The shared gaze is the center of the scene, the shared understanding of what is to happen next, in only a moment.

Turning the vase more to the right, you see that behind the Priest is a shoulder-high scaffold made of poles lashed together. There is a small ladder to the platform of the scaffold, where underneath a thatched roof raised on four more poles sits a man, not painted red, not masked, he is naked. He is bound: his legs are bound, his hands are bound, his arms are bound. His hair has been cut off, and his head looks notched, as if scalped. His eyes are lifted and rounded in terror—not slanted and pointed like the eyes of the others—his mouth is agape. Kneeling beside the scaffold, a man wearing a turban waits. He holds a bowl.

Turning the vase back to the left, behind the chief are four figures. Three painted red, red-kilted, wearing small headdresses, masked. One of them lifts his arms, ready to dance. The remaining figure, which might be a woman—the wrapped cloth comes up over her breasts—kneels on the ground and holds a rattle. The ritual that is about to begin has been documented from several other sculpted and painted scenes. These attendants will dance. She will shake her rattle. The Priest and the Cacique will step up to the stairs of the platform. The Priest will mount the platform and kill the bound man and throw his body down the steps. The Cacique will step on the sacrificed man as he walks up the ladder, and the jaguar pelt will be thrown on the bloody seat. The Cacique will now seat himself. He has acceded to his throne.

That is what will happen in a moment. At this moment on this vase, however, the Cacique does not look at the victim. His gaze is fixed in that of the Priest's. All the attendants fix their attention—even the sacrificial victim fixes his attention—on what happens between these two. The sacrifice is horrible to think about, frightening and sad to contemplate, yet seems only the occasion of the event, but not the event. From this look comes accession to power? An inauguration of a new moment in their small world, the petty kingdom that they share between them?

The Master chooses to paint this moment. The Master must master this moment—it is his only subject. Three times, at least, he invoked this moment, this shared moment, which is always in place, always waiting to be inhabited by any two companions, any two that would prevail by means of that gaze. Three vases, three times. Two vases might be by chance, but three vases?

## XI
## The New Wakefield Hotel

EVEN THOUGH MORLEY IS BACK IN CAMBRIDGE, she is not back home. While she copies the last vase, Morley lives in one more small hotel, the New Wakefield Hotel, a mile from her house and two blocks away from the University Museum, where the vase is located. In the mornings, she copies the vase. During the afternoons, she acts like any foreigner visiting Boston. She buys guidebooks, rents a car with her last bit of money, and tours the region. Cape Ann and Rockport, Cape Cod and Chatham. Then she gives the car back and walks all over the city.

Everything is thrilling for Morley. The dusty, decrepit museum is revealed to be overwhelmingly rich, all its shelves and shelves of treasures hidden in back rooms. Against the great granite ledges of Cape Ann, black ocean crashes, to Morley's almost unbearable delight. At Chatham, sea storms have carved the cliffs down to their core of slick clay. The Charles River is bright and shining, dotted with white sails. In Cambridge, late-blooming peonies hang heavy heads over peeling latticed fences, and their fragrance spills in with the perfume of the embowering honeysuckle—it must have been a long, wet, cool spring for everything is still at its fullness. Fronds waving in the slightest breeze, the wild ailanthus grows so swiftly in abandoned lots and untended yards, towering, powerful. In Somerville, a tight row of tall, peaked-roof white clapboard houses curve over a hill, the sun flat on their faces.

All around the town, people walking on the sidewalks are various, so various, in their bodies, each person—a boy burned into a single shining smooth scar, no ears, no hair, two fingers—suddenly picked out especially in light, given a clarity, a sharpness unforeseen. Everything is Morley's for this little while, turned toward her, gazing at her, making a home for her. Cats on porch steps and dogs behind fences and squirrels on telephone wires. Dead raccoons and opossums along the highway, the wind riffling their fur. On the sidewalk, ants busy with a crystal-red sucker. A cosmos of gnats suspended in the air.

Morley finishes her drawing of the last Master vase. Taking out all her drawings of all the Master vases, she tapes the separate scenes of each vase into a cylinder and sits looking at the three Master vases. The vase with the two fat, fantastic jaguars ready to dance. The vase of the child sacrifice with the dancing Jaguar Priest and the Fat Cacique in the man-god mask seated on his leaping jaguar throne. The accession vase, the two, meeting as men gods, about to accede through blood to their small power, to their petty kingdom, to this world. Maybe. Morley thinks of Michael Draw and laughs.

The paper vases tumble over.

One hot night, two nights before she finishes her drawing of the vase, after a dinner with an archaeologist she met at the museum, who talked all evening about her new dig in Belize and reggae in Belize, Morley walks along the street where her house stands. Her garden is blooming. The perennials are all up, up-right. Someone has weeded it, watered it—taken pity on it. Leaning against the fence, Morley thinks she sees a cat lying behind the bushy catnip, stretching to cool off. She says to herself, My red cat is dead, but my red cat isn't dead. Morley quickly walks away.

The night before she finishes her drawing of the vase, Morley walks along her dark street and stops in front of her house again. She thinks she sees faint lamplight glowing in her kitchen window and somebody sitting at the kitchen table, leaning on one elbow, reading, perhaps, in the lamplight. Morley is holding her breath. Then Morley says to herself, Maybe he is dead, but maybe he isn't dead. She walks back to the New Wakefield Hotel.

Morley finishes the drawing.

That night, Morley cannot sleep. She cannot sleep anymore in this small hotel, in this plain room. She has to go home. She grabs her clothes, her brushes, and her jaguar postcard, throws them into her bag. Her drawings she stuffs into the bag, too. She is careless in her hurry, but these things hardly matter now.

Then, at the last moment, Morley sits back down on the

narrow bed. Elbows on her knees, hands still and open before her.

"He's dead, he's not dead," she hears herself say out loud.

The statement is like a perfect riddle that doesn't need an answer, that has no answer. The statement is like a touchstone, or a small object you can hold in your hand, oddly shaped but perfect.

Morley leaves at dawn with her bags. She walks along her street and stops in front of her house.

The early sun sheets the house.

Morley gazes at the illuminated rectangle of the kitchen window.

The world begins all over again.

# *Author's Note*

The characters that appear in these five stories are fictional.

One of the motives for writing these stories was to find out more about certain objects and activities, which have always fascinated me. I am indebted to the work of the following authors.

For "The Island of the Mapmaker's Wife," I found R. A. Skelton's *Decorative Printed Maps of the Fifteenth to the Eighteenth Centuries* (Staples) an informative introduction to the map trade in the early-modern period; the lion map is a description of *Leo Belgicus: The Seventeen Provinces of the United Netherlands,* engraved by Pieter Van der Keeve, in *Germania Inferior* (Amsterdam, 1617). I drew upon Lloyd A. Brown's *The Story of Maps* (Dover) for details on the materials of early mapmaking.

Several books were very helpful in the writing of "Kites!" *The Penguin Book of Kites,* by David Pelham (Penguin), and *The Ultimate Kite Book,* by Paul and Helene Morgan (Simon and Schuster), both wonderfully illustrated, showed me the world of kites. I based the scenes of the Shirone kite festival and the Hamamatsu kite festival on the descriptions of those festivals by Tal Streeter in his beautiful *The Art of the Japanese Kite* (Weatherhill); I have quoted the Buson poem (from R. H. Blyth's *Haiku*) that appears in Streeter's book, and the lament of the Edo kite maker is also drawn from Streeter's book.

*The History of Beads: From 30,000 BC to the Present,* by Lois Sherr Dubin (Abrams), provided a gorgeous overview of bead history for "The Bead Trade"; the bead trader's exclamation that beads are "the small change of civilizations" is from Robert Liu's foreword to the same book. The suffragette's prediction of the imminent advent of women sculptors and preachers is that of Harriet Hosmer, a well-known nine-teenth-century American sculptor; this excerpt was taken from *Daughters of America, or Women of the Century*, by Phebe A. Hanaford (Russell, 1883); Hanaford is quoting a letter from Hosmer.

The "Master of the Pink Glyphs," the longest story, involved the most research. I quote Bernal Díaz from his *The Conquest of New Spain*, translated by J. M. Cohen (Penguin). Teodor Maler, in his "Explorations in the Department of Petén, Guatemala: Tikal" (*Memoirs, Peabody Museum, Harvard University*, vol. 5, no. 1), describes the site of Motul. *The Blood of Kings: Dynasty and Ritual in Maya Art*, by Linda Schele and Mary Ellen Miller (Braziller), a lavishly illustrated exhibition catalog providing a wealth of information, is where I first discovered the Master of the Pink Glyphs and his vases. *A Forest of Kings: The Untold Story of the Ancient Maya*, by Linda Schele and David Freidel (Morrow), is a narrative account of the rise and fall of the Maya Classic civilization; I drew upon their epilogue for the scene of the bloodletting rite. The description of the sky and earth as a blue-green plate and a blue-green bowl is from *Popol Vuh: The Definitive Edition of the Mayan Book of the Dawn of Life and the Glories of Gods and Kings*, translated by Dennis Tedlock (Simon and Schuster). My account of finding the scribal tomb is based upon the finding of a scribal complex at Copán, detailed in "A Royal Maya Tomb Discovered," by Ricardo Agurcia Fasquelle and William L. Fash, Jr. (*National Geographic*, October 1989), and in "An Elite Compound at Copán, Honduras," by David Webster and Elliot M. Abrams (*Journal of Field Archaeology:* 10). For my account of the ceramic vases, I am indebted to: Michael D. Coe's *Lords of the Underworld: Masterpieces of Classic Maya Ceramics* (Princeton University Press), *The Maya Scribe and His World* (Grolier Club), and *Old Gods and Young Heroes: The Pearlman Collection of Maya Ceramics* (Israel Museum); David Stuart's "The Río Azul cacao pot: epigraphic observation on the function of a Maya ceramic vessel" (*Antiquity:* 62); Anne Paul's "History on a Maya Vase?" (*Archaeology:* 29–30); and Justin Kerr's many beautiful roll-out photographs of Maya vases. *Tikal: A Handbook of the Ancient Maya Ruins*, by William R. Coe (University Museum: University of Pennsylvania), and "The Pennsylvania State University Kaminaljuyú Project—1968 Season" (*Occasional Papers in Anthropology*, no. 2, University of Pennsylvania) informed my visits to both of these sites. Joyce Marcus's *Emblem and State in the Classic Maya Lowlands: An Epigraphic Approach to Territorial Organization* (Dumbarton Oaks) helped me understand the changing power structure in the Maya lowlands. Stephen Houston and David Stuart, "The Way Glyph: Evidence for 'Co-essences' Among the Classic Maya" (*Research Reports on Ancient Maya Writing: 30*) and Peter T. Furst's "The Olmec Were-Jaguar Motif in the Light of Ethnographic Reality" (Dumbarton Oaks Conference on the Olmec, ed. Elizabeth P. Benson) shed light on what seems to be a basic tenet of the Maya belief system —the belief that animals and humans can share an essence or identity; Houston and Stuart underline the manifestation of this belief in the Maya writing system. *Guatemala: A Country Guide,* by Tom Barry (Inter Hemispheric Education Resource Center), tells the tragic story of the civil war going on for decades in Guatemala between the government and indigenous groups. The fascinating and moving *Unfinished Conversations: Mayas and Foreigners Between Two Wars* (Knopf), by Paul Sullivan, recounts the conflicts in the Yucatán and Chiapas; the reproach to Sylvanus Morley is an oral address by Paulino Yama, recorded in the 1970s by the linguist Alan Burns and quoted by Sullivan. I drew upon the documentary *Caracol: Lost Maya City,* directed by Robert Charlton, to describe the filming of and the dig into the double *cuyo* at Motul.

I would like to express my deep gratitude to Lily Pond of *Yellow Silk* for her encouragement from the beginning and to Christopher Begley and Carlos Dorrien for sharing their expertise in archaeology and sculpture, respectively. A Wellesley College Faculty Award in 1991 made possible the two trips to Central America that were crucial to the writing of "The Master of the Pink Glyphs," and I am most grateful for the college's support.

## ABOUT THE AUTHOR

MARILYN SIDES's stories have appeared in *The 1990 O. Henry Prize Stories*, *The Kenyon Review*, and *Yellow Silk*. She received the 1991 Kenyon Review Award for Literary Excellence for Emerging Writers. She teaches English literature and fiction writing at Wellesley College in Wellesley, Massachusetts.